Joe Jumpers

G. W. Reynolds III

This is a work of fiction. While, as in all fiction, the literary perceptions and insights are based on experience, all names, characters, places, and incidents are either products of the author's imagination or are used fictitiously. No reference to any real person is intended or inferred.

All rights reserved.
Copyright ©2003 by G. W. Reynolds III
ISBN 0-9759818-0-3

Published and distributed by:

High-Pitched Hum Publishing
P.O Box 49280
Jacksonville Beach, FL 32250

Contact G.W. Reynolds III at www.jettyman.com

No part of this book may be reproduced or transmitted in any form or means, electronic or mechanical, including photocopying, recording, or by any information storage and retrieval system, without permission in writing from the publisher.

PRELUDE

Mary C.'s right bare foot touched the bottom step of Miss Margaret's front porch. Her blood-splattered legs trembled as she lifted her left foot and it touched the second step. She wasn't sure if her legs would support her on the third step, but her hand on the wooden railing enabled her fatigued body to stand upright on the floor of the porch. Mary C. was afraid she would not be able to reach the front door of the house so she sat down in one of Miss Margaret's oak wood rocking chairs to gain control of her quivering legs. The screen door at the front of the house opened as Mary C.'s son, Jason, stepped out onto the porch and walked over to his mother's side. Miss Margaret followed close behind. Jason knelt down next to the wooden rocker.

"Mama, you all right?" Are ya hurt? Are ya bleedin'?" Jason was concerned and nervous. It made him a three-question man. Mary C. did not turn her head to face Jason. She stared straight ahead, but she did answer his three questions.

"I think I'm all right. I don't think I'm hurt. The blood ain't mine." Miss Margaret stepped up next to Jason. Her eyes opened wide when she saw the blood that coated Mary C.'s arms and face. Her shirt was blood soaked, as well. Miss Margaret could not contain herself.

"Dear God, child, what has happened to you, now?"

Mary C. continued to stare off into the distance. Her voice was monotone as she answered the question. "They killed Hawk and set my house on fire. It's burnin' down right now, but we saved the baby."

Miss Margaret looked at Jason as the screen door opened again and her youngest daughter and Jason's true love, Sofia, walked out onto the porch. She held the oak baby, Billy, wrapped in a blanket, in her arms. Sofia was her beautiful self. Her long silky blonde hair flowed as she walked and her big, sky blue eyes seemed to jump out of her head. Mary C. did not turn her head to greet Sofia, but she did sense the child's presence.

"I need to hold him."

Sofia walked over with the child and stood in front of Mary C. Mary C. reached out as Sofia handed Billy, who was still wrapped in the blanket, into his grandmother's bloody arms. Mary C.'s arms stopped trembling as she held her grandson to her chest. Both, Miss Margaret's and Sofia's eyes filled up with tears while witnessing the emotional moment. Mary C.'s eyes were clear and dry. She had no thoughts of crying as she continued her trance-like stare into space.

The scream of a siren interrupted the silence on the porch as another fire truck rolled toward Mary C.'s burning house. As the noise from the truck faded, Miss Margaret saw movement in the dark to the right of her porch. Even Mary C. turned her head when Miss Margaret screamed as the huge devil dog, Abaddon, stepped out of the darkness and stood panting with its tongue hanging out on the bottom step of the porch.

"Oh, sweet Jesus, protect us!"

Sofia screamed also when she saw the monster Rottweiler standing near them. Jason's heart jumped as he grabbed the wooden handle of a yard rake that was leaning against the railing of the porch. Jason moved toward the devil dog with the rake held high over his head in the attack position. It was Mary C.'s turn to cry out.

"Stop, Jason! Don't hurt him!" Jason stopped his forward motion, but still held the rake in a ready to strike manner. Mary C. continued. "He won't hurt us." Jason lowered the rake, keeping his eye on the huge dog.

"Mama, what are you doing?"

"Just leave him alone, that's all."

The monster seemed to sense what Mary C. had said and he lay down at the foot of the steps as if he was a member of the group. Miss Margaret looked at Mary C. and interrupted the bizarre moment with the mutant canine.

"Please bring Billy into the house and let's get you cleaned up. I hate seeing you look like this. I'm so afraid for you. A hot bath is surely in order here tonight. Are you sure you don't need to see a doctor?" Mary C. shook her head. She stood up from the rocking chair, handed her grandson to Sofia and followed Miss Margaret into the house.

Mr. Butler stepped out of his unmarked police car as officers David Boos and Paul Short walked toward him. A small crowd of the Mayport locals had started to gather in the road leading to the burning house. It was easy to see that Mary C.'s house could not be saved and the firemen were merely trying to contain the flames and put out the fire. It was also easy to see there were a number of bodies on the ground covered with blankets. Both officers shared the same bewildered look on their faces. They waited for Mr. Butler to take in the surroundings. His eyes opened wide as he scanned the battleground. He shook his head.

"I really don't want to know, but here goes." He took a deep breath. "Who and how many dead?"

Officer Short took the lead with the information he had at the moment. "We don't know if anyone was in the house or not. There could be more bodies inside."

Mr. Butler took another deep breath. "How many outside?"

Paul Short took his own deep breath and continued. "We've got Hawk Hawkins over by the porch with fatal stab wounds to the neck and chest. It looks like he was able to pull the knives out before he died. Or perhaps, someone else pulled them out. We can't tell. Both knives are on the ground near him."

Mr. Butler interrupted Paul Short's report. "The Hawk, huh? That surprises me. I didn't think he could be killed. Not like this, anyway. You can bet your ass he didn't go easy."

Paul Short nodded his head and continued. "There's three of those big dogs blown to pieces in the front yard and one burned in the front doorway. It looks like a shotgun was the weapon of choice."

David Boos spoke up and assisted his partner. "The body of our priest friend, shaved head and all, is in the back yard. The dogs must have gotten to him before they were killed. They tore him to pieces, and I mean pieces. Another dog is on the ground next to the priest. It's hind legs have been cut off. The priest didn't go too easy, either." David Boos stopped and looked at Paul Short. Mr. Butler knew they had more to say.

"What?" There was a silence. Mr. Butler's eyes moved back and forth at the two officers. "What is it?"

Paul Short took on the task at hand. "There's six dead black men in the back yard. Some have been shot, some sliced up and one burned to a crisp." Paul Short stopped to allow his information to settle in with Mr. Butler.

Mr. Butler had a question. "Are their faces painted white like last time?"

"No sir. I don't think so. But, there's more, sir." Officer Boos knew it was time to relieve his partner and finish the verbal report to Mr. Butler. "There's one more body, sir. It's definitely another black man. He's at the edge of the woods behind the house. He's got a big knife of some kind stuck between his legs." Mr. Butler shook his head as David Boos continued. "He's gonna be hard to identify. He took a shotgun blast to the face and head at close range. Actually sir, he's got no face or head."

Mary C. stood under the water spray from the showerhead above Miss Margaret's bathtub. The hot water washed the dirt and blood from her hair, head and face. The water at the bottom of the white porcelain bathtub turned deep red as Hawk's blood from Mary C.'s arms ran down her body. She felt as if the blood was running out of her, not off her. Her stomach turned as she watched the last of Hawk's blood swirl down the small drain hole at her feet.

Mary C.'s eyes widened when she saw Hawk standing in front of her with the water from the shower bouncing off his big rounded shoulders. She had seen that many times. The vision faded quickly in the steam smoke of the hot water. Mary C. knew Hawk was trying to say good-by the best way he could.

CHAPTER ONE

Mr. Butler looked down at Johnny D. Bryant's headless body. The blast of the round pellets from Mary C.'s shotgun had hit the devil man above his jawbone, leaving his neck, jawbone, bottom teeth and tongue attached. The rest of his head was scattered in small pieces on the ground and against a tree. Officers Boos and Short stood behind Mr. Butler. They had already gone through the recovery stage from the initial shock when they both saw Mary C.'s brutal handiwork. It was Mr. Butler's turn to recover from the awful sight. He could not contain himself.

"Jesus, Mary and Joseph, have mercy on us all." The two police officers didn't respond after Mr. Butler's plea for mercy. There was a moment of silence except for Mr. Butler's heavy breathing. The others waited for him to speak.

"We gotta find out if anybody was in that house. If Mary C. or Jason ain't in there, where are they? Where's that baby?" Mr. Butler turned to his two officers. "I wonder who this poor devil is?"

A new voice cut through the night air. "Surely you recognize him, gentlemen. That's the devil, himself. Don't you deal with the devil on a daily basis?"

The three policemen turned together in the direction of the strange voice to see a young, handsome and well-dressed black man standing with them. Mr. Butler took the lead. "Who the hell are you and who let you back here?"

The young man stepped forward. "Lamar Harris, sir. If I'm in the wrong place I'm sorry, I'll leave. I saw all the commotion and was curious. I didn't mean to interfere."

Mr. Butler was curious too and always suspicious. "Curiosity usually doesn't carry somebody this deep into the situation. Where'd you come from?"

"I just followed the crowd, noise and lights and here I am. In all your performance of duty you haven't noticed the crowd gathering out there to see what's going on. I'm not the only one here, sir."

Lamar looked past Mr. Butler and nodded his head so Mr. Butler would turn and see who was standing behind him. Mr. Butler turned to see the young Croom twins, Chuck and Buck, standing near them. Both boys were looking at the headless body of Johnny D. Bryant. The two boys did not say a word as they gazed at the bloody mess. Mr. Butler's eyes lit up as he gave directions to his two officers.

"Get those little toe heads out of here. This ain't no peep show. They'll be havin' nightmares and their mama will be blamin' me. You two boys, get!"

The Croom twins had been yelled at and reprimanded so many times in their young lives they really didn't care what anybody said to them, particularly authority figures. They were mean, rude and not scared of any adult. Mr. Butler knew of the evil twins through his association with his fellow lawman and now deceased friend, Jimmy Johnson, who was always trying to help the twins be better young men. Mr. Butler also knew the Mayport citizens would be gathering in big numbers as they followed the fire trucks and police cars to the fire and crime scene. He wanted to continue the interesting conversation with the well-spoken and handsome black stranger, Lamar Harris. Mr. Butler had more instructions for his two officers.

"I need to talk to this young man. Take these two with you and try and keep the people back as far as you can. They'll be all over the yard. How can we protect the crime scene with people walkin' wherever they want?" Paul Short and David Boos followed his directions without a word. Lamar Harris stood alone with Mr. Butler. The lawman had a question. "You know something about all this, don't ya mister?"

Lamar gave a little smile. "Not as much as you want me to know, but I do know that headless mass of black flesh is the Ax. He's Johnny D. Bryant to his mama."

The name hit Mr. Butler like a ton of bricks. "This ain't the man who was raised by the voodoo woman, is it?"

Lamar kept his smile. "That's him. Her name was Voo Swar. She made him what he was."

Mr. Butler's eyes opened wide. "And just what exactly was he?"

Lamar still had that little smile. "He believed he was the son of the devil. He was told that all his life. It was an awful thing to tell somebody."

Mr. Butler nodded his head. "He was after his revenge on Mary C. because of Voo Swar's death, wasn't he?"

"I would think that was a good guess."

Mr. Butler agreed with another nod of his head. "What else do you know about this? You ain't even from around here are ya?"

"I grew up here. I've been away at school and now I'm home for a while. My mama's sick and she'll pass soon. Hattie Harris, that's my mama."

"I've heard her name, but I don't think I've met her."

"No, you wouldn't have met her. I'm sure you don't run in the same circles as my mama. Besides she hasn't been out of the house in a year. I doubt you've even heard her name, but it was nice that you thought you might have."

Mr. Butler wanted Lamar's information. "I don't think you're involved in this, but you know more about it. Will ya talk to me? I'm tired of being in the dark about this Mayport stuff and the killin's gotta stop. Will ya help me?"

"I'll tell you what I've heard and seen, but I've only been home a few days."

"Thank you." They both turned back to the dead body of Johnny D. Bryant.

Mary C. stood on a small, soft bathroom rug and patted her wet body with a thick pink towel. The dirt and blood were gone and she was clean. Her reflection in the small medicine cabinet mirror above the sink revealed the only marks left from the struggle she had endured. The butt of her shotgun had left bruises on her right shoulder and bicep.

Mary C.'s expression did not change when she saw Hawk's reflection in the small mirror. He was standing behind her. She nodded to him as the vision faded again. She knew he was doing all he could to stay and be with her.

It has been said, when the strong are taken violently and they are not ready to go, they fight to stay and not cross over. They fight so hard that they leave thoughts, visions and feelings behind. Some people believe the things left behind could very well be the aberrations, entities and ghosts that are known to appear to the living from time-to-time. Mary C. turned from the small mirror when she heard a gentle knock on the bathroom door.

"Yes."

Sofia's soft voice identified who was at the door. "Miss Mary C., I have some clean clothes for you. May I hand them to you?" Mary C. stepped to the door and opened it. Sofia held her head down as she handed the clean clothes through the open door to Mary C. She had to smile at the young beauty's shy and modest nature.

"Thank you, Sofia. You are always so nice to me."

Sofia kept her head down. "You're welcome. We love you." Sofia moved away from the door.

Mary C.'s house was a pile of smoldering wood. The dirt road in front of her yard was filled with at least a hundred residents of Mayport, both black and white. Every child old enough to walk was watching the firemen and policemen at work. It was an exciting night in Mayport and it would be the topic of conversation in the small town for quite sometime.

Mr. John King, the owner of Mayport's haunted house, and Mr. Al Leek, the owner of one of the major docks in Mayport, drove up to the wild scene at the same time. Mr. King jumped out of his white Cadillac hearse, which was an appropriate vehicle for the occasion. Mr. Leek stepped out of his truck. Mr. Leek saw Mr. King first.

"John, over here." They walked to each other. "This is awful, John. We need to find our friends." They were moving toward the front porch when officer Boos stopped them.

"I'm sorry gentlemen, but we need you to stay back at your vehicles, please."

Mr. Leek responded. "Of course, we'll move back. Can you tell us anything about Mary C. and Jason?"

"No sir. I do know they're not among the bodies we found outside. We don't know if anyone was inside the house."

Mr. King looked to his left at a blanket on the ground. It was obvious it covered someone. He had to ask. "Who's under the blanket?"

Officer Boos looked at the blanket and then back at Mr. King. "That's Mr. Hawkins."

Mr. King and Mr. Leek were both shocked at David Boos' answer. Their faces revealed their disbelief. Officer Boos understood.

"I know what folks thought about the Hawk. It's a sad night when we lose a man like that." Mr. Leek and Mr. King moved back to their vehicles.

Mary C. walked into Miss Margaret's living room, drying her wet hair with the thick pink towel. She wore the clean cut-off dungaree shorts and cotton pull over shirt Sofia had given her. The shorts showed off her muscular legs and the shirt hugged her upper body tightly, revealing the obvious fact she had nothing on under the shirt.

Sofia was sitting on a couch holding Billy. Miss Margaret was in her favorite soft rocker and Jason was standing at the front door looking at the huge dog, Abaddon, still lying at the foot of the front steps. They all turned to Mary C. when she entered the room.

"You were right about the hot shower, Miss Margaret, I feel much better."

Mary C. was the ultimate woman. She had always been beautiful and her body was the envy of any woman who saw her. They all wanted to look like Mary C. Miss Margaret responded. "Come sit down, dear. Are you injured in anyway?"

"I don't think so. My shoulder's sore and bruised from the kick of my shotgun, but that's it." Mary C. changed the subject. "Where are the other girls?

The bright-eyed Sofia had the answer. "Susan and Peggy are at the store. Susan's working the front and Peggy's doing the inventory. We haven't seen Margie all day. She went out to Seminole Beach early this morning to see her friends, Jenny and

Stephanie. As usual, she hasn't returned. She is supposed to have the late shift at the store, but we can only hope she makes it on time."

Miss Margaret smiled. " Now Sofia, let's not judge your sister."

"Now, mother. You know we'll all be surprised if Margie shows up on time."

Mary C. smiled, too. "That girl does have an independent nature about her, don't she?" Mary C. sat down next to Sofia and the baby.

Margie stopped the family station wagon on the dirt road next to Mary C.'s destroyed house. She had driven off the road at the little jetties to allow a speeding ambulance to pass by her and then she followed it into the small town of Mayport. Margie couldn't believe her eyes as she looked out the front windshield of the wagon and saw her friend Mary C.'s house burned to the ground. Margie jumped out of the car and ran toward the front porch of the house. Officer Paul Short was on the job.

"You can't get that close ma'am. Please stay by your car."

Margie stopped, but did not turn back. "Can you tell me if Mary C., Jason and the baby are all right? They live here. They're my friends."

"I'm sorry, ma'am, we don't have any information on those three. It will be a while before we can search the remains of the house.

"Oh God!" Margie was sick to her stomach.

Mr. Butler and Lamar Harris walked up behind Officer Short. Mr. Butler recognized Margie. He knew she had been Jimmy Johnston's close friend. "Hello, Margie. Quite a mess, huh? You wouldn't know where the family is, would ya?"

Margie looked at the smoldering rubble. "No, sir."

She looked down at the dead dogs and the blanket, but didn't say anything about them. It was the second time she had seen death and destruction in Mary C.'s front yard. For some strange reason she knew Mary C. and Jason were not lying under the ashes of the house. Margie felt it deep in her soul. She wanted to tell Mr. Butler she knew they were not there, but she didn't.

Mr. Butler moved past Margie and Officer Short. "I'm gonna sit in my car and talk to Mr. Harris for a while. If you need me, holler."

Margie walked back toward the family station wagon and got into the front seat. Mr. Leek stepped up to the driver's side window. "Margie, you all right?"

Margie looked toward him. "Hey, Mr. Leek. I don't think any of us can be all right."

Mr. Leek nodded in agreement. Then he looked toward the house. "I hope they ain't in there."

Margie looked in the direction of the house, too. "They're not. I can feel it."

Mr. Leek looked at Margie. "I think you're right."

Miss Margaret's eyes were opened wide and Sofia had the open mouth syndrome as Mary C. finished the incredible story about her fight for survival against a pack of wild dogs, a group of black warriors and the devil himself. Mary C. told of firebombs and the shotgun stand she and Jason made on the porch. She broke their hearts when she told of Hawk's bravery and brutal death. The eerie silence in the room was broken when the baby gurgled as Sofia held him in her lap. It was as if the child knew it was all for him. All eight eyes in the room looked at Billy when he made his noise. There were also four smiles.

Mr. Butler was sitting in his unmarked police car with Lamar Harris waiting to get the information he wanted and needed. "You know you don't have to talk to me like this, but I'm tired of comin' out here to find dead bodies. I think you know something about what happened here tonight. Even though you haven't been around very long, I still think you have the information I need. Will you talk to me?"

Lamar Harris nodded his head. "It was pure revenge. Johnny D. Bryant, known to some as the Ax, came here tonight to kill the white woman because she killed his mother who raised him to be the devil. It's voodoo and evil at the highest level. Six dogs, six accomplices, six knives, you get the idea?" Mr. Butler was getting more information than he expected from the handsome young black man. "There's still a lot of hard voodoo followers in this little town and even the one's who don't believe are angry that the woman kills and continues to walk the streets. Too many black people are dying in this front yard. They'll keep coming after her. She'll have to fall before it ends now."

Mr. Butler had to speak up. "I was told it started with the baby. Black folks came the first time to take the child and kill the woman in the process. I'm sure it was a chilling surprise when Mary C., along with the Indian priest, defended themselves and saved the baby. It was definitely self-defense. The law could do nothing."

"I believe that. I know Voo Swar wanted the child and others still do. But, now they're only remembering the numbers that were killed. And after tonight it will only get worse. You got nine dead men somewhere in this yard. Seven are black, one is white and the other one is an Indian of some kind. The ratio speaks for itself."

Mr. Butler had to speak up again. "You do realize this will be self-defense, just like before? You can't just take an army of men, black or white, and go to somebody's house to kill them. It's against the law."

"Maybe I'll be wrong about others coming after her. I know I wouldn't, not after what she has been able to do to the members of the first two attempts. One interesting point is that her protectors are being wiped out with her enemies. The priest is dead. The Hawk is dead. The boy's not that strong. For the first time she may have to stand alone."

Mr. Butler didn't like the way Lamar was talking, but at least he had the true story about what had happened there that night. He had to ask one more question.

"You think anyone was in the house?"

Lamar Harris smiled. "No sir, I don't."

There was silence and sadness in Miss Margaret's living room. Mary C.'s tale of woe and trail of death had mentally drained Miss Margaret and Sofia. They were both lost in their thoughts of the incredible life Mary C. had brought to their attention. Jason was quiet, as usual, and he continued to look at the dog through the window of the living room. A set of headlights flashed off the front window as the family station wagon rolled up into the front yard. Margie was home.

Margie stepped out of the car and stopped when she saw the huge dog. Jason opened the front door and stepped out onto the porch. He could see the fear on Margie's face as she looked down at the dog. Jason had to ease her fear.

"It's all right, Margie. He won't hurt ya. Or that's what Mama says, anyway. I'm not too sure myself, but he's been right there for about an hour. He hasn't made a sound."

Margie had seen the dead dogs in Mary C.'s front yard. She still didn't move past the dog. "There's three or four other dogs just like him dead in your front yard. I don't think I like this one being in my front yard. This is a killer dog, that's what they do."

Jason stepped off the porch, took Margie's hand and guided her past the dog. They both watched the huge creature as they moved slowly toward the front door. When Margie realized they were safe at the door she turned her attention to Jason. She had not been that close to him in a very long time. Margie squeezed his arm and held it against her breast as they moved into the house. She held on tight, even after they were in the living room. Miss Margaret saw them first.

"Margie, I'm so glad you're home. This is another awful night for us all to bear."

Margie continued to hold Jason's arm. She looked at Mary C., but responded to her mother. "I know mother, I saw Miss Mary C.'s house."

Mary C. looked at Margie. "You was there?"

Margie nodded. "I just left there."

Mary C. stood up from her spot on the couch. "You saw Hawk?"

Margie's eyes widened. "No ma'am."

"What about the house?"

Margie released her hold on Jason. "It's gone." Mary C. walked to the front window and looked out in the direction of her house. Jason stepped over to her.

"What do you want to do, Mama?"

Mary C. did not turn to him, but she did answer. "Nothin'. Let 'em find us." Mary C. turned to Miss Margaret. "If me and Jason sleep on the boat tonight can Billy stay here 'til mornin'?" Margie and Sofia looked at their mother. They knew what her answer would be.

"My dear friend, please don't even consider sleeping on that boat any night. We have plenty of room here for all three of you and you're welcome to stay as long as you like. I couldn't bear to think of you on the boat when you have a clean soft bed right here."

Mary C. smiled and nodded her head. "Thank you Miss

Margaret. You are the kindest woman on this earth."

Jason nodded, Sofia smiled with her snow-white teeth and Margie looked at Jason with "want" in her eyes. Mary C. saw Margie's lustful expression and she knew the look of "want" when she saw it. She had another suggestion.

"If it's okay with you, Jason can shower here and then he'll stay on the boat."

Miss Margaret nodded her head. "Whatever you think is best, dear."

The huge black woman, known as Macadoo, stood in the crowd of shocked spectators as the body of one the victims from Mary C.'s firefight was being carried to the back of an ambulance. The body was wrapped in a blanket. She watched another body move past her and then another. It was obvious to all who were watching that no one under the blankets had survived. As Macadoo watched another body being placed into the back of a truck, she saw Lamar Harris walking away from Mr. Butler's unmarked police car. The fat woman moved as quickly as she could to be sure she stepped into Lamar's path. He stopped when she blocked his way. She spoke to him in a low and cautious voice.

"And what brings you to this vile ground? You be a curious cat?"

Lamar smiled. "I tried to get here in time to actually see the battle between evil and evil, but I was too late. I did get to see the outcome and who was the real devil. Your devil boy's head's been scattered all over the woods outback, so much for him being the Devil's son." Macadoo's face revealed her anger, but she still had enough control to whisper again.

"You see 'im?"

Lamar nodded. "It's him all right. Somebody blew his head off. I'll bet you can guess who. Six others are dead, too." Macadoo put her hand over her own mouth to keep from screaming. Lamar knew she was about to explode. He added to her pain. "Seven more black men are dead. Two of her protectors are dead. The one they call Hawk and the one they say is a priest. If you look closely you will see five dead Rottweiler dogs. These dogs were trained to kill, but they're dead."

Macadoo stopped his casualty roll call. "And the woman,

Mary C.?"

"Not here."

"Her boy?"

"Not here."

"And the oak baby?"

"Not here, either."

Macadoo was sick to her stomach and had to challenge Lamar. "You don't seem to care 'bout what happened here tonight. These be ya people and they is dying in this evil place. Have ya been gone too long to care for ya brothers?"

Lamar took a deep breath. "First of all, these men being black don't make us brothers, but I do care that lives have been taken. Many people suffer when a life is taken. If seven men with six killer dogs came to your house to kill you, you would fight for your life. We all would."

Macadoo interrupted him. "I heard the same thing when the Calypsos was kilt on this same spot. They was all warriors against that evil woman and her hold on this town. This has nothing to do with man's written law. This is of the world beyond the law. This comes from voodoo, magic, witchcraft, and the other side. This has to do with the oak tree and the true evil that walk the earth. It be our duty to rid the world of such a vile presence. It be proper to come at night. It be proper to try and outnumber 'em. It be proper to use the beasts so our people are not kilt. These are not human beings we dealin' with. Any way to destroy them be the right way. There is no wrong way as long as we stop 'em. If you don't consider it witchcraft then say it be Biblical. Consider it as, fighting the devil like in the Old Testament." Lamar had absorbed Macadoo's "kill the evil" rationale and he wanted to leave her to her strange thoughts.

"I don't know what to say about what you believe, but you need to know that I do care and I hate this woman for these things. You also need to know, I will not come in the night with killer dogs. I will not come to steal a baby. I will not burn a house down. Her reign of terror will soon end and when it does you will remember I was the one who told you so. Now, go and bury these pitiful fools you have sent here to die and go ask, who ever you are asking tonight, for forgiveness. And the next time you talk to me let's talk about something pleasant." Lamar Harris left Macadoo standing in Mary C's front yard. She glared at him in anger as he turned and walked away from her.

Jason stepped up behind Sofia as she laid Billy on a small single bed in one of the guest rooms. She turned to him when he spoke.

"Thank you for being so good with him."

Sofia threw her arms around Jason and kissed him passionately. Jason returned the kiss and then held her at arms length.

"That was very nice, but I don't think your mother would like it if she walked in here." Sofia pulled Jason close to her body again.

"I don't care. I love you. I love your son. I love your mother. I don't care." Jason smiled and returned her hug.

"I just don't know how your mother is going to take this. You're a lot younger than me and I know that doesn't matter to you, but it might to her." Jason held her away from him again. "And we seemed to be snake-bit when it comes to being together."

Sofia had to smile her beautiful smile when Jason made his funny, but true comment.

"Okay, it's our secret for a little longer." She kissed him again and left the room.

As Jason looked down at his son there were loud voices coming from the living room. It was Mr. Leek and Mr. King looking for their friends. They were both happy when they stepped into Miss Margaret's living room and saw Mary C. sitting there with her wet hair, tight shorts and even tighter shirt. Mr. Leek was first to come through the door.

"Thank the Lord, you're here."

Mr. King spoke next. "I knew it. I just knew it in my heart. And I'll just bet Jason and the baby's here, too." Mary C. nodded. Mr. Leek could not contain himself.

"Praise the Lord, praise the Lord." Jason walked into the room. Mr. Leek had to hug his good friend. "My heart is about to bust open, son. I don't think I've ever felt like this. Praise the Lord." Mary C. did not hug either one of them and they did not advance toward her. They were most respectful. For some reason Mary C. wanted to tell them what she knew. It was as if she wanted them to know the night had not been all that happy for her.

"Hawk's dead. They killed him. He saved us." The room went

silent once more. They waited for Mary C. "The priest's dead too. He came for his sword today and then came back tonight to save the child, like he did the first time." Margie screamed and interrupted the sober moment. They all turned to Margie and she was looking at the front door. The huge dog, Abaddon, was standing in the doorway. Mr. King was the closest to the door. He moved back away from the dog.

"Good God! What the hell is that?" Mary C. stepped to the dog.

"That's my new dog." Jason's eyes lit up.

"Mama, what are you saying?"

"I'm sayin' that's my new dog. His owner's dead. He followed me here and now he's mine." She looked at Mr. Leek. "Al, if you have to kill somebody and he has a dog, don't you get to keep his dog?" The room went silent once more. Mr. Leek was not quick enough with an answer to suit Mary C. She turned to Mr. King. "Now John, don't ya think it's only fair I get the dog. Hell, they burned my house down. At least let me keep the damn dog." Mr. King was a little faster with his reply.

"If you want the dog, of course you can keep the dog." The room was silent again. Mr. King made an observation. "But Mary C., you do know this is a mean breed of dog you got here? I don't think these dogs are good to have around little children." The room was still silent as they waited for Mary C.'s reply to Mr. King's calm and sensible comment. Mary C. didn't disappoint them.

"Well, if he gets too mean, Jason can shoot him like we did the others. Hell, Jason's ready to shoot him right now. Ain't ya, son?" Jason was surprised with his mother's question.

"I just don't want him to turn on us and hurt somebody, that's all." Mary C. reached down and grabbed Abaddon's huge head in both her hands, squeezing both of the dog's ears.

"Well, he's gonna be my new dog as long as he behaves. If he don't act right, I'll shoot him myself." Mary C. turned to the shocked looks on everybody's faces. "Oh, and his name is Abaddon. Ain't that a strange name? That's what his owner called him when he yelled for him to kill me. Abaddon, I like that." She turned to Mr. Leek. "Al, take me to get Hawk."

The fire was out, the bodies had been loaded into the vehicles and the Mayport crowd was moving away from the yard. Mr. Butler stood with his two best officers, David Boos and Paul Short.

"Well gentlemen, we've gotta find the three that live here. I've been waitin' for her to walk up here and tell us all about it." Paul Short looked past Mr. Butler as a truck drove up into the yard. He could see the passenger.

"I don't think you'll have to wait any longer, sir." Mr. Butler turned in the direction Paul was looking. Mary C. was stepping out of Mr. Leek's truck. Mr. Butler shook his head.

"Well, I'll be damned. She is somethin' else."

Mr. Leek accompanied Mary C. as she walked over to where Mr. Butler was standing. She was still barefoot and dressed in the skimpy clothes Sofia had given her. It was difficult, if not impossible, for the three police officers to look at Mary C. without looking at the female attributes she was presenting to the group. Mr. Leek greeted Mr. Butler.

"Mary C. came back to let you know she and her family were safe. She didn't want the firemen to be looking for them in the ashes." Mr. Butler looked at Mary C.

"That was good of ya. They would have been searchin' for y'all. We appreciate you comin' back." Mary C. nodded. Mr. Butler continued. "You know I have to ask you some questions? I also know you have suffered great loses here tonight, both personal and material. If you want to wait 'til tomorrow to talk to me that'll be fine. Your choice."

Mary C. smiled. "I'll see you tomorrow, Mr. Butler. Will you come to me or do I have to go to you?" Mr. Butler was surprised with her question and he hesitated with his answer. Mary C. asked again. "Your place or mine?"

Mr. Butler found his answer. "I'm startin' to get used to the ride out here to Mayport. What time and where would you like to meet?"

"On the boat at Al's dock in the mornin'. Are you a mornin' man, Mr. Butler?"

"I'm an early riser, if that's what you mean?"

"I'll just bet you are at that. Men like you don't sleep much 'cause y'all always scared you gonna miss somethin'."

"I don't miss much."

"I'm sure you don't. Don't come too early." Mary C. turned

away and walked back to Mr. Leek's truck. Mr. Leek nodded to Mr. Butler and followed her to the truck. Mr. Butler looked at Officer Boos and then at Officer Short.

"Close your mouths gentlemen, she's gone."

Margie sat on the couch in her living room staring at Jason. He stood at the front door watching Abaddon lying down on the front porch. He was still uneasy about the monster canine. He knew he would never be able to trust his mother's new dog and companion. Sofia walked into the room and reminded Margie of her duties.

"Margie, don't you have the late shift at the store tonight?" Margie looked at her younger sister with a glare in her eyes.

"You know I do, Sofia. If we're the only two here and the other two are at the store and you don't have it, you know I have it. But, thanks for the reminder. With all the excitement I had forgotten. I can always depend on little sister to keep me straight. Thank you again, Sofia." Sofia smiled at Margie's open sarcasm and left the room.

Jason didn't hear the conversation behind him. He was occupied with his own thoughts. He wanted to find that dark place in his head where he had been saved before and leave all the death and destruction, but this time he had a reason to stay. Jason would not leave his infant son, Billy.

It seemed as if every black resident of Mayport was inside the Blue Moon tavern. The number of citizens spilled into the street outside the one black honky-tonk in Mayport. The only other black taverns were Tony's Seafood Shack out at the end of Mayport Road and a small bar called the Honey Dripper across the river at American Beach. American Beach was the beach where the members of the black community could gather to picnic, enjoy the seashore and swim in the Atlantic Ocean.

A hand pulled the electric plug from the wall and the loud music from the colorful jukebox went silent. The huge black woman, Macadoo, stepped up on the small band stage and raised her hand up high to get everyone's attention. The crowd stopped talking and moving and each person turned toward where Macadoo was standing.

"Y'all be quiet and listen." She did not have to make a second request. The room was silent. She took a deep breath. "Once again a sad and evil night come to our town and we have lost loved ones and friends. I ain't got no words to give for the grievin', but to say they died as soldiers against the evil of this world." As Macadoo allowed her words to settle, she looked into the crowd and saw Lamar Harris standing near the bar. Her eyes met his as if they were the only two in the crowded room. A voice came from the crowd and took Macadoo's attention away from the handsome young man. One of the elders stepped from the crowd.

"This be the second time good men been lost in the name of fightin' evil. The number of families who have mourned and will mourn be too many. It not be worth the losses we have taken. I for one believe the tree protects her and as long as she stay here it will always protect her. I also think she know that. We are too divided in our beliefs. Some of us are God fearing while others fear the oak tree. Some are God fearing and still go to the tree. Some believe in the old way, the way of the islands, voodoo and the craft. We have some here tonight who want that child. They think the child will solve all our problems."

Macadoo knew the man and she did not like his challenge or him having the attention of the crowd he so quickly demanded. "Well, Mr. Cane, what be the point you tryin' to deliver to us here tonight?"

The old man was ready for her. "To continue to go after this woman be a mistake and will continue to be a mistake. You, Macadoo, must admit you have been wrong in sending our young men to their death in the name of your cause, what ever that be. Most folk in this room are good people and wish no harm to others. This talk of revenge, evil, voodoo, and what ever you say that moves men to kill, must stop."

Macadoo's eyes revealed her discomfort and anger at the old man's words. He continued. "I pray no others join with you in your misguided quest to harm these people. If any of our homes be attacked in the same manner we would fight to survive. I for one will not be part of this madness." Mr. Cane looked around the room. "And I beg you young strong men not to be taken by Macadoo's words of revenge for the black man. I have said what I come here to say and I thank you for listening. I hope what ever you believe guides you down the right road."

Mr. Cane walked through the crowd as they moved aside to allow him to leave the building. Almost half the others in the room followed him out of the room and into the street. The people who were standing outside squeezed their way into the building as the others left. Macadoo looked toward where Lamar Harris had been standing. He was gone. The huge woman still held the crowd's attention.

"We will mourn and bury our dead now. I won't and I can't rest 'til I rid our town of the evil that come to live among us."

The bell on the door sounded when Margie walked into the store. Peggy and Susan turned to see their older sister. They both smiled. Margie did not smiled back.

"Didn't think I was coming, did you?" Peggy shook her head.

"Sure didn't. When you left for Seminole Beach this morning, I just knew you were gone for the day and the night." Susan had to add her thoughts.

"We were just talking about which one of us would have to stay if you didn't come in."

"It makes me very sad that you two don't have more confidence in me."

Susan had more. "Let's just say we know you from past experiences, but we are glad to see you and I am sorry I misjudged you this time." Peggy nodded her head.

Margie smiled. "Apology accepted." Margie hesitated and took a deep breath. "I'm sure you've heard the sirens."

Peggy nodded again. "We didn't have anyway to go see what was happening. We knew it was serious and actually we were afraid to go look anyway. We knew it was too far away to be at our house and we knew someone would tell us if we were needed. We've just been waiting to hear." Margie shared what she knew and what she had seen.

Mr. Leek's truck stopped in front of Miss Margaret's house and Mary C. stepped out of the truck. "Thanks Al."

"Good night, Mary C." She walked past the huge black dog and up the steps to the front door. Miss Margaret was the only one in the living room when Mary C. walked in.

"That was quick, dear. Are you all right?"

"I'm fine, Miss Margaret. I'm just tired."

"I'm sure you are. Jason is taking a shower and he said to tell you he would go to the boat. Billy is sleeping in Sofia's room. That girl sure loves that baby. Margie went to relieve the girls. They should be coming in any minute and I was waiting for you. I'm sure Margie is telling them about the excitement and I know you don't need to go over it with the girls. Please go get some sleep so you will be rested for what the morning brings. I have turned the sheets down for you in the room in the back. You will hear nothing once you fall asleep back there."

"I do love you, Miss Margaret."

"And we love you, too, child. Good night." Mary C. walked to the small bedroom, entered the room and closed the door. Miss Margaret went upstairs toward her bedroom. Sofia's bedroom door was closed. Miss Margaret stopped and tapped gentle on the door.

"Good night, Sofia." Miss Margaret was pleased when she heard her youngest daughter's voice from behind the door.

"Good night, Mother. I love you."

Jason stepped out of the shower and began drying the water off his body. He turned quickly to the bathroom door when it opened and Sofia stepped into the small room. She closed and locked the door behind her.

"Sofia, are you crazy? What are you doing?"

She moved to him, pulled the towel away from his body and wrapped her arms around him. The front of her thin nightshirt got wet when she pushed her hard breasts against his chest. He stood there naked as she kissed him passionately and pushed her body against his. Sofia felt his heat when she reached down and touched him. Jason reached down and touched her, too. The moisture and heat he felt coming from her body moved him to the same sexual feelings Jessie had introduced to him years before. It was the first time he felt such passion and heat since he lost his green-eyed Jessie. He did not care about anything at that moment, except having Sofia. She moved with him as he slowly maneuvered her to the floor of the small room. He lifted her wet shirt, exposing her hard snow-white breasts as she pulled and kicked her panties off for him.

Sofia opened her legs wide as Jason continued to touch her. She moved her hips against his hand and he knew she wanted him to push harder. He had witnessed such a reaction many times with

Jessie and he knew exactly what to do to create the most pleasure for Sofia. Jason was a master at giving sexual pleasure to women. He began to work his magic on his inexperienced partner. He knew he could satisfy her and move her to another state before his manliness actually entered her body.

As soon as Sofia's body shuttered from his touch he placed his head between her legs and gave her pleasure to the point where she was holding on to his head with both hands. She tried to push his head and tongue even deeper than where they already were. Jason was an expert at pleasing the woman he lay with. Jason began his sexual experiences with Jessie and his one wild time with the older Peggy, Sofia's cousin and Uncle Bobby's old girlfriend. He continued the learning process during his physical encounters with all three of Sofia's sisters. Jason's earlier sexual encounters had given him a world of experience in comparison to the sheltered Sofia. His love for Sofia enhanced his effort. He would always be sure she was completely satisfied before he took any pleasure. Jason's experience with Jessie had resulted in a sexual prowess, which would benefit the women who would have the good fortune to have sexual relations with him. A knock on the bathroom door stopped Sofia's movements.

Jason's did not lift his head. He kept his head buried between her legs with the insides of her thighs pressed against his ears. It was obvious to Sofia that in Jason's present position and state of mind he had not heard the knock on the door. She reached down, grabbed a hand full of his hair and pulled his head away from her, lifting it high enough for him to see her. Sofia held Jason's head up and pointed to the door. There was another knock and a voice.

"Sofia, are you in there?" Sofia recognized her sister Peggy's voice. Even in his sexual state of mind, Jason was quick to react.

"No, it's me, Jason. Just give me a second and it's all yours."

Peggy was surprised. "Oh, I'm sorry. I didn't know you were here."

"Your mama said I could get cleaned up before I went to stay on the boat."

"That's okay, I'll just go upstairs to mother's bathroom. Sorry." She moved away from the door. Sofia stood up and hurried to put her panties and wet shirt back on her overheated body. She was scared and frustrated again.

"What should I do? How do I get out of here?"

Jason put his dirty pants on. "I'll go out first and see what we need to do. Be ready to move quickly when I come back to get you."

"I'm scared." She hugged Jason. Her perfect body trembled as he returned the hug.

"Just stay in here and wait for me. Lock the door and if anybody comes to the door you can say I left and you came in. Just wait for me." He left the bathroom and Sofia locked the door.

Jason stepped into the hallway. He had his dirty shirt in his hand and the towel he had been using. It looked empty downstairs as he made his way to the front of the house. He looked up the stairs and saw no one. He turned toward the front door and came face-to-face with Miss Margaret's daughter Susan. Susan had long auburn-red hair and a small group of freckles crossing her nose. Each one of Miss Margaret's daughters had their own touch of beauty. Susan definitely had hers. Jason remembered his one and only sexual encounter with Susan as she stood there in front of him. His mental flashback was interrupted when Susan pushed her body against his and moved him, forcefully, against the wall of the hallway. She kissed him and continued to push her body into his.

"God, you taste good."

Jason knew she was tasting more than just him. He grabbed her arms with his hands and pushed Susan away from him.

"Are you crazy?" She kissed him again and pulled his head toward her with one of her hands. Jason held her at arm's length once more. "Stop, Susan. Your mama will kill us."

She smiled. "And I care about that?" She reached down and touched him. "Oh God, I really got you excited fast, didn't I?"

He moved her hand. "I said stop."

She continued her smile. "I know what you said, but I know you want me, too. It's been so long. When Peggy said you were here I knew we would have a moment together. I know you remember the other time. I'll never forget that first time, that first and only time. There should be more. I know you think about it, too. I know about my sisters and you and I don't care." There was the sound of someone walking down the stairs. Susan kissed Jason again quickly. "When you want me, let me know. Bye!"

Susan left Jason standing against the wall. He watched her long red ponytail swinging back and forth, touching her buttocks as she moved toward the kitchen. She entered the kitchen where Jason could not see her. He stepped to the corner of the hall and he saw Peggy stepping down off the last step of the main stairway. She turned toward the living room and walked to the front door. Jason moved back to the bathroom where Sofia was waiting and he touched the door lightly.

"Sofia, open the door." The door opened a few inches and he could see Sofia's big sky-blue eyes staring at him. "Come out and go right up the stairs. Hurry." Sofia didn't open the door any further.

"I'm scared."

"Come on! Hurry!" Jason pushed the door open and Sofia reluctantly stepped out into the short hallway. "Go right up the stairs to your room. Go on!" Sofia ran a few steps, turned the corner of the hallway and ran up the stairs, covering two stairs at a time as she ran. Her stomping feet could be heard and felt throughout the old house. Susan came out of the kitchen to see who was running up the stairs. Peggy left the living room and stepped to the foot of the stairs to also see who was making such a noise. Jason stepped out of the bathroom and joined the two sisters as they looked up the stairs. Peggy made the first observation.

"It sounded like a horse was running up the stairs."

Susan stared at Jason and had her own thought. "What ever it was shook the whole house. Jason, you didn't fall down the stairs, did you?"

Jason looked up the stairs and shook his head. "No, I didn't. But, it sure sounded like somebody did." To Jason's delight, Peggy changed the subject.

"Margie told us what happened. I'm sorry about Mr. Hawk and your house. That whole thing must have been awful. How's Miss Mary C.?"

Jason nodded his head. "She's fine. She went to the house with Mr. Leek to talk to the police."

Susan knew more than Jason did. "Actually, she came back and she's asleep in the back room. Mother told me when I was up stairs." Peggy changed the subject again.

"Margie told us Billy was here, too. Is he okay?"

Susan had the correct information. "He's sleeping in Sofia's room. I peeked in, but it was too dark to see and I didn't want to wake them. I'm sure he's fine with our little sister watching over him."

There had been far too much talk, contact, close calls and subject changing to suit Jason. He had to get out of that house and away from the beautiful vixens that were in hot pursuit of him.

"I'm stayin' on the boat tonight. I've got some clean clothes there. Good night y'all." Both sisters turned and watched Jason walk out the front door. He stepped over Abaddon as he left the porch.

Miss Margaret had fallen asleep with her Rosary beads in her hand. She was a strange religious mixture. She was a Baptist who knew and enjoyed the prayers of the Catholic Rosary. Sofia was under her sheet still wearing her damp shirt. She was trying to recover from her latest "coitus interruptus" with Jason. When she touched herself where Jason had touched her it made her recovery more difficult, if not impossible. She had awakened other times from a dream and had touched herself, this time she would touch herself and then fall asleep.

Mary C. was in a deep dreamless sleep. She seldom had dreams. It was one of her gifts. The magic carousel had created her last dream. Margie was minding the store and hating every minute she was away from the house and Jason. Susan was taking a bath in the small bathroom where Jason had showered and Peggy stood on the front porch and watched Jason drive away in Hawk's truck.

Mr. Butler stood next to one of the tables in the coroner's lab at the Atlantic Beach Police Department. The naked and dead body of Lester "Hawk" Hawkins lay on the table. Mr. Butler looked over at Officer David Boos. He was standing next to another table with the mutilated body of the Punjabi priest, Sandeep Singh. Seven blankets covering seven bodies lay lined up on the floor along the wall. Each body under the blankets would have its turn on the two tables. Mr. Butler shook his head at the sight of the two men.

"It gets worse every time she's involved. I've got a growing list you know? It's got all the people who have died because of her or when they were with her. It's becoming quite a long list, especially, if I have to add nine at a time. Do I count the dogs, too?"

David Boos looked at his partner Paul Short to see how they should react to Mr. Butler's strange information and question. They just listened. "No tellin' how many have died that I don't know about. She's somethin' else." The coroner walked in and Mr. Bulter's walk down memory lane with Mary C.'s death count ended.

Jason lay in the narrow bunk on a thin mattress in the small captian's quarters of the shrimp boat, Mary C. He would have to operate the boat alone until he found someone to work with him. Jason knew he could run the boat, but he would miss his friend, Hawk. Jessie's face flashed in his head. He remembered the night they stayed on the boat when she was hiding from Jake, the Mayport phantom of the night. It had been a great night of sex with his lover who became his teacher. Sofia's face flashed across his mind. He liked the thought of being the teacher now. His sexual thoughts were interrupted when he heard a noise. It felt as if someone had stepped onto the deck of the boat. He jumped up from the bed and stepped to the wheelhouse.

"Who's there?" Jason looked out the door of the wheelhouse as a voice answered his question.

"It's me, Peggy. I didn't mean to scare you." Peggy stepped out of the darkness and stood with Jason at the door. "Want some company?" In less than a minute, Jason had her head between his legs. It was Peggy's specialty.

John King stood on the front porch of his haunted house. He could smell the smoke from the smoldering ruins of Mary C.'s house. It was late. He was mentally and physically drained from the violent deaths of Hawk Hawkins and the Punjabi priest. Mr. King went into his house and walked into the living room to extinguish the flames in the lanterns. Although the house was equipped with electric lighting, he preferred candles and lanterns. He only used the electric lights for the comfort of his guests when he entertained. When he told his ghosts stories to the Mayport children he always used the candles and lanterns. They created the frightful atmosphere he wanted to establish as he told his strange and gruesome tales.

Mr. King blew out the last lantern near the fireplace in the living room and turned to go upstairs to his bedroom. He passed a coffee table in the middle of the room and saw the magic carousel Mary C. had left behind. Mr. King smiled and shook his head when he thought of how foolish he must have looked to the others when he tried to use the carousel to enter the ghostly porthole to the other side. He thought that Mary C.'s confused state of mind caused her to forget about the beautiful antique music box.

After Mr. King thought the attempt to use the carousel had failed, he did not think the music box had any magical powers at all. It was just a beautiful antique to him. He had no idea the carousel had introduced Mary C., Jason and Hawk to the other side and the ghosts who dwelled in the walls of his haunted house. He would give the music box back to Mary C. when the opportunity presented itself. If the ghosts were on the move that night, Mr. King would sleep through their activities.

Jason and Peggy lay naked in the narrow bed on the boat. They were both exhausted from their late night sexual encounter aboard the Mary C. Peggy had done most of the work at first, but Jason used his tongue to add to her pleasure as the activity progressed. Her comment was music to Jason's ears.

"I can't stay here all night. I need to be home when morning comes. I need to go."

Jason only nodded, but he was relieved she was leaving. Peggy dressed, kissed Jason good-by and climbed off the boat onto Mr. Leek's wooden dock. Jason looked up at her standing above him. He knew the proper thing to say.

"I should walk you home. It's late and you don't need to be walkin' alone."

Peggy smiled. "I wouldn't be considering it if Jake was still walking around at night. I think he's gone. We haven't seen him in about a year. I wonder what happened to him anyway?"

Jason had a monster mental flashback from the past. It would be the second time he had thought about Jake in the last few days. The first time was when the magic carousel revealed the doorway to the other side at Mr. King's house and now Peggy had said the skinny black man's name. Jason knew he and Mr. Leek were the only two who knew the truth about Jake and how they had killed and buried him under the oak tree at the sand hill. Jessie knew, too, but she was gone. Peggy's words brought Jason back from the past.

"I walked over here, didn't I? Besides, I'm going to the store and ride home with Margie. She's got the car. Mother's been letting us close the store at midnight lately. We're all in shock over that, but no one's complaining. I'll just tell Margie I couldn't sleep with all the excitement and I came to help her close up. She'll be so glad to have the help she won't question me at all. I could tell her I was here with you." Jason's eyes widened. Peggy smiled again.

"Don't worry, I won't tell. You like having secrets, don't you? It's funny how we feel about you. We all know about each other, but we don't tell or talk about it. We know you like Sofia the best, but for some reason that doesn't matter either, at least not to me. I don't think you'll ever be with one woman and if you are I know it won't be me, so I'm going to play with you like you play with us. Pretty neat, huh?" Jason was surprised with Peggy being so forward and her cavalier attitude. He had no answer or response to make to her as she walked into the fish house and headed to the store.

Miss Margaret's house was dark and quiet. Sofia had fallen asleep with her hand still between her legs. Mary C. was in her normal deep sleep. Her ability to compartmentalize her feelings and actions was another one of her gifts. Not even Hawk's effort to stay with her could take her to a dream world.

The bell rang on the door when Peggy walked into the front of the store. "Margie, it's Peggy. Don't let me scare you." Margie didn't answer. Peggy saw a small stool on its side on the floor. There was glass from a broken jar that lay broken on the floor and some other items that had fallen, but didn't break. "Margie, you in the back?" Peggy didn't like the feeling going through her body. She was scared. She moved slowly to the back room, staying close to the wall as she walked. "Margie, please answer me! You're scaring me!" Even though Margie did not respond, Peggy's fearful moment diminished when she saw the light from the small bathroom shining through the space at the bottom of the door. She moved closer. "Margie, you in there? It's Peggy." Peggy felt a welcome relief at first when she heard her sister's voice coming from the other side of the bathroom door.

"Yes."

Peggy took a big breath. "You scared me for a minute. You okay?" Again there was no response from Margie. "Margie, what's wrong?"

Margie spoke to her sister in a low and painful voice. "I'm hurt. Help me." Peggy turned the doorknob and pushed the door open to see her sister sitting on the floor between the wall and the toilet. She moved to Margie.

"Margie, what's wrong?" She knelt down next to her sister. There was blood on the front of Margie's pants. "Oh God, Margie! You're bleeding."

Margie looked up at Peggy. "I was standing on the stool and fell. I really fell hard on my back and butt."

Peggy looked at the blood. "Did you cut yourself on the glass?"

Margie shook her head. "No. It's not that."

"Margie, you're scaring me. I'll go get Mother."

Margie grabbed Peggy's blouse. "No, you can't. Just help me. Just you and me."

"I don't understand. You're going to bleed to death."

"Just get me a wet towel and help me get up. Help me pull my pants off and sit me on the toilet." Peggy helped Margie up and pulled her blood soaked pants down to her ankles. She eased her older sister down onto the toilet seat and then she got a towel and wet it in the sink. She handed Margie the wet towel. Peggy's hand was shaking as Margie took the towel. Margie knew how scared her sister was because she was scared, too. Margie would always be the bravest and strongest one of all the sisters.

"I think I'm going to be fine. I know it looks bad, but I'm okay, really." Peggy watched her sister place the wet towel between her legs. Margie knew she had to explain.

"I think I've been pregnant for about a month, but I don't think I am any more. If I can stop this bleeding, I think I'll be fine. When I fell it did something to me. I really fell hard. I thought I had broken something inside me. I know what it was, now." Peggy's eyes were as wide opened as they had ever been in her life.

"You need a doctor for this. What if you can't stop it?"

"It's already stopping. I can feel it. I think we can do it."

"What can I do? Tell me."

Margie took a painful deep breath. "Find me some Kotex. I know Mother keeps a case hidden for her lady friends. And just stay with me until this is over." Peggy hurried to find the large and very absorbent feminine napkin. Margie allowed the towel to soak up the blood and then she applied pressure to stop the flow. Peggy returned with a large box of Kotex. She turned away a number of times as Margie rendered first aid to herself, but she did remain in the small bathroom as Margie had requested. After an hour of generic medical attention and clean up, Peggy helped her weak older sister to the family station wagon and drove them both home. The night of death, terror, sex, devil dogs and Margie's miscarriage was over.

CHAPTER TWO

The sweet and pleasant aroma of French toast cooking in Miss Margaret's kitchen permeated the entire house. It was Mary C.'s specialty and she knew all four sisters loved her French toast with a glass of milk. Still sleepy sets of eyes popped open when the aroma entered each bedroom. Margie opened her eyes, but she would be the last one to leave her bed. She would not partake of the tasty breakfast. Miss Margaret and Sofia were the first to join Mary C. in the kitchen. Sofia was excited.

"Miss Mary C., I knew what you were doing down here as soon as I woke up. I've thought about your French toast a number of times. This is a great surprise. Billy's still sleeping. Are you feeling okay?" Mary C. turned her head from the stove and frying pan.

"I was thinking about how you girls enjoyed my French toast the last time I was here, so what better way to say thank you. I love cookin' breakfast for y'all."

Miss Margaret remembered the last time, too. "I was the last one to enjoy it last time, but I'm first this morning, thank you very much."

"Oh Mama!" Sofia loved her mother.

Susan was the next one to join the trio in the kitchen. Mary C. began stacking the square egg soaked and fried slices of bread on a large plate. She spooned out the sweet combination of white sugar and cinnamon that speckled each piece. The heat from each slice stacked together created a syrup-like liquid from the sugar and cinnamon. Susan was excited, too.

"Our house smells like Cinotti's bakery."

Sofia's eyes lit up. "Oh, I love those Melt Away Danishes. I love to talk to Miss Doodles, she's so funny. She loves country music. She used to live in Mayport. Mama, did you know that?" Sofia's change of subject caused Susan to squint her eyes.

"What are you babbling about?"

Sofia was ready. "You're the one who mentioned Cinotti's. I just mentioned Miss Doodles."

Miss Margaret joined in. "Doodles was a child when she lived in Mayport. I know her mother, Patti Ann. Mary C. you know Patti Ann, don't you?" Mary C. placed another plate of the French toast on the table.

"Yes ma'am. I know Patti Ann, good. We used to run together now and then when we was younger. We done our share of dancin' at Bill's Hideaway and at the Fish Bowl. She's always been so pretty and she always had the men lined up for her on the dance floor."

Miss Margaret smiled. "You Mayport girls have always been so pretty. It must be in the sulfur water." Susan held her nose when Miss Margaret mentioned sulfur water.

Mary C. smiled. "You say the sweetest things, Miss Margaret. You always make folks feel good. Please, y'all eat your breakfast."

Sofia wanted to help. "I'll pour the milk." The third sister Peggy walked into the kitchen.

Jason stood at the window of the wheelhouse of the Mary C. He watched the Miss Becky and the Miss Flossie leave the dock. He waved to David Pack as the Miss Becky floated past him. He gave another good luck wave to Glen Jackson as the Miss Flossie made her way toward the mouth of the St. Johns River. Jason knew he would have to shrimp soon, but for now he would have to stay with his mother for a day or so to help her deal with the tragedy that had occurred. They would have to find a place to live. Hawk would have to be buried. Both of them would have to talk to the police. Jason stepped out of the wheelhouse and walked to the stern of the boat. A voice from above on the dock made Jason's heart jump. He wasn't expecting a visitor.

"Mornin'. Your mama here?" Jason turned to see Mr. Butler standing on the dock.

"No sir, she ain't here."

Mr. Butler nodded. "I figured I'd be too early. I didn't get much sleep last night and then I got up early. I guess ya mama was right."

"Right about what?" Jason didn't understand.

"She said I didn't sleep much 'cause I was afraid I'd miss somethin'."

Jason nodded. "That sounds like, mama."

Miss Margaret and three of her four daughters sat at their kitchen table enjoying Mary C.'s French toast. Miss Margaret wanted Mary C. to tell a story about their friend, Patti Ann.

"Mary C., tell the girls about the time Jack picked the wrong woman for one of his panty raids."

Mary C. smiled and shook her head. " Oh my God, Miss Margaret, I haven't thought about that in years." Sofia's eyes widened and she had to speak up.

"A panty raid? What's that?" Both Miss Margaret and Mary C. had big smiles. Miss Margaret looked at Mary C. as to say, "you know the story better than me". Mary C. had the floor.

"When y'all was just little babies, there was a man living in Mayport named Jack. He came here with his two aunts. They lived up on the hill across from the oak tree. Jack was…" Mary C. was searching for the right words …"well, let's just say he was different."

Miss Margaret chimed in her own explanation of different. "Jack was a little slow witted, girls. He didn't think as fast as most, or have the same thoughts, for that matter. Go on, Mary C."

Mary C. continued. "A strange thing started happening around Mayport. Someone started stealing women's panties right off the clotheslines. Folks didn't mention the first few times it happened. Then one day your mama had a Stanley party. Most of the women in Mayport were there. During one of the conversations someone said they had lost three pairs of panties off their clothesline in a weeks time. Well honey child that did it. All the women had their own story about panties being taken off the lines." Sofia and Susan were all ears. Miss Margaret was excited about Mary C.'s comment.

"Mary C., I haven't heard the expression "honey child" since Miss Carolyn moved away from us to live out on Mayport Road. Honey child was her words. It was her trademark. She loved to call you honey child. I get tickled when I think of her. Miss Carolyn's a great lady. I miss our times together. She always took me to Midnight Mass at her church on Christmas Eve. It's a beautiful Catholic ceremony."

Mary C. had been thinking about Miss Carolyn. "I'd like to live out there near Miss Carolyn."

Miss Margaret realized the others were waiting on the continuation of the "slow witted Jack" story. Miss Margaret wanted to join in on the fun so she started telling the part of the story she remembered.

"At first we all thought the black children were stealing the panties off the clotheslines. There was a rumor that two black women who were living in a shack next to Roland's dock were the culprits. Some of the men went down to the shack and searched for the stolen goods. They didn't find any of the panties, but they burned down the shack and ran the two women off." Sofia had to speak up.

"They didn't find anything, but they still burned their house and ran them out of town? Why?" There was a silence after Sofia's innocent and naive question. Miss Margaret responded to her youngest.

"Now, things are getting better, but we all know there have been serious problems in the past with those kind of things."

Susan wanted the story to continue. "Mama, it's not just in the past and things are not any better, but Sofia knows that too. Don't let her bleeding heart change the subject. Can you get on with the story?" Sofia stared at Susan. Mary C. went on with the story.

"Now everyone was on the look out for the panty thief. Some of the men even hid in the yards waiting for the thief to show. It got real funny when folks would leave their panties on the lines for days trying to tempt and catch the thief. Most of the stealing was done at night."

Miss Margaret wanted the girls to know about Miss Patti Ann. "Now you have to understand that Patti Ann was a very pretty woman. She was a little ahead of most of us in her thoughts about, let's say, fashion and appearance." Mary C. smiled as Miss Margaret attempted to be delicate with her information about their friend, Patti Ann.

Mary C. interrupted and was not as delicate. "Patti Ann was sexy. Her walk was sexy. Her clothes was sexy. Her make-up was sexy. She danced sexy. And she had the first pair of pink drawers I had even seen." They all laughed at the thought of Mayport's first pair of pink panties. "She showed 'im to me the day she bought 'im at May Cohen's in Jacksonville. I wanted a pair, bad." They all laughed again. Mary C. waited for the laughter to stop. "A few days had gone by and no one had lost any underwear. It seemed, the thief had stopped or was layin' low for the time bein'." Mary C. paused and looked at Miss Margaret. "But, I guess once Jack saw that pair of pink panties hangin' on that line, it was just too much for him to stand." They all exploded with howling laughter at Mary C.'s perfectly timed comical observation. Susan couldn't contain herself. She tried to talk through her belly laugh.

"You know when he saw those pink ones, he had to have them." They all exploded again. Mary C. knew it was time to add the finale to the story. She spoke loudly above the laughter.

"And when Patti Ann looked out her kitchen window and saw Jack running away from her clothesline with her new pink panties pulled over his head, she went wild." Mary C.'s audience burst into laughter as she added to the hilarious story. The small kitchen was shaking with movement and laughter. Mary C. didn't let up on her audience. She was a good storyteller. "Patti Ann grabbed a big butcher knife and ran after him yellin', 'Get my new draws off that big head of yours'. She chased him all over, but he was able to outrun her and he got away with her pink panties." The girls couldn't stop laughing. Miss Margaret knew about the story, too.

"They say that later the same day Patti Ann went to his house and his aunt found her panties under Jack's bed along with a pile of other ladies' under garments from other Mayport clotheslines."

Mary C. nodded. "That's true. I was with her when she went to Jack's house. He was a strange character." Peggy stopped laughing. She was curious about Mayport's panty thief from the past.

"This Jack, actually stole women's underwear off the clotheslines and took them home?"

Miss Margaret nodded. "And wore them on his head. The raid on Patti Ann's clothesline in broad daylight was his down fall."

Sofia had to jump into the conversation. "What was wrong with him?"

Miss Margaret had the answer. "He was just different, Sofia. There is always someone who is a little different. He used to walk the streets and talk to himself. That usually scared folks who didn't know about him. Except for his need to have silky panties on his head, I think he was quite harmless." They all laughed again. Susan had a question.

"What happened to him?" Miss Margaret knew the answer again.

"He got hit by a car that was coming off the ferry. He died right in front of Strickland's Restaurant. I guess God felt that poor Jack had struggled and been teased enough. Folks did make fun of him from time-to-time." Sofia's low and sensitive voice interrupted.

"Oh Mama, that's so sad."

Mary C. nodded. "Folks say he was better off. If bein' dead can ever be considered better off. Somebody would have always had to take care of him. His two aunts, Carmy and Pansy took care of him the best they could, but they were gettin' too old to have to deal with Jack's oddness and foolishness. They could hardly take care of each other, much less a handful like Jack. He was better off."

Miss Margaret's eyes opened wide when Mary C. mentioned Jack's two aunts. "Pansy and Carmy, now that was a wonderful and interesting couple. I don't know if it's true or not, but that sad and beautiful love story about Carmy is a classic. And what a character that Pansy was, she had some wild hats for church. Aunt Carmy introduced me to the Catholic faith. It is a beautiful faith, full of ceremony, and holy days. She gave me my Rosary beads and taught me the prayers. It is a beautiful tradition and way to present yourself to God." The kitchen was silent. The three girls had never heard their mother talk like that. Mary C. listened too, as Miss Margaret continued. "They lived on the sand hill across from the oak tree. The stories about those two angels should be told. It's a crying shame that we forget the ones who came before and made us what we are." It was easy for the kitchen group to see how moved Miss Margaret was by her trip to the past. Sofia had an observation.

"The story about Jack was such a funny story at first, but it ended so sad. Mayport stories are always sad at the end." Mary C. looked at the young blonde haired beauty.

"Sofia girl, you're so right about that. More toast, anyone?"

Mr. Butler and Jason sat together on the stern of the shrimp boat, Mary C. Jason had told him what happened the night before. Mr. Butler was clarifying Jason's last statement.

"And they threw gas bombs at the house?"

"Yes sir. They hit the back porch first, then the side of the house. It was an old house and that dry wood went up pretty fast. Mama stayed in the house with Billy as long as she could. After she pulled the knives out of Hawk, she made me take Billy to Miss Margaret's house. I don't know why I left her there. I just did what she said. I should have stayed with her. I feel bad about leaving her like that. Mama has a way of makin' ya do things." Mr. Butler didn't respond. He had never heard Jason talk so much. He let the young man continue. "We thought the dogs was gonna get the baby, but we was able to stop 'em. Mama's still got one of them dogs."

Mr. Butler had to interrupt. "What?" There's another dog?"

"Yes sir, a big ugly one. He's at Miss Margaret's guarding the porch. Mama wants to keep him. She said, 'if ya have to kill a man, you get to keep his dog." Mr. Butler just shook his head.

Peggy opened the door to Margie's bedroom and peeked inside. Margie opened her eyes when a creaking noise came from the moving door hinges. Peggy saw that her oldest sister was awake.

"Margie, I'm sorry if I woke you. Mother wanted me to check on you. I told her I saw you when you came in last night and you were not feeling well. We just finished a French toast breakfast with Miss Mary C. She told us a great story. I'll tell you about it later. I'll tell Mother you want to rest some more." Margie slowly raised her head off the soft white pillow.

"I love you, Peggy." Peggy stepped into the room and closed the door behind her. She knelt down next to the bed as she had done next to the toilet at the store the night before. She touched Margie's cheek.

"You feel warm. Are you in pain."

"I'm fine, really. It's not the pain. It's the pressure inside me."

"I hope we did the right thing last night." Margie forced a little smile and touched Peggy's hand.

"We did."

Peggy wanted to take care of her sister. "I'll go get you some aspirin. That might help your fever."

"That sounds good."

Miss Margaret and Mary C. sat at the kitchen table while Sofia cleaned off the table and Susan washed the breakfast dishes. The two true Mayport women were still reminiscing with old Mayport stories. The girls listened as Miss Margaret recalled a few more characters that had roamed the Mayport streets.

"The king of all the walkers was probably Jake. Now, he could really look scary if you didn't know about him." Sofia's eyes lit up.

"He always scared me. Where'd he go, anyway?"

Miss Margaret had her theory. "He's just gone. Sometimes people like that are just gone. You don't see them anymore. And then sometimes they come back, right out of the blue, like they never left. And other times they're gone for good, never to be seen or heard from again. I'd be willing to bet that no one has even looked for Jake. Isn't that funny."

Mary C. looked surprised. "You know, I didn't know he was gone." Miss Margaret wanted to get back to her top list of Mayport nightwalkers.

"There was another tall black man named Benjamin, now he was strange, too. He walked slowly, but he was everywhere. I didn't like seeing him near the house. I think he was a peeping tom."

Susan reacted. "He looked into windows?"

Sofia reacted, too. "Oh, now that's scary!" Mary C. knew about Benjamin and she wanted to add to the story and the girls discomfort.

"I'm pretty sure he looked into my bathroom window one night when I was drying off from a shower."

Sofia couldn't maintain herself. "Oh God! That gives my goose bumps. What did you do?"

"I turned the light off and looked out the window."

Sofia couldn't believe what Mary C. had done. "You looked out the window? I don't think I would have been able to do that. Was he still there?"

"I saw a man walking into the woods and I'm sure it was him. When I was looking out the window I saw where he had placed a shrimp box on the ground under the window so he could be high enough to see into the bathroom. I watched and waited for a few days for him to try again. I was gonna introduce him to my shotgun, but I don't think he came back. If he did I didn't see him. I really don't remember ever seeing him again around town after that night. He was probably avoiding me."

Susan nodded her head. "He probably heard about your shotgun." Mary C. and Miss Margaret laughed out loud at Susan's statement. Sofia's eyes popped open.

"I can't believe you said that." They all laughed again.

Mr. Butler had heard the entire story from Jason. The only thing missing was the details on Mary C.'s encounter with Johnny D. Bryant in the back yard. Only Mary C. could tell that part.

"Well son, if your mama will fill in the parts you don't know she won't have to answer all these questions over again. I appreciate you telling me all this. You and your mama seem to have a lot of enemies. This is really gettin' hard to deal with and harder to understand. I don't mind tellin' you I don't know what to do. It gets worse each time. We got nine people dead, five dead dogs and your house has been burned down. This is awful." Jason didn't respond. Mr. Butler had another question. "That woman you call Ruby, do you know where she lives? I think I need to talk to her, too."

"Yes, sir. She lives on the other side of the river. It's called Cosmos."

Mr. Butler nodded. "I know the place. Pretty rough part of that area. There ain't many houses there, just old shacks and a few trailers."

"No sir, she's got a nice house. I've been there."

"Really?"

"Yes, sir."

Miss Margaret was ranking her Mayport walkers and stalkers. "Let's see now, Jake, then Benjamin, then Jack, oh yes, and the Indian woman, Violet. Mary C., you remember Violet, don't you?" Mary C.'s eyes lit up like Sofia's.

"Oh my God, I sure do. I haven't thought about Violet in years, either. Now, she was a strange bird, too." Peggy walked into the kitchen holding Billy in her arms. They all turned to Peggy and Mary C. stopped talking.

"Billy was making his little noises and he wanted to come down here to be with us." They all smiled and looked at Billy. Peggy had an interesting observation.

"He is the best baby. I don't think I've ever heard him cry." Peggy sat down and held Billy in her lap.

Sofia wrinkled her forehead. "Me either. Miss Mary C., he sure doesn't cry much does he?"

"No, he don't." Mary C. changed the subject. "I was a little girl when Violet walked the streets. She carried a nasty old croaker sack around with her. She had some strange stuff in that sack. She was always trying to trade the stuff in the sack for money or food or what ever you would give her. Most of the time folks didn't really want what she had, but they would trade with her to make her go on. She smelled so bad and she was always filthy. She wore the same clothes and dirty Indian moccasins when she wasn't barefoot. Violet had some nasty toenails. I sure wouldn't have painted 'em." Miss Margaret laughed. So did Peggy and Susan. Sofia squinted her eyes and wrinkled that flawless forehead of hers.

"Poor lady. That's awful. I'll bet people made fun of her, too, didn't they?"

Mary C. nodded. "All the time. Most of the children stayed away from her because they were scared."

Susan wanted to know about the contents of the croaker sack. "What sort of things did she have in the sack?"

Mary C. loved that question. "She always had a few slimy eels. She must have eaten them and thought people would buy them to cook." All three girls made a face, but didn't interrupt. As usual they were mesmerized by old Mayport stories. Mary C. knew she had the girls hooked. "She had dead crabs, but nobody ever buys dead crabs. You need to cook crabs when they're alive." Sofia gave her patented forehead wrinkle as Mary C. continued. "She was always picking things out of the trash holes in the woods and she walked the docks each day, trying to pick up a handful of shrimp or a fish to trade at the restaurants. Mr. Strickland was always good about givin' her somethin' to eat and Al Leek would give her a big flounder now and then to trade or cook." Sofia smiled and nodded at the thought that some people did help her. Miss Margaret remembered her introduction to Violet's nasty sack.

"One time, your Aunt Margie and I were walking home from Miss Carolyn's birthday party. We had stayed too late and we knew we were going to be in trouble when we got home, so we were trying to hurry. We were walking past the King house and heard a noise, as we got closer to the back yard. Of course, it scared us because of all the ghost stories we had heard. For some reason Margie stopped to see where the noise was coming from. She has always been braver than me. I walked a few steps and realized Margie was not with me. I turned back and saw her looking into the darkness of the back yard. I couldn't believe she had stopped. Then Margie really shocked me when she started walking closer to the back of the house. I didn't want to, but I walked back to her. I wanted to get her to leave, but I didn't want to say anything. I was really scared."

Miss Margaret's three daughters were quiet and attentive as their mother told her story. Mary C. had ignited memories in Miss Margaret the girls had never heard before. They loved listening to their mother tell her tales.

"When I stepped up behind Margie I could see she was staring at something in the backyard. I looked in the direction she was looking. The noise we had heard at first was the Indian woman, Violet. She was dancing around in Mr. King's backyard and making strange noises. For some reason Margie wasn't afraid as she watched her. I was really scared. Violet had something in both her hands as she danced around. I couldn't see what she was holding at first. When I got my eyes focused, it looked like she was holding snakes in her hands. It was probably two of those slimy eels from her sack."

Sofia had a question. "What was she dancing for? Did y'all need rain?" The entire group exploded into laughter after Sofia's serious, but hilarious question. Peggy looked at Sofia.

"Sofia, you might be the funniest person on this Earth and you don't even know when you're being funny. I do love you."

Sofia looked at all the faces looking at her. "What?" They exploded again. When the laugher calmed, Mary C. took over the conversation.

"It is a fact that Mr. King's house was built on some kinda graveyard. Some say it is an old Spanish cemetery, but some think the house was built on top of Indian burial mounds, created by the Timucuan Indians that were here way before any of us. Maybe Violet was dancing to honor the dead Indians."

Susan had her own theory. "Maybe Violet was trying to raise the dead Indians so they could kill all the people in Mayport who were mean to her." Sofia's eyes popped open.

Mary C. smiled. She liked Susan's style and imagination.

"Maybe so."

Miss Margaret looked at her daughter, Susan. "Now, that's a pleasant thought. Perhaps you should go tell ghosts stories at the haunted house."

Susan smiled. "I think I'd like that."

Sofia wanted to hear more. "Mama, you've never told us stories like these. We should have breakfast with Miss Mary C. more often. What happened next?"

Miss Margaret smiled, nodded her head and continued her story. "We both stood there watching her jumping and dancing around for a few seconds, then it happened and we ran away as fast as we could." The room was silent. All eyes were wide opened and looking right at Miss Margaret. Mary C. smiled and knew the best part was coming. Sofia broke the silence.

"Mama, what did you see? What did she do that made you run?" Miss Margaret looked directly into Sofia's big beautiful sky blue eyes.

"She bit the heads off the two snakes and spit them on the ground. I don't know what she did next. I was running." All three girls made more faces and a noise of some kind as they visualized the snakehead biting ritual. Mary C. smiled at Miss Margaret. It was a great story.

Mr. Butler stepped out of his unmarked police car in front of

Miss Margaret's house. Jason stepped out of Hawk's truck and joined Mr. Butler at the steps. The huge devil dog Abaddon stood up when the two men approached the porch. Mr. Butler stopped in his tracks when he saw the huge mutant canine. He had seen his share of devil dogs lately. However, this was the first one that was breathing. The others had all been dead. Jason stepped up behind Mr. Butler.

"That's mama's new dog I was tellin' you about." Mr. Butler stood still as the dog sniffed his pant's leg. "Mama said if he hurts anybody, she'll shoot him herself."

Mr. Butler nodded his head. "I have no doubt she will." Mr. Butler slowly edged past Abaddon, walked up onto the porch and knocked on the front door. His knock ended the Mayport story time for the moment. Peggy handed Billy to his grandmother, Mary C.

"I'll get it."

Miss Margaret looked toward the front room. "A little early for visitors."

Mary C. nodded. "I have a feeling it's for me. I'm sure Mr. Butler was up early, if he slept at all, waiting to talk to me about last night. Men like him don't rest 'til they get what they want. I don't like him too much." Miss Margaret didn't respond. She was a woman who knew when to be quiet. She was smart and she listened carefully.

Peggy looked through the curtain that covered the small window on the front door of the house. She smiled when she saw Jason and opened the door quickly to greet her sexual partner from the night before. She didn't see Mr. Butler until she opened the door. His presence surprised her and she altered the greeting she would have otherwise given to Jason.

"Oh! Good morning, gentlemen. Come in. You're just in time for some of Miss Mary C.'s French toast." Mr. Butler didn't mean to say it out loud, but it just rolled off his lips.

"That seems to be the breakfast of choice around here after a night of killin's." Peggy looked at Jason with her eyes opened wide after Mr. Butler's course comment. Jason was concentrating more on not looking at Peggy and didn't hear what Mr. Butler had said. The three of them walked into the kitchen with Peggy leading the way.

The others were still at the kitchen table as Peggy and the two men entered the room. Mary C. looked at Mr. Butler and then at Miss Margaret as if to say, "I told you so." Miss Margaret looked at Mary C. as to say, "You sure did." and then greeted her new guests.

"Mr. Butler, Jason, good morning. Would you men like some breakfast?" Jason looked at the one slice of French toast left on the plate. Mary C. smiled.

"I can make some more, son, don't worry." Jason smiled. He did love his mother's French toast. Mary C. looked at Mr. Butler.

"If I remember correctly, you had some French toast with us the last time you were here."

Mr. Butler nodded. "Yes, ma'am, I did. I wouldn't refuse a few slices this mornin' either." Mary C. was surprised with Mr. Butler's admission that he liked her French toast. She smiled again and stood up. She handed Billy to Mr. Butler. He was surprised when she pushed the baby into his chest. He lifted his arms to support the child as Mary C. stepped away from him empty handed.

"You gotta work for your breakfast this time." All eyes were on Mr. Butler as he stood there holding the oak baby. Susan got up and offered her seat.

"Here Mr. Butler, sit down. I've got to open the store." Mr. Butler sat down with Billy cradled in his arms. Mary C. had moved to the stove with her back to the others. Mr. Butler couldn't see her face, but he knew she was smiling after she handed the oak baby to him. Sofia got up from her seat.

"Jason, you sit here." She moved to stand next to Mary C. at the stove. "May I make the toast with you. If I learn how, we can have it more often around here." It was easy for Mary C. to love Sofia. Mary C. had a better idea for the beautiful Sofia.

"Why don't you make it?" Sofia grinned from ear-to-ear.

Mr. Butler looked down at the baby he was holding. He couldn't believe he was there on police business, but he would have to hold a baby and wait for Sofia to get a lesson in the art of making French toast. He looked at the back of Mary C. as she stood at the stove. He had always liked to look at Mary C. from any angle. The backs of her legs were smooth and tan. Both her calf muscles flexed and bulged as she went up on the toes of her bare feet. Mr. Butler knew she was something else.

Miss Margaret, in her understanding and gracious manner, saved the lawman from his babysitting chore when she stood up and took Billy from him. Mr. Butler gave Miss Margaret a "thank you" nod of his head. He knew she was taking Mary C.'s little joke off his hands. Mr. Butler was more than happy to let her take the child.

"This little fellow needs a bath." Miss Margaret left the kitchen talking to Billy. Mary C. didn't turn around, but she still had that coy smile on her face.

Peggy caught Jason's eye and licked her lips at him. His manliness pushed against the zipper of his dungarees. Jason turned away from her sexual gesture and reminder of their encounter on the boat. His mouth went dry and he felt his heart pounding. Peggy couldn't let him off the hook. She was having too much fun.

"Jason, did you sleep okay on the boat last night? It seems like it would be so noisy over there with that old ferry crossing every half hour." Jason knew Peggy was playing with him. He looked up. She was looking directly into his eyes. "Of course the ferry stops running at eleven, so I guess after that it's pretty quiet, huh?"

Jason nodded. "I'm used to the noises and I'm a pretty deep sleeper." Susan walked into the room and didn't know it, but she saved Jason from her sister, Peggy.

"Peggy, if you want the car you'll have to take me to the store. I'm not walking this morning. I'm already late. Mother hasn't said anything, but I know she will if I don't get over there and get those doors open. You taking me or what?" Peggy continued looking at Jason, but she answered Susan.

"I'm taking you." Jason was relieved when Peggy broke her stare and the two girls left the kitchen. Peggy stepped out onto the front porch and took Susan by her arm.

"I need to talk to you when we get into the car." They hurried to the family station wagon. Peggy would tell Susan about how brave Margie had been during her miscarriage. They would both keep Margie's secret and they would protect and take care of their older sister. Sofia would not know until Margie told her.

Jason and Mr. Butler sat at Miss Margaret's kitchen table waiting for Sofia to cook her first batch of French toast. Mr. Butler tried not to look at the two beautiful cooks as they worked together. Sofia was young and beautiful, with all the attributes needed to turn men's heads and Mary C. was mature and as voluptuous as a women could be. She still wore the tight shorts Sofia had given her the night before, but she did wear a different shirt. They were both barefoot and seemed to spend time on their toes, causing their calf muscles to flex. Mary C.'s legs were tanned and muscular. Sofia's were long and white. They both had a different look about them. It was a great look for a woman to have, any woman. Mary C.'s voice surprised Mr. Butler and took him away from his leg trance.

"My goodness, Mr. Butler, you were in some deep thought there for a moment, huh? I didn't mean to interrupt you."

Mr. Butler cleared his head. "No, no that's all right. I guess I was thinkin' 'bout that French toast. It sure smells good."

Mary C. smiled. "I don't think it was the toast. You seemed to be thinkin' 'bout somethin' else to me, but if you say so. I can't read minds, you know?" Mr. Butler had his doubts about that. He could feel the blood rush to his face as it left another part of his body. He wondered how long she had been watching him as he watched the four legs at the stove. Mary C. poured two glasses of milk and placed them on the table.

"Can't eat French toast without milk." Sofia placed a plate filled with French toast on the table.

"Well, there it is. I hope it's okay. I'm so nervous. How embarrassed will I be if it tastes awful?"

Mary C. had to laugh at the young beauty's dramatic nature. "It's gonna be great, I promise."

Sofia handed Jason and Mr. Butler a clean plate and forks. "I'll let you get what you want. I'm so excited."

Mr. Butler tried not to laugh out loud, but he had to smile. The two men took the slices of toast and they both tasted one at the same time. Mr. Butler surprised Mary C. when he was the first to compliment, Sofia.

"Little lady, this tastes just like the toast Mary C. makes. And you know how good that is! I can't tell the difference at all." Sofia grinned and looked at Jason. Jason knew he had to respond.

"Are you sure mama didn't make this?" Sofia's face lit up with the smile of smiles.

"I'm sure. I did it myself with her directions, but I did it." Sofia could not contain herself. She hugged Mary C., then Jason and then

Mr. Butler. "I think I'm going to cry." Mary C. had to stop the emotional and dramatic, Sofia.

"Sofia, we're not crying over making French toast. Save those tears. I assure you there will be more important things to cry about." Mary C.'s thoughts were cynical at times, but she knew what she was taking about. Sofia smiled and turned to clean the mess she had made during her French toast lesson. Mary C. turned to Mr. Butler as he took a drink of his milk.

"I know we've made you stay longer than you wanted. Why don't you ask me your questions while you eat and you can get on with your business? Mr. Butler put the glass of milk down on the table. He looked toward Sofia.

"I thought we would talk privately."

"I don't care who hears me. I got no secrets 'bout last night."

Mr. Butler nodded his head. "Actually, Jason has told me most of it. I went to meet you at the boat and we sat and talked for about an hour. I just need to know what happened when he left and you ran into the one they call the Ax. He was messed up pretty bad."

Mary C. took a deep breath. "A shotgun at close range usually leaves that kinda mess. I was real close to him when I pulled the trigger. I almost shot that damn dog out there first, but I realized he wasn't gonna hurt me."

Mr. Butler had to ask. "And how did you know he wasn't gonna hurt ya? You had to kill the other dogs. Why was that one different?"

"I could see it in his eyes. He's mine now, ya know?"

Mr. Butler nodded again. "Yeah, Jason told me about the 'if I have to kill you, I get to keep your dog' rule. I never heard that before, but I'm sure I'll remember it from now on." Mary C. didn't change her expression. Sofia was quiet and didn't turn around, but she was taking in every word that was being said. Mr. Butler added to the strange thick atmosphere. "You have a lot of interesting rules you seem to live by, don't ya?"

Mary C. knew how to play the word game. "Ain't it funny how most folks say I never play by the rules at all and here you are sayin' I've got all kinda rules. How do you explain that?"

Mr. Butler was in as deep as he could get. He knew he couldn't handle her the way he wanted with Jason and Sofia in the room.

Mary C. was way too smart for him and he knew it. He would curb his tongue for now, but he would wait for his opportunity to meet her on fair and even grounds at another time. Still, he didn't want to run from the room with his tail between his legs.

"Maybe most folks don't realize that you do play by rules, they're just your rules."

"And you think that's wrong?"

"I'm not sure what I think when it comes to you, Mary C. I do know that you seem to be involved in the death of a large number of individuals. Some you knew, some you didn't. Some were friends and some were enemies. Some were relatives and some mere passing acquaintances. And some were loved ones. You told me to go ahead and talk to you here and I would rather not do that." Mr. Butler went back to his original topic. "I'm sure you killed that man in self defense and that's how I'll report it. Seven men with killer dogs can't go around trying to kill entire families." Mr. Butler stood up from the table. "Sofia the breakfast was excellent." The tension was heavy in the room as Sofia turned from the sink.

"Thank you, Mr. Butler."

Mr. Butler nodded to Jason and turned to Mary C. "You may already have one, but if you ever need a running count of the dead feel free to let me know, I'll be happy to supply one for you. I can show myself out."

Mr. Butler left the room and walked to the front door without looking back. He opened the door and stepped out onto the front porch. He stopped on the porch when he saw Abaddon standing at the foot of the steps. The huge black dog growled and showed Mr. Butler his teeth. Mr. Butler reached under his coat and touched the handle of his gun in his shoulder holster and once again, he didn't mean to, but he spoke his thoughts out load. "I will put a bullet in that big ugly head of yours if you take one step toward me." Mary C.'s voice ended the standoff.

"I'm sure you would."

The dog backed away from the steps when he heard Mary C.'s voice. She was standing at the door behind Mr. Butler. Mr. Butler didn't take his eyes off the dog as Mary C. stepped out onto the porch.

"You won't have to shoot him. If he bites you I'll kill him." Mr. Butler watched the dog as Mary C. stepped closer to him. She smelled like cinnamon. "How many ya think?"

The dog had clouded Mr. Butler's thoughts and he didn't understand her question. "How many what?"

He didn't turn around. Mary C. stepped as close as she could get to him without her body pushing him off the porch. Her hard breasts touched his back when she leaned forward and whispered in his ear. "How many dead? You must have a number. You made me think you had a number. You got a number or not?" Mary C.'s questions took the experienced lawman totally by surprise. Mr. Butler didn't know what to say.

Mary C. could sense the confusion and nervousness in his usually strong and confident posture. She knew she had him by the throat and that was one of her favorite places to have someone. His lack of response only strengthened her hold and triggered her ability to add to the dramatic situation. She held the front of her body against his back. He didn't move forward to break the contact. She whispered to him again.

"When you do get this count you are so interested in creatin', it won't be close to the actual number. You need to think about leaving me alone, but I don't think you can. And I don't think it has nothin' to do with dead people."

Mr. Butler actually felt his knees quiver. He did not respond or look back at Mary C. as he stepped off the porch and walked past the dog. He got into his car and drove away.

During the two weeks that followed Mary C.'s ordeal with the Devil man, Hawk's death and the loss of her house, she and Billy accepted the genuine hospitality of Miss Margaret and her four daughters. Jason stayed on the boat each night during that time. Peggy visited Jason on the boat a number of times late at night. Susan went to the boat to be with Jason once, but got too nervous before they even kissed when Mr. Leek came to the boat to talk to Jason. She had to stay hidden for about a half hour. She wouldn't return to the boat, but she would be looking for the right opportunity to have an intimate moment with Jason somewhere other than the boat.

Margie was recovering from her own serious and life threatening situation. She was getting stronger everyday. She was becoming a true survivor. Miss Margaret thought her oldest child was having a serious bout with the flu. Margie was known for her unusually severe colds.

Lester "Hawk" Hawkins was buried on his mother's land in Palm Valley next to his father. Mr. Leek and Mr. King rode together in Mr. Leek's truck. Jason and Mary C. drove there in Hawk's truck. Hawk's mother said nothing to Mary C., Jason or any of the Mayport people during the funeral. The casket was closed at his mother's request. There were three pictures of Lester Hawkins on top of the casket. One was of him in an Army uniform, the other was of him as a child standing over his first deer kill and the third picture was of Hawk standing like a giant on one of the jetty rocks. The third picture was the man that Mary C. knew.

It was supposed to be a quiet and unassuming ceremony in honor of Hawk's quiet and unassuming nature. When it comes to dealing with the dead, things don't always go as planned. Hawk had never mentioned much about his family to Mary C. He was so quiet all the time and Mary C. really didn't care. She had never questioned him about such things. Mr. Leek stepped up behind Mary C. He had some interesting information. He whispered into Mary C.'s ear.

"You see those two standing with Hawk's mother?" Mary C. nodded. "That's his younger brother, Hester." Mary C. thought to herself, "Lester and Hester, oh my God?"

Mr. Leek had more interesting information. "The pretty young woman to the left is his half sister, Mary Ellen. I think someone said she was a nurse. Hawk didn't know the girl that well. She came with their mother."

Mary C.'s eyes zeroed in on the pretty young woman standing next to Hawk's mother. It only took a few seconds for Mary C. to recognize the young nurse from the hospital over a year before who took care of Jason when he was recovering from his injuries.

Mary C.'s heart raced in her chest. It wasn't a feeling she had very often or she liked very much. She remembered how the young woman had fallen in love with Jason. She also recalled how pleased she was when Jason was released from the hospital and had gotten away from the aggressive and beautiful version of Florence Nightingale.

Mary C. looked for Jason. He was standing under a big live oak tree. She knew he had not seen Mary Ellen. Mary C. was also sure

Mary Ellen had not seen Jason, as well. Perhaps she could keep the old friends apart. She walked to Jason and stood with him as the minister asked everyone to gather around the casket. Mary C. reached out and held Jason's arm as he took a step forward at the preacher's request.

"Let's stay back here. Hawk's mother is not too happy with us being here. We'll be respectful and leave as soon as it's over." Jason stepped back to stand with his mother. Mary C. wanted to get her son away from Mary E.

As the preacher spoke about Lester Hawkins, Mary C. watched Mary Ellen. She knew Jason would not see her. He was never good at paying attention to people around him. Mary C. would keep Jason in the background and make sure no attention came their way. It is true that the best plans go astray when dealing with the dead. Mary C. didn't hear him, but the preacher asked everyone to "please bow your heads in prayer as Mary Ellen Norton sings the Lord's Prayer". Hawk's friends and relatives all bowed their heads.

Mary C. did not bow hers. She watched the young woman step forward and stand next to Hawk's coffin. Mary Ellen began singing her version of the popular, but difficult to sing, prayer. Mary C. didn't want to turn and look at Jason, but she had to see his reaction to Mary Ellen. He had his head down and his eyes closed. He had not, as yet, recognized his old admirer.

Mary Ellen's voice filled the air. The notes seemed to bounce off the Spanish moss laden limbs of the huge oak trees that towered above the mourners. As Mary Ellen continued, an unexpected cool breeze touched Mary C.'s face. It was pleasant and she took a deep breath. Jason felt it too and he opened his eyes. A small piece of moss fell on top of the casket. Millions of leaves began to move and quiver in the trees. Another blast of cold air made the others take notice of the building breeze. A piece of moss fell from above and hit Mary C. on her shoulder, then fell to the ground next to her. It scared her when it touched her. Jason saw it, too. He smiled at his mother when they both looked at the moss at her feet.

Mary Ellen was singing "Amen" as another blast of cold air rushed across the top of Hawk's coffin. The picture of Hawk in his Army uniform fell off the coffin and hit the ground. Then the other two pictures fell to the ground as the small crowd made a collective gasp at the strange occurrence. More moss fell from the trees as the wind continued to blow even harder. Hunks of moss rolled on the ground. The woman held their hats on their heads as the wind grew stronger. Leaves, sand and moss began to pepper everyone.

Some folks moved toward their cars to wait out the unusual weather change. A large moving, thick clump of moss hit Mary C.'s right leg. Then another piece of moss actually wrapped around her left leg. She reached down to pull the soft plant from her skin. Before she could free herself of the mossy grip more pieces flew into her body, as if she were a human moss magnet. Jason couldn't believe his eyes when he realized his mother was being covered in moss. It was clinging to her as if it was part of her body. Mr. King and Mr. Leek saw Mary C.'s struggle and both hurried to help her.

Mary C. was trying to kick free of the moss. Jason, Mr. King and Mr. Leek began grabbing the clumps of moss, ripping them away from Mary C.'s legs and shoulders. She pulled a piece from her face that had covered her eyes for a brief moment. The onslaught of moss was too much for Mary C. to bear. She exploded with a bloodcurdling scream. "Let me go!"

The wind stopped blowing. The moss stopped moving. Mary C. was breathing heavily as Jason removed the last small pieces of moss from her body. Mr. Leek and Mr. King had moved away from her when she screamed. All eyes of the people who had stood against the wind were on Mary C. Mr. Leek turned to Mr. King.

"What in God's name just happened here, John?"

Before Mr. King could respond Mary C. gave everyone listening the answer. "Hawk was holdin' on to me. He didn't want to leave me. He's been tryin' to stay and not cross over. A man like him can't go easy. He ain't finished, either. He'll be back."

There was a moment of eerie silence that was broken by Mr. King. "Let's get back to my house. Maybe he'll meet us there and we can help him stay." Mr. Leek couldn't believe what Mr. King had just said. Another voice cut through the air. It was Hawk's mother.

"Get these crazy, ignorant fools away from my son. This evil woman bewitched him. He is dead because of her. Somebody get them all out of here."

Mary C. took Jason's arm and walked toward Hawk's mother.

She stopped and looked deep into the old woman's eyes. Mary C. didn't blink, but the old lady didn't either. Hawk's mother broke the silence of their first eye-to-eye meeting.

"Be sure to leave the keys to my son's truck when you go. When do you think you'll be going?"

Mary C. never changed her expression. She held her opened hand out to Jason and he handed his mother the keys to Hawk's truck. Mary Ellen's heart pounded in her chest when she recognized Jason and Mary C. She was speechless and her body was frozen as she watched Jason walk past her. Mary Ellen's eyes met Mary C.'s evil stare and she knew Jason's possessive mother was telling her to "stay away". Mary Ellen's eyes told Mary C., "not a chance."

Mary C. rode back to Mayport from Hawk's funeral in Mr. Leek's truck. She sat between Mr. Leek and Mr. King in the cab seat. The two men had a normal conversation during the ride, but Mary C. did not talk at all the entire trip. The two men did not press her to join the conversation. They both knew when to mind their own business. Jason rode in the back truck bed. Palm Valley was fifteen miles south of Mayport. He didn't mind the cool wind touching his face and he was glad it wasn't raining. Jason had not seen the nurse Mary Ellen during all the turmoil and confusion at the funeral.

The mutilated body of the Punjabi priest, Sandeep Singh was turned over to the officials of the Presbyterian Church. Many foreign immigrants entered the country with the help of the Presbyterian Services. They would try to find a way to get his body back to his homeland, but if that was not possible, they would give him a proper burial. It was sad that no one from Mayport ever inquired about where the warrior-priest was finally laid to rest.

Macadoo attended the funerals for five of the seven men who died in Mary C.'s yard. Three of the men were related and their family had all three services at the same time in the big Pentecostal Church at the corner of Mayport Road and Church Road. The service took over three hours and had hundreds in attendance. Macadoo wanted to speak during the service. She knew it was the opportunity of a lifetime to talk to such a large number of the black citizens in the area, but her new nemesis, Mr. Cane, was an uncle to the three young men and he was in charge of the ceremony. He sent word to Macadoo that she would be allowed to attend and pay her respects, but she would not be welcome in the pulpit. She was angry about his message, but she would reluctantly honor his wishes. Lamar Harris attended the service for the three young men. Macadoo saw him, but he did not acknowledge her. She was angry about that, too.

One of the dead young men lived at American Beach on the other side of the river. Macadoo attended the small service in his mother's home on the beach. The remains of the man who had been burned beyond recognition were cremated and his ashes were sent to his family in St. Augustine. The last of the six followers was the oldest son of Macadoo's sister. Macadoo performed the service in Mayport for her fallen nephew.

There was a closed wooden box funeral for the Ax, Johnny D. Bryant, in a small graveyard in Cosmos. His girlfriend, Ruby, and three men she knew carried the wooden box and two city workers buried him. There are no prayers to say when you bury the devil.

Mr. Butler didn't talk to Jason or Mary C. about that night again. There were no other living witnesses to give him any more information about that evil and bloody night. No charges were filed against anyone. Mr. Butler was afraid Mayport was a time bomb and would explode again in the near future.

CHAPTER THREE

Every man and devil dog that died that awful night in Mary C.'s yard had been buried. Mr. King sat on his front porch wondering when Hawk would reveal himself as a new ghost and welcome resident of the haunted house. The magic carousel music box was still on the small table in his living room. It was strange that Mary C. had not mentioned the beautiful and valuable antique.

Mary C. and Billy were getting used to the cleanliness and comfort of Miss Margaret's home. The four girls were more than willing to attend to the baby's needs and Miss Margaret treated them both like family. Mary C.'s old friend Chichemo had returned to Mayport just in time to help Jason on the shrimp boat, Mary C. He would work with Jason as a favor to Mary C. until the young man could be the true captain of the boat. Jason wasn't very excited about the return of Chichemo and his monkey, Bosco, but he would do what his mother wanted and learn all he could from the old master. Jason wanted to provide for his mother and his son. He threw the bow rope of the Mary C. to Mr. Leek as the boat floated up to the dock pylons. Jason, Chichemo and Bosco were coming in from a three-day shrimping trip. Mr. Leek was all smiles as he tied off the bowline.

"Welcome home, son. The Lord kept y'all safe. That's a good thing."

Jason forced a smile for his friend as Bosco, the spider monkey, ran out of the wheelhouse and began swinging on the ropes and cables hanging above them. Mr. Leek could see the fatigue and disgust on Jason's handsome, but haggard face. Mr. Leek watched Bosco run across the top of the wheelhouse.

"I see the Lord kept all his creatures safe on the high seas." Jason tossed the stern line to Mr. Leek and sat down on the railing of the boat as Mr. Leek tied the rope to a pylon.

"You been sick for all three days ain't ya, son?"

Jason looked up at his friend. "I would have had to die to feel better."

Bosco ran on the railing and hit Jason on the head with his small hairy hand. The wild animal climbed up one of the ropes to get away. Mr. Leek fought back a smile when Jason didn't even blink at the monkey's antics. Jason shook his head and looked up. Mr. Leek was still fighting back the smile. He knew how awful it was to be seasick and he could tell Bosco had tormented Jason during the three days. Before either of them could say another word the boat engine went silent. Mr. Leek saw Jason shut his eyes when Chichemo's booming voice cut through the air as the old crusty seadog stepped out of the wheelhouse.

"Al Leek! How the hell are ya? Didn't get to see ya before we left. Got some big ones in the hold. I figure near twenty boxes." Mr. Leek looked at Chichemo with disbelief in his eyes. Chichemo smiled. "At least twenty boxes, Al. No shit." Mr. Leek looked at Jason as Chichemo continued. "We got fish, too. We hit the biggest batch of big flounder I ever seen. I ain't never seen that happen, and we got King Mackerel, too. I'll bet we got a thousand pounds of big kings in there. This was the damned'ist trip I ever been on." Chichemo looked at Jason, who was still sitting on the railing. "This is a good man here, Al. He was sick the whole time and he never stopped workin'. I ain't never seen nobody do that. I like this man. Bosco likes him, too."

The little monkey stopped running and sat down on the railing next to Jason. Chichemo smiled. "See what I mean, Bosco knows a good man when he sees one." Mr. Leek smiled as Jason touched the top of the Bosco's tiny head. Jason thought about squeezing the monkey's eyes out, but he didn't.

Mr. Leek knew twenty boxes of shrimp was a great catch for Jason and his new mentor. The word would go out for the headers to come and head the shrimp. Mr. Leek's dockworkers joined Chichemo and Jason and began unloading the boat. It would be a busy day on the dock. Jason would be excited with the catch once he got off the boat and back on dry land. A good nights sleep wouldn't hurt him either. Mr. Leek, Chichemo and the white residents of Mayport had no idea it was time to bury another Mayport citizen.

Hattie Mae Harris had passed away during the night. Her son Lamar was at her side when she closed her eyes for the last time. It was a peaceful passing. Lamar had returned to Mayport to be with his mother until she died.

The handsome, educated and well-spoken young black man had no idea when he first returned home he would become involved with the white woman called Mary C. His original plan was to be with his mother until the end. Then, he would take care of her funeral arrangements and return to his graduate work at Bethune-Cookman College in Daytona. He already had a degree in Political Science. He was now studying to be a specialist in the area of civil rights. Lamar felt out of place in the barbaric surroundings of his hometown. Even though he had been beyond the boundaries of Mayport and he had seen what the world held for men like him, he still had mean blood flowing slowly through his veins. All the education and thoughts he had been exposed to had not changed his blood. He was confused by his thoughts to challenge Mary C.

Lamar stood on a small porch in front of his mother's modest cinder block house. It was a little square concrete cracker box house like most of the houses in the black section of Mayport. The house and the front yard were filled with relatives and family friends.

Hattie had been sick for the past year and had not left her house. Before her illness she was one of the most influential and active members of the black community. Voo Swar and Macadoo were both jealous of Hattie's popularity and following. She had left a legacy of kindness and respect for all who knew her. Mr. Cane walked out of the house and stood next to Lamar Harris.

"How ya doin', son?"

Lamar nodded. ""I'm all right, Mr. Cane. I was with her when she left us. I couldn't have asked for more. I'm all right, sir."

"You're a good son to come home like this and put your life on hold."

"I wouldn't have a life if it wasn't for her, sir."

Mr. Cane put his arm on Lamar's shoulder. "And was she proud of you? We heard all about you. She read your letters to us. She would call us all together to read your school papers and show us your grades." Lamar had to smile as Mr. Cane went on. "And when you graduated, my God, what a day that was for us all. She talked about that hotel on the beach in Daytona for six months. We were all so proud of you. It was like we all went with ya."

Mr. Cane took his hand off Lamar's shoulder. They both looked down from the porch to see the obese black woman, Macadoo, waddle through the crowd that stood in the front yard. Her huge swollen face and forehead glistened with sweat. She was well over four hundred pounds and it was a true physical effort for her to walk around as much as she did. Her arms were as big as most people's legs and her cheeks looked ready to explode at any moment. Four men walked with her, two behind and one on each side. They looked like bodyguards. Mr. Cane made a low voice comment before the huge woman reached the porch.

"I know you're too smart, Lamar, for this fool."

Macadoo reached the steps on the small porch. "I come to pay respect to Hattie. I won't be able to 'tend the service so I come today. She was a good woman, maybe too good. She worked herself to death doin' for others, white folk and black folk. She just worked herself to death."

Lamar had no idea if Macadoo's comments were praising his mother or saying she was a fool. He didn't care what Macadoo said or thought. He was like Mr. Cane. He did not want the fat woman there at all. Mr. Cane was the first to respond to Macadoo's words. He couldn't help himself.

"I'll tell ya one thing. You and Hattie was sure at different ends of the stick. But, you know I never heard her say one word against you, not one word. I wonder if you ever said a word against her. She saw goodness in everybody, even her enemies."

Macadoo's eyes lit up like Roman candles. It was the third time in as many weeks that Mr. Cane had publicly challenged and spoken against her. As she glared at her new enemy, he had more for her burning ears.

"You're on your own now, Miss Macadoo. You're the last one. The last matriarch, if you will. Voo Swar's gone so she can't out craft you. Hattie's gone so she can't take your friends. You got a free reign to convert the entire black town of Mayport. You should be able to sweep through the streets with no opposition at all. It seems as if that should be enough for you, yet you have found a new enemy to defeat and try to outlive. Only, the new one's white."

Buckets of Macadoo's blood boiled in her huge body like four hundred pounds of Tom Green's peanuts. She put her hand over her mouth to keep from screaming or perhaps throwing up. She clinched her teeth and glared at Mr. Cane, but she spoke to Lamar Harris.

"I came here to show my respect to you and ya mama. But, you let me be insulted by this weak little man. I can see I'm not welcome here." Macadoo stepped closer to Lamar and with a whisper she challenged him. "I expect you to keep your word concerning the white woman. Hattie would expect you to keep your promise." The huge black woman turned and walked away with her four protectors.

Mr. Cane turned to Lamar. "You owe her nothin'. Go back to school. Your mother would tell you the same thing." Lamar watched Macadoo make her way through the crowded front yard. He thought how strange it was that he had said nothing to her, not one word during the entire encounter. It wasn't like him to be at a loss for words. His debate team awards had not helped him with Macadoo. He put his arm around Mr. Cane's shoulder and they both turned to walk back into the house. Loud talk from the crowd in the yard stopped their movement. They turned at the same time to see what was happening.

A huge smile came over Lamar's serious face when a red Ford truck pulling a horse trailer drove up into his small yard. The crowd moved aside as the red truck drove right up to the small porch. A young black man with perfect pearly white teeth stuck his head out the driver's side window of the truck and gave a huge, nothing but teeth, smile to Lamar. The young man's voice quieted the crowd.

"Damn, Lamar, I almost missed the Bar-B-Que. This is a hell of a party. You gotta buy ya mama a bigger house if y'all gonna throw parties like this." Lamar stepped off the porch to meet the loud young man as he stepped out of the truck. They embraced like brothers and Lamar whispered into his friend's ear.

"You already know mama's gone, don't ya?" The young man squeezed Lamar harder.

"I figured so when I saw all the people. Ya mama would have liked me comin' in here like a fool. She did laugh at what ever I did. I'm so sorry. You okay?" The manly hug ended.

"I'm good and I'm better now that you're here." Lamar turned to the crowd of stunned and not so happy family members and friends. "This is my best friend, Shadow Martin. His mother was a full-blooded Cherokee Indian and his father was blacker than a potbelly stove." A few of the mourners laughed at Lamar's description of Mr. Martin's parents, but most of the crowd were still recovering from his arrival. " Mama loved him like a son and he loved her. Please welcome him to our town."

Shadow waved to the large crowd. He knew they would not all approach him to shake hands. Mr. Cane was the first to step to him. "Welcome young man. That was the most exciting entrance I've ever seen under these circumstances."

"Yes sir, I hope Mama Hattie forgives me."

Mr. Cane nodded. "I'm sure she already has, son." Lamar caught Shadow's eye and shook his head. Shadow smiled and motioned for Lamar to come to him. Lamar knew what Shadow wanted as they walked to the trailer behind the truck.

"I can't believe you brought him all that way." The curious crowd was moving toward the trailer to see the contents of the wooden pen on wheels. There was a gasp from the crowd when the nose of a horse appeared through two of the boards. Lamar was glad to see that his pure black stallion, Raven, had arrived safe and well to Mayport. Lamar wanted to get the horse out of the trailer.

"How about pullin' around the back of the house and let him stand on solid ground. I don't think we should take him out with all these folks standin' around. He's pretty skittish ya know? Thanks for bringing him."

"I knew if you were gonna stay much longer, you would need to do something to ease your mind. You know how ridin' that horse makes you feel. Hell, you've told me enough." Shadow got back into the truck and drove the truck, trailer and horse to the back yard.

Mr. Leek's fish house was alive with dockworkers and shrimp headers. The heading tables were piled high with big Atlantic Ocean shrimp. Two other boats had docked and were waiting to unload. It would be a full workday and probably most of the evening for Mr. Leek and his workers. The smell of shrimp and fish filled the air. To Mr. Leek and Chichemo it was the smell of money. Mr. Leek sat down on a wooden shrimp box next to Chichemo.

"Good trip, huh?"

The old seadog nodded his weather beaten head and changed the subject. "That Jason, I ain't sure what to think of him. When I worked with him and Hawk before, I spent most of my time with Hawk. You know, man stuff. I didn't pay much mind to the boy. He's got a different way about him. I ain't never come across it before."

Mr. Leek smiled. He fully understood what Chichemo was feeling and saying. "You wouldn't believe how many times I've heard someone say that very same thing about that young man. He is a rare breed."

Chichemo took a deep breath. "No, it's much more'n that. I seen rare breeds before. This man's beyond that. He's much more." There was a few seconds of silence between the two men. Mr. Leek changed the subject.

"You know the Mary C. had the biggest catch, don't you?"

Chichemo nodded again and changed the conversation back to his subject. "She'll always have the biggest catch as long as he's on her. What do they call him?"

Mr. Leek smiled. "His uncle Bobby Merritt called him Jetty Man. Actually, Hawk Hawkins named him that and Bobby made sure it took with folks. You know how Bobby was about people havin' names."

Chichemo smiled a rare smile and nodded his head one more time. "Yeah, that's it. He's the Jetty Man." Both men looked up as

Jason walked into the fish house.

The embarrassing and strange ordeal for Mary C. at Hawk's funeral was over. She would not think about Hawk's mother again. She would, however, think about Hawk more times than she wanted. Mary C. knew his aggressive spirit had refused to crossover. His strong will and struggle to stay with her raged on. She didn't realize it at the time, but Mr. King's house was the perfect haven for such a ghost, if you believed in such things. She was concerned the young and beautiful nurse and hymn singer, Mary Ellen, would make an attempt to be with Jason again.

Mary C., Miss Margaret, Margie and Sofia sat on the front porch. Margie was still recovering from her bout with the miscarriage flu. Her two younger sisters, Peggy and Susan had nursed her through the painful and mentally disturbing ordeal. Margie would survive.

Billy, the oak baby, lay asleep on a blanket next to Sofia's rocking chair. The monster dog, Abaddon, lay at the bottom of the steps. Miss Margaret had an observation.

"I don't think folks appreciate the weather we have in this part of the country. You hear about the hard winters up North and here we are two weeks before Thanksgiving and look at this glorious sunshine. The Lord has truly blessed the South."

Sofia had to chime in with her thoughts. "I think we have crazy weather. One day it rains, the next day it's cold, and now today it's bright and sunny." Miss Margaret smiled at Sofia wanting to add to the conversation. She did love Sofia. They all did.

"The number of good days outnumber the bad ones ten fold. Praise the Lord for that." Miss Margaret looked at her eldest daughter, Margie. "You look much better today, Margie. I think you've got that old flu bug beaten. You always get so sick when the weather changes so quickly like it has lately." Margie nodded. Miss Margaret looked at Mary C. "You look like you're at peace, child. There is a calmness about you. What are your thoughts, dear?"

Mary C. took a deep breath. She continued to stare out into the yard, but she did respond to Miss Margaret's question.

"I was thinking about how wonderful it is here with you and the girls. You know we have to move on and find our own place?" Miss Margaret nodded and the two girls looked at Mary C. "My calmness comes from you and your words of love and encouragement. I like your moments of praising the Lord for the smallest things. Things I have never thought about. You give hope to the hopeless and substance to the empty. You shine a light for those lost in the dark. You are an angel. I've just never sat on a porch with one before."

Miss Margaret and her two daughters were overwhelmed by Mary C.'s revelation of goodness. There was a silence for a few seconds as Mary C.'s words echoed in Miss Margaret's head. Her eyes filled with tears.

"My dear child, that is undoubtedly the most wonderful thing anyone has ever said to me. I will never forget those beautiful words. Your sincerity flows around us. I have chills running through my body. Jesus surely sits on this porch with us."

Sofia and Margie had no room on their bodies for another goose bump. Sofia had to share her thoughts as her eyes also filled with tears. "Oh, Mama! I feel it, too. Praise Jesus."

Margie looked at her dramatic little sister. The eldest rubbed her arms trying to wipe down the raised hairs. The ugly devil dog stood at attention. Sofia saw the dog first.

"You see, even the dog feels it."

Margie had to speak up. "Sofia, are you always going to be so funny? I do love you."

Sofia stood up from her chair and hugged her mother first, then Margie, and then Mary C. She even patted the dog on the top of his big head. The moment of love, chill bumps and the Lord ended when Abaddon turned away from Sofia's touch and growled, showing his massive teeth. Sofia moved back onto the porch when she thought perhaps the dog was growling at her. When she realized the dog was looking away from her she looked in the same direction to see what had taken Abaddon's attention away. The other three ladies did the same. All four pairs of eyes widened, including Mary C.'s, when they saw what had made the dog growl and look away.

There was a man riding a beautiful black horse, a black man. The horse and the man would pass by them in a matter of seconds. None of the ladies had ever seen a horse on that road, much less a black man riding a horse on that road or any road. Abaddon barked and took a few steps toward the horse and rider. Mary C. broke the silence.

"You stay right there, dog." She turned to Miss Margaret. "You got a gun here?" Miss Margaret's eyes popped open.

"A gun? Do we need a gun?"

"It might not be a bad idea. This don't look a little strange to you?"

Miss Margaret was nervous about the thought of needing a gun. "Oh dear, God."

Margie ran into the house. The horse and rider were only about twenty yards away from the steps to the porch. The dog barked and the horse stopped in the middle of the dirt road. Lamar Harris greeted the three ladies.

"Evenin' ladies. I didn't mean to frighten y'all. I was just takin' Raven here out for his first look at Mayport."

Sofia talked too much. "He's a beautiful horse."

Lamar smiled and leaned back in the saddle. "Why thank ya, little lady. I'm sure he thanks ya, too."

Mary C. stepped to the edge of the porch. "Why'd you come by here?"

Lamar ignored her question. "That's a mean lookin' dog you got there. Thanks for not sickin' him on us."

Mary C. wanted an answer. "Why'd you turned down this road?" Mary C. noticed a bullwhip wrapped around the horn of the saddle. "Why you got that bullwhip?"

Lamar smiled again. "You sure got a lot of questions, ma'am."

"But you ain't answerin' none of 'em."

Lamar was glad to meet Mary C. "There ain't many roads to turn down here in Mayport. You make six or seven turns and you've been down all the roads. This was just my last turn. I'm actually headed back home. And as for the whip, my friend suggested I carry it just in case there might be a horse chasin' dog around here."

Sofia spoke up. "You hit dogs with that whip?"

"I've never had to hit a dog with it yet. I hope I don't have to. My friend gave it to me as a gift. His mother was a real Indian. He taught me how to use it. I've never used it on a living creature."

Mary C. wasn't finished. "You ever been hit with one?" Lamar Harris knew a threat and he knew a racist remark when he heard one.

"No ma'am, but I'm sure somebody in my family tree has felt the sting of a whip. But, I haven't."

Mary C. could play the word game. "Not yet, anyway. But, you're still young. Maybe someday."

Sofia had no idea or concept of the tension that was building in the air. "Is your friend a Punjabi Indian?"

"No ma'am, he's Cherokee."

Miss Margaret was one who knew how thick the tension was around them and she had to end the war of words. "You have to admit that a man on horse back in Mayport is a rare sight."

Lamar looked at Mary C. "Especially, a black man, huh?" Mary C.'s eyes locked on Lamar's eyes. Margie interrupted the stare when she came out of the house holding her father's single barreled shotgun.

Lamar saw her first. "Hold on there girly. If there's a gun involved, I'm leavin'. Please be careful with that thing. You don't look to steady to me." Miss Margaret turned to see Margie standing with the shotgun on her hip.

"Dear God, put that thing down." Mary C. stepped to Margie and took the gun.

"Thank you Margie. I'll steady it for him." She turned to Lamar. "I think you need to continue your ride home, don't you?"

Lamar ignored Mary C. again and looked at Miss Margaret. "Miss Margaret, I know you don't recognize me, but I'm Lamar Harris. I'm Hattie's son. I haven't seen you since I was a little boy, but I do remember when mama did the ironing for you and your family. Mama always said you were the kindest woman she ever worked for."

Miss Margaret smiled and took a breath of relief. "You do still favor that little boy, now that I get a good look at you. How is sweet Hattie?" Lamar continued his stare with Mary C., but he spoke to Miss Margaret.

"Mama passed away last night. She's been sick for a year. We'll bury her in a few days."

Miss Margaret's heart ached for Lamar Harris. "I'm so sorry. I didn't know she was so sick. I haven't seen her in ages."

"No ma'am, I'm sure you haven't." Lamar pulled back on the

reigns he held in his hands. Raven moved backward and turned away from the house. Lamar looked at Mary C., but he talked to the others. "Good evening ladies. You too, ma'am."

Mary C. held the gun as she watched Lamar and the black horse move down the dirt road and away from the house. Margie had an observation.

"That was strange. I don't like him coming by here."

Miss Margaret was trembling. "He meant no harm. Grieving folk do things out of character sometimes. I feel bad about his mother."

Sofia would not be left out. "Me too."

Abaddon growled and showed his teeth again. The wild dog looked at Mary C. His raised lips revealed as many of his teeth as possible. Mary C. nodded to the mutant devil dog. Sofia screamed when the huge dog ran into the dirt road. Lamar turned the horse back when Sofia screamed and saw the wild dog charging toward them. Abaddon ran under the scared stallion and began biting at the horse's front legs causing the massive creature to lift his legs off the ground.

Lamar held on to the reins as Abaddon's sharp teeth and powerful jaws snapped at the legs of the horse. When the horse's front hooves hit the ground, Lamar sunk his heels into Raven's sides and the frightened horse began to run. Abaddon was close behind continuing his vicious assault on Raven's hind legs.

Miss Margaret and her two daughters watched in shock. Mary C. just watched as Lamar turned Raven off the road and into the woods. Abaddon followed as they disappeared from sight. The stunned spectators could hear the dog barking, but the sound faded away as a new sound took its place. It was the sound of a truck engine. The horse-chasing trance on the porch was broken as Jason drove his Uncle Bobby's truck up to the front of the house. The sight of Jason moved Sofia to a new excitement.

"Jason's home!"

The moment Lamar turned Raven off the road and into the wooded area he knew he had made a serious mistake. The flat road would have been the better choice. Abaddon was relentless with his attack. Lamar had to use all of his riding skills to stay in the saddle as Raven ran to get away from the wild dog.

The frightened horse jumped over a small fallen tree and galloped into, what looked like, a narrow walking trail of some kind. Abaddon ran along side of the huge animal snapping his powerful jaws and teeth at his legs with every step. The dog was as fast as the horse in the restricting underbrush and low growing cabbage palms. Raven lost all traction when he stepped in a pile of pine needles and stumbled forward. The black horse fell to his knees, throwing Lamar over his head. Lamar Harris was airborne.

The ground shook when the huge horse landed on its side. The ground shook a second time when Lamar landed on his back. It was an awful fall for any man to take. All of the air exploded from Lamar's lungs. He was dazed, could not catch his breath and his mouth was bleeding from biting his own tongue. He thought he was going to die, if not from the fall, then by the teeth of the devil dog. He could hear Abaddon barking and growling, but he couldn't see him. He knew the wild hound would attack him soon and he would have to defend himself.

Somewhere deep inside Lamar found the strength and the courage to roll over onto his stomach. Perhaps true fear of what was to come gave him that strength. He lifted his head and saw Raven running away with Abaddon running behind him. It was awful for him to think that the dog would be able to seriously injure his great stallion. Lamar realized he was breathing again. He laid his head back on the ground and listened to Abaddon's cruel sounds in the distance. Lamar raised his head off the ground again when the barking stopped.

Lamar moved his head from side-to-side. His neck was sore and he could feel the deep gash in the middle of his tongue. He tasted his own blood. He was alone, no horse, no dog.

Lamar pushed off the ground with both his hands to raise himself out of the dirt and pine needles. His right hand touched something that felt like a snake. He got to his knees to move away from it with his eyes scanning the ground for the reptile. Lamar was relieved when he realized his hand had touched the bullwhip his friend Shadow had placed on the saddle horn as a protection against any horse chasing dogs in Mayport. Shadow's far sight and premonition had gone far beyond a mere coincidence.

Lamar reached down with his right hand and picked up the leather wrapped wooden handle of the bullwhip. His throat went dry and all of the blood left in his body ran cold when he heard the now familiar death rattle of Abaddon's growl. Lamar stood up and turned in the direction of the evil sound. Abaddon had returned to do Mary C.'s bidding.

The dog's powerful hind legs pushed off the ground as the bloodthirsty hound from hell charged forward with his huge head leading the way. The scared and hurt Lamar Harris stood tall and spit the blood from his mouth as Abaddon drew closer. The dog jumped, leaving the ground like a torpedo blasting out of the dirt. Lamar screamed as the crack of a handcrafted Cherokee bullwhip echoed in the air. Another classic battle between man and beast was raging in the woods of Mayport.

Jason stood on Miss Margaret's front porch surrounded by the four ladies. He had just heard the wild and bizarre story about Lamar Harris and his horse from an overly dramatic Sofia. The other three had allowed her to tell the story because it was so much fun watching the expressions on her beautiful face as she told her version.

"And then they were gone. We could hear the dog barking for a little while and then it faded away. I hope he's all right. The horse, too." Jason looked at his mother. He knew Mary C. had been waiting for Sofia to stop talking.

"Well son, y'all catch any shrimp?" Jason would never tease his mother. He knew she wanted the truth and not playing.

"Over twenty boxes of shrimp and even more fish." Mary C. didn't change her expression. Miss Margaret's eyes lit up. She knew what twenty boxes of shrimp meant. Sofia still wanted to talk.

"Is that good, mama?"

"That's more than good, Sofia." Sofia looked at Jason with love in her big sky blue eyes. Margie looked at him with "want" in her eyes. Jason knelt down next to Billy and put his hand on the babies little back.

"How's he doin'?"

Mary C. surprised them all with her answer. "Babies are always good when their daddy comes home."

Miss Margaret had a great idea. "Why don't you girls heat up some of that corn beef stew and rice for Jason. I'll bet he's hungry for some home cooking." Mary C. saw the look on Jason's face.

"You said the magic words Miss Margaret. He does love his corn beef stew."

Shadow Martin sat on the hood of his red Ford truck talking to Mr. Cane and Mr. Cane's daughter, Chiquita. Her full name was Chiquita Naomi Cane. Evidently, a woman of Spanish or Mexican decent had made a lasting impression upon her father in his younger days. Chiquita was nineteen years old and very pretty. She was tall and had a slender build body frame like Sofia. She wore bright yellow pedal pusher pants showing the muscles in the calves of her legs. A one-inch wide yellow headband matching her pants was stretched across her forehead and wrapped around her head. Shadow Martin was talking to Mr. Cane, but he was enjoying his eye contact with Chiquita Naomi. Mr. Cane was doing the talking.

"I'd like Chiquita Naomi to go to college like you boys." He always called her by her first two names. "She's smart as hell, but we can't afford it right now. She graduated high school last year in Georgia when she went to live up in Savannah with my sister for a while." Mr. Cane looked at his daughter. "She become too refined for us Mayport folk. I know she wants to go back to her aunts."

Chiquita Naomi shook her head. "Now that's not exactly true

daddy and you know it." She looked at Shadow. "I do miss my aunt and my friends, but daddy needs me here for now. I can visit there if I want, but I like helping here."

Mr. Cane was full of information about his smart and pretty daughter, Chiquita Naomi. Information Shadow Martin was not at all interested in hearing. He was only thinking about getting his hands on Chiquita Naomi.

"Chiquita Naomi came home to visit and saw we was havin' money trouble. She got a job in the kitchen at Strickland's that very day. She's been a God send." Even though he was not interested Shadow listened. He felt bad for the pretty young girl. He didn't like the sad fact she had to put her life on hold to help her father. Mr. Cane looked to be an able man and capable of providing for his own needs. Shadow smiled at Chiquita Naomi and shared his worldly philosophy.

"It's truly an admirable thing you've done for your family, but don't let anything interfere with your future and what you're destined to be. Too many young black men and women have sacrificed their dreams for others. You're smart and pretty. Those characteristics alone give you a fighting chance. Allow them to open the doors to your future."

Mr. Cane wasn't sure if he liked what the handsome young stranger had just said to his daughter. Chiquita Naomi had never heard such words. She was flattered, flustered, and speechless. Her heart raced in her perfectly shaped chest. If her father had not been standing there she would have fallen into Shadow's arms. She knew it was only a matter of time before she would thank him properly for his beautiful words of encouragement.

Jason sat at the small table in Miss Margaret's kitchen. Margie poured a ladle full of the red corn beef stew over a big bowl of piping hot white rice. The chunks of soft potatoes rolled to the sides of the bowl. Jason had not been able to eat during the three days of being seasick on the high seas. He was feeling much better now that his feet were firmly on the ground. His stomach was still queasy. His body rocked back and forth like he was still on the ocean, but he would not disappoint the two beautiful ladies who were serving him the food. Sofia poured him a glass of sweet tea and handed him two pieces of buttered bread.

"I know you like to dunk the buttered bread into the stew." Sofia smiled. Margie rolled her eyes. Sofia kept talking. "There's plenty more where that came from. Mama always cooks enough corn beef stew to feed an army." Miss Margaret yelled from the living room where she sat in her rocker holding Billy.

"Everyone knows corn beef stew tastes better when you heat it up as a left over."

Mary C. sat at the table across from Jason. "Shouldn't you be back at the dock helpin' them unload?" Jason put down his first spoonful of stew before it reached his mouth.

"Mr. Chichemo told me to come here and tell you the good news. He'll come here when he settles up with Mr. Leek." Mary C. nodded. She watched Jason eat the stew for a few seconds.

"You look bad. You been sick ain't ya?" Jason put his spoon down again.

"Yes ma'am, all three days. I don't think I'll ever get my sea legs."

The wild dog Abaddon walked slowly into Miss Margaret's front yard and sat down again in the guard position at the foot of the steps. He was covered in dirt and blood. He had a long, inch wide gash across his back. There were three other open wounds on his muscular body, but the wet blood soaked dirt covered them. The injured canine laid his huge head down on the ground and made no sound.

Mr. Cane was just organizing his thoughts so he could try and respond to Shadow's, "Use your beauty and brains to make your future" philosophy. A noise to their left took the attention of all three of them away from the subject at hand. It was Lamar Harris. He was walking in front of Raven holding the horse's reins. The horse was limping badly as it slowly followed, favoring his right front leg. Shadow jumped off the hood of the truck and ran to assist his friend. Mr. Cane and Chiquita Naomi followed him. They could all see that Lamar was hurt, also.

Lamar's face was splattered with blood and his mouth was still bleeding from the cut on his tongue. They didn't know the dried blood on his left arm was from two dog bites on the lower part of his forearm. The cuff of his left pant's leg was shredded and he was limping because he had been bitten on his left ankle. Shadow reached him first.

"Holy shit, Lamar. What in God's name happened to you?" Lamar took a deep breath, filling his once empty lungs with a blast of cool air.

"It ain't got nothin' to do with God's name. I've met the devil and he comes in many forms." Shadow didn't know what to say. Lamar had never spoken in such a manner before. Chiquita Naomi stood back as her father stepped up behind Shadow.

"My God son, you're bleedin' bad. We gotta get you to Aunt Matilda's Place. She'll know what to do. She's as much a healer as any white man doctor." Lamar looked at Shadow.

"See to Raven first. I'll go inside and clean this blood and dirt off me. Then we'll be able to see what I need. Take care of Raven." Lamar handed the reins to Shadow and walked slowly to the back door of his mother's house. Mr. Cane walked with Lamar and assisted him as he walked up the three steps to the small back porch. They went into the house.

Shadow bent over to look at Raven's right front leg first. He squatted down to get a closer look at the injured leg. Shadow knew the moment he saw the injured leg that it was badly broken. He knew Lamar must have seen it, too. He lowered his head in disgust and sadness. Chiquita Naomi stepped up behind him and put her hand on his shoulder.

"This is awful. Is it bad?"

Shadow nodded. "As bad as it can get." Chiquita Naomi put her hand over her mouth in sad shock. Lamar's strange words were bouncing around in her head.

"What do you think he meant about seeing the devil? That was scary. You think he was just talking like that because of the pain?"

"I don't really know. It's not like Lamar to say such things."

Miss Margaret was still rocking Billy in the living room. Jason was getting another bowl of the leftover corn beef stew. Margie and Sofia were sitting at the table watching Jason eat and waiting for him to finish so they could clean up. Mary C. sat quietly in the living room with Miss Margaret. She was thinking about the strange encounter with the black horseman and his sarcastic words. She was glad Abaddon had chased him away.

The sound of Abaddon barking ended the quiet moment in the

living room and the "let's watch Jason eat" vigil going on in the kitchen.

Miss Margaret stopped rocking. "Oh, thank the Lord that dog's back! I was fearful for him and the Harris boy."

Miss Margaret stayed in the chair. Mary C. was the first one to step out onto the porch. She saw Chichemo first, standing about ten yards away with Abaddon standing in a protective position between Chichemo and the porch. Mary C. had to tease her old friend.

"Well, he sure knows who to keep away from the house. He's a smart dog, ain't he? You must have been easy to smell. Money smells, too ya know?"

It was strange to Mary C. when Chichemo did not respond to her playful greeting. He only stared at the dog. Sofia and Margie had left Jason at the table when they heard the dog barking. Sofia saw the dog.

"He's back. The dog's back. He's okay. Thank the Lord." Margie was the first on the porch to notice the deep cut on Abaddon's back.

"Be quiet Sofia, he's hurt." After Margie's observation, Mary C. and Sofia saw the huge cut on the dog's back. Sofia could not maintain herself.

"Oh no! He's cut bad. Do something." Sofia started to go down the steps to the dog. Chichemo spoke for the first time since he had arrived.

"Tell her to stay on that porch, Mary C. Don't come down here, girl."

Mary C. took Sofia's arm and held her. Sofia didn't understand. "We have to help him."

Chichemo raised his voice. "I said stay on the porch." Chichemo's aggressive manner brought a growl from Abaddon. Chichemo stepped back a few steps. Mary C. wasn't sure what was on her old friend's mind.

"What's wrong? He won't hurt you if I'm here. Be a good dog and let Mr. Chichemo bring me some money." Mary C. stepped off the porch and stood behind Abaddon. "We need to look at this bad cut on his back." Chichemo's eyes met with Mary C.'s eyes.

"You need to shoot 'im right now." Sofia and Margie couldn't believe their ears. Margie beat Sofia to the punch.

"Shoot him? Why? He hasn't hurt you. He's just protecting us. He'll let you come in." Chichemo didn't move. He looked at Mary C. again.

"Call the bastard and make him turn to you." Mary C. still didn't understand, but she did what Chichemo requested.

"Abaddon. Come here. Leave that old grouch alone. He ain't worth bitten."

The huge dog turned his blooded body to face Mary C. Sofia and Margie both screamed when the dog faced them. Mary C. had to step back herself until she could regain her composure. They all knew instantly why Chichemo was acting so strangely. Abaddon's right eye had been torn out of the eye socket, but it was still attached by a long piece of skin. The round black and white eyeball was dangling on the side of his head. Every time the dog moved his head it would swing like it was keeping time. Sofia turned away and began vomiting over the wooden railing of the porch. Margie stared at the hideous sight with her newly hardened eyes and heart. Mary C. looked at Chichemo. Miss Margaret heard the girls screaming and stepped out to see that had happened. She saw the dog.

"Dear God, what has happened to this poor creature?" Chichemo had not seen Lamar Harris sitting on his black horse. He knew nothing about the verbal encounter with Mary C. He had not seen the bullwhip on the horn of the horse, yet he knew what had happened.

"This dog's been bull whipped. I seen it before. A whip crack in the eye tears it right out of the socket. That mark on his back, that's from the thick lash cuttin' him deep. Those round spots are where he's lost chucks of hair, that come from the end of the whip as it slashes and then snaps back. That part of the whip most likely took his eye out." The porch was silent after Chichemo's description of what had happened to the dog. All four of the ladies knew the old seadog was right. Lamar Harris had used his bullwhip on Abaddon.

Chichemo had another observation to share. " I know y'all are probably mad about the beaten this dog took, but lot's of people are scared of these kinda dogs. I know I am. If he tried to bite somebody, or somebody's child it would be big trouble. I'm just sayin' he ain't no everyday mutt." He looked at Mary C. "This dog's trouble I tell ya. You need to put him down."

Both girls yelled "no". Miss Margaret was quiet. Mary C. looked down at the dog. He moved his head and the hanging eyeball swung back and forth.

"If we put him to sleep can you put his eye back in?" The ladies on the porch were silent again after Mary C.'s question to Chichemo. He knew she was serious.

"We can probably get it back in, but he most likely won't ever see out of it again. There's been a lot of damage to that eye. It would be better to just cut that skin and patch the hole 'til it heals."

Mary C. nodded her head. "You got somethin' in that bag of yours to put him out?"

"Damn, Mary C. you want me to play doctor, do ya?"

"I just know you have done things like this before. If I can save him I want to. I know who did this and I want this dog to live and meet up with him again." Jason stood at the door of the house. He had been listening to the wild conversation between his mother and Chichemo.

"Mama, we don't need this dog. You said if somethin' happened you'd shoot him yourself." Sofia and Margie turned to Jason as he continued. "This poor thing's sufferin' and he'll be sufferin' for some time now. These are awful injuries and he needs to be put out of his misery. That's what you do when animals are sufferin'."

"I said I would shoot him if he bit any of us. And I will. He ain't hurt none of us. He was protecting us when this happened. We owe him the effort to keep his ass alive if we can." Mary C. looked at Chichemo. " I wouldn't shoot you if you was injured with one eye." Mary C. smiled. "Well, I might shoot you."

Chichemo did not smile. He was a serious man. "He ain't gonna die, but we need to sew up this big cut so it don't get infected. I seen one-eyed dogs before. They're ugly to look at, but that shouldn't matter to this poor devil, he was ugly before his eye come out."

Lamar Harris stood at a small bathroom sink. He was washing the dirt and blood from his arms and face. Mr. Cane stood in the hallway.

"Let me know if I can help you, son. I know it must be painful. Please, allow me to take you to the hospital so you can get proper treatment." He watched the blood run off Lamar's arm and into the sink. "Dear God, those are bite marks. Something has bitten you."

"One of those big dogs like Johnny D. had. The ones that got killed at Mary C.'s that night."

Mr. Cane was interested. "Where did you run into one of those?"

"I was ridin' and passed the lady they call Miss Margaret's house. You know the lady who owns the store over there. The one with all those daughters."

Mr. Cane nodded his head. "I know Miss Margaret. She's a good Christian woman." Lamar took a towel and patted the water off his sore arm.

"Christian or not, she's got the devil sittin' with her on her porch. And the dog was standing guard. If I hadn't seen it I would never have believed it."

Mr. Cane didn't realize who Lamar was calling the devil. "Who was with her?"

"The one they call Mary C. was there and she made the dog attack us. She would have shot me with a shotgun if Miss Margaret had not been there to witness it. I think one of those girls is one of her followers, that dark headed one. And the dog knew just what Mary C. wanted. She wanted me dead. I ain't never done one thing to her and she wanted me dead, because I was a black man on a horse and I stood above her."

"I wouldn't think Miss Margaret would have much to do with the likes of Mary C."

"Well, she was there with her dog."

"What happened to the dog?"

"He went up into the woods. I didn't see him die, but he was hurt bad enough to bleed to death. I used my bullwhip to defend myself. I know he's hurt. It was just too dangerous to follow him into the thick woods to make sure he was dead. I was too weak and couldn't let him get a hold of me again."

Abaddon lifted his big head up when Mary C. stepped out onto Miss Margaret's back porch. She had moved the dog to the back yard. She was waiting for Chichemo to return with the tools to put the injured dog back together. Mary C. had gotten used to the dog's swinging eye as long as it didn't get too close to her. She was alone with Abaddon.

"I ain't gonna shoot ya, boy. You still got things to do. That fancy nigger will pay for this. I should'a blasted his black ass off that horse when he first came up. Stayin' here's makin' me weak and cloudin' my good judgment. I just ain't thinkin' right with all this Lord praisin' around me." She reached into her pocket and pulled out a white envelope. It was full of the money Chichemo had given her before he left. It was a badly needed payday. Sofia and Margie walked out onto the back porch to join Mary C. She turned to see the two girls when the door opened. Sofia had a sad look on her face.

" Miss Mary C., I came out to wish you good luck. I've got to go to work and let Peggy come home. Susan will stay with me until Margie relieves her later. Mother's been making us work two at a time since she heard about the Punjabi priest wanting to take me away." Margie rolled her eyes at the dramatic comment as Sofia continued. "I hope Mr. Chichemo can help him." She looked down at the pitiful looking dog. "I don't think I could watch it anyway. I'll be better off working at the store." Sofia squinted her eyes when Abaddon looked up at her with his eye swinging like the round ball hanging from the elastic string of a Bo-Lo bat. Sofia went back into the house.

Margie sat down next to Mary C. "I'd like to help if you need me."

Mary C. smiled. "How you feeling? You over the flu?"

Margie smiled back. She knew Mary C. knew why she had been sick. She also knew Mary C. would never betray her. It was one of those secrets Mary C. would keep burned deep in her belly.

"I'm better. The pressure that was bothering me is gone. Thank you for asking."

"We're like sisters, remember. Sisters take care of each other."

Margie smiled again and changed the subject. "Why do you think Mr. Chichemo can fix the dog?"

Mary C. looked at Abaddon, but she answered Margie's question. "He's the kinda man who's done it all. Nothin' rattles him or surprises him. He takes on the jobs nobody else will take. He's hard and he has seen his share of blood and felt his share of pain. Men like him get used to pain. They accept it as part of their life. It becomes second nature to them. He has no fears. If he dies this very second his life has been full. He fights hard and gives no quarter. He wasn't scared of the dog today. He was scared for the rest of us. He knows how dangerous a wounded animal can be." Margie loved to hear Mary C.'s strange words of wisdom. Mary C. had another Mayport story.

"One night I was ridin' with Chichemo and my brother, Bobby on Mayport Road. We were going out to the end of the road to eat some Bar-B-Que at the Red Barn. Them damn two fools tried to trick me and leave me home, but I jumped into the truck and they had to take me with 'em. They was gonna go jukin' after they ate and they didn't want to have to bring me back home before they went on into Jacksonville Beach. They were goin' to a place called Smitty's. It was a bar, poolroom and dance hall near the Board Walk. Hell, I wanted to go, too. I wouldn't have bothered them at all. But it just so happened that we only made it to the Red Barn that crazy night." Margie's eyes were full of interest.

"What happened?"

"During the ride we were passing the Buccaneer Trailer Park out near Miss Carolyn's house." Mary C. stopped for a moment and shook her head. "My goodness, I haven't thought about Miss Carolyn since she left Mayport to live out on the main road. She had a little piece of land her gramma left her and she built one of them Jim Walter Homes on it. I need to see how she's doin'. I'd like to have me a Jim Walter Home out there right next to Miss Carolyn. She would be the perfect neighbor." Mary C. realized she had gotten off track. Margie was waiting for the other story. "Anyway, a car on the other side of the road hit a horse as it tried to run across the road. I saw the whole thing. The horse's head hit the front windshield of the car. The poor horse began to spin around in a circle like it was dancing before he fell to the road. There was a loud slapping noise when the horse landed on his side."

Margie squinted her eyes. "How awful. I like horses. What did you do?"

"Chichemo stopped his truck and jumped out first. Me and Bobby followed him. Chichemo ran to the car to see if the people was injured or not. The windshield of the car was shattered, but no one in the car was hurt. Then we walked to the horse. It was really a sight. He was layin' on his side and he wasn't moving none.

There was a great big cut on his belly. It wasn't just a little cut; it was about three feet long and six inches wide. You could see inside his belly. Part of his intestines and his stomach was actually hangin' out. I thought it was strange that there wasn't much blood. You would think there would be a lot of blood. I don't know how his belly got so cut. I saw the windshield hit his head. I just knew he was dead until I saw that he was still breathing. He was knocked out, but he was alive. Every time he took a breath his guts would move in and then out. Chichemo turned to Bobby and said, 'Holy shit, he's still breathing. This bastard's still alive.' Bobby looked at me and said, 'This bastard's still alive.' My brother was a fool, ya know?"

Margie smiled as she remembered Uncle Bobby. "I liked your brother. He was fun."

Mary C. smiled. "You're right. He was fun. Everybody like Bobby." She thought about her brother for a second and then went back to her story.

"For some reason I looked at Chichemo. He never changed the expression on his face. Bobby talked to Chichemo for a few seconds, but I couldn't hear what they were saying. Bobby ran back to the truck while Chichemo moved closer to the horse. He knelt down and put his hand on the horse. I saw Bobby looking into Chichemo's toolbox in the back of the truck. He jumped out of the truck bed and ran back to the horse." Margie's eyes were open wide as Mary C. continued. "I stepped closer to see what they were going to do. Bobby handed Chichemo a big shrimp net needle and a spool of nylon twine. I couldn't believe it when Chichemo threaded the needle with the twine and started sewing up the big cut on the horse's side. Bobby pushed the guts back up into that big belly as Chichemo sewed him up like he was hemmin' a pair of pants. A small crowd began to gather to watch the spectacle. I loved those two men that night. They were real men. They were men who took chances. They were men who did somethin', men who didn't stand back, men who didn't hesitate."

Margie could see the fire burning in Mary C.'s eyes. She liked seeing that fire. Mary C. had some more advice. "Don't settle for a man because you think you need one or you think your time is running out. Be sure it's a real man no matter how long you gotta wait." Margie had the same fire in her eyes that flashed in Mary C.'s eyes. Mary C. had to finish her great story.

"The big cut was closed. You could see the big wide stitches. Chichemo had never changed the expression on his face. Then things got even crazier. The damn horse came around and struggled to his feet. He stood right up there in the road. I couldn't believe it. Nobody could believe it. Bobby stepped back to where I was standing to be sure I was all right in case the horse went wild. Chichemo stepped right up to the horse and checked the damage to his head. The horse actually stood there and allowed Chichemo to touch him. The horse was probably in pain and dazed from the accident and couldn't run if he wanted to. Then Miss Patterson joined the crowd. She owned the horse and had been looking for him. He had gotten out of her pasture earlier in the day. Chichemo helped her put a rope around the horse's head. And believe it or not, she slowly walked the horse off the road and back to her pasture." Margie's mouth was wide open. Mary C. looked at her. "That's a true story."

Margie wanted more. "Did you ever see the horse after that? Did he heal and live?"

"We did hear that Miss Patterson called the vet to look at the horse. He said Chichemo did a great job. We also heard Miss Patterson had put him out to stud. I'll bet he was pretty gentle when he tried to climb that first mare." Margie smiled at Mary C.'s little stud joke. Mary C. had another ending to the story. "We didn't go dancing' that night, but we did go get some Bar-B-Que." It was a great Mayport story.

CHAPTER FOUR

Lamar Harris walked out of his mother's house. His mouth and tongue were swollen and cut. He had a slight limp from the dog bite on his ankle. His arm was bandaged. Mr. Cane walked behind him. Shadow Martin and Chiquita Naomi stood next to the black stallion, Raven. Chiquita Naomi turned to see Lamar and her father walking toward them. She touched Shadow's arm.

"Are you taking Lamar out to Aunt Matilda's Place, daddy?"

"I'm not sure. It's up to Lamar. Perhaps Mr. Martin will advise him to go."

Lamar moved past Chiquita Naomi to stand with his best friend. Shadow had to speak his mind. "You look bad, brother. I don't think it's a bad idea to have a doctor look at those bites. Dog bites ain't somethin' to play with or ignore. What do you want to do? You know what ever you say I'm with you. And who the hell is Aunt Matilda." Lamar forced a smile and put his good hand on Shadow's shoulder.

"She's the next best thing to an old time witchdoctor. She runs a store near the beach for the black and white folks in East Mayport.

She does seem to have a healing way about her."

Shadow raised his eyebrows. "A healin' way, huh?"

Lamar had to smile at his friend's doubtful look. "I'll probably be treated better at her place than I would be treated at the white hospital. And I ain't goin' all the way into St. Vincent's." Lamar looked down at Raven's crooked and broken leg. He changed the subject. "It's broke bad, ain't it?"

Shadow nodded his head. "You know it is. You knew it when you walked him in. I'm so sorry. I shouldn't have brought him here. I'm so sorry."

"This has nothin' to do with you bringing him here. You did the right thing for me. Don't you dare take the blame for this. I should be able to ride my horse wherever I want as long as I am not a danger to anyone. The devil is to blame for this." Shadow looked at Chiquita Naomi. She looked away and took her father's arm, walking him toward the house. Shadow looked at Lamar.

"You're scarin' me with all this devil talk. It ain't like you. You do know how crazy you sound, don't ya?"

"I'll explain it all to you and what I'm going to do when we ride to Aunt Matilda's and we're alone. Right now we have to decide what to do about Raven."

Mary C., Jason, Margie, Miss Margaret, Peggy and Chichemo stood in Miss Margaret's back yard. There was no fight left in the vicious, but seriously injured black Rottweiler as he lay at Mary C.'s feet. They were all there to watch and assist Chichemo's generic medical abilities and treatment. Chichemo unzipped a small leather case and took out a little glass bottle. Mary C. knew Chichemo would not give them much information, but she was unusually curious. Perhaps she asked the question for the benefit of the others. "What's in the bottle?"

Chichemo did not change the expression on his face. "It's ether. If I can get him to breath it in he'll be out for an hour or so. He won't feel a thing." Chichemo looked at Mary C. " Don't ask me where it came from." Mary C. understood. There would be no more questions. Chichemo moved closer to the dog.

"If we can hold him down long enough with out gettin' bit, I just need him to take one big whiff of this ether and 'good night Irene'." Chichemo turned to Miss Margaret. "You got a old blanket we can put over him?" Margie ran into the house before Miss Margaret could answer the question.

Chichemo took a pair of thick leather gloves out of his pocket and put them on his hands. "I don't think these will help much if he bites me, but it can't hurt to wear 'em."

It was easy for the backyard spectators to see the seriousness of what was about to happen. Margie came back with an old heavy and thick wool army blanket. She handed the blanket to Chichemo. He turned to Mary C.

"You should put the blanket on him. I think he'll let you do it. We can hold him down easier by holding the blanket down around him. Just be careful."

Mary C. didn't hesitate. She had been around men of action throughout her adult life and she had become a woman of action because of it. Margie watched Mary C. kneel down next to Abaddon. She knew Mary C. was a real woman with no fear.

"Hey ya ugly thing. Let Mary C. help ya stay warm out here. Don't bite me now with Jason standin' up there. He'll make me shoot ya. And I don't think ya want that to happen. Ya got things to do." The huge dog never moved as his new master placed the warm blanket around his torn body. Mary C. looked at Chichemo.

"So far so good." The crowd on the porch was silent. Chichemo looked at Jason.

"If you and ya mama can hold the edges of the blanket so he can't move, I'll try to hold his mouth closed and put the ether on his nose." Jason nodded and stepped off the porch to stand with his mother. Margie stepped off the porch, too.

"I can hold him with you."

Miss Margaret was surprised and concerned. "Margie, you get back up on this porch!"

Margie looked back at her mother. "Please let me do this. I can help." Miss Margaret didn't know about the story Mary C. had told Margie earlier. It was Margie's chance to be a true woman of action. "Mother, I'm fine." Miss Margaret crossed herself and began to pray. She wasn't Catholic, but she understood the religious concept and liked crossing herself before she prayed. The three medical assistants surrounded the covered dog.

Chichemo knelt down next to Abaddon's exposed head. He

could see the eye still attached by the string of skin. He knew the dog could not see him on that side. Chichemo took the top off the small bottle and poured the liquid ether onto a rag. He looked at the three others and nodded for them to hold the blanket down around the dog. As soon as they all pushed the edges of the blanket Chichemo grabbed Abaddon's mouth with of his gloved hands, holding a vice type grip on the dog's powerful mouth and jaws. At the same moment Chichemo wrapped the ether soaked rag around the dog's nostrils.

Abaddon kicked his powerful hind legs to free himself from the blanket. Margie's blood ran wild as her heart raced in her chest when the dog began to struggle. Chichemo's grip was as powerful as the dog's bite. The weak and distressed animal could not free his nose from the rag. In fifteen seconds the fight ended. The great devil dog, Abaddon, was sleeping like a newborn puppy. It was probably the deepest sleep the always alert and aggressive dog had ever experienced. Margie felt a sense of great pride as she released her hold on her edge of the blanket. She looked at a smiling Mary C. and nodded. Mary C. understood.

Lamar Harris stood next to his broken black stallion. He hugged the wide thick neck of the beautiful creature. Shadow stood behind him.

"He's sufferin' ya know. You want me to do it?"

Lamar shook his head. "No, it has to be me. We both know that. But, thanks for the offer." Lamar took a deep breath. "My mama's layin' in her coffin over at the funeral parlor. She'll be put in the ground in two days and I'm more concerned with a horse."

Shadow's eyes lit up. "That's not true. Your mama knows how you feel about her. You have proven it throughout your life. She would also understand what you're goin' through right now. You're really bein' too hard on yourself. You need to stop. You gotta put Raven out of his misery. That's what you do when the animal you love is sufferin'."

Chichemo held a long, thick, lit kitchen match under the four-inch blade of his favorite pocketknife. When the match went out he held the blade out toward Margie. The new woman of action poured alcohol over the scorched metal. Chichemo looked at Mary C.

"I don't think I can put this eye back in. He's gonna be blind on this side no matter what I do."

Margie couldn't help herself. "Even if he can't see won't he look better with the eye in?" Chichemo looked up at Margie. He didn't change his expression.

"I was gonna just cut it off. That's the easy thing to do. Hell who knows, he might be able to see out of it right now. It is still connected to somethin'." Chichemo looked at Mary C., but he talked to Margie. "Oh-key-doke-key, Miss Margie, lets put this eyeball back into that socket. If he can't see out of it at least he'll still be handsome." Chichemo never changed his expression. Mary C. looked at her old crusty friend. She had never heard him say, "Oh-key-doke-key". She had to smile.

Chichemo needed help. "I need somebody to hold his eye lid up so I can put the eyeball back in." Everyone was shocked when Margie stepped to assist Chichemo one more time. Miss Margaret couldn't believe her eyes. She shook her head, but said nothing. Margie knelt down next to the sleeping dog. "Tell me what to do." She was eye-to-eye with a real man.

No one in Miss Margaret's back yard could hear the two gunshots that rang out from behind Mattie Harris' house. They did not feel the ground shake as the huge black stallion fell.

Chichemo had more medical directions for his unregistered nurses. "Pour some of that alcohol on your hands and use one thumb on the top and the other thumb on the bottom. Pull the lids apart and I'll slide it in."

Mary C. poured the clear liquid on Margie's hands and stepped away. Margie turned to the dog. She did not hesitate to follow Chichemo's medical instructions. She used her thumbs to pull the dog's eyelids open. Chichemo took his gloves off, laid them on the ground and placed the loose eyeball into his bare hand. He looked at Mary C. again.

"Mary C., pour some of that in my hand. Cover the eye with it." There was no hesitation in Mary C. either as she poured the alcohol over the eye and into Chichemo's left hand. He took the eyeball out of his one hand and held it with the fingers of his right hand. Margie's throat and mouth went dry when Chichemo moved the eyeball toward the open socket. He took the loose connected skin and slowly tucked it into the hole in the dog's head. Margie took a deep breath and made a decision not to look away. It was a turning point in the young girl's life. She just didn't know it.

Chichemo pushed the eyeball into the socket. It was easier to slide back in than Chichemo had anticipated. Margie held the eyelids open wide. Chichemo turned the eyeball like a radio knob until it was in the middle of the socket and looking forward. Chichemo moved his head back to be sure the eyeball was straight and centered. He looked at Margie. "You can let the lids go. I'm hopin' they'll close around the eye."

Margie took a deep breath and removed her thumbs. The dog's eyelids closed around the eyeball. Chichemo nodded his head. "We're movin' right along here. Now the hard part." Margie wasn't sure what could be harder than what had already been done. She watched and waited with the others for Chichemo's explanation.

"I need to put a few stitches in both corners of the eye lids. If I don't, that eye's gonna fall out at any movement at all. After I stitch it we'll put a patch on it, but ain't no dog gonna keep a patch on too long. The stitches will keep the eye in a position for the socket to heal around it. Then we'll sew up that big cut on his back so it don't get dirty and infected. Somebody hand me that little bag over there."

Chiquita Naomi and her father stood at the driver's side window of Shadow's red Ford truck. The horse trailer was not attached. Mr. Cane was talking. "I'm sure glad you decided to let Aunt Matilda look at those bites. We're very sorry about your horse. I'll get some help and get the hole dug while you're gone. You want us to go ahead and bury him, or wait on you to come back." Lamar stared out the front window and didn't respond. Shadow responded for him.

"If you get the hole dug and get him in it, go ahead and cover him. No sense waitin'." Shadow had two things on his mind. Taking care of his best friend and finding the time to take care of Chiquita Naomi. Shadow looked out the truck window at his new female friend.

"We'll be back as soon as we can. I hope to see ya later." She nodded her pretty head as Shadow pressed the gas pedal and the truck rolled away.

Abaddon lay in a deep and healing sleep. The dark green army blanket kept him warm and comfortable. Chichemo reached down and held the ether soaked rag against the dog's nose again. "Maybe he'll sleep longer with another whiff of this stuff. Nothin' better for healin' than sleepin'."

The canine reconstructive ordeal was over. They would all remember what took place in Miss Margaret's back yard for the rest of their lives. It would be a great Mayport story. They all went into the house. Their relationship with Mary C. was creating a strange and bizarre history for Miss Margaret and her four daughters.

Lamar Harris directed his friend, Shadow Martin, as the red Ford truck stopped at an East Mayport cross road. "Turn here on Seminole Road. Aunt Matilda's Place is at the end of the road near the beach.

Shadow made the turn. He was concerned with his best friend. "How ya feelin', sport? You in a lot of pain?"

"My heart hurts more than anything. I can't believe we put him down. I hope it was the right thing."

"It was the right thing. And you know it." Shadow Martin had been waiting to be alone with Lamar. "Talk to me about what happened. You been sayin' some strange things. I thought it was some kind of shock from the attack and the dog bites. But, I can see it's more than that. Talk to me. What's goin' on?"

Lamar continued his stare out the front window of the truck, but he responded to Shadow's request. "I've been hearin' all this devil and evil talk since the day I got home. There's this white woman they call Mary C. She has a brutal history of evil and death, death of Mayport's black folks. Her actions are always ruled self-defense by the local law. The death count grows every year or so and sometimes even monthly. Her life has been full of other deaths and killings before she started on the black community. Last year a group of black men called Calypsos, who followed the teachings of a voodoo woman named Voo Swar, tried to steal a true-blooded oak baby from Mary C.'s house. Mary C. and some priest slaughtered all of the Calypso warriors and killed Voo Swar, who was Mayport's resident queen of the black arts, too."

Shadow Martin was in a daze as he listened to Lamar's rendition of Mary C.'s trail of blood and death. Lamar had much more. "Then a day or so after I got home, Voo Swar's son called the Ax, took six black men and six of those big dogs and tried to kill Mary C. His real name was Johnny D. Bryant. I knew him from our childhood. Somewhere during his life with Voo Swar, she convinced him he was the son of the devil and he was invincible."

Shadow had to stop Lamar. "You gotta slow down a minute. I can't handle all this at once. This Ax took six men and six dogs to kill this one white woman?"

Lamar nodded. "That's right. You know sixes are a devil thing?" Shadow couldn't believe Lamar had more. "You're gonna think I'm lyin', but all seven men died including Johnny D. Some were cut to pieces, some were shot and one was burned alive. I saw the remains of Johnny D. myself. His head was gone. Five of the six dogs died and the surviving dog just killed my horse and tried to eat me."

Shadow took a deep breath and interrupted Lamar. "How could one woman kill all these people? You have to admit it is not an easy story to believe."

"I know it sounds crazy, but let me finish." Lamar knew Shadow would try not to interrupt him again. "The first time with Voo Swar a soldier priest of some kind from a foreign country did most of the killin'. This last time her son, the priest and a monster of a white man, called Hawk protected Mary C. and the oak baby. Hawk and the priest died with the others." Lamar stopped for a second, but Shadow waited to see if there was more. There was. "Macadoo wanted me to join forces with her and rid Mayport and the world of this death machine in the form of a woman. I had given it some thought and actually told Macadoo that I would take care of Mary C. in my own way."

Shadow's eye lit up. He had to speak. "You have gone crazy. Comin' home to all this voodoo crap and devil talk has had some strange effect on you. Maybe it was your mama dyin' that weakened your mind and allowed you to be taken in by all this foolishness."

Lamar nodded his head. "I thought about that. At first I was sorry I had made that comment to Macadoo. The fat bitch even mentioned it to me at the house before you came up. She is expecting me to kill Mary C."

"You're not a killer. You are an educated man. You are going to take the black man into the next century. You have come a long way since you walked these streets and headed shrimp on the docks. I really don't think you are going to jeopardize your wonderful future to stay here and fight his woman. We need to bury your horse when we get you patched up. We need to bury your mother in two days. We need to go back to Daytona and never come back here again. There is nothin' here for you now that your mama's gone. You don't belong here anymore."

Lamar looked at his friend. "You are one silver tongued rascal ain't ya?" Shadow smiled and thought the subject matter would change. He was wrong. "I saw it myself today. I saw the evil and the devil. I never thought I'd ever say it, but this woman is the devil. She told that dog to kill me."

Shadow wanted it all to stop. He interrupted. "I want to talk about all this, but we need to get you some medical attention."

Shadow saw a small wooden building with a tin roof. He knew they had reached their destination when he saw the sign with big red letters that read: Aunt Matilda's Place. There were smaller letters on the sign that read: cold drinks, meats, smokes, bait, sweets and potions. Shadow looked out the front window of his truck as the truck rolled to a stop. "It's actually called Aunt Matilda's Place?"

Lamar had to smile. "I said we were going to Aunt Matilda's Place."

Shadow read the rest of the sign. "What the hell kind of store has potions? Are we really goin' in there?"

"You ain't seen nothin' yet. What til' you get inside and meet Aunt Matilda and her daughter Zulmary."

Shadow turned to look at his passenger. "Aunt Matilda has a daughter named Zulmary? What kind of name is Zulmary?"

"It's probably from somewhere in the islands or maybe Africa, hell I don't know. I never heard where it came from."

Shadow laughed out loud and laid his head on the steering wheel of the truck. Lamar smiled too and had to ask. "Now, what the hell is so funny to you?"

Shadow lifted his head. "Here we are, two young, handsome black men here to honor your wonderful mother. We were to say good-by to your mama and go change the world. Now, we are going to see a witch doctor named Aunt Matilda, who just happens to have a daughter named, Zulmary. There was a voodoo queen who had "Voo" in her name. A woman called Macadoo wants you to kill a devil woman who has something called an oak baby, what ever that might be. I don't think I really want to know. You told me about a killer priest, a monster white man, a man who thought he was the devil and devil dogs. Don't you think somewhere in all this ridiculous crap there is something we can laugh about. Come on, think about it."

Lamar didn't want to respond to his friend's question at that moment. He changed the subject. He opened the passenger's side door. "Come on my friend, let me introduce you to Zulmary. She will get all this off your mind. I promise you won't be disappointed."

Mary C., Miss Margaret, Peggy and Margie sat at the kitchen table. Jason had taken Chichemo home. He didn't stay after he finished his medical business. Jason would stay on the boat again and he would not return to Miss Margaret's house until breakfast the next morning.

The subject at hand was the canine surgery that had taken place in the backyard. No one could believe the major role Margie had played in assisting the operation. Miss Margaret had a question for her older daughter.

"My dear Margie, what possessed you to get into the middle of all that cutting and sewing? I never would have thought any of my girls would be able to handle seeing such a thing as we saw today. For that matter, I never imagined we would have anything like this going on in our back yard. It's not something you think about. This has been a strange day for all of us. I'm looking forward to a new day tomorrow. I'd like to put this one far behind us."

Peggy looked at her older sister. "It was great the way you jumped right in there. I couldn't believe it. I can't wait to tell Susan and Sofia. They won't believe it."

Margie smiled at her sister's praise and kind words, but she didn't care what anyone thought. She knew she was now different and would never be the same. It was the moment she had been waiting for. Margie's head flashed with the changes that had taken place inside her during the last year.

She had become a real woman of action only an hour ago. She

had learned to satisfy her sexual needs with a man or the tree. She had suffered through the mental and physical pain of a miscarriage. She wanted to be the mother of an oak baby. She had held a shotgun with the intention to protect others. She had stood in Mary C.'s house when Voo Swar's head was splattered all over the door. She was standing next to Mary C. when she shot the big black man called Truck. She had watched bull gators kill her friend and sexual partner. Margie was ready to handle whatever came her way. She wanted to stand next to the tree and see if it would recognize her. She wanted Jason.

Shadow and Lamar walked into the small building. Lamar was first. One light bulb hanging from a single brown electrical cord was the only light in the entire room. The walls were lined with shelves from the floor to the ceiling. Pots, cans, bags, bottles and other containers filled the shelves on one side and books, old newspapers and magazines filled the other side. There was a strange smell. Shadow knew what it was and he had a thought to share with Lamar.

"I've always liked the smell of formaldehyde when ever I entered a room, haven't you?" Shadow did not wait for Lamar to answer the sarcastic question. "I have a feeling the sign out front isn't right. I really don't think they still sell meat in here? At least I hope they don't."

A raspy voice came from a far corner of the dimly lighted room. It was slow and deliberate. Shadow and Lamar both knew who ever was talking had a serious speech impediment.

"You wight, we don't. We haben't sold none in years. I been meanin' to take dat sign down, but I just can't seem to get awound to doin' it. Ain't got no bait or told dwinks either. Got smokes, but they just for special customers. I gotta know ya pretty good to sell you those smokes." Lamar tried to focus his eyes on the person talking. He could see that the person was sitting in a rocking chair.

"Is that you Aunt Matilda?"

The voice cracked again. "Mama's sweeps a wot watewy. That's what you do when you pert-near a hundwed. Hell, she might alweady be a hundwed. Nobody knows and she don't care."

Lamar knew who it was. He had forgotten Zulmary had difficulty with certain letters of the alphabet. Some times she substituted B for V and W for R and L. She also left out a letter now and then, like an S at the end of a word. She struggled with Th and usually replaced it with a D. Once in a while she would get the tougher words right, but not very often.

"Zulmary, is that you?"

The rocker stopped moving. "Who say my name?"

Shadow looked at Lamar. "This is some scary shit, here. I got a strange feelin' Elmer Fudd's sittin' in that chair." Lamar had to smile as the voice interrupted Shadow's cartoon flashback.

"I asked who's sayin' my name?"

Lamar stepped toward the chair. "It's Lamar Harris, Zulmary. I used to come here with my mother, Hattie, when I was a little boy. You and I met one time on the beach when you were getting' sea turtle eggs with your mama, Aunt Matilda. We were both about fifteen then. You kissed me when we ran up into the sand dunes."

Shadow's head turned toward Lamar. His eyes were wide opened. "Oh shit!" He looked back into the dark corner as Zulmary stood up.

"You was da fiwst boy I eber kissed." Shadow Martin could not believe his eyes when Zulmary stepped toward them and stood under the one light bulb.

Zulmary had very dark skin. She had a different look than Shadow had ever seen. She was a combination of beauty with a worn look about her. It was obvious she had done more in her short lifetime than most do their entire lives.

She wore a long white dress that touched the tops of her bare feet. The top of the dress was pulled down over her arms exposing her dark brown shoulders. The front of the dress cupped the white material over her breasts with a piece of elastic across the top. She looked like a Mexican peasant. Her black hair brushed her bare shoulders. She stepped closer as she recognized Lamar.

"I sowwy 'bout you mama. She was a good woman. Her and my mama was fwiends for years. I weawy wilked her."

Shadow stood in amazement as Lamar responded. "Thank you. I know our mothers were friends a long time." Zulmary stepped even closer to the two young men.

"Mama can't go to da funewal, but I was gonna try and go for her."

Lamar nodded his head. "That would be nice. Mama would like that."

Shadow couldn't take his eyes off Zulmary. There was something in her eyes that gave her an unusual appearance. His eyes widened when he saw a long thick scar on her right cheek that went from the corner of her mouth to the back of her jaw. He couldn't tell how far back it went, but he knew a knife of some kind had caused such a scar. Lamar made the introduction.

"Zulmary, this is my friend Shadow Martin. We met at college and became roommates. He's here for the funeral, too." Zulmary stepped to Shadow. They were eye-to-eye as the light was at it's brightest on her face. She stuck out her hand.

"Nice to meet you."

Shadow shook her hand. It was softer than he thought it would be. She did not release his hand after the normal handshake. Shadow waited for her to release her grip. He had to say something as the strange young woman held his hand.

"Zulmary is an interesting name. I'm sure you're tired of folks asking you about it. Where did it come from?"

Zulmary held his hand. "It don't bother me none, but ebewybody that I see alweady know 'bout my name. I tell you 'bout my name, you tell me 'bout you name." Lamar and Shadow both had to smile at the informational deal Zulmary had offered. Shadow nodded his head.

"That's a good idea. I guess my name is different, too." Zulmary nodded, but there was no smile. Both men could tell the strangely attractive woman didn't smile very much or possibly not at all.

"Mama tell me it came fwom the Haiti iwends. She thought maybe it came fwom the swaves that was took dere on da boats. Dey was fwom Afwica. When mama was down dere she found out dat she had da sight. She got it fwom her mama and she gibe it to me. The woman who told her 'bout the sight was name Zula Marie. Mama changed it a wittle bit and call me Zulmary." She had not released Shadow's hand. He was uncomfortable, but he didn't want to hurt Zulmary's feeling. She looked at Lamar. "I didn't know I had da sight when we kissed. I would have told you if I knew."

Shadow looked at Lamar and then he looked back at Zulmary.

They were still eye-to-eye and she still held his hand. He saw one of the reasons she had such a different look about her. Zulmary had one deep blue eye and one dark black eye; it wasn't brown, it was black. Shadow had never seen such eyes. He didn't know if Lamar knew about her eyes or not, but since Lamar had kissed her before, Shadow thought his friend probably already knew. Zulmary scared Shadow with her next comment.

"The black one give me da sight."

A chill went through Shadow's body. He pulled his hand away, forcing her to break the marathon handshake. His throat went dry. Zulmary apologized.

"I didn't mean to scare you. I just know when somebody wooks at my eyes. Sowwy." She turned away from Shadow and looked at Lamar's bandaged arm. "You hurt?"

Lamar nodded. "Yes, it's a dog bite. A devil dog bite." Shadow turned quickly to face Lamar after the devil dog comment. He still had no words. Zulmary nodded her scarred, but pretty head.

"Dere be lots a dogs dat bite for da debil; oder animals, too. Da debil libes here. Me and mama saw her."

Lamar looked at Shadow, who was still staring back at him with a bewildered look on his face. Lamar had to ask the question.

"When you and Aunt Matilda see the devil, it's a woman?" Another chill ran through Lamar and Shadow when she answered the question.

"If you see the debil awound here, it be a woman."

Lamar understood. He was excited. . "I've seen her, I have! She made the dog bite me!"

Shadow didn't like what was happening to his friend, but he would stay with Lamar. Zulmary's eyes were alive, even the black one, as she continued the devil talk.

"She has many pwotecters. I didn't know she had da dog. I do da heawin' now dat mama went bwind. Dat's when I got da sight. I go bwind one day and will weave da sight to my daughter, if I eber have one." For some reason Zulmary changed the subject. "My mama's daddy was bwack, fwom da iwands and her mama was fwom Spain. My daddy was Portuguese. He came here when da Portuguese ran away fwom da Bwack Manorcan in St. Augustine."

Shadow had heard enough. "Zulmary, we came here to see if

you could help Lamar with his wounds. We don't know much about dog bites, but these look bad. Can you help him and y'all can get back to the devil and the Black Minorcan while you take a look at him? I don't want him foamin' from the mouth at his mother's funeral."

Mr. Cane and his daughter, Chiquita Naomi, stood next to a large hole that had been dug in a small wooded area behind Hattie Harris' house. A beach skeeter made from a cut down 1955 Chevy rolled past them dragging the huge dead body of Lamar's horse, Raven. Chiquita Naomi put her hand over her mouth as the horse was pulled next to the large hole a number of her father's friends had dug. He wanted to get the horse into the ground before Lamar returned. Lamar had enough to deal with without adding the burial of his horse. Mr. Cane was a good man and did the right thing.

The Chevy skeeter stopped when the carcass was next to the hole. Two men jumped out of the skeeter and untied the rope from the back bumper. They left the rope tied to the horse's leg. One of the men jumped back into the driver's seat of the skeeter and drove it around to the other side of the big hole. The other man took the loose end of the rope and carried it to the back of the skeeter. He retied the rope to the back bumper. It was obvious to Chiquita Naomi that they were going to pull the horse from the other side into the hole. Mr. Cane raised his hand to the driver.

"We need to hang on a little longer. Don't put him in yet. I called the police to talk to them about what happened. They'll probably want to see the horse. I hope we'll have it done before Lamar gets back, but if we don't, we don't."

Chiquita Naomi had a question. "You think somebody will come, daddy?"

"I don't know. I hope I didn't make a mistake in callin' 'em." There was a noise behind them. They both turned to see a police car stopping in front of Hattie's house. Chiquita Naomi saw the car first.

"We'll know soon enough."

It would soon be dark in the little fishing village near the mouth of the St. Johns River. Jason sat on the dock next to the shrimp boat named after his mother. He looked across to the Fort George side of the river. The sun was half way down. It had always been his favorite time of the day. That time when night is taking over the day, but it hadn't quite happened yet. It was neither day, nor night.

His heart jumped when the Mayport ferry horn blasted as the huge floating carrier left the slip on the Mayport side headed for the Fort George side. Jason loved to hear that horn. It would always be a symbol of the time he moved into manhood. The sight of the oak tree flashed in his head. His thoughts from the past allowed him to drift away.

Officers Paul Short and David Boos stood next to the deep and wide grave that had been prepared for Raven's burial. Officer Boos shook his head.

"This was some horse, here. What a beauty. You had to put him down?"

Mr. Cane nodded his head. "There was nothin' we could do. Lamar knows about these things. He just couldn't bear to watch him suffering."

Officer Short took the lead as he wrote in a small pocket spiral notebook "And the horse broke his leg because a big dog made him fall in the woods while the dog was trying to kill this Lamar Harris, fella?"

Mr. Cane nodded his head again. "Yes suh. The dog belongs to the woman called Mary C. Lamar was riding the horse and passed Miss Margaret's house. He stopped to tell Miss Margaret about his mother's death. That's when Mary C. made the dog attack."

Paul Short looked at David Boos. "And Lamar thinks Mary C. did this on purpose? It wasn't just a big dog chasing a strange horse that had never passed that house before?"

Chiquita Naomi didn't like Officer Short's tone of voice. "I knew you shouldn't have called them. They're not gonna do anything to help Lamar."

Officer Short didn't like Chiquita Naomi's tone of voice. "Hang on there, little missy. We're hearin' this story from a second and third party. We need to talk to Lamar, Mary C. and anyone else that saw this happen." He turned from Chiquita Naomi and faced her father.

"Mr. Cane, you must understand that if this happened in the woods like you said it was only Lamar, the horse and the dog. Mary C. was at Miss Margaret's house while the dog was supposedly attacking in the woods. We all know dogs will chase horses. That particular dog, if it's the one you say it is, will probably chase anything and try to kill it, I might add. Mr. Butler told us that Mary C. had kept the big dog after her house burned."

Chiquita Naomi interrupted Paul Short. "And seven black men died. Could you add that, too?"

Officer Short had reached his limit with the pretty young Chiquita Naomi. She was nice to look at, but that did not interest him at all. He took a deep breath and looked at Mr. Cane again.

"If you don't send her away from this discussion we're getting' back in that car and we won't be back." Chiquita Naomi looked at her father after Officer Short's demand. She was expecting her father to defend her to the policeman. It didn't happen.

"Go on up to the house and let the men talk. You don't need to be in the middle of all this."

If mad, glaring looks could kill, Chiquita Naomi's father would have dropped dead next to the already dead Raven. The angry young woman wanted to scream and tell her father "no", but he had already embarrassed her enough in front of the two white men. She turned away as the tears of anger filled her eyes. It would be hard to forgive her father for not standing up for her.

Mr. Cane turned back to Officer Short. "I'm sorry about her. She thinks she's grown."

Officer Boos had a question. "You do know that Lamar has to be the one who initiates the investigation. You hearin' the story and then tellin' us will not be enough."

Mr. Cane shook his head. "I know all that. I just wanted to tell the authorities and maybe it would help the young man. He came home to bury his mother and now this. A man can just take so much, ya know?" Mr. Cane looked at the two men standing near the cut down Chevy skeeter then he looked back at Officer Boos. "Can we put the horse in the ground? We were hopin' to have it done before Lamar came home."

"Where is Lamar, anyway? We'll be able to decide what to do next when we talk to him."

"He's gone to Aunt Matilda's to see if she can help him with them awful dog bites. What about the horse?"

Lamar sat on a small wooden stool, as the novice Mayport

witchdoctor examined the dog bite marks on his arm. Shadow stood next to the glass top counter watching Zulmary's every move. In spite of the large scar on her face, her speech impediment and her weather beaten look, Zulmary was dripping with sexual magnetism. Lamar grimaced in pain when Zulmary unwrapped the white gauze from his injured arm.

"I try not to hurt you. I need to see how deep da bite go." Lamar nodded and looked up at Shadow. Shadow forced a smile.

"You all right?"

Lamar licked his dry lips. "I'm a little queasy in the stomach."

Shadow had his own problem. "I've got an awful headache from smellin' that damn formaldehyde." He addressed Zulmary. "How you get used to a smell like that?"

Zulmary continued to examine Lamar's arm, but she responded to Shadow's question. "I don't know what that is. I can't eben say dat word. I don't weally smell it. What do it smell wike?"

Shadow couldn't resist the opportunity to add to the bizarre encounter. "It smells like dead people smell."

Zulmary didn't look up. "Oh Shadow, dat scare me. I don't wike dead people."

Shadow looked at Lamar, but spoke to Zulmary. "I guess you could say formaldehyde is used to preserve things."

Zulmary nodded her head. "You mean wike figs?"

Lamar saw a little smile on Zulmary's face. He couldn't believe it. She was actually playing with Shadow. Shadow looked at Lamar and moved his index finger in a circle as he pointed at his ear, indicating to his friend that Zulmary was crazy. Lamar saw Zulmary's little smile again.

"Shadow, dink Zulmary cwazy?"

Shadow stopped twirling his finger. His throat went dry again and his heart raced in his chest. He felt bad about his childish gesture.

"I'm sorry, Zulmary. I was just bein' rude and silly. Forgive me."

Zulmary turned to Shadow. "Dat's okay, Shadow. I was bein' siwwy 'bout the figs, too. The smell is fwom the jars on dat shelf ober dere in da corner. Dey fill wid animal parts." Shadow really struggled with Zulmary's strange language. It was time for him to try and paraphrase what he thought she had said.

"So the smell is coming from the jars on those shelves." He pointed at the shelves in the corner of the room with the same index finger he had twirled earlier. Zulmary nodded. He continued. "And those jars are filled with animal body parts?" Shadow was like Lamar. He couldn't believe it when Zulmary smiled.

"Bery good Shadow, you say ebewy ding I say. You say it good."

Shadow and Lamar had to smile at Zulmary's moment of humor. Shadow needed more information about the jars.

"These animal parts, what do you do with them?"

Zulmary stood up next to Lamar who was still sitting on the little stool. "When mama die I will drow dim all away. Mama used dim when she did the heawin'. I neber used dim when I heawin'." She turned back to Lamar and pulled another wooden stool up in front of him. She sat down, pulled up her dress, and bent down, pulling Lamar's shoe off his injured foot. She picked up his foot and placed it between her opened legs. The bottom of his foot lay flat against her flat crotch. Only a sock, bandage and a piece of her white dress separated his foot from her womanhood. Zulmary pulled off the sock and then took off the white gauze bandage. She moved her hips forward pressing harder against the bottom of Lamar's barefoot. Lamar looked up at Shadow. His friend's eyes were as wide open as they could be. Shadow recognized an advanced stage of "footsy" when he saw one. Zulmary examined Lamar's other dog bites.

"These not as bad as da one's on you arm. Look wike you pant's weg sabed you." She kept the bottom of his foot pressed against her crotch. "There one bad one on you arm. I can keep it fwom gettin' fected."

Lamar couldn't help himself. He had to push his foot against her to see how she would react to his movement. He tilted his foot forward and pressed against her. He was surprised and it scared him when she looked up at him the moment she felt his change of position. She gave him that little smile he had seen earlier.

"My, my Lamaw, dem wittle piggies was stayin' home at first and now dey twyin' to go to da market." Lamar stopped pushing his foot. Shadow burst into laughter. Zulmary looked at Shadow.

"I was just pwayin' wid him." She looked back at Lamar. "It was feewin' kinda good. I ain't neber had no body put der foot der."

Lamar stood up off the little stool. His sudden departure surprised Zulmary and she smiled again.

"I didn't mean to 'barras you. I thought it was funny."

It was obvious by the look on his face Lamar was embarrassed. "I should be the one apologizing to you, Zulmary. I took advantage of you and I'm sorry. But, can I say you really have an interesting way about you. I had forgotten how pretty you were."

Shadow had stopped laughing when his friend began the sincere apology. Zulmary was surprised again by Lamar's comment. She held her head down as if she was the embarrassed one now. Strangely enough, Zulmary broke the awkward silent moment.

"Dat was a nice ding for you to say to me. I know I was bery pwetty one time. De edge of a knife bwade took dat away."

Shadow had to speak up. "That's not true." Zulmary looked up at Shadow with her one blue and her one black eye. "That's not true at all. Lamar's right when he says you have a certain quality about you. The scar does not cover your beauty. I'm just concerned with the fact you are breathing in these chemicals everyday. That can't be healthy. You're gonna age real fast if you don't get rid of that stuff."

Lamar looked at Shadow as to say, "That was a little too much of not minding your own business." Both men were baffled when Zulmary looked at Shadow and changed the subject.

"You did not keep you part of da deal. How you get name wike Shadow?"

Shadow knew she did not want to talk about her surroundings. Zulmary was right. It was his turn to present his information.

Shadow smiled. "Well, it's like this. My mama was a full-blooded Cherokee Indian."

Zulmary wanted more. "You wook diffwent, too. What bwood was you daddy full of?" Lamar and Shadow smiled at the interesting question.

Lamar had to add to the moment. "Yeah Shadow, what was your daddy full of?"

Shadow looked at Lamar. Zulmary's head turned from one to the other. She was smiling again.

"You bewy funny. I can see y'all are good fwiends. I wike you comin' hear to see me and get my help. I go get you good medicine." Zulmary left the two men alone for the first time since they had entered the strange store. She walked to the back of the room and disappeared into a dark hallway. Shadow moved next to Lamar with one "Mother May I?" giant step.

"What have you gotten us into, here? Are you really gonna let her put her medicine on those bites? Hell man, you ain't started foamin' at the mouth yet, so you must be okay. That just might change if you let her put somethin' on you." Lamar did not have time to respond to Shadow's concerns. Zulmary walked back into the room holding a small glass jar in her hand.

"After I put dis on you bites, Mama said she would wike to see y'all."

CHAPTER FIVE

Darkness had finally taken Mayport. The boats were tied to the dock and the holds were empty. Mr. Leek's fish house was clean, quiet and also empty. Susan, Miss Margaret's red headed daughter, was restocking the store shelves while her little sister, Sofia was wiping the dust off the empty shelves. The bell on the door of the store rang. They both turned to greet the next customer. Four beautiful eyes lit up when the girls saw that the bell ringer and next customer was Jason. Sofia could not contain herself.

"Hey Jason!" She stepped over to him.

Susan smiled. "Hey Jason."

Jason wasn't too crazy about being with the sisters in numbers. He preferred to see them one at a time. He did like Sofia's excitement as she approached him, but he was always a little disappointed when ever he did not get the original and official "Miss Margaret" store greeting. He knew the girls were supposed to say, "Good evening. May I help you with something?" That was Miss Margaret's store rule and he wanted to remind the girl's of their duty to honor a fine tradition, but he never would.

Sofia stood next to him. "What brings you here? I thought you would be sleeping, or at least resting. You've been gone for three days an I know you must be tired."

"I'm fine."

Susan wanted to talk, too. "Everybody's talking about all the shrimp you caught. It's like you're a hero, again."

Jason knew he was no hero. "Chichemo's the reason we caught the shrimp, not me. I think folks pretty well know that."

Susan wasn't finished. "They say it's because you're an oak baby."

Sofia turned to her sister. "He's golden. Sandeep said he's golden. That's why good things happen to him." She turned back to Jason. He was surprised, but glad when Sofia changed the subject. "Oh, that reminds me, what happened with the dog? Is he all right? Did Mr. Chichemo fix his eye?" Her excitement made Sofia a three-question girl. Jason was more than ready to talk about the dog rather than oak babies.

"He put the eye back in and stitched up the big cut on his back. Margie held the dog's eye lids open while Chichemo shoved the eyeball back in the socket." Susan's lower jaw dropped. Sofia squinted her eyes. Susan was the one who could not contain herself, now.

"Oh my God! Are you serious?" She didn't care if Jason answered her or not. "Oh my God! She'll be relieving me in an hour. I can't wait to see her." Susan looked at Jason. "Margie's gone nuts, you know?" Sofia reacted to Susan's negative remark about their older sister's state of mind.

"Stop saying such things. Jason will think you're serious."

Susan smiled at Jason and turned back to her work. Sofia gave Jason a condensed version of the proper store greeting. "May I get something for you?"

Jason knew he would have to be satisfied with what he considered a very poor greeting. "I was cravin' a honey bun and a strawberry Nehi to wash it down." Jason walked to the cold drink box, opened it and pulled out a tall ice-cold bottle of the red soda. Sofia got a honey bun off the Merita Bread rack and walked to the cash register. Jason stopped at the candy shelf. He stuck his hand into one of the boxes and grabbed a handful of Squirrel Nut Zippers, then walked to the counter where Sofia was standing. He dropped the small rectangular shaped pieces of brown candy onto the glass top of the counter. Sofia noticed Jason had not opened the bottle of Nehi.

"You want me to open your drink? I have an opener right here under the counter."

Jason nodded. "Yes, thank you."

Sofia bent down and reached under the counter for the opener. Jason could see down her blouse. The tops of her lovely white breasts were exposed as her blouse fell away from her upper body. She stood up and took the bottle of Nehi in one hand and popped the top off with the silver opener. She looked at Jason with those eyes. "There you go."

Sofia bent down to put the opener back. Jason made sure he watched her blouse open and reveal her female attributes once again. He thought about how he had held and squeezed both of those firm round beauties in the bathroom and how he had his tongue inside her. The sexual flashback caused his manliness to push against the zipper of his dungarees. Sofia's voice sounded like it was far away as she interrupted his exciting vision.

"I just love these Squirrel Nut Zippers, don't you?"

Jason only heard the two words, "nut" and "zipper". He was eye-to-eye with Sofia. He looked down at his crotch, and then back at Sofia. He thought maybe she had noticed the movement he had felt in that particular area.

"What?"

Sofia looked down at his crotch and then back at Jason. "The candy. They're called, "Squirrel Nut Zippers".

Chiquita Naomi stood next to her father's car. She was still mad and outraged at the way her father had treated her in front of the two white policemen. She looked up when she heard the Chevy skeeter's engine start and saw the cut-down vehicle rolled forward, dragging the huge black horse into the hole.

Chiquita Naomi was sad as the two men began shoveling the dirt back into the grave. She could hear the thud of the heavy dirt as it hit the tight skin of the dead horse. The disturbing noise did not last very long as the dirt started to pile up and cover the animal. Chiquita Naomi saw that her father and the two policemen were walking back toward the house. She could hear Officer Boos voice as they came closer.

"It's gettin' late. We can't wait on him any longer. We'll go out to Aunt Matilda's and see if he's there. He can tell us what he wants us to do." Chiquita Naomi stared at her father for a second and then walked into the house.

The strangely attractive and scar faced witchdoctor with the "sight" in her black eye, held a small green jar in her hand. Shadow watched with a mixture of skepticism, caution and interest. Lamar Harris was his true best friend and he did not want their visit to Aunt Matilda's to be a mistake at Lamar's expense. Lamar held his arm up while Zulmary opened the small jar, stuck two fingers in and scooped out an oily substance. She gently covered the wounded area with the mysterious ointment. Shadow looked at his friend as Zulmary wrapped white gauze around Lamar's arm, covering the deep dog bite and the strange substance. Zulmary broke the silence.

"You ankle has a small cut, I know it must be sore and you are wimping because it is bwuised and I habe a feewing you habe a sewious ankle spwain. The cut is not bad. You should be better in a few days." Zulmary smiled and looked at Shadow. "Come on now you two handsome debils, come say 'hey' to my mama."

Mr. Cane walked into Hattie Harris' house as the police car drove away. His upset daughter, Chiquita Naomi, met him at the door. "I will not be disrespectful to you. I want you to know that I am not a child any longer, even though you think I am. I came home to help you and for some strange reason, I thought that would create respect between us both. It is obvious you are more concerned with what others think of you. Why do you care what those two white crackers think? After Miss Hattie's funeral I will be gone. I'm going back to Savannah. He called me, little missy, like I was a character from "Gone with the Wind". Her father shook his head and tried not to smile at his daughters ranting.

"I think her name was Prissy."

Zulmary led the way down a dark hallway. Lamar and Shadow walked behind her. Shadow put his hand on Lamar's back and pushed him forward. Lamar reached back and slapped his friend's hand away, but Shadow continued his humorous harassment. Zulmary stopped next to a door at the end of the hall. She placed her hand on the door and pushed it open. The room was dark except for the light from an oil lantern that was sitting on a mirrored dresser on the far side of the room. Shadow didn't recognize the smell that slammed into his nostrils, but he knew he would not be able to stay in the room very long.

"It me again, mama, I bwought Miss Hattie's boy Lamaw and he fwiend Shadow. You awake?"

Zulmary reached back and took Lamar's hand, pulling him into the room. She maneuvered him in front of her. It only took a second for Lamar to realize he would be the first one to reach Aunt Matilda's bedside. Shadow stopped at the door. That was close enough for him. He didn't even know Aunt Matilda or Zulmary existed before then, so he would allow Lamar to be reunited with his childhood witchdoctor. Zulmary stood behind.

"Wake up. You say you want to see 'em."

Lamar was standing next to the bed. The light from the lantern flickered off the wall above the headboard. Zulmary was blocking the light and a shadow covered Aunt Matilda's face. He reluctantly leaned forward, but he still could not see the old lady's face.

"Hey Aunt Matilda, it's Lamar Harris, Hattie's son. It sure has been a long time. Zulmary helped me with some dog bites. I'm here for my mama's funeral. She passed on last night."

Zulmary moved to Lamar's side causing the light from the lantern to shine on Aunt Matilda's face. Her eyes were wide open and glaring at him. Her mouth was also wide open and there was a huge cockroach crawling on her cheek. Lamar jumped back from the bed.

"Oh, my God! Holy shit!"

Shadow had no idea what Lamar had seen, he just knew instantly he did not want to see it. He moved completely out of the room and back into the hall. He even contemplated leaving his friend alone with the mother-daughter witchdoctor tag team. Shadow looked back at the door as Lamar backed all the way out of the small bedroom and into the hall. Lamar could see that Zulmary had walked to the side of the bed. Lamar turned to Shadow.

"I think she's dead! No damnit, I know she's dead."

Shadow took another step backward. "What?"

"Aunt Matilda's dead."

Shadow's eyes were as wide open as Lamar had ever seen them. "She can't be. She asked to see you." They both turned to the bedroom door as Zulmary walked into the hall. Their hearts were racing in their chests.

"Mama dead. I guess da 'citment of bisitors was just too much for her." She walked to Lamar and hugged him. He stood still and touched her back with his hands. He felt her hard breasts as she squeezed him. Lamar had no idea what to do. Zulmary whispered in his ear.

"You mama die, my mama die. It always good when ol' fwiends die and cwoss ober togeder and ol' fwiends wike me and you meet again. You need to go to you mama and leave me wid my mama."

She released Lamar from the hug and surprisingly tender moment. Shadow turned and led the way back to the front of the store. Lamar turned to Zulmary as they approached the front door.

"We should stay and help you. You shouldn't be here alone."

Zulmary's different colored eyes looked deep into Lamar's soul. "Mama was a hundwed years ol'. I have been weady for dis day a wong time. I be fine."

She walked past both men to the front door, holding it opened so they could walk through. When they were both outside Zulmary followed them to Shadow's truck and waited for them to get into the front seat. Shadow was sitting behind the wheel and Lamar was closing the passenger's side door. Zulmary stepped up to the driver's side window. She was black and blue eye-to-eye with Shadow.

"Maybe you tell me more 'bout you name anoder time."

Shadow didn't know what to say. He was quite sure there would not be another time. He nodded his head. Zulmary looked across to Lamar. "It was good to see you, Lamaw."

"You too, Zulmary."

Shadow started the truck, but he couldn't leave without asking one more question. "The ointment you put on Lamar's arm, was that from one of your mama's secret potions?"

Zulmary nodded. "They call it "Bick Sabe". Eberybody know it take da soreness out of any ding. She stepped away from the truck.

Shadow looked at Lamar. "Vick's Salve?"

Lamar smiled. "I thought I recognized the smell."

Jason walked past the empty ferry slip. He was glad he saw Sofia and Susan, but he was also glad he had left the store. Due to his past separate sexual encounters with all four of Miss Margaret's daughters, he would always be nervous when the girls outnumbered him. He looked across the river and could see the huge floating automobile carrier docking on the Fort George side. He wanted to hear the ferry horn blow. He needed to hear her blast away. Jason kept walking.

Margie stood on the sand hill next to the huge oak tree. Her recent revelation with Mary C., Chichemo and the wild dog, Abaddon, had ignited her to make one of her mysterious visits to the oak. With her new strength and considering herself a woman of action she thought it was time to return to the tree.

Margie had become a true believer in the power of the great oak tree. She wanted to be an active player in the mystic of the tree. Her relationship with the oak was emotional, spiritual and definitely sexual. It was important for her to touch the tree. Margie had straddled the lowest limb of the tree many times and rubbed herself against its hardness. She reached out and touched the huge trunk of the tree with one hand and then her other hand. Margie pushed her body away from the trunk and walked around the tree sliding her hand over the rough bark.

As Margie made the ritualistic circle she thought of hearing Mary C.'s voice telling her about being the next one to have an oak baby. Margie believed in the oak babies. She also believed it was not a dream when she stood with Mary C. in the white sand under the tree. Margie smiled as she completed her circle. She reached up with both hands and grabbed the limb above her. She grimaced in pain when her stomach muscles contracted as she pulled herself up on the lowest limb of the great oak tree. Margie sat there in her usual position, with one leg on one side of the limb and her other leg on the other side. She started moving her body slowly at first, stopping when she felt pain. Margie would endure the pain as she began another ritual of pleasure with the oak tree.

Mary C. sat on Miss Margaret's porch in one of the comfortable rocking chairs. Miss Margaret sat in another chair next to her. The wild day with the dog, the horse, Lamar Harris and Chichemo had drained them both. Miss Margaret took a deep breath of the cold night air. She had a pleasant thought.

"You can feel Thanksgiving and Christmas in the air. I like it when it gets a little nippy out. We've had such warm days lately I'm afraid it will be eighty degrees Christmas morning. I hope not. It should always be cold on Christmas Day." Miss Margaret was surprised when Mary C. joined the conversation with a total change of subject.

"You know I haven't been to see what's left of my house since that night? It was still smolderin' when I went over there. I don't think I really looked at it."

"No, I didn't realize that. You planning to rebuild out there?"

"I don't know. I ain't thought much about it. I guess I need to do somethin', don't I?"

"There's no rush, dear. You can stay here as long as you want. We love you and Billy being here."

"I really love you all for the way you have taken us in, but I can't live here. This is your home. I need to move on."

"I do understand that you need your own place, but you don't have to rush into anything, just to do it."

Mary C. smiled. "Thank you."

Mr. King sat on his front porch and watched a huge tanker move down the river headed for the mouth of the St. Johns River and out to the open Atlantic Ocean. The single deep blast of the ship's whistle punctured the evening silence as the ship entered the channel. Mr. King dearly loved sitting on the porch of his haunted house. He looked to his right and saw Sofia leaving the store. She was walking home and had to pass right by him as he sat enjoying the same cool early evening air Mary C. and Miss Margaret were feeling. Mr. King waved to Sofia. She waved back and walked to the latticework railing of his porch.

"Well, Miss Sofia, no ride home tonight?"

Sofia stepped up next to the porch. "No sir, but I've walked home before. Susan let me go home because she wants to talk to Margie. Margie's supposed to be here. I know she hasn't thought about any of us having to walk home. It is a nice evening for a walk, don't you think?"

Sofia had no idea Margie was deep into her sexual perch on the limb of the oak tree. Margie hadn't realized how quickly the night was rolling in. Sofia was right about Margie not thinking about her. Mr. King responded to her question.

"It is a nice evening for a walk. You always see the best parts of everything, don't you, Sofia?" She smiled, but didn't have an answer. He pointed to his white Cadillac hearse. "I can give you a ride home if you'd like."

Sofia was quick with her answer. "Oh, no sir. That's okay. I'll just walk." Mr. King smiled, nodded his head and didn't ask again. He did have another question.

"How's everything at your house? Things settled down some? Your guests doin' okay?" Sofia knew what he meant.

"Yes sir, it seems so. We like having Miss Mary C. and Billy staying with us. They're like family. We did have some excitement today when a black man rode by the house on a big black horse and Mary C.'s new dog chased after him." Mr. King was interested.

"Your mama didn't know the man?"

"She knew him once he said who he was. His name was Lamar Harris."

Mr. King nodded his head. "Hattie's boy. I heard he was back to stay with his mama. She's bad sick, you know."

Sofia knew more than Mr. King. "She died last night."

Mr. King had one thought about Hattie Harris. "Hattie was a hard worker. I'll give her that." He changed the subject. "Your mama has always helped folks when they were in need. She's the true "Good Samaritan"

Sofia smiled. "That's mother." Sofia surprised Mr. King with an interesting question. "Any new ghosts lately?"

He looked at the curious beauty. "What?"

She looked down as if she was embarrassed at first. Mr. King repeated her question with his own question. "You want to know if any new ghosts have come here?"

Sofia kept her head down, but answered him. "With all the people dying around here lately, and so close by, I just thought some of them would end up here at your house with you and the others." Mr. King smiled the biggest grin he could muster. He loved what Sofia said to him.

"You know, I've been so preoccupied with the sadness of Hawk's death and the death of that priest, that I haven't been paying any attention to what might be going on right here under my roof. Now that you have brought such possibilities to my mind I will be more observant and be on the look out for new visitors. Thank you, Sofia."

Sofia had stopped listening to Mr. King when he mentioned the death of the priest. During all the talk and the information about that awful night, no one had mentioned the sad fact that Sandeep Singh had died along with Hawk. Mr. King knew by the look on her face something he said bothered her. Her beautiful sky-blue eyes were as wide open as they had ever been.

"What is it, Sofia?"

"Sandeep died, too?"

"Yes. He tried to help fight off the men who attacked the house."

"He was so nice to me. I didn't know he was there."

"I don't know all the details, but he was surely there and gave his life to save them. I think he was a good man. His relationship with Eve was strange, but I think he wanted to do the right thing. Some folks can keep others from doing what is right."

Sofia was sad. "He was a good man." Sofia did not think to tell Mr. King about Abaddon losing an eye and the surgery that took place in her back yard. She was too upset about the death of her friend and professed admirer, Sandeep Singh, the Punjabi priest.

Officer Paul Short turned his police car onto a dark Seminole Road. He had no idea the red truck that was passing them headed in the opposite direction was Shadow's red truck.

"I feel like we're wastin' our time goin' out here."

Office Boos shrugged his shoulders. "It doesn't matter. We've still got an hour on duty, so what difference does it make where we are. Besides, I wouldn't mind seein' what that wild Zulmary's wearin' today. You never know about that one."

Paul Short smiled at his partner. "Why do you think there's always somethin' exciting about a woman of low moral fiber?"

"I don't know. I guess it's the unknown. Like ya don't really know what's gonna happen. And it doesn't hurt if she looks good, either. Even with that scar, Zulmary looks good."

Officer Short nodded. "I wish we would have caught that bastard who cut her like that. There wasn't any reason for him to do that. Damn, I can't believe we couldn't find him!"

Paul Short looked out of the front windshield of his patrol car and couldn't believe his eyes. David Boos saw it at the same time. Aunt Matilda's Place was on fire.

The old dry wood had ignited and the entire building was engulfed in flames. Officer Boos picked up the hand held microphone of the police radio and made his emergency call into the Atlantic Beach Fire station.

"We've got a big fire at Aunt Matilda's Place. Just arrived and have no further details. We'll try and see if anybody's here."

Sofia walked into her front yard. Her mother and Mary C. were sitting in the rockers on the front porch. "Well, you two look very comfortable in those chairs." The two ladies looked up at Sofia as she walked up the steps. Miss Margaret greeted her youngest daughter.

"Hey, Sofia."

"Hey, mother." They both smiled. "Hey Miss Mary C."

"Hey, Sofia." They all smiled. Sofia sat on the top step.

Miss Margaret shook her head. "Margie didn't come get you?"

Sofia smiled again. "Now, mother. Did you really expect her to be on time?"

Miss Margaret shook her head. "I don't know where Margie's mind is sometimes."

Margie climbed down off the lowest limb of the tree. She had not felt the cold air until her feet touched the white sand. She had not realized it was so dark. Once again, her relationship with the tree had caused her to lose track of the time. She looked up into the tree as a cold breeze cut across her body. The wind moved the many ropes still hanging from the tree. They were left there as a reminder of the Duckin' games in the past. Margie smiled. Her masturbatory encounter with the tree had satisfied the fire inside her. She did not think about Sofia having to walk home at all. She turned away from the tree and started her descent to the bottom of the sand hill. Margie walked toward the family station wagon.

Sofia broke the moment of silence on the porch. "I didn't know Sandeep died at your house that night." Mary C. and Miss Margaret were both surprised with Sofia's abrupt statement. Miss Margaret was surprised because she didn't know the Punjabi priest had died there either. She looked at Sofia then at Mary C.

"That young priest was with you that night?" Mary C. nodded her head.

"Yes. I thought you knew that."

"No. I didn't. I don't recall anyone saying that."

Sofia shook her head. "I didn't either. Mr. King told me." Miss Margaret could see the distress on her daughter's face.

"You liked him, didn't you, dear?"

"Yes, ma'am. He was very nice to me. He told me I was special. He called it golden. He said Jason was golden, too and that Billy was the most golden of anyone ever. I liked the way he talked to me. He had a wonderful way of saying things. He made you feel good about yourself." Even though the warrior priest had given his life to save hers, Mary C. would always have hardness in her heart.

"Some say he was going to try and take you away with him. Once he became your friend and you trusted him he was going to lure you away and steal you from ya mama. He would have made you his love slave in a far away country. Those people do that to beautiful women all the time. One day you would have been missing and no one would have been able to find you." Sofia's eyes and mouth were wide open. Miss Margaret's eyes were as wide open as Sofia's. Miss Margaret had to respond.

"Mary C., do you think this could have been his motive for talking to Sofia?"

Mary C. was ready. "Everyone was keepin' an eye on him when it came to your girls." Miss Margaret was amazed at the information Mary C. was presenting.

"What do you mean?"

"Well, Al mentioned it to me first. How that fella was hangin' 'round Sofia at the store. Al didn't trust him with her at all. Al knew the story about that fella and Eve and how he was her love slave. He had to do what ever she told him to do. He even tried to kill Hawk because Eve wanted him to. She wanted to hurt me by killin' Hawk. That's how we got that big knife of his. Hawk took it away from him when they fought." Miss Margaret and Sofia were both speechless and engrossed in Mary C.'s new story.

"He came to the house earlier to get that big knife."

Sofia interrupted. "The Kirpan Sword. It's called the Kirpan. It's holy." Miss Margaret looked at Sofia.

"You do know a lot about this man. This scares me. How come I didn't know about this plot to steal you?"

Sofia didn't know what to say. She knew her relationship with the Punjabi priest had been blown out of proportion. She also knew that anything she said would have made no difference at that moment. Mary C. looked at Miss Margaret.

"Well, what ever he called it, he wanted it back real bad. He was the one who helped me the first time when them painted faced devils and that voodoo woman came to take Billy. He cut 'em up bad with that Kirpan. I didn't know about him doin' that 'til later when he told me. We gave him the knife back and he left. I don't know what made him come back. All of a sudden he was in the back yard cuttin' up dogs and them black devils. He was a fighter. I couldn't have asked for two better men to defend me that night." The two shocked listeners had no intentions of interrupting Mary C.'s reenactment of that night. "Then there was too many dogs. He couldn't fight 'em off." Sofia put her hand over her mouth and she began to breath heavily. "He was fightin' hard 'til the dogs took him down to the ground." Sofia gasped and held her hand over her mouth as Mary C. continued. "Before he died he managed to throw that Kirpan knife and it stuck in that devil man. It hit him right up here between his legs." Mary C. pointed to her crotch. Miss Margaret made a face and Sofia kept her hand over her mouth. "The devil man couldn't pull the knife out and he crawled into the woods. That's when the dogs got to the priest. They tore him to pieces." Mary C.'s typically insensitive remarks sent Sofia running into the house. Mary C. looked at Miss Margaret.

"That devil man was the last one I killed. I kept his dog." Miss Margaret nodded her head and for an instant she was concerned with Mary C.'s state of mind. She was uncomfortable.

"I need to check on Sofia. Do you really think he was planning to steal my baby?"

"John didn't seem to think so, but Al did. I think Al seen him at the store a number of times. He didn't like the way he was talkin' to Sofia. Them kinda people got different ways. They don't think 'bout things like we do."

Miss Margaret had heard enough. She went inside the house to assist her youngest child. Sofia was in the small downstairs bathroom. Miss Margaret heard her throwing up. She pushed the door open and Sofia was leaning over the toilet, vomiting in the white bowl.

Margie reached for the door handle of the family station wagon. She loved being a true woman of action. She turned back to look at the tree one more time before she left. Margie smiled with respect for the great oak and turned to open the car door. Her heart jumped in her chest when she realized she was standing eye-to-eye with her true love, Jason.

"Oh Jason! You scared me. What are you doing here?" What Margie really wanted to say was "how long have you been here?" She didn't want to think he had watched her during her sexual encounter with the tree.

"I didn't mean to scare you, Margie. What are you doing here? It's too dark and too cold for you to be out here like this."

Margie was excited to be standing there with Jason. She had not been alone with him in a long time. "You came to visit the tree, didn't you?" He hesitated with his answer. Margie didn't care. She was too excited about being there with him. "It's true what they say about you being an oak baby, isn't it?"

Jason didn't like the oak baby subject. "I don't know what I am or what is wrong with me. I know I'm different, but I don't know why. Some times I feel like it's a good thing, but then other times it don't seem so good."

Margie's eyes lit up like candles in the night. She loved the way Jason was sharing his feelings with her at the foot of the sand hill with the oak tree above them. "You're different because you're an oak baby."

"I like the tree because I feel stronger when I'm here. My life changed a number of times because I was here."

Margie could not contain her excitement. Jason had never talked to her in that way before. It was as if he was opening up to her, and only her. She truly understood.

"I know what you mean. I feel stronger here, too. There's something here and it's real." Margie's next comment made Jason's blood flow change directions. "When does your mother want us to breed so I can be the next one to have an oak baby?" Jason's mouth went dry. He had no idea what Margie was talking about. Margie was in her own oak baby, tree-humping mindset. She had another crazy thought. "Did Miss Mary C. send you here tonight, because she knew I was here? Is tonight the night? I'm ready, you know."

Margie stepped to Jason and put her arms around him, kissing him passionately. Jason had never interfered with a passionate kiss before and he would not start then. He returned the kiss. Margie did not hesitate to reach down and touch him between his legs. Her eyes sparkled.

"Oh Jason! You're ready, too. This is so exciting." Margie knew she would be a woman of action no matter what she had to do. She took Jason's hand and turned to walk toward the sand hill. "Come on." She stopped herself. "Oh, wait a minute. It has to be after midnight for it to work, doesn't it? Oh my, I was so excited I forgot that." She let Jason's hand go. "Miss Mary C. didn't send you, did she? You were just walking by, huh?" Jason nodded his head. Margie smiled. "Come on, get in the car. It's cold out here."

Shadow's red truck rolled into Lamar's front yard. Their entire conversation during the ride back was about their outrageous visit to Aunt Matilda's Place and her beautiful and speech impaired daughter, Zulmary. Lamar looked toward the back woods and could see the pile of dirt that marked the freshly dug grave.

"Let's just go on in the house, Lamar. This has been one hell of a day." Shadow stopped the truck and they both got out. Mr. Cane stepped out of the house to greet them.

"I was getting' worried about you boys. I thought maybe y'all might have gone on to the hospital in Jacksonville Beach or maybe Aunt Matilda had cooked ya and ate ya."

Mr. Cane did not know the poor timing of his joke. Shadow walked past him and went into the house. Zulmary had ignited a sexual fire in his black and Indian blood. He was looking for Chiquita Naomi. Lamar responded to Mr. Cane's concerns.

"We've been out at Aunt Matilda's all this time. Zulmary doctored me up a little and Aunt Matilda died while we were there. Other than that."

Mr. Cane had to allow Lamar's statement to sink in. "What was that?"

"Aunt Matilda, she died while we were there. Right in her bed."

Mr. Cane scratched his head. "That's two in two days. There

will be a third, ya know. It always goes in threes. I wonder who's next?"

Lamar had a thought. "Do horses count? Maybe Aunt Matilda was the third one. Thank you for burying Raven. I'm not sure I could have done it."

Mr. Cane put his hand on Lamar's shoulder. "You're welcome, son. I need to leave you to your friend and get on to my house. My daughter's not too happy with me and I need to talk to her. I'll see you at the service."

Shadow walked out of the house. He did not hide the fact he was looking for the double named beauty. "Mr. Cane, where's Chiquita Naomi?"

Lamar smiled and shook his head at his friend's aggressive question. He could tell Mr. Cane wasn't very pleased with Shadow's abrupt style.

"My daughter went home to get ready for work. She waited to say good-by, but she would have been late if she had waited any longer." He turned to Lamar. "We'll see you at the service." He turned back to Shadow Martin. "Good night, Mr. Martin."

Aunt Matilda's Place was blazing. There was no way to enter the burning building. The jars and bottles filled with chemicals were popping and exploding. The firemen recognized the sound of shotgun shells exploding, as well. The firemen and policemen would have to wait until the fire was out to see if anyone was in the strange store. Officer Boos stepped up next to his boss, Mr. Butler.

"It's a strong possibility Aunt Matilda and Zulmary are in there. Aunt Matilda was bedridden and Zulmary didn't go out much. They just might be in there."

Mr. Butler nodded his head. "That damn old dry wood and all those so called potions she had in there, sure made for one fast and hot fire. If they're in there we'll only find teeth. I ain't sure Aunt Matilda had any. Why were you two out here, anyway?"

David Boos looked at Paul Short. Mr. Butler wanted an answer. "Well gentlemen, what brought y'all out here? You boy's weren't lookin' for a quickie from Zulmary, were ya?" David Boos responded to Mr. Butler's crude and rude remark.

"No sir. We came out here to talk to that man named Lamar Harris. We went to his house after being called to investigate a dog attack on him and his horse. The horse was injured. It had to be killed. We were told this Lamar Harris was at Aunt Matilda's, so we came out here to talk to him."

Mr. Butler was puzzled and interested. "A dog attacked this Harris fellow and then the dog killed his horse? That's some damn dog."

Officer Short took his turn. "Not exactly sir." Mr. Butler took a deep breath. He had heard the "not exactly" response quite a few times in the last few weeks.

"Well, Officer Short what exactly did happen?"

"We only heard this from a Mr. Cane. Mr. Harris has not verified it. We were told Mr. Harris was riding his horse. He was passing Miss Margaret's house and he stopped to tell Miss Margaret that his mother had died." Officer Short blew air from his mouth. "During the conversation it seems Mary C. made the dog attack Mr. Harris and the horse." Mr. Butler's eyes popped open. He had to interrupt.

"Mary C. turned a dog loose on this man?"

"That's the story, but like I said, we haven't talked to Mary C. or this Harris fellow. We were gonna talk to Mr. Harris first. He may not be pressing any charges. We just don't know."

Mr. Butler shook his head. "You do remember that Mary C. took in that big dog from the devil man? She said if you kill a man you get to keep his dog. The dog probably just chased the damn horse. All dogs chase horses."

"Yes sir. That's probably the case here. We just wanted to talk to Mr. Harris and then Mary C."

Mr. Butler turned to walk back to his car. "Let me know if they find the witchdoctor family and call me when you talk to Harris."

Officer Boos had a question. "After we finish up here can we head home? Don't you think Mr. Harris and his dog bites can wait until tomorrow?"

Mr. Butler nodded. "I didn't think about how late it was. Take care of the dog stuff in the mornin' first thing. How did the dog kill the horse, anyway?"

"The horse fell and broke its leg while the dog was chasing it in the woods. Mr. Cane told us Mr. Harris had to put the horse down."

Mr. Butler shook his head. "That's a damn shame. I like horses.

See you two in the mornin'."

The windows of the family station wagon were completely covered in moisture. The cold night and the heavy hot breathing of Jason and Margie had caused them to fog up. Jason and Margie were in the back seat where there was plenty of room for any sexual position and maneuvering they desired. Margie was completely naked. The first chosen sexual position was for her to sit across Jason. Margie had sat across Jason in a car before. That was the first time they were together. They left Bill's Hideaway, had sex in the car and saw the big sea turtle.

She had undressed so quickly and jumped into the back seat there had been no time for the foreplay Jason was noted for. The tree had given Margie all the foreplay she needed so Jason was already deep inside her. Jason held her hips as she worked her body against his for deeper penetration. Margie pulled her head back and looked into Jason's eyes.

"I'd like you to do it from behind me before we have to go."

While Margie was burning in the cold night, the fire was out at Aunt Matilda's Place. The building was completely gone. A single fireman was spraying water on the last small pile of burning wood. It was still too hot to search for human remains. The work at Aunt Matilda's Place would resume in the morning. Officers Boos and Short went home.

Shadow drove his red truck up to the back of Strickland's Seafood Restaurant. Lamar sat on the passenger's side of the seat. Shadow looked at his friend.

"You sure she's right here in the back?"

Lamar nodded. "She said she was working the prep area of the kitchen. It's right through that screen door. She should be at one of the tables. If you don't see her, ask for her. They won't care." Shadow jumped out of the truck and pushed the screen door open and stepped into the back of the kitchen. As soon as he walked in he saw Chiquita Naomi sitting at one of the tables breading fantail shrimp for frying. Shadow could see the surprised look on her face when she realized he was standing next to her.

"Shadow, what are you doing here?"

"I came to see you. I want to see you after you get off. Either meet me or I'll come get you."

She smiled. The look on her face went from surprise to excitement. "My friend, Lulu, was going to give me a ride, but she'll understand. I'll get off about eleven. Is that too late?" Shadow loved her reaction to his suggestion. No time would be too late for him on that night.

The family station wagon rolled up to the front of Miss Margaret's store. Margie had preformed her ritual at the tree and had wild sex with Jason in the back seat of the wagon in three different positions. She had also taken Jason back to Mr. Leek's dock, where he would stay on the boat for the night. Margie stepped up to the front door of the store. Susan opened the door, ringing the bell before Margie had the chance to walk in.

"Where have you been?"

Margie stepped past her sister and entered the store. She looked around. "What are you doing here, anyway? I thought it was Sofia's turn."

"Like an idiot, I told her to go on home and I would take her turn."

Margie didn't understand. "Why would you do something like that?"

"Because I wanted to talk to you. I wanted to see if you were feeling better and I didn't want the others around. I also wanted to hear about what you did with Mr. Chichemo and the dog. I wanted to here it from you and not from our naive little sister."

Margie smiled. "Oh, Susan. You love me."

Susan smiled, too. "You know you're a pain in the butt, don't you? And yes I do love you, but I can't for the life of me remember why. Are you all right?"

Margie knew she had her sister right where she wanted her. "I went for a ride to get out of the house after all that stuff happened and I got sick. I had to stop the car and throw up on the side of the road."

Susan interrupted her older sister. "You did too much. You can't over do things. You have gone through a terrible thing and you are still not back too normal. Go on home and I'll cover your shift. Try and get some rest. Tell Peggy to pick me up at midnight, she's usually lurking around that time of night anyway." Margie smiled and hugged Susan.

Mary C. sat alone in one of the rockers on Miss Margaret's front porch. A set of car lights caught her attention as they approached the house. It only took a moment for Mary C. to recognize the family station wagon as it pulled up into the yard and stopped. Margie stepped out of the car and walked to the porch. Mary C. smiled. "I'll bet your ears have been burnin' tonight."

Margie smiled as she thought to herself. "I've been burning, but it hasn't been my ears," but that was just a private thought. "Why, were y'all talking about me?"

"You didn't give Sofia a ride home when she got off work at the store. She had to walk home."

Margie didn't change her expression and it was more than obvious she didn't care about Sofia's problem. "Oh, like I've never had to walk home from the store before. She is such a baby. I don't remember saying I'd be there to pick her up. Well, she'll get over it I'm sure. How are you tonight?" Mary C. smiled when Margie suddenly changed the subject.

"I'm good. I think I upset Sofia when I told her about the dogs killin' that priest fella at the house that night. Ya mama went in quite awhile ago to check on her." Margie shook her head. Her heart was becoming as hard as Mary C.'s heart.

"Those policemen told me about how he got killed. It's sad that he died that way, or died at all, but there was something strange about him. I didn't like being around him. He scared me. I think he was trying to do something to Sofia, like hypnotize her or brainwash her. He had plans to do something to my little sister and that scared me. I watched him like a hawk when he was in the store. He always tried to talk to Sofia. I had the feeling that he thought he could influence Sofia in some way, her being so young and pretty. He was a smooth talker and you know how innocent and trusting Sofia is with everyone. I guess I'm sorry he died like he did, but I'm still glad he's gone."

Mary C. nodded. "I understand. Mr. Leek was concerned about him and Sofia, too. Usually when more than one person senses something it should be a concern. Sometimes it just takes one person's deep feelin's to know somethin's wrong. If he hadn't of died, he probably would have tried to take Sofia away."

The Punjabi warrior priest who saved Mary C. and her grandson on two separate occasions and unselfishly gave up his life to do so, would not be thought of again as far as Mary C. and Margie were concerned.

Mary C. had been worried about Margie, but she had not had the opportunity to talk to her. "How you been feelin'? You were so sick for a while there."

"I'm much better, now. It took a week for that flu bug to leave me, but I'm getting back to normal. Whenever you want me to have the next oak baby, I'm ready. I thought it would be tonight, but I knew I couldn't wait until midnight."

Mary C.'s eyes lit up. "You ain't still been thinkin' 'bout that crazy dream you had, have ya? I thought all that foolishness was done with." Margie shocked Mary C. with her first statement, but Margie's next statement was the double whammy.

"I'm sick about your house burning down. How will you be able to come to me in a dream and tell me when to go to the sand hill if you don't have the carousel?" Mary C.'s heart jumped in her chest. Margie had never seen such an obvious change of expression in Mary C.'s face. Mary C. reacted.

"Oh my God! The music box! Oh my God!"

Margie shook her head. "You lost Hawk, your house and the carousel, what will you do?"

Mary C. thought for a second about Margie's dramatic and heartfelt question. She remembered she had left the magic carousel at Mr. King's house after his attempt to open the door to the other side. Mr. King had no idea the ghosts had walked through the door he opened. Mary C. and Jason knew it and so did Hawk. Mary C. had her answer.

"I'll build another house. I'll be with Hawk when he comes to me. I'll go to Mr. King's house and get the carousel." She looked at, the now quiet, Margie. "You want to take me for a ride on a cold night?"

. Sofia sat on her bed. Billy lay next to her. Miss Margaret stood at the bedroom door.

"Are you sure you're all right, Sofia?"

Sofia looked up at her mother with bloodshot eyes. "Yes ma'am. I told you I'm just sad about Sandeep dying like that. I'm also very tired. Today was a strange day. Did they bury Sandeep around here?"

Miss Margaret only knew what Sofia knew. "I don't know anything about that, honey. I was surprised to hear about it, too." Miss Margaret was more concerned about the other things that Mary C. had told them. "Sofia, you think that man was going to take you away?"

Sofia was surprised at her mother's question. "No, ma'am, I don't. I don't know why people are saying that about him. He was just nice to me and everyone wants it to be more. Sometimes I hate the way people think." Miss Margaret could see how sensitive Sofia was about the situation. She would not continue with more questions.

Mary C. and Margie stood at the front door of John King's haunted house. Mr. King opened the door. "Well, well, this is a pleasant surprise. Please come in and get out of the cold. What brings you two lovely ladies to my humble, but haunted home?" The two women stepped into the front of the house as Mr. King closed the door behind them.

"This way ladies." Mr. King directed them to his large living room. "I knew you'd be coming to see me Mary C. I just didn't know you would bring Margie with you. Please sit down. Can I get y'all something to drink?"

The ladies shook their heads to the offer of a drink and sat down. Margie looked at the skull on the mantle over the huge fireplace. Mary C. did not look toward the fireplace. She already knew James Thorn's skull was there. She didn't like the reminder of her act of revenge from the past. Mr. King knew why they had come to visit. "You want the music box, don't ya?" Margie's eyes popped open and Mary C. smiled.

"Yes. I forgot I had left it here. I thought it might have been lost in the fire and then I remembered we didn't take it with us when we left you the last time. I need to talk to you about that too, John. I should have told you when we were here, but it was just too strange."

Mr. King nodded his head. "I know it was strange and I'm sorry for getting you mixed up in one of my crazy schemes. I was so embarrassed after it happened. I really did appreciate the way you three handled my foolishness."

"John, it worked."

Mr. King wasn't sure what she meant. "What worked?"

"The carousel. It worked. It opened the door to the other side."

He wasn't sure how to respond to what Mary C. said. "I'm not sure what you're sayin' to me. Is this a joke of some kind?"

"No joke, John. It opened the door, right here in this room." Margie's eyes were wide opened. Mr. King was still uncertain.

"I was sitting here too, ya know. I saw what didn't happen."

Mary C. nodded. "I know you didn't see anything and I don't know why, but the rest of us saw it all. I saw it. Jason saw it. Hawk saw it." Mr. King knew Mary C. was playing with his emotions.

"What did y'all see?"

"I can only tell you what I saw. Me and Hawk didn't get a chance to really talk about it, but I know he saw somethin'. Jason told me he saw Bobby and I knew he was tellin' the truth 'cause I saw him, too." Margie was quiet and all ears. Mr. King's eyes lit up.

"You actually saw your brother, here in this room?"

"He danced through the room and went into the hallway. Jason saw him, too. He had his black and white bebops on and he was lookin' good."

Mr. King wanted more. "Where did he come from?" Mary C. pointed to the spot where the light had opened the door to the spirit world.

"Right over there. The lights from the carousel gathered right there and became one big round light. They all came through the light."

Mr. King was in shock. He had to ask. "They came through the light? Who is they? Who else was here?" Mary C. thought for a second. She had to be careful with her information and what she was about to say.

"I don't know who or what Jason and Hawk saw. We'll have to ask Jason later. I know I saw a lot." Margie and Mr. King were mesmerized by what they were hearing. Mary C. continued. "Bobby was first. I didn't know 'til later Jason saw him, too. It was all so fast." Mary C. looked at the skull about the fireplace. "I saw James Thorn, too." Mr. King's eyes were opened their widest.

"You saw James Thorn in this room?"

"Yes. He tried to hand me a drink, like he used to do at the Fish Bowl." Margie's mouth dropped open and Mr. King took a deep breath. "Who else?"

Mary C. would be more careful with the rest of her information. She had said far too much already. "I'm not sure who the others were. My old friend Skinny was here, I think. There was a few others I didn't recognize." Then Mary C. remembered the most important vision of all. "Oh! The dogs were here." Margie broke her deep trance silence.

"What dogs?"

"You know them big devil dogs, the ones that attacked us at the house, like Abaddon.

"You saw the dogs in this room?"

"They ran through the light. That's how I knew they was comin'. When that black girl that likes Jason, that Ruby, came to the house and told me about the man with the dogs, I knew she was tellin' the truth 'cause the carousel had already showed 'em to me. I knew they was comin'."

Mr. King was being pounded by Mary C.'s words. "You know I didn't see anything? My God, Mary C. is all this true?"

She nodded her head. "I don't know why it didn't work for you, but it's all true."

Mr. King smiled a huge grin. "Maybe next time." He walked to a table in the corner of the room and picked up the beautiful carousel music box. Mr. King walked to Mary C. and placed the carousel next to her on a small table by one of his lanterns.

"Here it is. I hope you'll bring it back and we can try again. I would love to see that door open." He looked at Margie. "How 'bout you Margie, would you like to see the other side?"

Margie swallowed and took a deep breath. "I don't know much about that sort of thing. It sounds scary, but I'm trying not to be afraid of things." She looked at Mary C. "If Miss Mary C. will be with me, yes sir, I'd like to see it." Mary C. smiled and looked at Mr. King.

"Margie has seen what the carousel can do with your dreams. She brought it to me. Jason left it at her house for safe keeping, like it wouldn't be safe with me."

Mary C. and Margie stepped out into the night air on Mr. King's front porch. Mary C. looked back at the door as Mr. King followed them out. She had changed her mind and decided to leave the magic music box at the King house, while she was staying at Miss Margaret's. Mr. King was excited that she trusted him with such a valuable antique.

"I think it would be better to leave it here with you, John. Just be careful using it alone, especially with all the ghosts you have in there."

"I won't use it at all unless you're here, I promise."

Mary C. smiled. "You don't have to make that promise, John. It's pretty tempting to have it around, if ya know what I mean?" She looked at Margie. Margie didn't smile or react, but she definitely knew what Mary C. meant. Margie was addicted to the oak tree and the carousel. She wanted Mary C. to bring the music box back to her house, but she didn't interfere with Mary C.'s decision to leave it at the King house.

The family station wagon was rolling away from Mr. King's house without the magic dream maker. Margie turned toward home. Her head was spinning with the incredible story she had heard.

Shadow Martin had picked Chiquita Naomi up at the back door of Strickland's at eleven sharp. They were taking a shower together at Lamar's house. It had been Chiquita Naomi's suggestion. She told Shadow that she needed to get the smell of fried shrimp off her body and he was welcome to assist her if he would like to. After a first date of sex in the shower, they would drive out to Tony's Seafood Shack on Mayport Road for a late night dinner. They would eventually return to Lamar's house where she would spend the night with Shadow.

During the night Lamar would wake up to the sounds of sexual pleasure coming from down the hall. Lamar had a great deal on his mind, but he still enjoyed listening to Chiquita Naomi make her unique sexual sounds. She yelled "Oh God!" at least a dozen times and one time actually made what Lamar considered a noise like a screaming monkey.

It seemed as if most of the Mayport citizens were settling down for the cold night. Sofia had fallen asleep in her bedroom with the oak baby, Billy, sleeping in a wicker bassinet a few feet away from her bed. Jason was also sleeping on the boat after Margie had drained him of his manly body fluids and what little energy he had left. Mary C. and Margie walked into Miss Margaret's quiet house. Peggy had fallen asleep on the couch. Margie would not wake her or tell her to go get Susan. Susan would walk home at midnight. Abaddon was in the deepest sleep of all.

CHAPTER SIX

Lamar Harris woke up when the smell of fresh coffee brewing and bacon frying filled his snoring nostrils. The aroma seemed to pull him out of his warm bed. He walked down the short hallway to see what was happening in his mother's house. He stepped into the small kitchen where his friend Shadow's smiling face greeted him.

"Mornin' Mr. Harris. How 'bout some breakfast. She can cook, too."

Lamar looked over at the small white stove where Chiquita Naomi was standing. She smiled at Lamar and flipped the sizzling strips of bacon. The young, pretty woman wore one of Shadow's Bethune Cookman sweatshirts that only hung down past her butt cheeks. She was barefoot and her legs were prefect. Her breast wobbled and it was obvious to Lamar that she wore only white cotton panties under the school spirit shirt. He could see the edges of her white panties as she moved in front of the stove. Lamar forced himself to move his eyes away from Chiquita Naomi and responded to Shadow's greeting.

"She sure looks good.... I mean.... it sure smells good. That's what woke me up." Shadow and Chiquita Naomi both smiled at Lamar's little Freudian slip. Shadow had to comment.

"Now ya see Chiquita Naomi, that's what a black man's face looks like when his face turns red from embarrassment. You can't really see the red, but you just know it's there."

Lamar had to smile at Shadow's remark. Chiquita Naomi stepped to the table and placed a hot cup of coffee on the table in front of him.

"Thank you for the compliment."

Lamar picked up the coffee cup. "Thank you for the coffee."

Shadow was concerned. "How ya feelin?"

"I'm sore, but I'm fine."

Shadow couldn't resist. "The Vick's Salve didn't take the soreness away?"

"I guess not." Lamar knew that Shadow was being sarcastic and he was very skeptical about Zulmary's ability to do anything in the realm of healing. He changed the subject.

"You two must have hit it off last night."

Chiquita Naomi smiled and placed a plate of scrambled eggs and crispy bacon on the table in front of him. "What was your first clue?"

Lamar was like Shadow; he couldn't resist a smart remark. "I think it was when the house was shaking during the night." Chiquita Naomi turned to Lamar.

"Now my face is red."

Shadow had to tell Lamar something important. "Lamar, after we eat breakfast I'm drivin' Chiquita Naomi back to Savannah so she can stay with her aunt. She needs to get away from here. Hell, we all need to get away from this crazy town."

Chiquita Naomi chimed in. "I'm sorry I won't be at the funeral."

Lamar understood. "Y'all just be careful."

Shadow had more. "I'll be back for the service in the morning. It's only about a four-hour drive. If we get on the road I'll probably be back tonight."

"Don't worry about that. Make sure Chiquita Naomi gets settled. Mama would want you to take care of her." Chiquita Naomi kissed Lamar on his cheek.

"You two are the kindest men I have ever seen. I didn't know men like you two actually existed. No wonder you are such good friends."

Shadow had to make one of his comments. "Don't be fooled by his sweet voice and handsome face. This man does have a mean streak. Believe me, I've seen it."

Miss Margaret's house was quiet in the morning, as usual. Three of her four daughters were sleeping. She had no idea her oldest, Margie, had gotten up early and went to have more sex with Jason on the shrimp boat. Margie was already kneeling down in the small bunk. Jason was holding both sides of her beautiful buttocks and pounding her from behind. It was Margie's favorite sexual position.

Miss Margaret was going to open the store and let the girls have the morning off. She liked working at the store at least three times a week. She was careful not to make any noise as she prepared to leave the house. Miss Margaret stepped out onto the front porch and closed the front door behind her. She turned to walk down the porch steps. Miss Margaret stopped when she saw the patched eye Abaddon lying in his guard position at the bottom of the three porch steps.

The dog lifted his big head and looked at her with one visible eye. His other eye was covered with the taped bandage Chichemo and Margie had placed there. Miss Margaret was amazed that the wild dog had not found a way to remove the bandage. She was not scared of the pitiful looking beast.

"How are you doing this morning, Abaddon? You don't have to be on guard duty all the time. You should be getting your rest. You do need some beauty rest." Miss Margaret smiled to herself at her early morning dog humor. She moved past the hound from hell and got into the family station wagon. Abaddon laid his big deformed and scarred head back down on the ground. Mary C. walked out onto the front porch as the family station wagon rolled away from the house. Abaddon raised his throbbing head.

"I ain't never been scared of much, dog. And now, with you here, I ain't scared of nothin'." Abaddon stood up and moved his butt back and forth, trying to wag his nub of a tail.

Lamar was finishing his breakfast. Shadow and Chiquita Naomi stood in the kitchen with him. Shadow was talking to Lamar, but he looked at Chiquita Naomi. "I'm gonna take her home and leave her there. She'll get a ride back here in thirty minutes."

Chiquita Naomi spoke up. "It will be better if I go to the house alone. My friend Lulu will bring me back and then we'll go."

Shadow had an idea. "Lamar, come go with us and I promise we'll get back tonight. Let's get away from here."

Lamar shook his head. "I can't do that. I got all Mama's relatives comin' in from all over. I'd like to go, but I really need to be here. Besides, I've got a lot of things to take care of before I go back to school."

There was a heavy knock at the front door. Lamar stood up. "You see. They'll be comin' in any time all day." He answered the door and came eye-to-eye with the chief lawman, Mr. Butler. Officers David Boos and Paul Short stood next to their patrol car in the front yard.

"Mornin'."

Lamar looked past his early and unwanted intruder and recognized the two officers. Mr. Butler didn't look back at his men. "I'm interest in what happened yesterday with you and the dog."

"How did you find out about yesterday?"

Mr. Butler looked back at the other officers. "They found out and told me. They went out to Aunt Matilda's to find you, but you had left. You didn't get mad and set fire to Aunt Matilda's did ya?" Lamar's eyes widened as he absorbed Mr. Butler's off the wall comment. Officer Boos walked to the front door as Mr. Butler's question ignited Lamar's curiosity and caution. Shadow stepped up behind Lamar in the doorway. Lamar responded to Mr. Butler, but he watched Officer Boos as he approached the front door.

"I'm sorry, but I don't understand or appreciate your question about Aunt Matilda's. Please explain yourself." Mr. Butler didn't like Lamar's response.

"You don't understand or appreciate it, huh?"

"That's right I don't. And I don't know what you're talkin' about. We saw no fire."

"Who's we?"

Shadow Martin stepped to Lamar's side. "I was with him. The young girl helped him with his dog bites and we left. We saw no fire."

Mr. Butler turned his attention to Shadow. "And you are?"

"I'm Mr. Martin. I'm a friend of the family."

"Well, friend of the family." Shadow knew that Mr. Butler would not call him Mr. Martin. He hated the lawman already. Mr. Butler continued. "Zulmary was there?"

"Yes. She bandaged Lamar's arm."

"Did you two boys see Aunt Matilda?" Shadow hated him even more. He turned and looked a Lamar. Mr. Butler didn't like the hesitation. "Well did you see the old lady, or not? I don't think I like the look you two boys just gave each other. Did you see Aunt Matilda when you were there?"

Lamar knew Shadow was at his limit with the bigoted lawman. He answered the question. "Yes we did. Zulmary took us to see Aunt Matilda. Zulmary said her mother wanted to see me."

Mr. Butler turned back to Officer Boos, who was standing near them. "I guess they were in there. When we decide what to do with these two y'all go on back out there and see if they found any remains this mornin'. I'm goin' to talk to Mary C." Mr. Butler turned back to Lamar and Shadow. Neither of them liked Mr. Butler's comments and it showed on their faces. Mr. Butler reacted. "You two boys need to get those bad ass looks off your faces. It would be awful to spend a few days in jail and miss your mama's funeral." Lamar and Shadow wanted to kill Mr. Butler. " I got you two leavin' Aunt Matilda's two minutes before it goes up in flames. I'm investigatin' the claim that you got attacked and bitten by a dog. When the dog attacked you it caused your horse to fall and break his leg. Then you had to kill your horse." Mr. Butler stopped for a few seconds and then continued. "How'm I doin' here, boys."

Lamar was too smart to fall into a trap and loss his temper. "We did not do anything. They were there when we left and there was no fire. They were my friends."

"What did y'all talk about with Aunt Matilda?"

"We didn't talk to her. Zulmary took us to her room, but she had fallen asleep and we didn't want to wake her. We figured at a hundred years old she needed the rest more than she needed to talk to us."

Mr. Butler shook his head. "We got some crazy shit goin' on here, don't we. But, that's kinda the way it goes around here, huh?" He really didn't want an answer. "Tell me about this dog, Lamar."

"There's nothin' more. You already know the whole thing. I

don't know how you found out what you did."

Chiquita Naomi stepped to the door. "Daddy called them. He thought they would help you." Lamar turned to Chiquita Naomi. Mr. Butler looked at her, too.

"And who is this third voice with information?"

"I'm…" She looked at Shadow. "I'm Miss Cane another friend of the family."

"Well, were you at Aunt Matilda's with 'em?"

"No, I was here with my father, talking to your officers."

David Boos nodded his head in agreement and joined the conversation. "Mr. Cane called us and told us about the dog attack. She was here the whole time."

Mr. Butler was tired of being there. "What do you think we can do about this wild dog that bit you?" Lamar was tired, too. He wanted to be rid of the awful lawman.

"I haven't asked you to do anything. I didn't ask you to come here. Mr. Cane was mistaken about what I wanted."

"Really? Then there's no reason for us to investigate this situation."

Lamar shook his head. "Not as far as I'm concerned. It over. I'm leavin' as soon as I bury my mother."

Mr. Butler looked into Lamar's eyes. "You wouldn't be playin' with me would ya, boy? I don't think I'd like that." The stare continued for a second. "Damn boy, you lose your mama one day and your horse the next day. Your luck ain't runnin' too good lately, is it? "I'm sorry 'bout your horse. I've always like horses." Lamar, Shadow and Chiquita Naomi all wanted to beat the hell out of Mr. Butler as he turned away from them. The redneck needed a lesson badly.

Mr. Butler gave orders to his two officers. "Go on out to Aunt Matilda's and see what's goin' on. Our work's done here for now." Mr. Butler turned back to the three at the door. "Maybe you're tellin' the truth about the fire, but you two boys are the closest thing we've got to a suspect. We'll talk again, so don't get too far away unless you let me know where you're goin'. See y'all later, boys." Mr. Butler turned and went to his car, leaving Lamar, Shadow and Chiquita Naomi with their blood boiling at the door of Miss Hattie's little house.

Mary C. picked up her grandson, Billy, from the wicker bassinet in Sofia's bedroom. The blonde haired sleeping beauty was still in a deep sleep. Billy's green eyes were wide open as Mary C. moved him up and out the small crib and into her arms. She whispered to the baby. "I don't want to see your mama's eyes. You ain't got baby eyes." She moved quietly out of the room, down the stairs and sat in the rocking chair in the living room down stairs.

Mary C. had no idea, Margie, the new woman of action, was lying naked next to Jason in the bunk on the boat. Margie was waiting for him to recover. She was ready for another sexual pounding.

Mary C. held Billy and began to rock the chair back and forth. She heard the noise of an engine as a car rolled up to the front of Miss Margaret's house. She stood up and looked out the front window. Mary C. didn't like it, but Mr. Butler was making another one of his early morning visits. She talked out loud to herself as she watched him get out of his car. "I hope you don't think you're getting' any French toast here this mornin'.

Lamar, Shadow and Chiquita Naomi sat at the small kitchen table. Shadow was talking. "I don't care what that red neck son-of-a-bitch says, I'm takin' you to Savannah today. He can kiss my ass and hunt for me all he wants. Do you believe that sorry bastard?"

Chiquita Naomi was concerned. "Maybe we should go later. He scares me."

It was Lamar's turn. "Shadow's right. He's not gonna do anything today. You'll be safe at your aunt's and Shadow will be back here for us to leave together. Now, go get your things and get the hell out of here. I feel bad about Zulmary and Aunt Matilda."

Officers Boos and Short stood next to the ashes and burned wood that had once been Aunt Matilda's Place. A fireman stood with them. "We found the remains of one person. If you could call it remains. They took what we could pick up to the lab. It was layin' on mattress springs. It was probably the old lady.

Paul Short nodded. "What about the girl?"

The fireman shook his head. "'Nothin' so far. All those liquids and chemicals in there made it a hot fire. She still could be under those ashes somewhere. But, if you ask me, she's gone. She probably caused the fire. It could have been an accident and she got scared. And then again, it could have been on purpose and she's on the run. I wouldn't put anything past these crazies out this way. Either way, she's gone."

Officer Short nodded. "I didn't think about that. It couldn't have been easy for her to live here and take care of Aunt Matilda. She could have reached her limits."

Officer Boos had his own opinion. "I think the accident theory is probably the right one. She's runnin' scared." He looked at his partner. "I don't think those two boys had anything to do with this, do you?"

Paul Short shook his head. "Not at all. I think Butler was way out of line with those two."

"You know how he gets when he thinks he can scare one of those black boys. He's like a wild dog himself."

"Well, I didn't like it."

Shadow Martin sat in his red truck. Lamar stood next to the driver's side window.

"We're leavin' in a few minutes. I'm just goin' back to the house and pick her up. Her friend couldn't give her a ride back. I'll try to be back before mornin'. I've got my key so go on to bed if it gets too late. I'll try not to wake you."

Lamar nodded. "She's awful young, my friend."

"Ain't she though? She's way ahead of her time. I really like her."

"Just be careful. Don't worry about getting' back here. Make the right decisions for you and her as you go." Lamar patted Shadow on his arm. Shadow couldn't help himself.

"If things work out with me and Chiquita Naomi maybe we can double date with you and Zulmary." Shadow hit the gas pedal and the truck moved away before Lamar could respond to Shadow's Zulmary joke. He heard Shadow laughing as the truck moved away. Lamar knew Shadow wasn't thinking about Zulmary being in the fire.

Mr. Butler stood next to his car keeping his distance from Mary C.'s mutilated guard dog. Abaddon had stood up when the car pulled up next to him. Mary C. watched from the window. Mr. Butler was too busy watching the dog to notice Mary C. at the window.

"Good God, dog, what happened to you. If you attacked somebody, you damn sure got the worst of it."

Mary C. knew the persistent lawman would not go away until he talked to her. She laid Billy on the couch and placed a couch cushion next to him so he would not roll off and fall to the floor. Mr. Butler took his eyes off Abaddon when Mary C. opened the front door and walked out onto the porch.

"Damn Mary C., this dog gets uglier every time I see it."

Mary C. did not smile. "That's funny, I was just getting' ready to say the same thing about you. The kitchen ain't open this mornin'."

"I didn't know you got mean this early in the mornin'. Each time I've seen you you've been so kind. Could it be that it depends on what company you're keepin'?" If those pretty little girls are around you seem different. Hell, you even shared breakfast with me. I 'spose you need that French toast to sweetin' you up."

Mary C. didn't like his tone, but she never did. "I can assure you the kitchen you ate breakfast in did not belong to me. I am a guest here and contrary to what you think, I do know how to act."

"Well, I'm here on official business. It seems like your new pet might have caused a horse to break his leg and then sunk his teeth into the rider. You wouldn't happen to have any interesting information for me, would ya?"

"I might be able to shed a little light on your official investigation. Come on up and sit with me." She looked at Abaddon. "Down dog!"

Mr. Butler was surprised at Mary C.'s invitation to sit with her and he was even more surprised when the patched eyed guard dog lay back on the ground when she made her command. Mr. Butler stepped around the dog and joined Mary C. on the porch.

Miss Margaret turned to the front door of the store when the bell rang. She was ready to greet her first customer of the morning. She was surprised when her oldest daughter, Margie, walked into the store. Miss Margaret had no idea Margie had been with Jason in the boat's bunk.

"Margie, good morning. What are you doing here so early? Are you all right?"

Margie smiled. "Yes ma'am, I'm fine. I heard you leave this morning and I couldn't fall back to sleep. I thought I'd come help you. If you have things to do I can take care of things here." Miss Margaret smiled at Margie's kind offer.

Mr. Butler wasn't sure how he ended up sitting in a rocker next to Mary C., but he was. He tried to keep eye contact with her, but he could see Mary C.'s round bare breasts and protruding nipples through the thin material of the tight shirt she wore. Mary C. was ready to get to the official business.

"What do you need to know?"

Mr. Butler's struggle to keep his eyes looking in the right direction began. "Just tell me what happened with the man and the horse."

Mary C. knew what she wanted to say. She believed it from the bottom of her cold and dark heart. "He didn't belong here. He came to see me. He can say he was riding by and stopped to talk to Miss Margaret, but that's a lie. He was here to see me. I knew it and the dog knew it. He'll be the next one to try and take the child."

Mr. Butler wasn't expecting to hear such a statement. He was speechless for a few seconds. Mary C. had more for him to hear. "He's a vigilante for his kind, anybody could see that. The black horse, the bull whip, oh he's got meanness deep inside that black body. He made a few smart-ass comments about his slave ancestors and rode on down the road. The dog chased after him and followed him into the woods. That's all we saw until later when the dog came back all cut up with his eye ball hangin' out his head. That bull whip sure tore him up."

Mr. Butler looked at the dog, mainly because he didn't want to look at Mary C. "He had a bull whip?"

"I told you he was a vigilante man with a black horse and a bull whip. He was here to scare me and let me know he was comin'. He'll come alone. He wants me to be ready. That's why I have to leave this house. They have nothin' to do with all this and I will not put them in danger."

Mr. Butler had to stop her for a second. "You know the horse fell and broke his leg. It had to be shot." He could see Mary C. didn't know the horse was dead. She didn't respond for a few seconds. Then she nodded her head.

"On one hand that's good. It takes away from him and makes him less of a threat for a little while. Losing the horse will fuel his anger and he'll recover and be stronger. After he buries his mama, he'll come for me."

Mr. Butler couldn't take it. "Mary C., what are you talkin' about? This man came here to see to his mother's last days and to take care of her affairs when she died. I think he's a smart-ass, know-it-all, that don't know nothin'. But, I don't think he came here for you."

"He didn't come for me at first, but he's comin' for me now. As a vigilante, he looks for ways and reasons to eliminate those who threaten his people. I am the biggest threat he's ever seen or heard of. Macadoo will use him like she used the others."

Lamar Harris sat in his front yard with two of his male cousins, who had arrived that morning after Shadow and Chiquita Naomi left. All three men turned when a car pulled into the yard. Lamar recognized the small black man who stepped out of the car.

"Banjo, I can't believe you're here. Mama would have loved to see you."

Banjo walked to Lamar and hugged him. "I'm sorry 'bout ya mama. She was an angel. Everybody loved her."

Lamar introduced his cousins. "I don't know if you've met my cousins. This is Ralph and Amos. They just came in from Woodbine."

Banjo shook their hands. "I think maybe when they was youngin's and runnin' 'round here, but not as men. Pleased to meet y'all." He turned to Lamar. "I need to speak to you privately if that's all right. I just got back into town and heard about your mama. We need to talk."

Banjo had left the area, fearing for his life, after Ruby literally pumped him for information about the attack Macadoo and Johnny D. Bryant planned against Mary C. The information was the reason Mary C. and her protectors were successful in defeating the devil man and his followers, both human and canine.

Lamar stood up from his lawn chair. "Excuse me y'all." His two cousins nodded to him. Lamar and Banjo walked to Banjo's car. He took the lead.

"I came home, but I didn't know about Hattie's death 'til I saw Macadoo." Lamar raised his eyebrows as Banjo continued. "She sent me here to see if you will meet with her before you leave, after the funeral, of course.

Lamar had been thinking about talking to Macadoo. Banjo was surprised at Lamar's response. "I'll see her today. I don't know what I'm doing after the services tomorrow. Tell her I'll treat her to lunch at noon at the Blue Moon. She seems to like it there."

Banjo smiled. "That's true, she does. I'll tell her. She'll be pleased about the meeting and the lunch."

Mr. Butler was glad he was back in his car and leaving Mayport. He had no conversation left in him for Mary C. Her strange way of looking at things had totally drained him. Every time he talked to her she was different, except for the way she looked. That attribute was always the same. She was sexy, desirable and all woman. He was uneasy about what was to come. He wasn't sure how to deal with Mary C. Was she insanely paranoid? Was she a true angel of death? Was she a constant victim of bizarre circumstances? Was she the cold-blooded calculated killer he thought she was? Mr. Butler's head was pounding with questions, thoughts and even desires about Mary C.

It was eleven o'clock when Jason woke up from his post Margie deep sleep. He got no sleep while she was there. Even when he fell asleep she would wake him for another sexual pounding. It was easy for Jason to fall back asleep when she left. It was the latest he had slept in a year. He knew Chichemo would be coming back to the boat in the afternoon so they could prepare for another trip. It would only take a few hours to ice and fuel the boat and get the needed supplies and groceries. They would leave some time the next morning. Jason knew you had to shrimp when the shrimp were there. His Uncle Bobby taught him that.

Miss Margaret had gone home and Sofia had joined Margie at the store. Sofia was surprised and interested in Margie's early arrival. "You actually came in early to help mother?"

Margie nodded and smiled. "Couldn't sleep. Thought I'd try and make up for missing so much time when I was sick."

Sofia wasn't convinced her oldest sister's actions were as honorable as they appeared.

"If you wanted to make-up for the time the rest of us covered for you why didn't you take our time instead of mother's time? She's hardly here anyway."

Margie had never heard Sofia speak in such a tone. "My goodness little sister, I do believe you are a bit upset with me. Would you like me to stay for your shift today so you can go play?"

Sofia was mad now. "I'm always going to do my job. I just think it's very strange that you jumped up out of bed before daylight and ran down here to help out." Sofia began stocking the Tom's peanut rack.

Lamar walked into the front door of the Blue Moon tavern. It was brighter inside during the day. The customers were there for lunch and a beer, instead of the usual nighttime dancing and hard liquor. He saw Macadoo sitting in the far corner of the room at her regular table. It was as private as a table could be in the open environment. Banjo sat with her. Lamar approached the table. Macadoo greeted him.

"I'm happy about you meetin' with me. I know you've got a lot on your mind and I'm sorry to take away from those important things. What I have to say is important, too."

Lamar nodded and sat down across from the fat woman. "I came here to tell you I believe what you said about the white woman. I've seen her in action for myself. I do think she's of the devil." Macadoo looked at Banjo. Her eyes were wide open and seemed to pop out of her huge head. She looked back at Lamar.

"You take my breath away, Lamar. I had no idea you understood what we are up against and what has to be done."

Lamar wanted Macadoo to know one more thing. "There can be two movements against her. If one fails the other can proceed. I'll work alone and you will know nothing about what I am doing. Neither one of you will talk of this meeting and what we say here. After my mother's funeral I'll stay here until one of us has ended it. This is the only way I'll be part of this."

Macadoo wanted to be sure she understood his plan. "I'm gonna continue with my plan to end it? You'll have another plan only known to you? When one of us succeeds we'll all rejoice?"

Lamar nodded. "That's about it."

Banjo entered the conversation. "Is there any thing we can help you with?"

Macadoo interrupted Banjo's offer. "Banjo knows I'm mad about him leavin' like he did. He wants to suck-up now and get back in my good graces. He got scared of Johnny D. and ran like a rabbit. He heard the Ax was dead and now he's come home. He ain't told why he got so scared, but I'm sure he will."

She looked at Banjo, but he would not make eye contact with her. He would never tell Macadoo how Ruby's sexual favors loosened his tongue and made him sing like a canary. He knew Ruby used his information to warn Mary C. about the evil plan.

Lamar responded and saved Banjo from Macadoo's verbal beating. " I don't know what to ask about. I just know what I saw and how I feel now. The rest will come to me."

Macadoo had to tell what she knew. "There's a woman." Banjo's heart raced in his chest, but he still did not make eye contact with Macadoo. "Her name is Ruby. She lives on the other side of the river in Cosmos."

Lamar knew the area. "I know where that is. We used to play sandlot football against the boys over there. They were some bad boys."

Macadoo continued. "I heard Johnny D. stayed with her when he was in town. I also know for a fact she was a good friend of the oak baby's mama, Jessie."

Lamar stopped Macadoo. "Hold on. I don't care about this oak baby thing. I'm doing this for other reasons. I don't believe in any of that crap. You need to know that up front before we go on."

Macadoo had more. "You didn't believe she was the devil, 'til something happened and made you understand. The power of the tree might just jump up and grab you, too. Good lookin' man like you probably get all kinds of information from Ruby. They say she can't say, 'no'." Banjo looked at Lamar. Macadoo wasn't finished. "She knows Mary C. and the oak baby. They say she even knows the son, Jason. Yes sir, she might just know a weakness or a habit we can use to better our chances. It sure wouldn't hurt the cause for some one to get to know Miss Ruby. I have a feelin' you'd enjoy meetin' her even if she didn't tell ya nothin'." Macadoo looked at Banjo. "Banjo's seen her. She's a looker ain't she?" Banjo's throat went dry. He knew she was the best-looking woman he had ever had the privilege of holding in his arms. He knew he had to answer Macadoo's question.

"She's a beautiful woman."

Macadoo smiled. "Ya see. You might just enjoy yourself and get somethin' we can use. Couldn't hurt to try."

Lamar nodded. "And exactly how do I get introduced to this Ruby?"

Macadoo had more. "Well, if you wanted to just take a look at her, I hear she always goes to the Honey Dripper at American Beach on Saturday night. I know with ya mama's funeral and all tomorrow, it ain't likely you'll be goin' to a honky tonk tonight. Maybe you can take a ride over there and see her. You don't have to dance or drink, just see her. That might help you decide on what to do with her." Macadoo changed the subject. "I heard ya mama wanted to be buried on a Sunday. I ain't seen many Sunday funerals."

Lamar reacted. "Mama loved Sunday mornin' at church. A person should be buried at their favorite time." There was a moment of silence and then Lamar continued. "I'll decide if I need to talk to this Ruby character or not. If I do, I do."

Macadoo looked at Banjo and smiled. "He do, he do. He don't, he don't. I think we need to leave it at that, don't you, my little Banjo man? I want pulled barbeque pork for lunch."

Mr. Butler was having his lunch at Cinotti's Bakery on Penman Road. He had asked Officer's Paul Short and David Boos to meet him there. The three lawmen sat at a window table enjoying the lunch spaghetti special. Mr. Butler put down his fork.

"So we're sure the three teeth and the other remains belong to Aunt Matilda?"

Paul Short responded. "Yes sir. The daughter's remains could be in there somewhere, but we're goin' with the premise she didn't die in the fire."

Mr. Butler nodded. "She's on the run. We might never find her. And when you think about it, why would we look for her. That was a nasty place they lived in out there. Don't spend any more time lookin' for that crazy, Zulmary. We got bigger problems ahead of us in Mayport. Let's eat and I'll fill y'all in later."

Jason was making the bunk of the boat when he felt the boat move. He knew someone had jumped onto the deck. He was hoping it wasn't one of the sisters looking for him to perform more of his sexual magic. Jason's pounding heart was eased when

Chichemo walked into the wheelhouse.

"You know we need to get back out there, don't ya? Them shrimp ain't gonna stay much longer." Jason nodded. Chichemo nodded back. "Let's get ready."

Mr. Butler and his two officers stood outside Cinotti's next to their cars. Mr. Butler had told them about his strange conversation with Mary C. "Let that boy get his mama buried tomorrow and then pick him up Monday mornin'. I want him in custody first thing. We'll question him again about the fire. And if we have to, we'll make him leave town for sure. That could end the possibility of Mary C. being right about him. It ain't likely she's right, but I've been shocked before with her predictions. Just get him in to the station."

Lamar sat with his cousins in the lawn chairs. The house was again filled with relatives and friend. He knew there wasn't enough room for them all to stay at his house, but he would do the best he could. He also knew his Mayport relatives would take some of the burden off him. The right thing to do was to stay with his relatives, but Lamar was curious about the woman called Ruby.

The last one hundred pound block of ice was sliding down the wooden chute and into the ice grinder. Jason held the hose over his shoulder and aimed the end of the flexible tube into the hold of the boat as the last bit of crushed ice fell behind the wooden slats. Chichemo yelled down into the hold. That's it, Jason. Come on up." Jason climbed out of the hold as Chichemo pulled the five-inch hose up and onto the deck of the boat. Mr. Leek stood above them on the dock.

"Ya think that's gonna be enough ice? Y'all hit 'em again like last time and you might need some more."

Chichemo nodded. "Hell, I hope we don't have enough ice. We'll be haulin' ass in to deliver 'em fresh."

"Better be safe, than sorry."

Chichemo looked at Jason and then at Mr. Leek. "Okay, shoot three more blocks in there."

Susan had relieved Sofia earlier that day and now Peggy was relieving Susan. Mr. King sat on his front porch and watched the family station wagon roll up to the front of the store. Susan waved and he waved back. Peggy met her at the door.

"Right on time. You are a good sister."

Susan smiled. Peggy was out the door and into the station wagon. She was hoping to see Jason. She drove past Mr. King's house and went straight to Mr. Leek's dock. Peggy didn't care who saw her. She was becoming extremely aggressive with her drive to be with Jason. She pranced through the fish house like she was one of the regular shrimp headers. Mr. Leek turned to her when she walked out onto the dock. She could see instantly that the Mary C. was gone.

"Can I help you, Miss Peggy?" She was at a loss for words. "Miss Peggy, you lookin' for somebody?"

Peggy realized Mr. Leek was talking to her. "Oh no sir. I mean, yes sir. Mama wanted me to see if Jason was coming home for dinner."

"Well, they're gone. Left twenty minutes ago. They're past the jetties by now. I know Jason went home to tell his mama they were goin' out. Wonder why she didn't tell Miss Margaret?"

Peggy shook her disappointed, but pretty head. "I don't know, sir."

Mr. Leek knew why the hot-blooded sister was there. He decided to have a little fun with Peggy. "That mama of yours is a great cook. What's she fixin' tonight. I might have to stop by and see if I can have Jason's helpin'."

The beautiful young black woman, Ruby, stood next to the juke box in the Honey Dripper bar in American Beach. She was Jessie's best friend and one night danced for Jason and shared his sexual magic. The shagging song, "Work Out" by Jackie Wilson was coming from the huge lighted record player. Her three male friends who helped her carry Johnny D. Bryant's wooden box casket, sat at a corner table near the jukebox. Ruby moved her incredible body to the upbeat rhythm of the well-known dance tune. She loved dancing with or without a partner, preferably without. There were a number of other men and women sitting at the bar and the other tables.

The Honey Dripper was a very popular watering hole for the black residents of American Beach, Fernandina and the surrounding areas. It was always crowded on the weekends when the music was loud and hot. There was no better place on Earth to go dancing.

Ruby usually stopped by on Saturday night whenever Johnny D.

was gone. He didn't allow her to leave her house when he was in town. She could go to the Honey Dripper anytime she wanted now that the devil was dead. She mourned his passing during her dance to the Jackie Wilson song. When the song ended, so did her time of mourning.

Ruby danced to the table where her three friends were sitting and watching her. She held out her hand to one of the men. The young man took her hand, stood up and they moved to the small plywood dance floor in front of the jukebox. Rudy would dance away the small amount of grief she had inside her hot blood and her cold heart.

Lamar Harris sat at the bar and watched Ruby as she danced away from her partner. Even with his mother's funeral a night's sleep away he was compelled to seek her out. She began to put on her personal show for anyone who would watch her. They all did, even the women and especially, Lamar Harris.

Another pretty young woman danced from a table and joined Ruby on the plywood floor, adding to the impromptu floorshow. Ruby's male dance partner walked back to the table and sat with his friends. He knew no one wanted to watch him and he wanted to enjoy the show himself.

Ruby's big brown eyes met with Lamar's eyes as she danced and moved around the room, but she didn't stare at him very long. She was too deep in her exhibition and exotic world of dance. She loved it. Everyone else loved it, too. Especially, Lamar Harris.

American Beach was located on the Atlantic Ocean between Fort George and Fernandina on the Florida coast. The majority of the black citizens from Jacksonville, Mayport and the beach towns, frequented American Beach for swimming, fishing, picnics, barbeques and other water activities. It was the place to be on Saturday and Sunday nights. Ruby danced past Lamar Harris and smiled with her perfect white teeth.

The Honey Dripper bar had filled to capacity with drinkers and dancers. It was standing room only. The slow song, "Twilight Time" by the Platters came softly from the jukebox. In a mater of seconds the dance floor was full. It was always full when a slow dance song was playing. Men who wouldn't dance to the fast songs seemed to find a way to struggle through the slow dance process.

You could sure lose a woman quickly if you did not, at least, slow dance.

Ruby had tried not to make it very obvious that she had been watching Lamar, but she had looked at him as much as he had looked at her. There was not a bashful or inhibited bone in Ruby's unbelievable body. She strolled toward the bar as if the rhythm of the slow song was moving her. Lamar watched her as she danced and stood in front of him. She offered him her hand and he took it without hesitation. Ruby gently pulled Lamar off the bar stool and led him to the dance floor.

When Lamar reached for her waist to pull her closer, Ruby put both of her arms around his neck and pressed the front of her body against him like they had been intimate dance partners for a long time. Her breasts were like two jetty rocks making two dents in his chest. There was no gap between their pelvic areas as Ruby pressed and humped against him as they danced. Ruby had no idea who he was or that Lamar Harris had come to the Honey Dripper looking for her. He had no idea it was going to be so easy to make contact with the beautiful black woman who knew all about the devil woman and her son.

Mary C. walked into Miss Margaret's kitchen. Miss Margaret was at the stove stirring a large pot of shrimp purlieu. Miss Margaret turned to greet her houseguest.

"Supper's ready."

Mary C. smiled. "Nothin' smells better than shrimp purlieu boilin'."

"Thanks to Jason's skill on the high seas, we have the freshest shrimp in the world."

Mary C. liked the thought of Jason's shrimping success. She was proud. She was also ready to tell Miss Margaret she had to leave.

"Miss Margaret, you know how I feel about you and the girls and all you've done for us. No one could have been a better friend."

Miss Margaret knew what was coming. "You don't have to leave. You can stay here as long as you like, but I do understand your need to have your own place. What ever you do will be the right choice. Now, sit down and pour some of this purlieu over that rice and let's talk before the girls follow the aroma in here."

Ruby turned the key and opened the front door of her house in the Cosmos woods. She stepped into her front room as Lamar Harris followed her.

"Let me get a light on in here. I usually leave the porch light on when I go out, but I left so early and it was still light out. I didn't think about it. Please sit down and make yourself comfortable." Lamar moved past her and sat down on her couch. He looked around.

"This is a nice place you have here. I didn't know there were any houses like this around here. I just remember old rundown shacks and a few rusty trailers."

Ruby smiled. "I try to keep it nice. My mama left me and my brother this house and she always took such pride in keepin' it up. I'm tryin' to do the same thing. I know she's watchin' me. My brother used to stay here with me. He's a great handyman, but he went shrimpin' in Texas and found a girl he likes. I don't think he's comin' back too soon, if at all. I miss him, but he seems to be happy and that's a good thing. It ain't too easy to be happy sometimes." Ruby stepped to the couch and stood in front of Lamar. "I need to take a shower and get a little of this dancin' dust off me. Would you like to join me?"

Lamar looked up past Ruby's huge round breasts and into her eyes. "Most definitely."

Ruby was an expert at taking showers with men. It was one of her many favorite things to do. Lamar had his own ulterior motive for being with her, but he was rather excited he was going to be Ruby's wild and wet partner for the evening.

The water from the shower bounced off Lamar's shoulders and chest. Ruby lathered him up with a bar of soap. She looked into his eyes and reached down to hold his wet and exposed manliness in her soapy hands. Ruby had held many other men in that same manner, but her hands had never been as full as they were at that moment. She knew he was huge and a true cut above the others. She was compelled to look down.

"Oh my God, it's real." She couldn't take her eyes off it as the water washed the white lather away. She spoke to Lamar, but continued to stare at the massive hunk of blood filled, fleshy organ pointing at her.

"I'll bet you get light headed every time that thing fills up, don't ya? I heard about men like you, but never thought I'd see one in person. I've seen 'em in those nasty magazines, but I thought they used a special camera for that. You could hurt somebody with a thing like that, maybe even put an eye out. I never thought I'd ever say this, but it's kinda scary."

Lamar smiled and took the bar of soap from her. He lathered up her huge breasts first and then worked his soapy hands and bar of soap down past her stomach. Lamar stopped the soapy journey when he had two of his fingers inside her. Ruby pushed against the palm of his big hand as she continued to hold him in her little hand.

She released him when Lamar turned her around and began using the bar of soap on her back and then on her butt cheeks. Ruby placed both her hands on the shower tile squares and couldn't believe it when Lamar moved the bar of soap up and down the crack of her butt. She was even more shocked, but pleased when she felt his soapy fingers move in and out. Ruby had never had anyone clean her like Lamar Harris.

Peggy walked into the kitchen. She was glad Mr. Leek did not follow her home with his nosey and incriminating questions. "What smells so good in here?" Miss Margaret and Mary C. looked up from their piping hot shrimp purlieu.

"Sit down my sweet daughter, and mother will fix you a plate." Mary C. loved the way Miss Margaret talked to her daughters.

"I can get my own plate, Mother."

Miss Margaret smiled. "You are a good daughter, Peggy. All you girls are so good to me."

Peggy took a plate out of the cabinet. She didn't like the fact that Margie had gone to work early that morning. She knew Margie was up to something. "Margie's the best daughter today, isn't she?"

Miss Margaret gave a little smile and raised her eyebrows. "Now, now. Do I hear a bit of sisterly sarcasm in your voice, Miss Peggy? Your sister's just happy to feel good again. She's getting her energy back." Peggy rolled her eyes. Mary C. smiled. She liked the way Margie kept them all guessing. Peggy wanted to change the subject.

"Will Jason and Mr. Chichemo be eating with us?"

Miss Margaret smiled again at the fact that Peggy's question included Chichemo. "Well, since Mr. Chichemo has never eaten here, I don't think he's coming. As for Jason, who eats here on a regular basis, he will not be here today because he and Mr. Chichemo are out in the ocean looking for shrimp."

Peggy wanted to ask her mother if she sensed a bit of motherly sarcasm, but she thought it would be better not to share that thought with her mother.

Lamar Harris lay on his back in Ruby's bed. He looked up at her as she maneuvered her incredible body so she could straddle him. Once again she reached down and held his abnormally huge manliness in her hand. In a matter of seconds she placed him inside her and she sat down on him with one sinking motion. Ruby lost her breath and made a painful noise. She knew it was the deepest penetration she had ever felt inside her body. It did scare her for the moment. She rotated her hips and could feel the difference. As she moved and allowed him to go deeper, she realized it was a perfect fit. Lamar would enjoy her sexual favors and become her lover for the night so he could learn what she knew about Mary C. and Jason.

Ruby stopped making her sexual groans and stopped moving her hips. "Did you hear that?"

Lamar stopped moving, too and listened. "What is it?"

"Listen how quiet it is outside, no dogs barkin'. I love it." She started moving her hips again. It took a second or two for her "no dog barkin'" comment to sink in for Lamar. He realized she was talking about Johnny D. Bryant's six devil dogs. Even though he knew the dog that attacked him was one of the six dogs he did not mention it to her. Ruby was a true sexual pleaser and she took her destiny role seriously.

While the Saturday night crowd was dancing and drinking at the Honey Dripper bar on American Beach another Saturday night crowd had gathered in Mayport at the Blue Moon. The song, "Stagger Lee" by Lloyd Price was rocking the room from the jukebox. Macadoo sat at her usual corner table with three of her male followers. She liked the noise and music. No one would hear what she was saying unless they sat at her table. And it was public enough to make people think she was merely enjoying an evening with friends. Her diabolical motive, however, was to find more human instruments for her next attempt at revenge against Mary C. and her family. She had been thinking about the fact that Mary C.

had lost two main protectors when Hawk and the Punjabi warrior-priest were killed.

She had decided to do what Lamar Harris wanted and make her own plan to rid Mayport of the devil's white woman. Macadoo wanted to trust Lamar, but she had seen him talking freely to the policeman, Mr. Butler. If Lamar ended Mary C.'s reign of terror Macadoo would be grateful to Hattie's handsome son, but she would not depend on him. She surprised her friends at the table when she unfolded the details of her next attack.

"We need to strike now while there's so many possible suspects. The longer we wait the more people forget or go away. They'll not be expecting it."

The three men were surprised again when Macadoo revealed her second motive for the attack. "I want the oak baby. I want to avenge the deaths of our brothers and sister, Voo Swar. I want the child."

One of the men had a question. "I understand wanting the white woman dead. I myself, lost a brother and a cousin, but why do you want the child, now? You have never talked of wanting the child." Macadoo's eyes glared through the dimly lit room.

" You forget, Mr. Demps, that I be the one who felt the child's power. Voo Swar felt it, too. She went to take the child and lost her life. I want the child." Mr. Demps didn't understand and wanted to know more.

"What will you do with the child?"

Macadoo had the answer. "You forget that both bloods flow in his veins. His mother was of mixed blood." The man nodded his head.

"We all know about his mother, Jessie. The child has less pure blood than she did. He is more white then black. Leave him with the protected woman. If he is of the oak and you believe in such things, you already know the tree will protect him against you and anyone else who tries to take him. If he is not of the tree, he is just a child, and nothing more. There is no reason to take him." Macadoo was obsessed with her self-imposed mission of revenge.

"I felt his power. It be true and he be of the tree. He'll bring good fortune to those who protect him. The white woman don't deserve such good fortune. She won't understand it and she won't appreciate what he is. There must be some way to defeat her and use the child's power to do good." Mr. Demps was not convinced.

"Use his power to do good? What would that be? What good could come from killing someone and stealing their grandchild? You are not learning from the lessons you are being taught. This child is protected and more will die if you continue to recruit assassins. I'm not sure what you are saying to these fools to convince them to do your bidding. I will not be part of your plans of revenge." Mr. Demps stood up and left Macadoo and the other two men at the table. He moved to the bar area to sit with other friends.

Macadoo was outraged at his questions and his aggressive attitude toward her. She was used to being in charge and doing the talking, but in the last few days she had been challenged by the young newcomer, Lamar Harris, one of the elders, Samuel Cane and now her friend, Clayton Demps. Macadoo did not like being questioned or opposed in anyway. Since the violent death of her rival, Voo Swar, the voodoo queen, Macadoo had moved up in the ranks of spiritual leader to the true believers and the strange cults that festered in the little town of Mayport. She was hoping to bring them all together as one under her leadership when she had defeated Mary C. and had the oak baby to raise as her own. Macadoo knew how Voo Swar had raised a child and she would do the same. Her child would be different from the devil child Voo Swar nurtured to manhood. Macadoo's child would be golden and would bring light instead of darkness.

Ruby and Lamar lay naked side-by-side in her bed. Their first sexual encounter was more than satisfying for them both. Lamar had indulged in Ruby's many sexual specialties and he was ready to move on to the second part of his informational agenda. Ruby's face was buried in her pillow. Lamar grabbed her hair and lifted her head up from the pillow. She smiled at his aggressive caveman maneuver. She was a true pleaser. Ruby had no idea she was getting ready to be introduced to the mean streak that dwelled inside Lamar Harris. His best friend Shadow Martin had seen it and even mentioned it to his new friend, Chiquita Naomi.

"Tell me what you know about the white woman, Mary C. and the child they call "oak baby." Ruby didn't expect such a request and she hesitated with her response. "I was told you know about the family. You were there that night before it all happened."

Ruby wasn't sure what to say. She pushed her body up off the bed with her arms, but Lamar held her hair and turned her onto her back, pushing her down on the bed. Ruby's eyes widened. She was scared.

"I asked you to tell me what you know about the woman they call Mary C. What is your tie to her and the child? Please don't make me ask you a third time." Ruby 's mouth went dry and she felt her heart pounding under her huge breasts. She knew it would be in her best interest to answer Lamar's questions.

"I'm not sure why you've decided to treat me like this. I don't know much, but I'll tell you what I do know. You really don't have to hurt me if that's what you have come here to do. You won't be the first. Men have hurt me before. I've been with the devil himself for the last year, so there ain't much you can do to me. I'm scared, but it don't matter."

Lamar released his grip on her hair. Ruby pulled the pillow with her as she stepped away from him and covered her naked body. She moved from the bed and sat in a chair on the other side of the room. Lamar sat on the edge of the bed. He did not cover his naked body. Ruby's eyes showed him her strength and her fear.

"I won't hurt you. You've been hurt enough. I need to know about the woman and the child."

Ruby realized what was happening. "You're gonna kill her, ain't ya?"

"I didn't say that."

"You didn't have to."

Lamar paid no attention to Ruby's revelation. "Tell me what you know."

Ruby gave him a puzzled look. "I'm not sure what you mean."

"I mean everything from the beginning."

She nodded her head. "Jessie was my best friend. She was the baby's mother. She's dead, now. Her and Jason stayed with me one night before they went to find the man called, Tom Green. He lived in a place called Ruskin. When they were there the child was born. Jessie died during childbirth and Jason brought the baby back here." Ruby was hoping she had given him enough information, but she knew he wanted more.

"You went to see her before the attack, didn't you?" Ruby was afraid he would ask that question. She hesitated with her answer. "You went to save them from Johnny D., didn't you? You knew what he was going to do and you told them. That's why they were ready to defend themselves." She didn't know what to say, but it didn't matter, he had more. "Why would you care about these white people?" Ruby was still afraid, but she had the answer.

"I couldn't allow the child to be harmed or killed. Jessie was like my sister. The child has her blood and I saved him because I loved Jessie. I don't care about any of them, just the baby. My best friend died so this child could live. I did it to honor the sacrifice she made. You know they think the child is a true oak baby? The first pure one, from two true oak babies."

Lamar smiled. "Do you really believe that old tree gives its power to a baby conceived in the sand beneath it?"

"I don't know if I believe that. I know there's a lot of folks swear by it and I know at one time Jessie believed in it. She may have changed her thinking when she found out that Miss Bell had lied to her all those years about coming from the tree."

Lamar interrupted her. "Jessie changed her feelings?"

"I think so. Let's say, she wasn't as sure of things when she found out about her real mother. Miss Bell had raised her, but was not her real mama."

Lamar shook his head. "Damn! Y'all got more people around here raising children that don't belong to them. Don't you think that's strange?"

"I ain't had no reason to think about it. And I really don't care. As long as they leave me alone, that's all I care about."

"You sure got involved that night."

"I've already told you why I did that and I think you know I'm tellin' the truth. It seems you have used me in a number of ways so would you please leave me alone now? I don't want to know anything about what you're going to do. Please don't hurt the child."

Lamar stood up and moved to where Ruby sat. He took her hands in his hands and pulled her back to the bed. "Let's play some more and then when you fix me breakfast in the morning I'll tell you what we're going to do."

CHAPTER SEVEN

. Miss Margaret walked down her upstairs hallway. It was house cleaning day for her and three of her daughters. She started waking up the girls and giving them their responsibilities. She didn't wake her houseguest, Mary C. Sofia was already up making her bed as part of the cleaning ritual when Miss Margaret opened her bedroom door.

"Good morning, Sofia. Look at you, already working. You are a dear. Get something to eat first. Breakfast is ready downstairs."

"Good morning, Mother. Thank you."

Miss Margaret left Sofia and knocked on Margie's locked bedroom door. "Margie, dear! Get up for breakfast and join the cleaning crew." Margie rolled over and put her pillow over her head hoping to block out her mother's loud and much too perky voice. Margie moaned as she felt soreness between her thighs from her physical encounter with the oak tree and Jason. She would be the last one to start her cleaning chores. Susan was at the breakfast table and Mary C. was up and dressed. She would help in the cleaning ritual and consider herself as a member of Miss Margaret's family.

Ruby woke up with Lamar Harris sucking on one of her huge breasts and three of his fingers inside her. It only took a few seconds for her to adjust to his rude awakening. He turned her onto her side with her back against his chest and entered her from behind.

Lamar pushed hard and deep and Ruby knew he was only concerned with his own pleasure. She tried not to react to his animalistic behavior, but he was too big and she felt pain as he pumped her. Ruby tried to move her hips so his penetration would not be so deep, but he held her with his strong hands and would not allow her to pull away. Ruby had recently buried the devil that victimized her and now she was a victim once again. It was her nature.

Miss Margaret's house was buzzing with a four woman cleaning brigade, as the fifth member, walked down the stairs. As usual, Margie was the last and most reluctant one to join the group. Susan and Sofia looked at the late arrival with disgust. Mary C. smiled at Margie's defiance and Miss Margaret had a motherly morning greeting and instructions.

"Good morning, sleepyhead. Eat some breakfast and then start with your room. Your other cleaning duties are the two bathrooms and the kitchen, including defrosting the icebox. I said, 'Good morning'." Margie looked up. She hated the way her mother called it "cleaning duties", like they were in the army or something. She also knew her mother's tone had punishment written all over it. Margie was almost twenty-three years old and she didn't like having chores. She understood about everyone keeping the house clean, but she just didn't like the way her mother still treated them like little children.

"Good morning, Mother."

Lamar Harris stood next to Ruby, as she lay naked curled up in her bed. It was obvious she was in pain and was trying to recover from the abuse she had taken from her new and now, unwelcome friend. Like Miss Margaret, Lamar had instructions for Ruby.

"I'm gonna take a shower and get your smell off me. Fix us some breakfast and we'll discuss what we need to do. I take my coffee with four sugars. I'm always sweeter after I have my coffee."

Ruby did not respond to his attempt at a moment of humor. She did roll over to show him she was getting up to do as he ordered. Lamar walked over to the door of the bedroom and looked back at Ruby as she stood next to the bed.

"Stay naked. I like seeing you naked." She didn't look up at him as he gave her more instructions and moved out of the doorway.

Ruby walked slowly toward the kitchen. Each step she took was painful as she heard the water from the shower bounce off the bottom of the bathtub. She wanted to run out the back door and hide in the woods, but she stopped in the kitchen and started fixing breakfast for her new abusive houseguest.

A fire engine red Corvette Stingray was rolling up State Road A1A with the destination of Mayport, Florida, U.S.A. Steve "Crane" Robertson was at the wheel of the streamlined, jet-like machine, as it seemed to float above the road. At ninety miles an hour the car looked like it would leave the road at any moment and take flight. He would stop at the Oasis outside of St. Augustine for some fried shrimp and a cool one before he continued his trip to Mayport.

Miss Margaret's house was spotless and smelled of Pine-Sol. Miss Margaret, Sofia and Susan were out front on the porch. Sofia was sitting on the bottom step petting the monster dog, Abaddon. Susan was sitting on the step behind her little sister brushing Sofia's long blonde hair. Miss Margaret sat on one of the wooden rockers crocheting a white circle doily for the arms of one of her chairs in the living room. Margie was still defrosting the icebox.

Mary C. stood in the bathtub and had just turned the shower on. She adjusted the temperature of the water to be as hot as she could stand it. She wanted to recreate the fog of steam she had seen before in the small bathroom. Mary C. was hoping Hawk was still fighting to stay with her. She looked for him in the steam, but he did not appear.

Mr. King stood in his living room staring at the magic music box. His thoughts were of his good friend, Ana Kara, the voluptuous belly dancer. He touched the magic carousel and wondered if the antique music box would bring his thoughts of Ana to him in a dream. Mr. King put his finger on the small lever that turned on the carousel. He remembered his promise to Mary C. so he pulled his hand away and went to the kitchen for his third cup of coffee.

Lamar Harris walked into Ruby's kitchen looking for his first cup of Sunday morning coffee. The aroma of scrambled eggs cooking in butter filled the room. He had one of Ruby's big thick towels wrapped around his lower body. Ruby was still naked, as he had ordered. She stepped to the small kitchen table and spooned the yellow eggs out of the black cast iron frying pan into a white plate. Lamar sat down in the chair as she shoved the plate of eggs in front of him. Ruby placed a full cup of piping hot coffee next to the plate.

"You said three sugars, but didn't say cream or not."

Lamar picked up the piping hot cup of coffee and put the rim of the cup to his lips. He blew air into the cup, and then touched his top lip to the hot liquid, sipping a small amount. He moved the cup away from his lips.

"This is the way I like it; hot, sweet and black. Just like my women. After breakfast I have to meet my aunt at church. They're having a prayer group for my mother." Ruby forced a smile after his chauvinist and religious comment as he took another sip of the hot coffee.

"Damn, Ruby, you are the total package. You've got the looks, the body, the know-how, you cook and this is the best cup of coffee I've ever had." He took his biggest drink from the cup. "How'd you get it so sweet?" Ruby forced another smile at his poor excuse for a compliment.

"I put three big spoonfulls of that Dixie Crystal sugar and a touch of pure honey."

Lamar gulped down the last drop of coffee and put the cup back down on the table. Ruby filled the empty cup as soon as it hit the table. Lamar couldn't wait to pour the second full cup down his throat. Ruby sat down at the table across from her guest. Lamar put the cup down again.

"You should do this more often. A woman like you should always cook in the nude. Promise me when I'm here you'll always cook breakfast for me naked."

Ruby smiled again. "I promise."

Lamar dipped a fork into the scrambled eggs and began to eat. Ruby shoved a small plate of toast coated with white sugar and butter toward him.

"Try my new sugar toast with your eggs." Lamar took a piece of the sweet bread and ate it along with his eggs.

"We're going to make a good team, Ruby. I've been looking for someone to take care of me."

Ruby forced another smile. "I'm your girl."

Lamar finished his second cup of coffee. "I truly believe you are."

She filled his cup again. "How can I help you?"

"You can help me kill the woman. We won't harm the child." Lamar sipped his coffee.

"Are you goin' to take the baby?"

"I was thinking about that. If we have to kill her son, too, why don't you take care of the child? What better way to honor your friend, Jessie? You'll get the child away from that awful family and if he's a true special child of the tree, perhaps you'll be the one to direct his future. You would be a better choice then Macadoo."

Ruby's eyes lit up. "Macadoo? Macadoo is a crazy power hungry witch who hides behind a false veil of being a child of God. She may be even more dangerous than the voodoo woman, Voo Swar. She ruled with black magic and fear. Her death was no great loss to the black community."

Lamar surprised Ruby when he seemed sad and changed the subject. "The black community has lost an angel, you know? I'll bury my mother today. That's why I'm here."

Ruby couldn't believe what her new tormentor had just said. "You're here for your mother's funeral and it's today?"

"Two o'clock." Ruby hated him even more.

Lamar's tongue felt strange. He had that sandpaper, cat tongue feeling you get when you have burned the top of your tongue. It felt thick and too big for his mouth. His mouth went dry as he tried to swallow. There was a burning sensation deep in his throat and down in his stomach. Lamar looked across the table where Ruby sat. His eyes burned and he could not focus on a clean image of his naked host. He felt the coffee, eggs and sugar toast leave his stomach and explode upward into his throat and mouth. Before he could empty the nasty mixture from his mouth it plunged back down into his stomach. He was able to breath for a few seconds and his eyes were clear again as he focused in on Ruby's huge brown eyes. Lamar Harris knew something was terribly wrong with him.

"What's happening to me? What have you done to me?" Ruby stood up and picked up a shirt off the counter next to the sink. She put on the shirt and covered her naked body. Lamar wanted to throw up the fire in his belly, but it would not come up. He tried to talk, but he could not. Ruby stood by the sink and watched Lamar struggle. She could read the question screaming in his eyes.

"Let's see, now. What made the coffee so sweet? And that sugar coating on the toast was sweet, too. Like I told you, there was that good ol' Dixie Crystal sugar and pure honey. Oh, I forgot my secret ingredient." Lamar's burning eyes were able to focus in on the box of rat poisoning Ruby placed on the table. He grabbed the box, spilling the small white tablets on the table.

"They were easy to crumble up and add to the coffee. They dissolved as fast as the sugar did. I even put some in the eggs. And yes, it was on the toast, too. You really ate a lot of rat poison in the last few minutes. More than I thought you would. But, don't you think that rat poison is an appropriate breakfast for someone like you? " Lamar lunged across the table at Ruby, but it was only a futile effort. He fell to the linoleum-covered floor.

Ruby talked as she cleaned off the table. "The thought of raising Jessie's baby was a good one. If you would have told me that earlier and treated me with respect I might have helped you. I'm tired of men like you using me for their needs. And when you took a shower at my house to get my smell off you, I knew right then I was goin' to kill you no matter what. I don't think you're gonna make it to your mama's funeral, but I think you'll be seein' her pretty soon."

Lamar Harris would die on Ruby's kitchen floor in a matter of ten minutes. He watched Ruby clean off the table and wash the dishes as his throat swelled shut and he suffocated. Mary C. would never know she had an unlikely protector and the beautiful black woman called Ruby had saved her life once again.

Miss Margaret's icebox had been defrosted and Margie had finally completed her cleaning duties. She would relieve her youngest sister, Sofia, at the store later in the afternoon. Margie felt she had already done enough work for one day and she was not happy about doing even more work at the store. She had rebellious thoughts against her mother's taskmaster philosophy, but they would remain only thoughts. Margie was not yet ready to speak up against her mother's wishes and she knew she might never be ready. Sofia had already gone to relieve Peggy. Susan would have the late shift and work until midnight. Margie was standing on the front porch when Peggy drove up in the family wagon. Peggy got out of the car and walked up to the front porch steps, side stepping Abaddon.

Peggy knew the look on Margie's face. She had to smile and make her comment.

"Hey Margie, cleaning day went well, I hope." Margie's eyes showed her anger. Peggy did not let up on her angry older sister. "Don't tell me." She stepped toward the front door. "You got the bathrooms and the kitchen?"

Margie responded to her sister with pretty, straight, white, clinched teeth. "I had to defrost the igloo, too." Even though she knew how serious Margie was, Peggy couldn't help herself. She burst into laughter as she pushed the front door open and left Margie steaming on the front porch. Margie was going to follow her heartless sister into the house to confront her, but Mary C. walked out of the door as Peggy was going in.

"Hey Peggy."

"Hey Miss Mary C." Mary C. stepped out onto the porch and smiled at Margie.

"Girl, your mama sure put the whammy on you today, didn't she?" Margie had to smile at Mary C.'s observation.

"Yes ma'am she sure did." Mary C. sat in one of the wooden rockers.

"Sit here with me. It's always so pleasant on this porch." Margie sat in the other chair. Mary C. took a deep breath. "You know Margie, if you're gonna be different and stand alone, you have to take responsibility for your actions and be ready and willing to take the consequences. I do like your style."

Margie's face lit up. "You think I have a style?"

"Of course you do. And it's yours and yours alone. I think your life is much more exciting then you will admit, but I think you know. I watched you work with Chichemo on that dog. You have it."

Margie wrinkled her forehead. "My life? You think my life is exciting?"

Mary C. shook her head and smiled. "Now, you're playing a game with me." Margie didn't respond. She waited for Mary C. to say more. "You have had more excitement around you in the last year to last most people a lifetime. You need to open your eyes and take a good look."

Margie was hoping Mary C. would continue to give the reasons her life was exciting. Mary C. had the list memorized. "Until those big gators ate your man, you was having plenty of good sex. When I saw y'all that time in your room I knew that wasn't your first time. If you was wild enough to do that right here in your house with your mama downstairs, you did it in other exciting places before that time."

Margie's eyes were wide open after Mary C.'s reference to her friend officer Jimmy Johnston being eaten by the gators at the Gator Farm. Margie was speechless, but Mary C. was not. "You have witnessed life and death. You have lost a lover. You have enjoyed dreams from the carousel. You have known the oak tree in a way not many have attempted. You have conceived and lost a child." Margie's heart raced in her chest after Mary C.'s last comment. Her mouth went dry as Mary C. stared at her and had a question. "So you think there is no excitement in your life?"

The only thing Margie was thinking about was Mary C.'s comment about her losing a child. She had to get her thoughts together. Mary C. knew Margie wanted to respond so she rocked in the chair and waited. Margie looked into Mary C.'s eyes.

"How did you know? It was the carousel, wasn't it?"

Mary C. shook her head. "You and that carousel. I didn't need that thing to tell me why you was so sick last week. I knew you were with child right after Jimmy died. I knew when you were no longer with child. I don't have a reason for knowin' it. I just knew it. I know things sometimes."

Margie did not know what to say. She didn't like Mary C. knowing and talking about her situation. Mary C. knew Margie was struggling with the conversation at hand so she gave Margie some relief.

"Maybe I should have kept it to myself, but I think you need to have somebody on your side. Your sisters can't give you the support you need. Like your other secrets, this one is safe with me. Hell, you wouldn't believe all the secrets I've had to burn deep in my belly. I'm the best secret keeper you'll ever know." Mary C. reached out her hand and touched Margie's arm. "We might even make some secrets together, you and me."

Margie's eyes lit up. She thought about the words in her dream and again she wanted to be the next mother of an oak baby. Margie smiled and touched Mary C.'s arm.

"I understand. Just tell me when." Mary C. smiled and shook her head.

Ruby watched her two male friends drop Lamar Harris' poisoned and dead body into the back bed of a rusty red truck. She threw an old green army blanket over the body and turned to her friends standing near her. Her house was isolated in the woods and she knew no one would see their activity.

"You two are the best. I'm sorry to get y'all involved in my craziness. I've had two devils come my way lately and I hope I've seen my last. This one had to go, too." She kissed each of the men on his lips. "I do love you two handsome rascals. Where y'all gonna take him, Carl?"

Carl looked at his partner. "We're gonna take his cold sorry ass for a boat ride and we'll decide what to do during the ride. You don't need to know nothin' 'bout what we do. He'll make some good chum for the fish. You did your part. We'll do ours. We love you, too."

"You two come on over tomorrow night and I'll fix supper. Just the three of us, unless y'all want to bring somebody with y'all."

Carl smiled. "Why don't you invite a couple of those big butt friends of yours? The ones that like to party. Me and Jerome trust your judgment." He looked at the other man. "Don't we, Jerome?" Jerome smiled and nodded his head. Ruby smiled, too.

The three had been friends since childhood and the men thought of Ruby as a sister and there was no physical involvement between them. Ruby did set them up with women she knew every now and then, especially to repay them for favors. Disposing of Lamar Harris' swollen dead body was the biggest favor they had ever done for her. She was more than happy to cook them a great meal and supply them with female companionship.

"Four for supper. You got it. Y'all be careful. Don't get caught with this devil in the back of your truck. Don't speed." Jerome got into the rusty truck and Carl got into Lamar's car. They left Ruby at her house in Cosmos.

Mr. Butler sat at his desk in his office at the Atlantic Beach Police Station. He was staring out the window and thinking about the remarks Mary C. had made to him the last two times they stood together on Miss Margaret's front porch. He hated the way she had taunted him the first time and even challenged him to admit his feelings for her. She also challenged him about the death count he was keeping. Now she had given him thoughts of a new battle to come with the black man with the bullwhip. He would admit to himself that she was good to look at and he had moments of sexual fantasies about her.

Any man with blood running through his veins would have physical desires for such a woman. He did not like the fact she was aware of his thoughts, but he also knew a woman like Mary C. most likely thought every man had those thoughts and fantasies about her. She would probably be right in most cases. He had been careful not to give any indication he thought about her sexually, but she knew. As far as the vigilante comment, Mr. Butler was at a loss.

Mr. Butler also thought of Mary C. as having the traits of a black widow spider, because of the way the men who had dealings with her seemed to die violently. He had called her an angel of death. He had reasons to believe he would be arresting her a number of times, but she always managed to clear herself of all wrong doings. She was an expert at not being responsible. She was the ultimate victim of circumstances. He knew she had killed in self-defense. She had also committed cold-blooded murder and would most likely never pay for the crime. He also knew Mary C. had more secrets buried in her head, heart and belly, than any normal person could take. She was far from normal. He hated her for being with Jimmy Johnston when he died. Mr. Butler hated her for the army of people who had died because of her and yet he would crawl into bed with Mary C. at the drop of a hat. He wanted to just forget about her vigilante talk.

Steve "Crane" Robertson drove his fire engine red Corvette Stingray away from the Oasis. He had been enjoying the music and liquid spirits. He stayed too long and drank too much with his St. Augustine friends. He had planned to be in Mayport before late afternoon, but he knew that would not be the case. The Crane was back in his car and on the road. He knew he was about an hour away from the little fishing village or even less if his Corvette took flight, which was possible at the high speed he usually drove. He had Jason and Mary C. on his mind. Not necessarily in that order.

Margie drove away from her house in the family station wagon. She had to relieve Sofia at the store in an hour. She was thinking about Mary C.'s words of praise and encouragement. She liked Mary C. telling her how exciting her life was and there was even much more to come. Margie still felt deep in her misguided heart that she would be the next one to breed with Jason and she would be the mother of the next oak baby.

It was almost two o'clock in the Mayport afternoon. Hattie Mae Harris' funeral service was to begin within minutes. The Pentecostal Church on Mayport Road was filled to capacity with mourners left outside in the churchyard. The number in attendance rivaled any previous funeral in Mayport, black or white.

Shadow Martin drove up to the church in his red truck. There were no parking places so he drove up to the church steps and created his own. He had delivered his new female friend, Chiquita Naomi, to her Savannah home and returned in time for Miss Hattie's funeral service as he had promised. The church was too crowded for Shadow to sit up front with Lamar and members of the immediate family. He would wait until the service was over to let his best friend know he was there.

Mr. Cane eulogized the beloved Hattie and the popular Reverend Johnny Wells presided over the ceremony. Reverend Wells was known for his God given ability to move the members of his congregation to a dancing and singing holy frenzy in the name of the Lord. The rafters would shake in the old wooden building whenever the good reverend slammed his big fist down on the wooden top of the pulpit and denounced the devil. He would not raise his voice or pound his fist on that day. He would not preach or try to save souls. He only prayed with the crowd after Mr. Cane completed his one full hour walk through Hattie Mae Harris' life filled with sacrifices for others.

Joe Croom stood on the soft white sand at the bottom of the sand hill. He was looking for his twin brothers, Chuck and Buck. He knew the boys were playing on the oak tree earlier that day and he thought they might still be up there. The two bad boys should have been home an hour ago. The twins never seemed to do the right thing. It wasn't in their nature.

Joe began making his way up the hill toward the tree. He was on the grape arbor side of the hill and had to walk through the palmetto fan tunnel. It was an area of the hill where the fans grew on each side. Through the years of the game the boys swinging on the ropes had created a tunnel like hole through the green palmetto fans. It was where the swing downs took place when Duckin' was played in the past. Some young Mayport boys still enjoyed swinging through the fan tunnel, but they didn't play the game. Joe stayed clear of the briers and the prickly bushes.

As Joe was about to reach the end of the tunnel he heard a low muffled laugh and he knew the sound came from one of his brothers. He stopped and listened, hoping he would be able to spot the boys, sneak up on them and scare them. That is what older brothers are supposed to do to little brothers. Joe crouched down and moved in the direction of the noise he had heard. He moved a large palmetto fan that was blocking his view to one side and there they were, Chuck and Buck, hiding behind a large clump of fans.

One of the boys put his hand over his mouth to keep from laughing out loud. Joe moved closer to them ready to scare the devil out of the two boys. He noticed the twins were looking up from their hiding place in the direction of the tree. Joe looked up, too. His eyes popped wide open when he saw Margie sitting on her favorite sex limb of the oak tree. With Jason out shrimping she would use the tree to satisfy her physical needs. She straddled the limb and was sliding her lower body back and forth across the bark. Margie was deep into her oak tree ritual of ecstasy.

Joe couldn't believe his eyes. He always liked Margie, but he knew she thought she was too old for him. He didn't think so, but he knew she did. Margie's moans of pleasure and sexual movements mesmerized the three Croom brothers. Joe forgot about scaring the twins. He could not take his eyes off Margie.

Chuck turned to laugh and saw Joe looking up at Margie. He tapped his brother Buck so he would see Joe, too. Joe did not know he had been spotted. He was busy watching Margie as the twins jumped up from their hiding place and ran through the palmetto fan tunnel. Joe saw the boys move with his peripheral vision, but Margie began to moan louder as her ritual was coming to a climax. He felt his manhood move and press against the zipper of his cut off dungarees. Margie moved her body back and forth, faster and faster against the limb. She threw her head back and grimaced with pain and pleasure. Joe could not turn away from Margie's sexual performance. Margie screamed as her stomach muscles flexed and she released her body fluids. Joe would find the twins later.

Margie leaned forward touching her breasts and stomach against the huge limb. She had a burning sensation between her legs, sore stomach muscles and cramps in one of her thighs. It was a pleasurable discomfort. Margie slowly climbed down off the limb and stood in the sand beneath the tree.

As Joe continued to watch Margie there were frightful blood curdling screams that brought Margie back from her ecstasy and Joe back from his fantasy. Joe knew the twins were making the awful noise. He knew his bad little brothers were in serious trouble.

Margie turned in the direction of the screams, but could not see anyone because of the palmetto fans. Joe moved from his observation post and ran through the fan tunnel to find the twins. Margie straightened her blouse and began moving down the sand hill in the direction of the tunnel. Her legs were shaky, but they always felt that way after a visit to the tree.

Joe ran to the end of the tunnel of palmetto fans. Both boys were screaming with pain and fear. Joe looked to his right to see both boys on the ground crying and holding their feet. Joe saw the problem instantly. The boys had run through a bed of Joe Jumpers and the small needle spiked cacti had attacked with no mercy what so ever. Each boy had at least five of the thorny plants in both of their feet. It may have been the worst Joe Jumper attack in the history of the spiny green cactus.

"Joe Jumpers" were a member of the cactus family that not only had spines like sewing needles, but the spines had ridges on them making it difficult to extract them from the flesh they had penetrated. The cacti grew in peanut shaped long green clumps so a moving foot stepping on one would throw the green spiked cacti up higher on the leg. It was very painful.

Chuck and Buck were bad little boys, but no one deserved such a vicious attack. Joe didn't know what to do or which brother to help first. Both boys were in an uncontrollable panic mode. Joe knew there would be no way to reason with them or calm them down.

It has been said that Joe Jumpers sit and wait in the sand for unsuspecting human feet to draw near. As the fleshy foot and five digits pass by, the vibration of the stepping foot alerts the Joe Jumper and it actually propels itself toward the foot, sticking its one inch needle sharp thorns into the soft flesh of the heels, ankles and toes. It was traumatic enough for a person to have one of the demon plants stick them in the foot, but to have a nest of them strike at once was too much for anyone to handle. Then it became even worse when someone would try to remove them, as fingers and hands would be stuck as well. Joe knelt down next to his brothers.

"Oh God, boys!" Chuck and Buck were beyond reason. Joe reached for Chuck's foot, but Chuck pulled it away and continued to cry.

"Don't touch it." Joe looked at Buck. He was crying, too.

"You'll both have to hold still so I can get 'em out." Joe heard another voice in between the boy's screams.

"Oh dear God!" Joe looked up to see Margie standing next to him. The twins saw her, too and they both stopped screaming. "You poor darlings. Let me help you get those things out of your feet." She stepped between the boys. "You are so strong. Both of you lie back and relax. Don't look at them. Find something else to look at or think of something pleasant."

Margie knelt down between the two boys and bent over to talk to them. The two boys had no problem finding something else to look at and think about as they looked down Margie's blouse and saw her bare breasts. The twins looked at each other, smiled and turned back to Margie's nipples.

The boys were trying not to cry now that Margie and her bare breasts had joined them. They were making painful and pitiful noises and repeated, "oowee, oowee, oowee, in oowees of three at a time. Margie smiled up at Joe and nodded to him, telling him with her eyes that he needed to begin the removal of the merciless Joe Jumpers from the feet of his little brothers. Margie patted Buck on his chest.

"How did this happen?"

Joe pulled two of the small thorny cactus out of Buck's foot. "Oowee, oowee, oowee!"

Margie touched his cheek. "It's okay. You are very brave." Margie looked at Chuck. "You doing okay, over there?" Joe pulled the biggest Joe Jumper out of Chuck's heel and held it up so Margie could see it.

"Oowee, oowee, oowee!"

She touched Chuck's forehead. "That big one's gone. The others are just little ones. That must have been the daddy Joe Jumper." Chuck smiled at her attempt to humor him, but he was too old to hear about the daddy Joe Jumper. He decided his best bet was to zero in on her exposed breasts as his big brother, Joe, continued to remove the sharp ruthless intruders. Joe pulled two of the smaller stickers out of Chuck's ankle. Each time Joe pulled out a Jumper, blood would trickle from the hole it left behind. Margie's soothing techniques and exposed nipples allowed Joe the time to remove all the nasty Joe Jumpers from the twins' feet.

Joe pulled the last Joe Jumper from Chuck's foot then the last one from Buck's. He had alternated back and forth from one foot to the other so he was fair with his timely removal of the stickers. The boy's feet were on fire and lined with blood. Margie stood up, taking the view of her breasts away from the two little demons.

"You boys need to go home and clean those feet. You don't want to get an infection from those opened wounds." She turned to Joe. "The Joe Jumpers didn't jump you, did they, Joe? It seems like you were the more appropriate victim. They are called Joe Jumpers aren't they?" Chuck and Buck rolled their eyes at the same time at Margie's silly little comment. Joe didn't care how silly the comment was, he just wanted to stay with her as long as she would stay. Margie had another concern.

"Can you two walk home?" The two boys looked up from the ground with pitiful looks on their faces. Margie turned to Joe. "My car is on the other side of the sand hill. I can give you boys a ride home so they don't have to walk."

Chuck, Buck and Joe were going to ride in the family station wagon. Joe was happy and ready to spend as much time with Margie as she would allow. The twins sat in the back seat of the wagon and were very quiet during the ride home. The traumatic experience with the swarm of Joe Jumpers had taken the noisy meanness out of Chuck and Buck for the time being. Margie and Joe sat in the front seat and they were as quiet as the boys. Joe didn't know what to say and Margie was not that interested in talking to him. She still considered Joe Croom too young for her.

Six male pallbearers walked out of the front door of the church carrying the body of Hattie Mae Harris. Shadow stood at the bottom of the steps waiting to greet Lamar. The somber crowd was quiet except for a few women who were crying. Reverend Johnny Wells led the procession of family members as they followed the moving casket. For some reason Shadow's eyes met with Mr. Cane's glaring eyes. Perhaps it was a coincidence that their eyes met, or perhaps Mr. Cane was looking for the man who took his daughter away. No matter the reason, Shadow's heart raced in his chest when Mr. Cane left the procession and walk toward him. Shadow was hoping he was not going to face an angry father and have an ugly confrontation at the foot of the church steps. He didn't like the look on Mr. Cane's face, but he thought, "Surely this friend of Hattie Harris would not cause a personal scene at her funeral." Shadow stood his shaky ground as Mr. Cane drew near him. He could see the concern in Mr. Cane's eyes.

"Mr. Martin, where is Lamar?" Shadow was shocked by the question and could not respond. "I was hoping he was with you."

Shadow found his missing words. "He's not here?"

Mr. Cane shook his head. "Hasn't been here at all. Maybe he couldn't come. That happens to folks now and then. When the time arrives they just can't face the fact their mama's gone."

Shadow shook his head. He knew better. "No sir, not Lamar. That's not Lamar. Something else happened. You think they arrested him?"

Mr. Cane's didn't understand. "Arrest him for what?"

"That cracker cop, Butler, questioned us about the fire at Aunt Matilda's Place."

"I heard about the fire, but why did they question y'all?"

"I guess it started right after we left. They thought we might have seen something, or maybe we were the cause of it."

Mr. Cane had a sensible idea. "I'll get Hattie buried, you find Lamar."

Mary C. stood in her front yard facing the pile of burned wood that had been her house. She had walked over from Miss Margaret's house. The mangled, but recuperating devil dog stood next to her. She looked at the pile of charred wood. Mary C.'s eyes fell upon her blue Ford Falcon. It was all she had left. She had not driven it since that night. Grass and weeds had grown up around all four tires. As she walked over to her car, Abaddon barked and ran toward the burned ruins.

Mary C. watched the wild creature as he ran around the black ashes, barking and sniffing the ground, as if he was looking for something. She opened the car door and sat down behind the wheel. Abaddon was still running in circles. Mary C. shook her head when she saw the car key still in the ignition.

"I wouldn't blame you ol' girl if you didn't start, but I think you're gonna fire right up. Don't let me down, now." Mary C. turned the key and pushed down the gas pedal. Abaddon stopped running when he heard the car engine. It sputtered for a second or two and then roared as much as a Ford Falcon could roar. "That's my girl."

Abaddon ran to the opened car door and stood there. Mary C. looked down at her living trophy. "You lookin' for all your friends? Poor baby. They're all dead. Ain't you glad you switched sides when you did?" Mary C. closed the car door, put her in gear and pushed down the gas pedal. Abaddon watched the Falcon as the tires rolled out of the tall grass. He did not follow.

Shadow Martin walked into the front door of the Atlantic Beach Police Station. A woman sat behind a small desk in the middle of the room. There was a concerned look on her face when she looked up at Shadow. She stood up from her chair. "Harley, get in here, quick!"

Shadow wanted the ease her discomfort and his. "Excuse me, ma'am, I was tryin' to get some information about…" She interrupted him. Her voice was even more urgent.

"Harley, I said get out here!"

Shadow turned to a side door as a uniformed police officer ran into the room holding a black nightstick in his hand. The woman stepped away as the man walked past her. Shadow stepped back as the man stopped a few feet away from him. The officer was patting the nightstick against his open hand making the sound of wood slapping on skin.

"What ya want here, boy?"

Shadow's heart was racing and his lips went dry. "I'm not here to get hit with that stick, for one thing."

The woman wanted to add to Shadow's discomfort and possible billy clubbing. "He just barged right in. Scared the life out of me."

Shadow knew that the less he talked, the easier it would be on him, if it were to be easy at all. He heard the front door open behind him and he turned to see if anyone else had a big stick. Officer David Boos walked through the door followed by Officer Paul Short. David Boos looked at Shadow and then at Harley.

"What's goin' on Harley?"

Harley was excited. "This boy scared Martha. Come in like a wild monkey." Shadow's Cherokee blood wanted to give out an Indian war cry and scare Martha some more and scalp the idiot holding the nightstick, but he knew better. Shadow felt a small amount of relief in his racing heart when David Boos talked to Harley.

"Put the damn stick down Harley. Have you even talked to him yet?"

"He won't say nothin'. Just a smart-ass remark about not wantin' to get hit with a stick.

David Boos shook his head in disgust at Harley. "Go on in the back." He turned to Martha. "Go fix us some fresh coffee."

Martha stared at Shadow. "I ain't fixin' him none."

David Boos looked at Shadow, but he talked to Martha. "I don't think you have to worry about him drinkin' your coffee, Martha." She left the room. David Boos addressed Shadow. "What can we do for you?"

Shadow was trying to calm down from the last few minutes. He didn't want the two white officers to see his fear and anger from the racist confrontation, but he knew it was obvious that Martha and Harley had scared and irritated him. He took a deep breath and tried to gain his composure.

"I didn't come here to cause a problem. I never knew blacks had to knock on the door to enter a police station. I'll know better next time."

David Boos knew sarcasm when he heard it. "I wasn't here when you came in, so I don't know what happened. Just tell me what you're here for and I'll try to help. If not, go on."

"I'm lookin' for my friend, Lamar. He didn't make it to his

mama's funeral. I thought that might have somethin' to do with you."

David Boos looked at Paul Short. "Why would you think that?"

"I thought maybe you arrested him."

"Why would we do that? Did he set the fire?"

Shadow was afraid to say anything, but he had to find Lamar. "I think you know we didn't set the fire. I'm just concerned that somethin' has happened to him. It's not like him to miss his mama's funeral."

"Well, we don't have him. And we haven't seen him since we talked to you both."

Another voice added to the tensioned filled air of the room. It was a familiar voice that caused Shadow's heart to race again. He knew Mr. Butler had entered the room.

"Don't look good for ya boy to be missin'. I told y'all to stay put 'til we could iron this thing out. Him runnin' looks bad. Hell, he might be runnin' with Zulmary."

Shadow knew how ridiculous Mr. Bulter's comment was, but he knew not to respond. Officers Boos and Short knew it was ridiculous, too. They were like Shadow and would not respond.

Mr. Butler continued. "I hope you find that boy and talk some sense into his thick head. He's a suspect, especially now that he's gone. If and when you do find him, tell him to come on in. Zulmary, too."

Shadow knew he needed to get away from the crazy misguided lawman before he found himself behind bars. Mr. Butler had more. "You go on now and tell that boy to give himself up."

Shadow walked out of the police station and walked quickly to his truck. He was relieved as he drove away, but he had no idea where to start looking for Lamar.

Hattie Mae Harris was in the ground. Mr. Cane was exhausted and he went home after the burial service. The family members would stay at Hattie's house to greet and feed the friends who came by after the service. They would leave before dark and go back to Georgia. Many of Hattie's friends went to the Blue Moon tavern to eat and drink to her life.

Macadoo was still sitting at her favorite table in the Blue Moon tavern. She knew most of the people who had gathered there after

Hattie's funeral. She kept her word and did not attend the service. Many of the mourners stopped at her table to pay their respect for the local black female religious leader. The huge black woman adored the attention and bathed in the words of praise. As a group of well-wishers stepped away from Macadoo's table, a single man remained standing next to her chair. Macadoo looked up at the lone stranger.

He was so black he was blue. His face was weathered to the ultimate extent. Even though his bloodshot eyes screamed of a life of gin and moonshine, there was something familiar to Macadoo about them. The small amount of hair that circled his ears was white and sparse from age.

"Can an ol' friend buy Macadoo a slab of ribs?"

Macadoo knew his voice. She smiled, making her fat cheeks squeeze her eyes closed. "You can buy me ribs, even if you ain't my ol' friend. I never thought I'd live to see you again, especially here. I guess when you start gettin' ol' nothin' really matters or scares ya much."

"Some things still scare me, but not many. I had to come for Hattie's funeral, even if they hang me."

Macadoo smiled again and shook her huge head. "Tom Green, how the hell is ya?"

CHAPTER EIGHT

Mary C. walked into Bill's Hideaway, the honky tonk built high on stilt pylons near the jetties on Seminole Beach. She wasn't dressed for the Fish Bowl where she preferred the classy clientele, so Bill's would have to do. She hadn't planned on going anywhere, but once the Falcon got rolling, Mary C. drove all the way to Seminole Beach. Even though she was not decked out in her regular sexy jukin' attire, she was still the sexiest and best-looking woman in the building. All eyes were on her when she walked through the main dining room and made her way to the bar. She had sat at that bar many times. Mary C. was in her element and liked the eyes being on her. Many of the customers knew about the killings and the fire that had taken her house. It had been quite a while since Mary C. sat at any bar. Hawk had taken her out to dinner and even dancing, but not just to sit at a bar like she did when Hawk was not her man. She recognized the bartender.

"Well, well, if it ain't the wizard himself. I thought you was through with mixin' drinks. Where ya been, Hank?" Hank smiled when he saw his old friend sit down on one of the bar stools.

"Mary C., you are a sight for sore eyes. And these eyes of mine ain't even close to what they used to be, but they see you real good right now. You never change, do ya? Ain't nobody called me the wizard in years. How'd ya think of that?"

"You'll always be the wizard to me. Nobody'll ever mix drinks like you, Hank. "Oh and yes, I have changed plenty. You always did say the kindest things to me."

Hank was much older than Mary C. He had a hard look to him with deep crows feet cracks in his face streaming from both sides of his tired eyes. Hank wore long mutton chop sideburns like the sea captains of old. He looked out of place behind the bar where younger men usually made a good living. Mary C. leaned across the bar and kissed Hank on his lips. He touched her hand and smiled.

"I was sick when I heard about your brother, Bobby. I was in Texas and couldn't make it home. I thought about y'all though."

Mary C. smiled. "I know ya did, Hank. Now, what are ya doin' here behind that bar and where have ya been for the last five years?"

"Bill needed some help this week end and he roped me in last night. I'm gonna work 'til Monday and that's it. I have to say it's been fun bein' back here. I still remember the drinks. There's a few new ones, but most of 'em are the same. I was in South America for a year, spent three years shrimpin' in Texas, tryin' to make my fortune. That, by the way, seems to continue to elude me."

"You gonna stay a while?"

"I didn't plan to, but I'll probably get on a boat and see what happens. Mary C., it's hard for me to believe I was there the night you was born. I guess I was about fifteen years old. Your daddy was older than me, but he was my friend. I always had older friends. He was a good one, too. Your daddy helped me be a man. Real men help others be better."

Mary C. could see the respect and seriousness in Hank's eyes after his little trip to the past and a moment of manly philosophy. He changed the subject. "You all right, Mary C.? There's a lot of talk about the battles you've had to fight lately. You do know you're somewhat of a legend in your own time. I even heard you was indestructible and had made a deal with the devil and that big oak tree. Is it true? Did you make a deal? They say that's why you don't age. It's part of the deal."

Mary C. knew Hank was playing with her. "I know for sure that you don't believe any of that stuff. People do say the craziest things about me, but they always have."

Hank smiled. " I just tell 'em you're mean as hell and the devil wouldn't come near you with his hot poker."

Mary C. shook her head. "One easy Jack Black, Mr. Wizard."

Margie stopped the family station wagon in front of the Croom house. Joe opened the passenger's side door and got out of the car. He stepped to the back door to assist Chuck and Buck. The boy's four feet were bloody and swollen from the attack of the Joe Jumpers. The twins limped as they walked slowly on the sides of their damaged feet toward the house. They never thanked anyone for anything. Joe stepped to the driver's side of the station wagon.

"Thanks Margie. My rude little brothers ain't much on manners, but this was a nice thing for you to do."

"You're welcome. I hope they're all right. I know they're bad sometimes, but they are cute. I hated seeing them in such pain. They were really scared."

"They'll be fine. They're pretty tough boys, too tough sometimes. It might be good for them to be scared now and then. I don't want them to get hurt either, but a little humbling might just do them some good."

Margie smiled and nodded her pretty head. "Listen at you with such a grown-up philosophy. Be careful there Joe, you sound like a man's supposed to sound."

"I'll be nineteen in three weeks, Margie. My boy days have been over for some time, now."

"I guess you're right, Joe. Folks change so fast and most of the time no one's looking, are they?"

"No ma'am. No one's ever lookin'."

"It was nice to see you again, Joe. You take care of those two. They need a man like you around."

Margie pushed down the gas pedal and left Joe standing there. She would be late relieving her sister, Sofia, at the store. Margie knew that once she told her story about the Joe Jumpers to her sensitive little sister, she would understand and be proud of Margie's role as a Good Samaritan. Joe would think about Margie's sexual antics at the oak tree for the rest of his young life and afterward.

Mary C. finished her first easy Jack Black. Hank was serving another customer at the end of the bar. The sound of Elvis coming from the jukebox gave Mary C. a chill as she thought of her brother, Bobby, and how he did love Elvis. She smiled and tapped her foot to the beat of the song. A deep voice interrupted her thoughts.

"It's times like these that I wish I was a dancin' man." Mary C. looked up at the huge man standing next to her bar stool. Even though Mary C. was surprised she never changed the expression on her face.

"You can always learn to dance, Mr. Robertson. And men like you can always find a partner. The hard part is findin' the right partner."

Steve "Crane" Robertson sat down on the bar stool next to Mary C. He was a huge man. He was even bigger than Hawk. Uncle Bobby called him the Elvis of the crane operators and king of the big rigs. Mary C. had a short and sexual past with the Crain. She had forgotten how big he was. She looked at his huge arms and hands, hands that maneuvered her quite easily during their sexual encounters.

"What brings such a famous man to my neck of the woods?"

The Crane touched Mary C.'s hand. "We'll talk about why I'm here later. You drinkin' Jack?"

"I was just havin' one. I'll leave it at that."

Steve nodded and motioned to Hank. "Jack and coke, when ya get a second, please." Hank poured the drink and placed it on the bar in front of the Crane. He turned the bottle toward Mary C.'s empty glass. She held her hand over the glass.

"None for me, Hank." Hank nodded and moved to his other customers.

Steve shook his head. "You always look so good, Mary C. Men love to see you comin' and women love to see you goin', don't they?"

Mary C. looked into his eyes and gave a little grin. "I've heard that a few times in my life. I don't know how true it is, but folks seem to think it's true."

"There's a lot of talk about this beautiful woman in a small Florida town fightin' to save her family. This beautiful woman survives against unnatural odds and gives no quarter when it comes to life or death. Seems quite a few folks, mostly black, are bein' buried when they cross paths with this wild woman. When I first heard about her I knew it was you. I was compelled to see you and Jason, so here I am."

"There's a lot of wild women in these parts, Mister. What makes you think I'm the one you're looking for?" A new voice from across the room interrupted Mary C. and joined the conversation.

"Of course you're the woman he's looking for." Mary C., as well as everyone else at the bar, turned toward the rude voice to see Mr. Butler walking toward the bar. It was obvious he had been drinking and the alcohol had set his tongue free. Mr. Butler stopped a few feet away from Mary C. He looked at the Crane. "Do be careful, sir. She is the angel of death, you know?"

Mary C. smiled. "Now Mr. Butler, please don't say things you'll be embarrassed by later. It's not like you to put yourself in a situation where you may act a fool."

Mr. Butler continued to stare at the Crane. "I don't have an official count yet, but it's a lot."

Steve looked at Mary C. "What's this drunk fool talkin' about?"

Mary C. touched Steve's leg. "This drunk fool is the law around here and I think he's got the night off. I didn't know he would take a drink. I ain't never seen him like this."

"What's he countin'?"

Mary C. looked at Mr. Butler then back at Steve. "Dead bodies. He's countin' dead bodies."

Steve wrinkled his brow. "Your dead bodies?" Mary C. nodded. Mr. Butler nodded along with her and moved closer to the Crane.

"Be careful, mister. Men don't last long with this one." Steve put his hand on Mr. Butler's chest and pushed him away.

"You're kinda crowding me a little there, sport. Let's keep a friendly distance."

Mr. Butler held on to the bar stool to keep his balance. "It's my duty, sir, to warn you against possible harm. If you buy her a drink it could be a hazard to your health."

Mary C. looked at Steve. "Is he the cutest thing or what?"

"Cute's not the word I'd use, but nothin' ever surprises me when I'm with you."

Mary C. touched Steve's leg again. "You're still a silver tongued devil, ain't ya?"

Mary C. and Steve turned in the same direction as two uniformed police officers stepped up next to Mr. Butler. Officers David Boos and Paul Short had arrived to save Mr. Butler from further embarrassment. Both officers took Mr. Butler by an arm. David Boos looked at Mary C.

"It's his day off. Sorry about the problem."

Mr. Butler looked at Mary C. "Let's compare numbers sometimes." He looked at David Boos then at Paul Short. "Hey, fellas, what are you doin' here?" The two officers escorted Mr. Butler away from the bar and out the main door. Mary C. turned to the Crane.

"You still got that fast red car?"

Margie stood behind the cash register at the store. She had just finished telling Sofia about the Joe Jumper attack on the Croom twins. Sofia had a look of pain on her face as if she had a foot full of the little green cacti.

"Those poor boys. It's a good thing you were driving by and heard them screaming."

Margie changed the subject. "You should see their older brother, Joe. He's turned into quite a handsome young man."

Sofia surprised her older sister with her reply. "I've always thought he was good-looking. And he's always been manly and more mature for his age."

Margie nodded her head. "Really?"

Sofia had more. "I like the way he takes care of his brothers."

"How do you know if he takes care of them or not?"

"I've seen him around and in the store. I do notice things whether you think I do or not." It was Sofia's turn to change the subject. "Why were you driving over there anyway?" Sofia's quick question took Margie off guard and she hesitated with her response. Sofia had her own answer. "Don't tell me you went to that tree again." Margie still had no answer. Sofia knew the answer. "You did! You were at that tree again! Are you crazy? You know that means nothing but trouble. When are you going to learn your lesson? I was hoping you had gotten that out of your system." Margie had to stop her overly dramatic little sister.

"Hey, hey, take it easy. I never said I was through with the tree.

I told you I'm not afraid any more and the tree helps with my courage. And by the way, you sound more and more like mother everyday. " Sofia's eyes were like big round blue saucers.

"Every time I think about that tree I think about that dream we had together and I get scared all over again. I never will forget that. It was the most scared I've ever been, except for the night in the cemetery when Charlie Klim scared me, or the night Jake scared me when he tried to hurt Jessie, or the night I saw the Werewolf girl on the sand hill, or the time Miss Mary C. shot that big black man in her front yard." Sofia stopped her scary recollections and remembered another. "And when gators ate Jimmy." The two sisters were silent as they stared at each other. Sofia moved closer to her older sister when she realized how many times she had been afraid. "I've been scared a lot, haven't I?"

Margie nodded and then hugged her little sister. "We've all been scared a lot."

Steve Robertson's fire engine red Corvette rolled across the packed down white beach sand like it was on rails. The top was down, as usual, as Mary C. laid her head back on the headrest of the passenger's seat. The cool ocean breeze touched her face and she closed her eyes.

"I forgot how it felt to ride in this car." Steve smiled, but kept his eyes on the beach in front of him.

"I think you like ridin' fast more than I do." Steve's next comment surprised Mary C. "I'm sorry about Hawk. I liked him."

Mary C. opened her eyes and looked at Steve. "I liked him, too. He wouldn't like me bein' with you like this."

"No, I don't reckon he would. I'll take ya back if ya want, if it's too soon for us to be ridin' fast together." Steve slowed his Corvette and stopped on the wooden ramp that lead to Seminole Road. He revved up the engine and gave Mary C. her options.

"Back to Bill's or the tar of Seminole Road?" Mary C. smiled and stood up, holding on to the top of the front windshield.

"One flight on Seminole and then back to Bill's." Mary C. fell back in the seat as Steve floored the gas pedal and the red machine went flying into the night.

The huge black woman Macadoo still sat at her favorite corner table finishing her slab of barbequed ribs. Her lips and cheeks glistened from the grease and sauce she had failed to wipe away. Three black men sat with her at the round table. The song, "Come Softly" came softly from the jukebox. Tom Green was gone. Macadoo talked to the man sitting directly across from her. He was the oldest of the three men. He was bald on top with salt and pepper hair still growing on the sides and back of his head. The man looked like the Uncle Remus character from "Song of the South".

"I'm glad you've decided to join us, Milton. Your influence will help our cause and give us direction."

Milton nodded. "I lost my son and now my brother because of that woman. I don't want her to take another breath of air."

Macadoo reached out and touched Milton's hand. "You do realize her protectors are gone. The one they called Hawk and the priest are both dead. Only Jason remains to defend her. The longer we wait, the more things can develop to interfere with our mission." Macadoo was talking more and more like a military general and less like a spiritual leader. Her obsession with Mary C. was more than obvious and her thirst for revenge would not be quenched until the white woman was dead. The two younger men remained quiet as Macadoo continued. "What do y'all know 'bout Lamar Harris?"

Milton shook his head. "Not much. I know he's Hattie's son. He went off to study at some school. He's supposed to be a smart young man."

One of the younger men joined the conversation. "His mama died. Her funeral's today. He ain't stayin' here. He ain't one of us no more."

Macadoo needed more. "I've talked to him about joining us. He wants her stopped, too. He won't join us, but he did act like he was gonna do somethin' on his own. I'm just not sure 'bout him and what he says. He's a little too smooth for me. Besides, I hate the way he talks to me. I would try and deal with him if he talked to me with more respect."

Milton had a thought. "If you have doubts about him, leave him out of our plans. Your first instincts are usually the right thing to do. He's been gone a long time and he may not be what we need."

Macadoo took a deep breath and nodded her huge head. "You're right. I liked the way he talked and carried himself at first, but he's not really one of us. We'll deal with him if he comes to us, but we won't go to him. We'll have to see if he helps us." She hesitated and then had more to tell. "We might not need him. Guess who was here with me before you came in?"

A small rowboat floated along the St. Johns River shoreline near the area called Ocean Way. Ruby's two friends stopped the boat along side of a thick growth of water grass and hyacinth plants. Both men took hold of Lamar Harris' poisoned and dead body, rolling it out of the boat and into the plant filled water. Lamar's body sank under the water for only a few seconds and then floated to the surface. It didn't matter that the body was floating because the thick vegetation would keep it hidden until the fish, crabs and natural water deterioration process took it's toll on the flesh, organs, blood and bones of Lamar Harris. The two men knew there was a strong possibility the body would never be found and if it was discovered the white folks living in Ocean Way would not be concerned with a black floater.

As the two men took up the oars and the boat floated away, a huge manatee stuck its ugly snout and head up through the thick green hyacinths leaves, blowing air and water into the air. The large water creature, also known as a sea cow, scared both men until they realized it was not Lamar Harris rising like Moby Dick from the water. Their hearts jumped for a second and then they both smiled at the relief it was not Lamar.

The red Corvette stopped next to the East Mayport monument. Mary C. looked at the white column towering above them. The last time she was at the monument was the night she seduced James Thorn and led him to the Indian burial grounds where she ultimately, tortured and killed him. She had to settle her heart beat when she saw the monument. It didn't take her long to end her short memory flash and return to her cool and calculating self. The Crane looked up at the white column.

"Isn't it strange that this historical monument sits out here in good old East Mayport. Most folks don't even know its here."

Mary C. looked at her admirer. "It's always been here. East Mayport was the place to be in the ol' days. A lot of famous people stayed on Seminole Beach. There was big houses, hotels, beach cottages and even a place called the Wallace Mansion right on the beach. They say Mr. Wallace was a railroad man. That was way before our time. I would have liked to have seen the beach in those days."

Steve smiled. "You would have fit right in with those rich folks." Mary C. didn't look at Steve after his compliment, but she sure liked what he said.

"I've always known I should have been born to a rich family. I feel like maybe I was rich in another life."

Steve was surprised at her response. "Mary C., I never knew you believed in such things. You think we've lived in another time?"

"You probably didn't, but I'm sure I did." Steve smiled at her remark. He did like Mary C.

Evening was falling in Mayport with John King sitting in a rocking chair on his front porch. He watched the activity on the street in front of his house and on the river. He held his evening cup of coffee to his lips. The vision of Ana Kara, his female friend and sometimes belly dancer, flashed in his head. He thought about the carousel music box sitting in his living room. He wondered once again if his thoughts and fantasies would become real through the lights of the magic box.

The red Corvette slowed down as it rolled onto the wooden ramp at Seminole Beach. The car fishtailed in the beach sand and the spinning wheels threw sand into the air. Mary C. didn't scream or flinch at all. She loved the speed and the danger. She was a rare breed of woman and Steve "Crane" Robertson knew it. And even though his body was filled with complete animal lust for his one time sexual partner, he would not pursue Mary C. until her time of mourning for Lester Hawkins had passed. He didn't realize Mary C. never really took time to mourn anyone. She was an expert at going on with her life. They were headed back to Bill's Hideaway. Mary C. smiled.

" I do love ridin' in this fast car."

Steve had to speak his mind. "I know it's too soon, but when this all settles and you need to move on and have some excitement, please consider me."

Mary C. smiled again. "It ain't that things need to settle. My blood's runnin' as hot as yours right now. The real problem is that Hawk ain't left yet."

Steve took his foot off the gas pedal and the red rocket began to slow down. Mary C. knew she had surprised him with her comment. She did not give him time to respond.

" I know you'll think I'm crazy and most likely I am, but it's true to me."

Steve took a deep breath. "You really believe his spirit is still here?"

"I know it is. I've seen him. I've felt him. I've smelled him. He's still here, all right. Folks that die violently and before their time always fight to stay. You see, they ain't ready to go and they don't believe it really happened to 'em."

Steve drove the Corvette next to the pylons under Bill's Hideaway and stopped next to Mary C.'s blue Ford Falcon. He turned the key off and the engine went quiet. He looked at Mary C.

"You do know that no man can compete with a ghost if a woman keeps that thought in her heart." Mary C.'s next comment was too much for the king of the big rigs.

"I think he just wants to be with me one more time and then he'll realize he has to cross over to the other side. I think he'll go after that."

Steve's eyes were wide open. "You think he'll leave after what?"

"After he has his way with me one more time." There was a silent moment that Steve ended.

"You gonna have sex with your dead lover? Your dead and buried lover?"

"I don't see no other way to help him pass over. I don't think he knows he's dead."

"Well, you know he's dead. Tell him when you see him again. Maybe he'll just move on without crawlin' into your bed."

Mr. John King was still on his front porch. Customers had been in and out of Miss Margaret's store for most of the time he had been sitting there and watching. He had been thinking about Sofia's questions and the possibility he would be having new ghosts join the old friends he already had residing in his wonderful haunted house. The sight of a naked and dancing Ana Kara flashed in his head. He stood up, looked around to be sure he was alone and walked back into his house. He wanted the magic carousel to bring Ana to him.

Mary C. told him the music box had worked and it opened a porthole to the other side. He wasn't thinking about the ghosts at the moment. He wanted Ana Kara.

Steve "Crane" Robertson stood next to his red Corvette. He watched Mary C. drive away from Bill's Hideaway in her blue Ford Falcon. The fast ride and the strange subject matter of the conversation had left the Crane in a daze of lust and ghosts. He wasn't sure how long it would take Mary C. to clear her mind about Hawk's death. He also thought that with all the death and turmoil in her life, she could very well have gone crazier than she already was. He walked back up the wooden steps of the honky tonk on stilts. A few more drinks were in order.

Mary C. turned her Falcon onto Julia Street between Miss Margaret's store and Mr. King's haunted house. Mr. King was walking up his front steps. Mary C. stopped the car next to the house and called to Mr. King out of the driver's side window. "Hey John, you seen Hawk, lately?"

Mr. King turned to see who was asking such a strange, but interesting question. He remembered Sofia's question about any new ghosts at his house.

"You think he's here?"

Mary C. stepped out of the car. "If he ain't here all ready, he's comin'."

John was now standing on his big porch. He put his hands on the wooden white railing. "Really? And what makes you so sure of that?"

"He won't cross over. He knows the carousel will bring him to me. He was here when the door opened. Hawk wants to have me one more time."

Mr. King's eyes were wide open. "He wants you one more time? You mean...." Mr. King didn't say it. Mary C. did.

"That's right. I mean he wants to ravish me one more time. And I have to say I wouldn't mind at all. I know it will have to be here. This is the only place. John, can I come in, we need to talk?"

Chichemo looked back toward the stern of the Mary C. He could see Jason was vomiting over the side of the boat. It was time to pull the nets up from the first drag. He hated Jason being so sick, but it was time to go to work.

Mary C. sat in Mr. King's living room with James Thorn's smiling skull on the fireplace mantle behind her. Mr. King was anxious to see what the wild woman wanted from him.

"Like I told you, the carousel worked. It opened the door to the other side just like you thought it would. The skinny man told you the truth. He knew it would work here. I know you didn't see what we saw. At first I wasn't sure why."

Mr. King was interested. "And now you know why?"

"I think so." Mary C. took a deep breath. "I'm not sure how to say this. I couldn't say it unless I trusted you. I have to know you will burn what I tell you in your belly and never tell it."

Mr. King was intrigued. There was only one answer he could give. "I'll take what ever you tell me to my grave."

Mary C. nodded and smiled at her friend. "I know you will, John." There was a moment of silence before Mary C. continued. "I had a dream that you were leaving Mayport for a while, is that true?"

Mr. King had a strange look on his face. "Actually, I was thinking about going to Gibsonton to see my circus friends."

Mary C. smiled. "The belly dancer was in my dream, too."

Mr. King nodded. "Ana was in your dream?"

"Dancin' her ass off."

Mr. King knew he was flushed and red faced when Mary C. mentioned Ana Kara, the belly dancer. He had been thinking about her for the last few days and he was planning to go see her. "I really haven't decided if or when I was goin'. I was just in the thinkin' stage, right now."

Mary C. had a great deal of strange thoughts on her mind. "John, I can't stay with Miss Margaret and the girls anymore. I need to leave for a number of reasons. They've been wonderful, but I'm afraid for their safety with me in that house."

Mr. King had to interrupt her. "Why would you worry about that?"

"They're comin' after the baby again. I can't be there when they come in the night. They'll kill 'em all."

Mr. King was concerned about Mary C.'s state of mind. She was scaring him and he was a man who didn't scare easily. "Mary C., you have been through an awful year of tragedy and personal loss.

Perhaps you should get away from Mayport for your own sanity."

"I know how crazy my life is. I don't know why it has unfolded like it has, but it has. John, they want me dead and they want the baby. It sounds crazy, but they've tried twice, now, and each time I've become weaker. I don't know if I can stop them again."

Mr. King was at a loss for words. He wanted to say the right thing and comfort her in some way, but he had no idea what to say. Mary C. didn't care if he had a comment or not. "John, this is gonna sound crazy, too, but here goes. I'll be stronger here. I'll have no protection at Miss Margaret's or on the boat. In fact, I don't think they'll come here at all. Not many folks want to deal with ghosts. The carousel, your resident spirits, Hawk, Bobby, the priest, they'll all be here. I know this is where we'll be safe. It's one of those sanctity places."

Mr. King understood what Mary C. was thinking. "It's a sanctuary. A safe haven."

Mary C. was excited. "Yes, that's it! Our sanctuary. That's it."

Mr. King's eyes sparkled with the thought of his haunted house being considered hollowed ground. "I never thought about how safe it is here. You're right. It's been a sanctuary for the dead for years. Why can't it be the same for the living?"

The owner of Mayport's haunted house was the perfect partner for Mary C.'s insane solution to her vigilante problem. He wanted to know more and get back to the original subject. "Mary C., what do you want me to burn in my belly and take to the grave? Why was I the only one who didn't see the door open to the other side?" Mary C. was ready to tell some of her secrets.

"John, have you ever killed anybody?"

Mr. King was shocked by Mary C.'s strange and serious question. He hesitated with his answer. "John, have you killed before?"

"No, I haven't. Why?"

"I think that's the reason you didn't see the ghosts come through the light. The lights on the carousel moved together and made one big light. The light was the opening and the spirits came through it. The only one in the room who had never taken another life was you. The three of us had killed before. I'm not sure why Bobby was able to come to us, but the other ghosts were people who had died at our hands."

Mr. King was not ready for Mary C.'s moment of true confessions. "I don't want you to tell me anymore. Keep your secrets in your belly, as you say. I'll do anything to help you and your family, but I don't want to know about these things."

Mary C. had been willing to tell her deepest secrets so Mr. King would help her. Now that he offered his services without her spilling her guts, she was excited and pleased with the possibilities ahead. She stood up and hugged Mr. King. She held him close as she talked.

"Thank you, John. There ain't many men like you on the Earth. I'm gonna come stay here until this is over. If you want to take your trip now, we'll be fine. If you want to stay that's fine, too." She released her hold on Mr. King's neck. "Oh John, one more thing." She stepped back. "I'm gonna use the carousel to let Hawk have me one more time so he can crossover. What bedroom should I use?"

As the two exceptionally eccentric Mayport citizens continued their morbid and supernatural conversation, Lamar Harris' body was floating at the bottom of the seafood chain.

Steve "Crane" Robertson stepped off the last step and onto the beach sand under Bill's Hideaway. He had Mary C. on his mind and Jack Daniels on his breath. He was sorry and disappointed he had let her drive away. The Crane knew with the Corvette under him he was only fifteen minutes away from Mayport. The Jack Black had added to his lustful thoughts and feelings, as well as his poor judgment. The ragtop of the red convertible was still down. He stepped into the front seat of his car without opening the door. He had plans to hold Mary C.'s hard butt cheeks in his huge hands.

Shadow Martin walked into the Blue Moon tavern. He had been looking for his friend Lamar since he left Martha and Harley at the police station. He saw Mr. Cane sitting at the bar. Shadow knew Mr. Cane probably didn't want to talk to him, but it was the only face Shadow recognized. Their eyes met. Shadow felt better about his intrusion when Mr. Cane motioned with his hand for Shadow to join him. Macadoo noticed the handsome new face as Shadow sat on the bar stool next to Mr. Cane. Nothing got past Macadoo. She watched and listened. Mr. Cane greeted the nervous and confused Shadow Martin.

"Well Mr. Martin, any word on Lamar?"

"No sir. I don't understand it. I don't know much about the area either, and that doesn't help when you're searching for someone. I went to the police station and those nasty crackers scared me even more. I have a number of theories, but I don't like any of them."

Mr. Cane felt bad for the young desperate man. "I can imagine a few things myself. None of them very good."

Shadow nodded. He had to speak his mind. "Maybe he's had some kind of mental breakdown and he left. I never thought I'd hope such a thing to be true. Maybe, I'll go back to school and he'll be there. If he had been in an accident we would have heard by now. It scares me to think that white woman, he told me about, did something to hurt him."

Mr. Cane's eyes widened. "You mean Mary C.?"

Shadow nodded. "He called her the devil. I have another thought. I wouldn't put it past that cracker cop to have done something, either." They were quiet for a few seconds. A huge shadow covered them both from behind. They both turned on the bar stools at the same time to see Macadoo standing behind them. She was huge and full of barbequed ribs. She looked like a massive black water filled balloon ready to explode any second. Shadow had not dealt with her before. Mr. Cane knew her well. She addressed Mr. Cane.

"I couldn't help hearin' you two talkin'." She looked at Shadow. "You come here with Lamar didn't ya?"

"Yes ma'am."

"You school boys are all so good lookin', ain't ya?"

"I don't know about that ma'am. Thank you."

"You lookin' for Lamar?

"Yes ma'am. He didn't come to his mama's funeral. I'm really worried about him. It's not in his character to just leave like this. I'm worried that something bad has happened to him." Macadoo turned and started walking away from the bar. "Can't stand here like this. I might be able to help you, but I've got to sit down." The fat woman walked slowly back to her favorite table.

Steve "Crane" Robertson had no idea the needle of his speedometer had moved to ninety miles an hour. His tunnel vision had only one thing at the end of it, Mary C.

The muddy smell of low tide filled the night air as the rocket red car flew across the small wooden bridge located a mile from the curve at the little jetties. The Crane had plans to steal Mary C. away from the ghostly hold Hawk had on her. He never took his big foot off of the gas pedal as the Corvette hugged the sharp curve.

At first the Crane didn't realize the two left tires were not touching the road as the car leaned into the curve. He held onto the steering wheel with his big strong hands as he felt the car roll to its right side. The car began to flip. The rotation of the first complete roll broke the Crane's neck. On the second flip, he was thrown from the car like a limp two hundred and eighty pound rag doll. The Elvis of the big rigs was dead before his huge body slapped the low tide mud.

Mary C. had an empty feeling deep in the pit of her secret burning stomach. Mr. King noticed a change in her facial expression. "Mary C., are you all right?" She turned quickly to James Thorn's skull on the fireplace mantle behind her. It was as if the skull had called her name. Mr. King knew something was wrong. "Mary C., what is it?"

She turned back to Mr. King. "Something's wrong, John. I need to get back to Miss Margaret's and check on the baby."

Mr. King thought about what Mary C. had said earlier. "You don't think they're comin' tonight, do ya?"

Mary C. shook her head quickly. "No, not yet. This is something else. I feel it. Can I come to see you tomorrow and we can decide what to do?"

"Of course. Do you want me to go with you?"

Mary C. was moving to the door. "No, I'm fine. I'll see you in the mornin'. Thank you for listening to me." She was out the front door and into her Falcon. A concerned Mr. King walked out onto his big front porch as she drove away.

Macadoo sat at her favorite table in the far corner of the Blue Moon tavern. Mr. Cane and Shadow Martin sat with her as she gave them the information they needed to know.

"I had lunch with Lamar here yesterday." Shadow's eyes lit up. "He came to talk about the devil woman." Mr. Cane's eyes lit up. "I was hoping he had come to join us, but he hadn't. He said he would work alone, but he was going to do something. But now, I hear y'all talkin' 'bout him bein' gone. I think maybe we can't count on him. I had my doubts about him in the first place, so it don't surprise me none."

Shadow had to stop her. "What was he going to do on his own?"

Macadoo stared into Shadow's soul. "Help us rid the world of the white devil. Lamar saw her close up and in person. It was easy for him to see her for what she is. Now, he's up and run off. Not everybody can face the devil."

Shadow had to defend his best friend. "Lamar hasn't run away. Something has happened to him, I just know it. He would have never missed his mother's funeral."

It was time for Macadoo's eyes to light up. "He wasn't at the funeral?"

Shadow shook his head. "No ma'am he wasn't."

"I have to say I think you be right about him not runnin'. I thought he had left after the funeral. If he didn't show, you're right, something be wrong." She looked at Mr. Cane. "I told him to go see the woman they call Ruby and she could tell him about the white woman and the oak baby. I didn't think he was goin', but maybe he did. You need to start with her and see if he found her. It's Sunday night, I think I know where you can find her."

Mr. King walked into his living room to extinguish the two burning lanterns. He had been using the lanterns ever since he talked to Sofia about the possibility and probability of new ghosts arriving. Mr. King's theory was to make his home more inviting for the confused and sad souls who may be searching for a safe haven. The old house was equipped with electricity and the modern conveniences needed for the comfort and entertainment for the living. The candle and lantern atmosphere was more inviting and suitable for the dead.

Mr. King bent down toward the first lantern and lifted up the glass cover. The flame on the wick flickered and went out before he could blow his breath on it. A strange and cold chill ran through his body as the flame from the second lantern on the other side of the room went out. The room was completely dark. A cloud drifted ominously over Mayport covering the night sky and blocking out any light from the moon. Mr. King could not see his own hand in front of his face. He knew the location of the furniture around him so he began to move in the dark toward the entrance to the front foyer and the stairway. He reached for the electric light switch on the wall as he passed through the doorway, exiting the living room. Mr. King felt the metal light switch cover and pushed up the switch with his index finger. The light bulbs in all three living room lamps came on and illuminated the dark room.

Mr. King's heart began to pound and his mouth went dry when he saw a shadow of a big man move away from one of the lights. The shadow moved across the far wall of the room and into the small dark kitchen area. Mr. John King was scared.

"Who's there?" He turned to his gun cabinet and opened the front drawer. He took out his loaded Colt 45 pistol. "I have a gun, here! I don't want to hurt you, but you are in my house. If you're cold and hungry, I can give you food and blankets. If you're here to steal from me I will shoot you."

Mr. King walked slowly toward the kitchen. He knew there was a light switch next to the open entrance. He also knew there was not an exit from the kitchen and the intruder was trapped. Mr. King cocked the hammer of the six-shooter back, held the gun out in front of him in his right hand and turned on the light switch with his left hand. His eyes widened when he saw that the small room was empty.

There was a cracking noise in the living room behind him. He turned to see his aunt's empty green rocking chair rocking back and forth. He had seen the chair move many times before. Mary C. words and Sofia's question echoed in his head. Mr. King pulled the trigger of the gun and eased the cocked hammer back into the safety position.

"Hawk, is that you?" The three lamplights flickered for a few seconds at the same time, and then they stopped and stayed lit. The green rocking chair stopped moving and the cool chill left the air. Mr. King had a new ghost in his haunted house. Steve "Crane" Robertson was looking for a safe haven and he was looking for Mary C.

Mary C. opened the door to Sofia's bedroom. A small lamp near the wicker bassinette gave her enough light to see her grandson sleeping. Her heavy heart was lifted, but there was still emptiness in the pit of her stomach. Miss Margaret stepped into the room.

"Oh, Mary C., I thought you were one of the girls up here. I didn't hear you come in. Are you all right, dear?"

"I'm fine now that I've seen him."

Miss Margaret smiled. " Isn't it funny how beautiful little babies seem to make things fine? How was your evening?"

"It was nice. I went out to Bill's and saw some old friends. Took a fast ride in a fire engine red convertible. Stopped to see John on his haunted house porch. It was nice."

Miss Margaret smiled. "You do have that magic touch when it comes to having exciting evenings. Come on downstairs and we'll dunk some spice cake in our coffee."

A red ford truck rolled onto the Mayport ferry. Shadow Martin looked across to the Fort George side of the river. He had no idea where he was going. Macadoo had told him to turn right when he drove off the ferry on the other side and stay on State Road A1A until he saw the Honey Dripper on the right hand side of the road. He couldn't miss it. He was on a mission to find the woman called Ruby.

Ruby stood next to the jukebox at the Honey Dripper. She moved her incredible body to the slow instrumental, Sleep Walk. Ruby had been on her own mission. She had prepared and served dinner for four at her house for her two accomplices. She had supplied them with female companionship with big butts, as requested. Carl and Jerome were wrapped around their two healthy women in a slow dance squeeze. Ruby watched her two friends and smiled at the fact they were lost in the moment.

Mr. King sat on his living room couch directly across from the green rocking chair. One candle flame was the only light in the room. He was hoping to create the perfect and proper atmosphere for his new ghostly arrival. He looked at the magic carousel and thought about Mary C.'s theory of why he could not see the spirits when they emerged from the door to the other side created by the spinning of the carousel lights. Mr. King was proud of the fact he had never killed anyone.

Shadow Martin walked through the front door of the Honey Dripper bar. Macadoo's directions were easy to follow. There wasn't a standing room only crowd, but every table and barstool were occupied by Sunday night customers. As soon as Shadow walked into the dimly lit room he saw Ruby standing by the jukebox. He didn't know she was the woman he was looking for. He stepped to the bar. The song ended and Ruby moved away from the jukebox and sat at a table. Jerome, Carl and their two lady friends joined her. The bar tender was a pretty young black woman dressed in a white shirt and black bow tie. She stepped to her new customer.

"What can I get for you, sir?"

"I'll have a rum and coke, please. No lime."

The female bartender quickly poured the drink in front of Shadow and placed it on the bar. "You're a new face in here, ain't ya? Just passin' through?"

Shadow smiled. "I came over on the ferry. I'm stayin' in Mayport. I'm lookin' for a woman called Ruby. I was told she might be here."

The bartender smiled, too. "There's always some good lookin' man lookin' for Ruby." The young woman pointed passed Shadow. "She's sittin' right behind you."

Shadow turned to see the beautiful woman whom he saw standing at the jukebox when he first walked in. He placed two dollars on the bar. "Thank you." Shadow stepped away from the bar and walked toward the table. He had no idea he was getting ready to meet the woman who killed his best friend, as well as, the two men who dumped Lamar's body into the river.

"Excuse me." All five at the table looked up at the stranger. "My name is Shadow Martin. I'm looking for my friend Lamar Harris. I was told there was a possibility he was here last night looking for you." He looked at Ruby. Her expression never changed.

"Now, why would your friend be lookin' for me?"

Shadow was uneasy about the hard looks he was getting from the two men at the table.

"A woman in Mayport called Macadoo sent him here to talk to you about the death of some devil man. Macadoo said you could help him."

"I know fat ass, Macadoo. I don't know you or your friend. And if you believe anything Macadoo tells you, you're really dumber than you look."

"My friend didn't attend his mother's funeral today. I was hoping you had seen him."

Ruby smiled. "You sure ain't from around here, are ya, Shadow? That is what you said your name was ain't it?"

Shadow nodded his head. "Yes ma'am."

Ruby couldn't resist. "I think we have an educated man with manners here with us tonight." They all looked at Shadow.

"I was hoping you could help me. I'm sorry I disturbed your evenin'." Shadow turned away from the table as the slow song, My Prayer, came from the jukebox. Ruby stood up.

"Shadow, do you dance?" He turned back to face Ruby. She stepped to him and took his hand, leading Shadow to the dance floor. Ruby had led Lamar to the same dance floor in the same manner the night before.

Mary C. sat at the kitchen table with Miss Margaret. They had shared coffee and spice cake. Miss Margaret was concerned and puzzled about their conversation.

"Why do you feel it is not safe for us if you stay here?"

Mary C. had the answer. "You saw the vigilante. You saw the bull whip. He'll come again. He'll come to kill me and take the baby. I won't put you and your girls in that kind of danger. You could all die with me." Miss Margaret knew it was one of those times to be quiet. She also knew Mary C.'s crazy talk always scared her. Mary C. continued. "I talked to John and we're gonna stay with him 'til it's over. We'll be safe there. It's our sanctuary. We'll leave in the morning."

Shadow Martin was body-to-body with the sexiest woman he had ever encountered. Her right thigh was buried between his legs gently rubbing his genitals. She also allowed his thigh to push against her in the same manner. He had never danced that way and it was only their first dance. It was as if they had been intimate for a lifetime. Ruby had danced with Lamar the same way only twenty-four hours before. She pushed her breasts against his chest and whispered in his ear.

"You're really exciting me. Keep rubbin' me there with your leg. If I make any noises don't stop. I'll try to be quiet."

Shadow couldn't believe her forward and sexually aggressive request. They had just met and she was actually going to have an orgasm right there on the dance floor at the Honey Dripper bar in American Beach. Shadow wasn't prepared for such a wild and untamed encounter. No one could be.

Ruby made a whimpering noise and squeezed his leg with both her legs, rubbing back and forth as hard as she could. Shadow held on to her so she wouldn't fall to the floor when he realized she was at her sexual peek and exploding inside. He watched her eyes glaze over as her stomach contractions ended. She blew hot air from her mouth into his ear.

"Oh my God! Shadow, Shadow, Shadow." Ruby chanted in his ear. "When the song ends I'll have to go straight to the lady's room. I've got to take off these wet panties. Pull a chair up to our table, they won't bite you."

Chichemo and Jason sat on the stern deck of the Mary C. picking out the shrimp and fish from the second drag. The first drag had yielded about three hundred pounds of shrimp and twice that many choice fish. The second drag was not as big, but it would add substantially to the overall catch. The nets were down in the water for number three. Jason turned from the pile of sea creatures and vomited near one of the drain slots on the side of the deck. Chichemo shook his head.

"Damn Jason, there can't be much left inside ya. I don't want you spittin' out a vital organ. I don't think I could put it back in like the dog's eyeball."

Jason was too sick to smile at Chichemo's crude attempt to make a joke. Jason wiped his mouth with his shirtsleeve and looked at Chichemo. "I think you could probably do it if you had too." The spider monkey, Bosco, ran out of the wheelhouse and jumped on the wooden hold cover. Jason vomited again. Chichemo looked at the monkey.

"We're witnessin' the worst case of the dry heaves in the history of bein' seasick. When we pull up this last drag let's head on home." Bosco grinned as if he understood. Jason wanted to grin too, but he couldn't.

Shadow Martin sat at the table with Ruby's four friends. He was waiting for her to return from her emergency trip to the restroom to remove her wet panties. There was no conversation. The two women were rubbing and kissing the two men. Shadow thought that

Ruby's activity on the dance floor had excited the others too. It was obvious the two couples were not at all interested in Ruby's new friend. She stepped up behind him and whispered again in his ear.

"I don't have any panties on." She sat down next to him and immediately touched him between his legs with her hand. "Shadow Martin, where did you come from?" She didn't wait for his answer. "These are my good friends, Carl, Jerome, Thelma and Nellie. Y'all say hey to my new friend, Shadow." The two women said, "hey", at the same time. Carl nodded and Jerome had a question.

"You a Indian or somthin'?"

"My mother was a full blooded Cherokee. My father was blacker than you."

Jerome wasn't sure he liked Shadow's comparison, but Ruby did. "Damn Jerome, that's a black man, if he's blacker than you." They all laughed, except Jerome and Shadow.

Mr. John King fell asleep on his couch waiting for his new ghost to reappear. He just knew Hawk had joined the other spirits that walked his halls a night. He would dream about the belly dancer, Ana Kara, without the help of the carousel. He would also prepare for his new houseguests to arrive sometime during the next day.

The shrimp boat Mary C., was headed to Mayport with nine hundred pounds of shrimp and fifteen hundred pounds of select fish iced down in the hold. Chichemo was pleased with the amount they had caught in such a short period of time. Jason was glad they were going home.

Miss Margaret's house was quiet. Three of her daughters were home and one was still at the store until midnight. Margie would be the last one to come home that night. Mary C. had showered and looked for Hawk in the cloudy steam of the hot water. Again, he did not appear to her. She would be with him again when she was able to make the carousel spin.

Mr. Butler would sleep like a baby with the hard liquor soaking inside of him. He had no idea about Steve Robertson's body lying broken and mangled in the mud near the little jetties. It would be his first call in the morning.

Shadow Martin stood next to his red Ford truck in the lime rock covered parking lot of the Honey Dripper bar. Ruby had followed him outside.

"I can't believe you're leavin' me. My damn ass is cold because of you and now you're just leavin'."

Shadow turned back from the truck to face her. "Ma'am you are the most unbelievable woman I have ever seen in my young life. I'm sorry about your panties. I'm not sure why you would want me to go home with you. I'm sure when I'm on the ferry going back to Mayport I'll regret not going with you, but I told you, my best friend is missing. I need to think about him before I think of anything else. Perhaps you'll make that offer again at a better time for me."

Ruby stepped to Shadow and kissed him passionately, driving her body through his. Their first kiss ended.

"After you find your friend, come see me. I want to prove that I am the most unbelievable woman you have ever seen."

Shadow nodded and got into his truck. Ruby turned and walked toward the front door of the Honey Dripper. Shadow waited for her to turn and look at him. She didn't disappoint him, but her comment did. "Even if you don't find Lamar, come see me."

CHAPTER NINE

The sun was rising out of the Atlantic Ocean as the Mary C. floated up to Mr. Leek's dock. The dockworkers had been on the job for over an hour and they were prepared to unload any of the boats that would arrive throughout the day. Jason threw the bow rope to one of the workers and then ran to the back of the boat to throw the stern line to another worker. Chichemo shut down the boat engine when the Mary C. was securely tied to the dock pylons. Jason pulled the top off of the hold of the boat. He climbed down into the hold and waited for one of the dockworkers to lower the empty metal basket down to him so he could fill the basket with the ice-covered shrimp. He looked up and saw the metal basket coming down to him. The unloading process began.

In a matter of minutes the Mayport headers would be making their way to the fish house to begin popping the heads off the shrimp. Jason would stay down in the cold hold until the entire catch was unloaded. Even though Chichemo had made the decision to pull up the nets and go home early because of Jason's seasickness, Jason would not go home this time until the boat was unloaded and he had done his share of the work.

Miss Margaret's house was alive with the usual morning activity. Sofia had already gone to open the store. Peggy and Susan sat at the kitchen table with Miss Margaret serving them eggs and grits. Mary C. sat on the front porch in one of the rocking chairs. The devil dog sat on guard at his normal position at the bottom of the porch steps. Mary C. was disturbed by the feeling she had the night before. She hoped something had not happened to Jason. She looked down at Abaddon. The bandage was gone from the dog's eye.

"Well now, you done gone and scratched the patch off that eye of yours, didn't ya?" The dog stood up as if he had to move to attention when Mary C. spoke. "I have to admit. You're lookin' pretty good here this mornin'." Miss Margaret walked out onto the porch.

"Mary C., how about some breakfast?"

Mary C. turned away from the dog. "Yes, thank you. I need to tell the girls 'bout us leavin'." Miss Margaret held the door open as Mary C. walked past her and into the house.

Officers David Boos and Paul Short stood next to a fire engine red pile of broken and mangled fiberglass that used to be a Corvette. They watched two firemen wearing high rubber boots walk out of the water carrying the dead body of Steve "Crane" Robertson on a canvas stretcher. The two firemen put the stretcher down on the ground. One of the firemen looked at the two officers. "He's a big man. The ambulance is on the way."

David Boos looked at his partner. "You know that's the man who was with Mary C. last night. Mr. Butler's gonna have a fit when he hears about this."

Shadow Martin woke up when a car horn blew out on the road in front of Lamar's house. After having a difficult night, Shadow had fallen asleep on the couch sometime during the early morning hours. He got up off the couch and walked slowly to the window to see who was blowing the horn. He didn't recognize the black and chrome Studebaker parked in front of the house. He couldn't see who was in the car from where he was standing. An arm came out of the driver's side window and waved for Shadow to come to the car. He was sure it was a woman's arm. He walked out onto the small front porch. The arm beckoned him again. He stepped down off the porch and moved toward the car. He stopped when the driver's side door opened. A woman wearing a black long dress stepped out of the black car and faced him. Shadow's eyes opened wide when he saw who had come to visit. It was Zulmary. She was nervous and on the run. Her scarred, but pretty head was on a swivel.

"Hey Shadow! I can't stay here wong. I weavin' and won't be back for wong time. I had to see you first. You can't find Lamaw, can you?"

Shadow was shocked to see her, but when she mentioned Lamar he came to his senses. "How do you know about Lamar? Have you seen him? Tell me if you know where he is."

"I see him with my eye."

Shadow was not sure about Zulmary's "sight", but he was desperate to know anything about Lamar. "What did you see?"

Zulmary looked around to be sure no one was around. "I was swimmin'. I don't know where. Not the Ocean. I saw him in the water. His body was different."

Shadow interrupted. "What was different?"

"It was Lamaw's face, but he had the body of a Manatee. I don't dink you find him." Shadow Martin stood at the driver's side window of the black Studabaker. Zulmary was behind the wheel.

"It was a dream Zulmary, just a dream. You saw Lamar the other day and he was on your mind."

Zulmary shook her head. "Don't keep wookin' for him. He gone. He a Manatee, now." Shadow knew he would not be able to reason with Zulmary. He needed to let her go and continue his search for his friend. Zulmary had one more comment before she left. "I was gonna ask Lamaw 'cause I know him, but I dink you be good too. Zulmary need to weave my gift of the sight to my daughter. I have you baby if you help me. I pwomise you will wike makin' baby wid me. You dink about it and I see you 'nother time. Zulmary got to go." She turned away and looked out the front windshield of her car, then turned back to Shadow. "There a evil storm comin' here. You should weave dis pwace." Zulmary hit the gas pedal and was gone, leaving Shadow with his mouth wide open, scary thoughts of being the father of Zulmary's sighted daughter and the vision of his best friend being a Manatee.

Breakfast was over. Miss Margaret's girls were sad when Mary C. told them that she and the baby were leaving. Miss Margaret was doing the breakfast dishes and the girls were doing their morning chores. Abaddon was on guard duty and Mary C. was sweeping off the front porch. The noise of an engine made Mary C. turn and look down the road leading to the house. It was Uncle Bobby's truck. She knew Jason was driving.

Mary C. had that empty feeling in her stomach again. She was afraid something was terribly wrong. The truck rolled up to the front of the house. Jason stepped out from the driver's side door.

"What's wrong?"

Jason moved to the steps of the porch. He stopped when he saw Abaddon. "Nothin's wrong, Mama. I just got sick and Chichemo felt sorry for me. We came in."

Mary C.'s heart was cold. "Can't make any money like that." Jason was used to his mother's insensitivity. It usually bounced off him.

"We did pretty good, but I know it would have been better if we would have stayed. I didn't ask to come in."

Mr. Butler walked into the small coroner's lab at the police station. The broken body of the Crane lay on one of the two tables. Officers Short and Boos stood next to the table. Mr. Butler shook his head. "I wasn't in the best shape last night as you two know, but I do remember talking to this man. He was with Mary C. wasn't he?" The two officers nodded their heads, but had no comment. They knew Mr. Butler would continue.

"I know this was an accident. I also know he was with Mary C. and now he's dead. I'll bet my pitiful paycheck that he was either going to Mayport to see her or he had just left her and was headed home." There was still no response from the two officers. Mr. Butler made an unusual change of subject. "Y'all heard anything more about that Lamar Harris fella? Y'all found Zulmary yet?"

Officers Short and Boos didn't know how to respond to Mr. Butler's surprise questions. Paul Short took the lead. "You didn't ask us to look for Lamar Harris and you told us not to look for Zulmary. If you've changed your mind about those two we'll get right on it."

Mr. Butler blew air from his mouth. "No, not Zulmary. I would like to see Lamar Harris again. Mary C. said he was gonna try and kill her and take that damn oak child or what ever they call him. If Lamar's still around be sure he leaves town. Be sure his friend leaves with him. I want both those boys out of here."

Mary C. and Jason sat in the cab of Uncle Bobby's truck. They looked out the front window at the burned ruins of their house. The devil dog Abaddon, jumped out of the back bed of the truck. The dog began to run around the yard barking and sniffing the ground as he had done before. Mary C. looked at her house. Jason watched the dog.

"Mama, why you keepin' that crazy dog?"

Mary C. did not hesitate with her answer. "I earned him."

"I'm scared he's gonna turn on you or get mad and hurt someone else, even Billy. I think we're takin' a big chance keepin' him around. I don't trust that dog. You know those dog's are trained to hurt folks. I don't want it to be one of us."

Mary C. was never paying attention when Jason had one of his better moments. He did make sense from time-to-time, she just didn't notice. Mary C. was ready to defend Abaddon. "If he was gonna hurt any of us he would have already done it. He won't hurt nothin' that's mine." She opened the passenger side door of the truck and stepped out into the yard. Jason would not question his mother about Abaddon again, but he would keep his son away from the mutant canine.

Jason stepped out of the truck and walked over next to his mother. He knew she was in deep thought about that night when she lost so much. He was surprised when Mary C. broke the silence.

"We have to leave Miss Margaret's house today. It's not safe for her family to have me there." Jason was silent He knew his mother had more to say and he knew when to listen. He had always been a good listener. "I was thinkin' 'bout sellin' our land and getting' another place, maybe out on Mayport Road like Miss Carolyn did. She built a Jim Walter Home on a little piece of land right off the road. There ain't many houses out there in the woods. I'd like to live in the woods. I was thinkin' 'bout livin' on the boat and helpin' you, but that was stupid. That wouldn't be good for the baby."

Jason did not respond, but he was glad his mother had abandoned her ridiculous notion to work on the boat with him. Abaddon ended the one sided conversation when the huge dog ran up next to Mary C. and sat at her feet. She reached down and touched the top of the dog's big head.

"Poor baby, all your friends are gone. You got new friends now."

"Mama, you act like he understands what you're sayin'."

Mary C. continued rubbing the dog's oversized head. "He knows."

Jason was concerned with the idea of his mother leaving the comforts of Miss Margaret's home. "Mama, why can't you stay with Miss Margaret a little longer? If you're not gonna stay on the boat, where ya gonna go?"

"We're movin' in with John. You gotta help us get settled over there before nightfall. I've already told the girls. We're stayin' at the haunted house, ain't that a hoot?"

Jason had no reply. Abaddon growled as a car rolled up into the yard. Mary C. recognized the car. Mr. Butler had come to visit. The car stopped and Mr. Butler stepped out.

"I went by Miss Margaret's and she said you were over here. I need to talk to you about a few things."

Mary C. looked down at the devil dog and stepped toward the lawman. "Stay here dog." She stood eye-to-eye with Mr. Butler. "You can always talk to me, Mr. Butler. I told you that before. What can I do for you this mornin'?"

"I need to apologize for the way I acted last night. I had too much to drink and got out of line. I'm sorry that happened."

Mary C. was as cold as ever. "Don't worry 'bout it. It doesn't matter. What else?"

Mr. Butler looked at Jason, then back at Mary C. "There was an accident out on the curve at the little jetties last night. A man was killed. It was your friend from last night. It was Steve Robertson."

Mary C.'s facial expression didn't change. She showed no emotion at all. Once again, Mr. Butler was amazed at her ability not to care. Mr. Butler had to continue with his information. "It looks like he was headed into Mayport. That car of his must have been clockin' a hundred. The mixture of the speed and the booze was too much to make that bad curve. I just thought you would like to know."

"Thanks for lettin' me know. Is that it?"

Mr. Butler hesitated. He was looking deep into Mary C.'s eyes. She didn't blink.

"There is one more thing. I'm gonna run that Lamar Harris out of here. He won't cause you any trouble. I promise you that."

"You don't have to promise me anything. You won't be able to stop him. If he comes, he comes. You can add him to your body count."

Mary C. turned away from the lawman and got back into the passenger side of Uncle Bobby's truck. Jason said nothing. He walked to the driver's side of the truck and climbed in behind the steering wheel. Abaddon's hair stood up on his neck and he growled at Mr. Butler, then jumped into the back bed of the truck. Mr. Butler stood in Mary C.'s front yard as the truck rolled away.

Shadow Martin sat alone in Lamar's house. His evening with the voluptuous Ruby had left him with an empty feeling as well as a distraction. He thought that perhaps his friend had fallen under her sexual spell and the black beauty knew more than she had told. He had only planned to stay until Miss Hattie's funeral was over. Shadow was packing the few clothes he had brought with him. He hoped a return to Daytona Beach would find his friend safe and sound at their apartment near the Bethune-Cookman campus. If Lamar was not there, Shadow had decided his friend would have to find him. With Ruby's tempting sexual offer, Zulmary's insight and invitation to fatherhood, the lawman from southern hell and the devil woman, Mary C., he would not return to Mayport.

Jason stopped the truck in front of Miss Margaret's house. Mary C. got out and the devil dog jumped from the truck bed onto the ground. Mary C. looked back into the cab of the truck. "It won't take me very long to get our few things together. I want us to sleep at John's tonight." Jason didn't fully understand his mother's hurry, but as usual he did not question her about the situation.

There was activity on the dock. Mary C.'s big catch after only three drags had caused another stir in the fish house. The shrimp headers were popping and the dockworkers were weighing and packing fish. Mr. Leek had a big smile on his face. Chichemo never changed the hard expression on his weather worn face.

Mr. King heard a noise on his front porch. He could see movement through the white curtain on the window of the front door. A knock on the door followed by the sound of a familiar voice told him his new houseguests had arrived.

"Woohoo, John."

Mr. King was afraid and really didn't want Mary C. to stay at his house, but he had not and would not, express his concerns and misgivings to her. He opened the front door with a big smile on his face.

"Come in, come in." Mary C. carried her grandson, Billy, in her arms. Jason stood behind her holding a navy issue duffle bag. "Any more luggage?"

Mary C. smiled. "Not much left. Most of this stuff came from Miss Margaret and the girls. I'm gonna take some of Jason's money and buy us all some new clothes this week. I ain't been shoppin' in quite a while." Jason passed her and walked into the living room.

"That's your money Mama, not mine."

Mary C. smiled again and looked at Mr. King. "He's a good boy ain't he, John?"

Mr. King nodded his head. "Always has been."

Jason placed the bag on the floor of the front foyer at the foot of the stairs. Mr. King was the perfect host. "Mary C. I've fixed up the big bedroom upstairs for you and the baby. I found a little crib in the attic."

Mary C. looked at Jason, but she talked to Mr. King. "Ain't no baby been pitchforked to death in that crib fifty years ago, has it?"

Mr. King had to smile at Mary C. remembering about his Aunt Viola being pitchforked to death on the green rocking chair. "No ma'am. No ghost stories about the crib. Jason, you can sleep in the back bedroom upstairs. It has a door to the back steps. You can come and go as you please. You will be stayin' too won't you?"

Jason looked at his mother. Mary C. answered the question. "He'll be on the boat some nights, but I'm sure he'll take advantage of your hospitality every now and then."

Mr. King smiled at Jason, but didn't understand. Mary C. continued. "John, let me assure you we won't be here very long. We'll be out of here in no time at all. We need to move on and get our own place. I'm gonna sell my land. I was thinkin' 'bout movin' out on Mayport Road near Miss Carolyn."

Mr. King nodded his head again. "Pretty woods out there. I've always liked the Patterson place with those horses runnin' in that big field. Mary C., that's a good idea. I know some folks with land out there. I'll talk to 'em. With your land you might be able to make an even trade."

Mary C. noticed Jason was looking at the magic carousel on the table in the living room. "I left it here that night we saw your Uncle Bobby. John's been keeping it for us. It's safe here."

Mr. King walked to the foot of the stairs. "Come on up y'all and I'll show you your rooms."

Shadow Martin stopped his red Ford truck in front of the Blue Moon tavern. He was on his way back to Daytona Beach, but he wanted to see if Macadoo was sitting at her favorite table. She was. The fat woman looked up when he stepped to her.

"Well, well, did ya find our boy? Was he shacked-up with that black hussy?"

Shadow knew he should have been shocked by her crude question, but nothing surprised him when it came to the characters in Mayport.

"I didn't find him. I found her, not him."

Macadoo eyes popped open. " You shack-up with her?"

Shadow didn't answer the question. "I just came here to tell you I did go there like you suggested. I think she knows something, but maybe not."

"Your first impression is usually right, ya know? You do understand that Ruby protects the oak baby. She has ties with that white family. With Mary C. tryin' to hurt Lamar, I wouldn't put it past Ruby to do Mary C.'s evil bidding for her. Sit down and have a drink or something to eat. I have two others meeting me here. I'd like you to meet someone before you leave. Shadow thought it wouldn't hurt to eat a little something before he hit the open road. He sat down with the fat woman.

Jason walked out onto Mr. King's front porch. He was going back to the dock to help Chichemo with whatever had to be done to prepare for their next trip on the ocean. He also wanted to see what they were going to be paid for the catch they had just delivered. As he stepped off the porch the sound of a sweet and familiar voice made him stop and look toward Miss Margaret's store. "Jason, over here!"

It was Sofia. She was standing at the front door of the store. Jason hadn't thought about the possibility she was working across the street. He had been too busy with unloading the boat and unloading his mother. His heart raced in his chest when he saw Sofia's shiny long blonde hair. Even from that distance, he could see her sky-blue eyes. Her body was perfect. Her teeth were perfect. Jason waved and walked toward her.

As Jason approached her, Sofia stepped back into the store. The bell on the door rang as Sofia grabbed Jason's shirt and pulled him to her, kissing him passionately. She kept pulling him across the room and into the back storeroom. They did not break the lip-to-lip contact as they moved.

Sofia's aggressiveness ignited Jason's wild blood. He thought of Jessie and how she made him feel. The kissing continued. Jason pulled Sofia's shirt up and moved his hand under it to touch her breasts. Sofia pushed against his hand as he moved from one nipple to the other. The kissing continued. Jason was surprised when Sofia reached down with her hand to unbuckle his belt. He reached down to assist her, giving her the opening she needed. Sofia liked feeling the heat in her hand as she held and squeezed him. The kissing continued.

The elastic waistband on Sofia's pants made it easy for Jason to pull them down over her narrow hips. His hand went under her cotton panties and he plunged a finger inside her. Sofia moaned as his finger penetrated. Her body fluids made Jason's work easy as a second finger joined the other probing digit. She moved her hips in a pumping frenzy. She reached down with her hand and pushed against Jason's hand, wanting his fingers deeper. He loved the feel of the liquid heat coming from Sofia.

Sofia's pants and panties were at her ankles. Her butt cheeks were snow white and flawless. Jason turned her around and she put her hands on the top of a table. He pressed the palm of his hand against her butt crack and continued to use his fingers. Sofia had never made such noises. She moaned, grunted and even squealed once. She trembled as her body fluids covered his hand and dripped down his wrist. He removed his hand.

Sofia was ready and willing for him to enter her from behind. She looked back at Jason with her eyes glazed over with lust and passion. She whispered.

"Do it now, please."

Jason reached down to guide his blood filled organ. The heat and moisture gave him the direction he needed to enter her. Jason's first push was deep and hard. Sofia made a whimpering noise and her eyes popped open. She didn't expect the pain and pressure she was feeling. There was no comparison to his two fingers and what she was feeling inside her now. Jason was in a wild animal pumping frenzy. Sofia held onto the table as he pumped her. There was a slapping noise each time Jason's pelvic area would slam against Sofia's butt cheeks.

Sofia felt pain and pleasure for the first time in her life. She wanted to scream, but she didn't. She even wanted him to stop at one time, but the urge to stop passed. Sofia went up on her toes trying to relieve some of the pressure, but that only made Jason pump harder. He was in another dimension. Sofia held on to the table and wondered how long it would last. They could barely hear it, as the sound of the bell on the front door tinkled in the distance. Sofia stood up. Jason dropped out of her. She reached down for her pants. "Oh God! Someone's here! Oh God! It might be Margie coming to replace me."

Sofia was tucking her shirt into her pants. Jason wasn't as quick. His divining rod was still erect and looking for water. He had very little blood left in his brain. Sofia took over.

"Go out the back. I'll take care of who ever. I love you." Sofia turned and left Jason standing there. He heard her sweet voice.

"Good afternoon, may I help you with something?"

Jason knew it was a customer. Sofia's greeting was perfect and gave him a good signal. He stepped to the small bathroom and washed his hands. He was still hard so he placed it over the edge of the sink and lathered it up with a bar of soap. Jason dried it off and forced it into his dungarees. He stepped to the door of the stock room and looked through the crack in the door to see if the customer had left yet. He wanted to be with Sofia again to finish what they had started. He watched a woman customer turn away from Sofia at the counter and walk out the door. The bell sounded as the woman left. It was another signal for Jason. Sofia looked toward the stockroom door as Jason pushed it open and stepped into the store. He could see that Sofia wanted him, too. He could also see the family station wagon rolling up to the front of the store. Margie was coming to relieve Sofia. Sofia turned to the front store window when she heard the car engine. She looked back at Jason.

"Go out the back, please. I don't want her to know we were here alone. I love you."

Jason heard the bell on the front door as he went out the back door. Margie entered the store. ""Well here I am, little sister. Right on time."

Sofia thought to herself, "Of all the days for you to be on time."

Margie stepped closer to the counter. "You don't look so good, Sofia. You look flushed. I hope you're not coming down with something. Do you have a fever? Let me feel your head." Margie put her hand on Sofia's forehead. "You're a little hot." Sofia knew her sister had her hand on the wrong place if she was looking for heat.

Jason walked to Mr. King's house and got into his Uncle Bobby's truck. He looked toward the store, waiting for Sofia to get into the station wagon. He knew he had to go to the dock, but he wanted to talk to her before he did. Jason wanted to be with Sofia. He smiled when she walked out of the store and got into the car. Sofia wanted to get home and take off her wet panties. Jason wanted to take her wet panties off, too.

As the station wagon moved away from the store, Jason dropped the truck key in his lap when he took it out of his pocket. He made a disturbing discovery when he reached down to find the key. His belt was gone. It was, no doubt, on the floor in the stockroom of the store. He knew Sofia would be embarrassed if Margie found it. Jason wanted to help the blue-eyed beauty keep her secrets. He started the truck and drove across the street to Miss Margaret's store.

Mary C. walked up the stairs in John King's haunted house. She was carrying the magic carousel music box. Mr. King stood at the foot of the stairs. Mary C.'s words sent a chill through his body. "I'm gonna keep this in my room with me. I'm gonna see if it will bring Hawk to me tonight. I know he's here. I can feel his eyes on me. I gotta get this thing with him done and over with so he can cross over." Mary C. was at the top of the stairs. Mr. King had a thought he wanted to share with her.

"What if he does come to you and he doesn't want to leave after he's shared your bed again?"

Mary C. looked down at her friend. "You know John, that would be my luck."

She turned to the room, leaving Mr. King at the bottom of the stairs. He was waiting for his heart beat to slow down. He knew Mary C. had no equal. She could have very well been the most insane of all the Mayport characters, but she sure was exciting.

Margie met Jason at the front door of the store. The bell rang when she pushed the door open. "Well, good afternoon. This is a pleasant surprise. What brings you here?"

Jason couldn't tell her about the belt so he lied. "If you don't mind I need to wash my hands. They still smell like shrimp."

Margie was smiling from ear-to-ear. "Sure, you know where the bathroom is in the back." She looked toward the stockroom door as Jason moved past her. He entered the back room and saw his belt on the floor under the table. He picked it up quickly and moved to the small bathroom. Jason closed the door, turned on the sink faucet and put his belt on.

As he hurried to buckle his belt, Jason had no idea Margie had closed and latched the front screen door. She also closed the main door and turned the bolt lock. Margie made sure they would not be disturbed. Jason washed his hands and dried them on a towel that was hanging on the wall next to the sink. There was a noise in the stockroom. He was amazed when he pushed the bathroom door open.

Margie stood by the sex table. She was completely nude all the way down to her bare feet. Her butt cheeks and the back of her legs were smooth. Her hands were on the table exactly where Sofia had placed her hands fifteen minutes before. Margie was wild and aggressive. Her body was dark and muscular like Jessie's. He could not resist her. He would not even try.

"I thought you would like this. Hurry please. And do it as hard as you can."

Sofia eased her young and perfect naked body down into a

bathtub full of hot water. She tingled and was sensitive in the area of Jason's welcome sexual attack. She rubbed the bar of soap between her legs and felt the hot water and suds cleaning her. Sofia had no thoughts of Jason being deep inside her sister, Margie, at that very moment. What little sister Sofia had started, big sister Margie was finishing.

Margie was up on her tiptoes, flexing her calf muscles, as Jason followed her request and pumped her as hard as he could. Margie made her noises as the sex table rocked and hit the wall to the rhythm of Jason's stroke and motion. She told Jason to "Come on!" with her teeth clenched in sexual pleasure and desire. Jason was drifting into his animalistic sexual trance when he heard Margie's voice over the noise of the table hitting the wall. Her calm request did not fit the situation or the "Come on!" request only seconds before.

"You have to pull out before you explode inside me. You can stay in when we do it at the oak tree." Jason stopped his movement. Margie looked back at him. "You don't have to stop. Just pull out before it happens. When you pull out I want to hold it in my hand."

Jason started pumping again. Margie was driving him crazy. He liked the crease down the middle of her bare back where her back muscles pushed together. Jessie had that same crease. It was a great focal point to excite Jason even more. He felt his juices rising as if they were boiling from down in his toes. Jason didn't want to pull away from her, but he would honor her request. As soon as he stepped back, Margie turned her naked body to face him. She grabbed his wet manliness in her hand and pulled as Jason exploded. Margie held him tightly as if she was holding the nozzle of a water hose. Her eyes were glued on every drop until the eruption ended. It was in her hand, on her leg, on her stomach and on the floor.

She released her hold on Jason and moved past him to the bathroom. Jason could not move. He heard the water running in the sink as Margie washed him off her hands and body. Jason found the strength to pull his pants up and make sure his belt was attached. Margie stepped from the bathroom wiping herself off with a towel. She was still naked. She bent down and cleaned the floor with the towel. Jason looked at her breasts and her butt. Margie broke the silence.

"We need to get up front. I can't believe no one interrupted us. It was great, wasn't it?" Jason smiled and watched Margie as she dressed.

Shadow Martin sat at Macadoo's table in the far corner of the Blue Moon Lounge. Two other men had joined them. Macadoo made the introductions.

"This is Mr. Shadow Martin. He's a friend of Hattie's long lost son, Lamar. He came for the funeral and now he's leaving our town." Shadow nodded to the two men as Macodoo continued. "This old hard face here came for Hattie's funeral, too. He's most likely leaving pretty soon, too. I should whisper his name just in case the law might be hiddin' in here somewhere. His is the notorious Tom Green. If that's the name you're using these days."

The small black man stuck his hand out to Shadow. "Don't let Macadoo's dramatics scare ya, son. I've always been Tom Green. Nice to meet ya. I loved Hattie. She was a great lady. I hope I get to see Lamar."

Shadow shook Tom's hand. "I hope you get to see him, too. He's been missing since the night before the funeral. He didn't even make it to the funeral. I'm afraid something awful has happened to him."

The other man spoke up. "I'm Clayton Demps. Macadoo told me about Lamar. Anytime you cross paths with that white woman bad things happen. Lamar just didn't understand what he was gettin' into. He wasn't ready for the evil."

Tom Green shook his head. "Let's just scare the hell out of this young man. He's got enough on his mind without you two comin' down on him with the devil and doom talk."

Macadoo had to join in. "You been gone too long, Tom. You've forgot how awful and evil that woman is. Clayton drifted away like you, but he's back with us now. He knows the evil we're facing. Tom, you've always been blinded by your love for the boy. We all know the story 'bout how he saved you and helped you kill Sheriff Floyd."

Tom Green had to stop her. "I did the killin'. The boy was gone. He gave me the machete to free myself. The cutting was my idea. And remember he was just a boy." Shadow couldn't believe he was listening to another incredible conversation. He was mesmerized by his three new acquaintances.

Jason sat in the driver's seat of Uncle Bobby's truck. He was thinking about how Margie had the nerve to lock the front door of the store. Margie stood outside the driver's side window.

"This was a great surprise today. I love being with you. We need to plan the "breeding" so I can be next." She touched Jason's shoulder. He had no words for her. He started the truck and moved forward slowly. Margie stepped away from the truck to allow him to leave. Jason's lack of response did not dampen her enthusiasm. She was still smiling. "Talk to you later."

Shadow Martin wasn't sure that he had made the right decision in stopping at the Blue Moon. He did not like the way Macadoo was talking. "You all know we're here at this time to join forces. Clayton, you and I have lost many of our relatives and friends to her death filled hands. Tom, we need your strength and courage. We need you to fight for the cause of the black men and women of this town. Shadow, she has done something to Lamar or had it done to him. Your youth and love for your friend will lead us all. Gentlemen, there is a reason why we're here and a power driving this quest. We're the perfect four. Destiny has brought us together at this place, at this time, for one reason. We'll stop the evil that has been a plague for many years. Together we have the power."

Shadow Martin was speechless. He knew in his heart he wanted no part of Macadoo and her plan. At the same time he was interested in this strange and compelling woman. Clayton Demps' eyes showed his excitement with Macadoo's words. Even though he had his doubts about Macadoo's motives he was ready to avenge the death of his loved ones. Tom Green would not be swayed by any of Macadoo's preaching or her persuasive tactics.

"Macadoo, I didn't come back to join one of your crusades. I came to honor my friend, Hattie and see the boy. When I see Jason I'm gone. I have a new life. I have nothing to do here."

Shadow watched Macadoo's face change. "When you think about my words you'll realize you should help your people. You'll always be Mayport. It's in your blood."

Tom Green looked at Shadow. "Young man, you need to get away from here as soon as you can. I hope you find Lamar." Tom looked at Macadoo. "I'll be gone some time during this night. I will not think of you again." Tom stood up. He looked at Clayton.

"It was good seein' you again, Clayton. Good luck." Tom turned to leave. Macadoo wasn't finished.

"You're not the man you was, Tom Green." Tom did not look back as he walked out the door of the Blue Moon.

Jason walked through the double door entrance to Mr. Leek's fish house. He did not see Chichemo's old truck parked outside. He thought perhaps the old seadog had taken the money to his mother. The shrimp headers were gone and the dockworkers were adding the final touches of cleaning the fish house. Jason nodded to one of the workers as he walked toward the dock, making his way to the boat. He boarded the boat and walked into the wheelhouse. Jason felt the boat move and he knew someone had jumped from the dock and had followed him. He thought it was Chichemo, but he was wrong. Jason couldn't believe his eyes when sister Peggy the "Succubus", stepped through the narrow door of the wheelhouse. She had that hungry look on her pretty face that Jason had come to know so well.

Shadow Martin did not want to be rude, but he did want to leave Macadoo and Clayton Demps to their revenge plot. "Miss Macadoo, I don't think I'm part of your situation. I don't even think I'm capable of participating in such a thing."

Macadoo's eyes were wide open. "You believe in the future of the black man, don't ya?"

"Of course I do. My entire life, as short as it has been, I have fought for our rights. I will continue to do so, but not in revenge." Shadow stood up. "It was interesting meeting you. I need to go home." He nodded to Clayton Demps and walked out of the tavern.

Jason lay in the small bunk on the boat. The Succubus had performed her specialty and she was gone. Jason could still feel her mouth on him, even though he knew she was not there. The sensation of her hard work would stay with him for hours. He wondered if he would see the fourth sister, Susan, before the day ended. The thought of being with all four girls in the same day intrigued and excited him. Jason was more like his mother than he realized.

Mary C. sat on the bed and stared at the magic carousel. She knew she would try to bring Hawk to her bed during the night. Mary C. hoped he was watching her and he would make her efforts worthwhile. Mary C. had no equal. She was the craziest one of them all.

Jason sat in the captain's chair of the Mary C.'s wheelhouse. He was recovering from his sexual encounters with Sofia, Margie and Peggy. His cup and loins truly runneth over and over and over. The boat moved and he knew someone had jumped aboard from the dock. Jason actually thought it was either Peggy looking for a return match or Susan ready to complete the foursome. It was his sexual mindset at the moment. He moved from the captain's chair and looked out the narrow wheelhouse door to see who was coming to visit him.

At first Jason did not recognize the small black man standing on the boat. It was Tom Green's voice and big smile that let Jason know his old friend had arrived.

"I hope I didn't scare ya, young man."

Jason's was happy and concerned at the same time. "Tom Green, what are you doin' here?" He knew Tom was taking a grave chance returning to Mayport. Tom was still grinning.

"An old man can't visit his best friend?"

Jason motioned for Tom to come into the wheelhouse. "Come inside, please."

Shadow Martin took his foot off of the gas pedal of his Ford truck as he approached the sharp curve at the little jetties. He was happy to be leaving Mayport. The truck rolled slowly past the twisted wreck of the Crane's fire engine red Corvette. The sound of a car horn took his attention away from the pile of broken fiberglass. He looked into his rearview mirror to see a black car following him. Shadow recognized the car. He knew Zulmary was blowing her car horn for him to pull off the road. He turned onto the white crushed shell road that ran behind the little jetty rocks.

Zulmary's Studabaker was bumper-to-bumper to his truck as both cars moved down the narrow road and toward the rocks. When Shadow stopped his truck, Zulmary stopped her car behind him, locking his truck in with the jetty rocks at his front bumper and her car at his rear bumper. Before Shadow could turn off the truck motor, Zulmary jumped out of her car and into the truck.

"Hey, Shadow Martin."

Shadow was shocked, but he had to smile. "Hey, Zulmary."

"You must dink I pweety cwazy, don't ya?"

"I don't know, Zulmary, are you?"

She smiled a great smile. "Pwababwy."

Shadow smiled with her. "Being different doesn't make you crazy, Zulmary. What you want from me is most unusual. I know you have your certain conviction and belief. I respect you for that. You have to understand I don't think like you do. My way of thinking might be strange to you, but neither one of us is crazy."

Zulmary's smile could not have been any wider. "You say the nicest dings to me. How you get to be so nice?"

Shadow knew Zulmary had made sure her appearance would entice him. It was obvious by the way her two big round breasts pressed against the black crape material blouse she was wearing. She still wore a long black skirt that was clinging to the skin of her legs. She smelled great. Shadow thought the pleasant aroma was from one of her love potions that would make her irresistible to him. He smiled at such a ridiculous thought. Shadow was comfortable sitting there with Zulmary. He knew there were no such things as magic love potions or black eyed women with the sight to see things that can't be seen. Zulmary took Shadow's moment of deep thought and silence to make her first move.

She slid her body next to Shadow and kissed him passionately, placing her hand on his crotch. She shoved her tongue as far as she could into his mouth. Shadow was not sure why he did not resist or stop her aggressive advances, but he didn't. He returned her wild French kiss as she sucked his tongue. Zulmary pulled him toward her and away from the obstructing steering wheel. Shadow moved with her and they did not stop kissing.

Jason and Tom Green sat across from each other at the small galley table. Tom was explaining his situation. "I couldn't leave town without seeing you and, I hope, the baby. I had to come for Hattie's funeral. You look good, boy."

"I'm fine. I'm scared for you bein' here. This place is crazy. If someone recognizes you it could be trouble. Folks don't forget things 'round here. You know that."

Tom nodded. "I know. I'm a little worried about the few people who know I'm here. Folks can turn on ya so quick. I'm leavin' tonight. Is there a way I can see the child?"

"I'll go get him right now. What's wrong?"

"I think your mama and the child are in danger. Macadoo and her henchmen want your mama dead, and I think you already know they want the child. It's the craziest thing I've ever seen. That mama of yours has made many enemies. Y'all will never be safe here."

Jason understood. "They've been trying to take Billy ever since we got back. A lot of people have died over him."

Tom Green had a most serious look on his face. "What's wrong with you, Jason? Why haven't you left this place for the baby's sake? It's the easiest and best solution. Get out of here. Come with me to Ruskin. You and the child will be safe there. Your mama, too, if she'll come. You'll be with Big Bob and the others. They'll protect you and Billy. Just leave. There's no other right choice. Can't you see that? Again I say, what's wrong with you?"

Zulmary's hand was rubbing Shadow between his legs. He maneuvered his hand under her blouse to touch and squeeze her bare breasts. He pinched one of her nipples between his thumb and index finger. Zulmary's sweet smell filled Shadow's nostrils. He felt strange, but he knew there was no such thing as a love potion. The kissing continued. Shadow knew Zulmary was unbuckling his belt and unzipping his pants. He felt her hand when she pulled "it" out and held "it". She pulled her head back ending the wild kiss. For only a second Shadow saw her one black eye and her one blue eye. He took a deep breath of the sweet aroma that filled the cab of his truck. Zulmary moved her head down into his lap. Shadow felt her hot lips on his exposed skin. He had never experienced such heat in his young life. He laid his head back on the seat and relaxed like he had never relaxed before. Shadow knew what was happening, but he had no will power or desire to stop it. He was in a conscious trance.

Jason looked into Tom Green's worn and aged eyes. "What about Mama and the boat. She ain't gonna leave. Sometimes I think she likes the danger and the killin'."

Tom Green answered with another question. "What about your son? That's the only question here. When he was born your obligations changed. A man always loves his mama, but his own children come first. Grandmothers understand such things. If your mama stays, she stays. You left her once before. It'll be easier the second time. Once you leave you'll realize you have done the right thing. You'll be fine." Tom could see Jason was thinking about the crucial decision. "Don't just get the child for me to see. Go get him and then leave with me. We can be in Ruskin before midnight. You can leave all the evil, death and danger behind you. People make changes in their lives all the time. It's time for you to do the same." Jason was silent again. Tom added more for his consideration. "You should make your mother go, too. I fear for you all."

Jason was not aware of the fact his mother was planning to make her next stand surrounded by ghosts at John King's haunted house. Jason knew it would be difficult to make her leave, no matter what danger was to come.

Tom Green gave Jason another reminder. "You found the courage to leave once before. You even have more reason now. You could have a good life with us. You can always work with me or I know Big Bob would welcome you and Billy with open arms."

Jason smiled when he thought of his friends at the Giant's Motel. Tom made a strange and interesting comment. "I've never been too sure what I believe about the oak tree, but if the child is special, what better place for him to grow than with other special people."

Zulmary took her mouth off Shadow's manliness and lifted her head. She stroked him with her hand.

"You must hold it. Don't wet it go yet." She pulled up her long skirt exposing her dark bare legs. She took her free hand and guided Shadow's hand under her skirt. He felt no hair, just smooth skin. Zulmary was shaved clean. Shadow had never felt a shaved woman. As his finger entered her, Zulmary's finger joined his, another first for Shadow Martin. Their fingers were side-by-side and moving together like they were dancing to the same beat. Zulmary touched him and herself at the same time. Shadow wanted to see her smooth shaved skin. He pulled his hand away and looked down. Zulmary sensed his desire and curiosity. She moved her own hand and pulled her skirt up higher so he could see her. The look in his eyes excited her as he looked down. She touched herself while Shadow watched her, another first for the college student from Bethune-Cookman.

It was time for Zulmary's next move. She pulled up her dress and moved to sit across Shadow's lap. As she straddled him, she guided his manliness inside her. When Zulmary sat down on him her wetness caused instant and deep penetration. As soon as Shadow was at the deepest part he could reach inside her body, the heat caused him to explode all the body fluids he had inside him. He opened his eyes as the explosion was ending. Shadow Martin found himself eye-to-eye with the black and blue eyed, Zulmary, the daughter of the local and now dead, witchdoctor.

Jason stood on the dock with his friend, Tom Green. "You go get the child. I'll meet you back here in a half-hour. We can talk later and you can decide what to do." They walked out of the fish house together.

CHAPTER TEN

Mary C. stood on John King's upstairs outside balcony looking out at the St. Johns River. She had a bad feeling in her heart. She had come to know that feeling well. For a brief moment she thought about her friend Steve Robertson. She was sorry he had died. Mary C. knew he was coming to see her when he lost his life. A chill ran through her body. She knew Hawk did not want her thinking about the Crane.

Shadow Martin opened his eyes when he heard someone knocking on the driver's side window of his truck. The knock scared him. At first, his vision was blurred. It took him a moment to focus in on the lawman from hell standing outside his window. He was scared even more when he recognized Mr. Butler. Shadow rolled down the window. Mr. Butler was first.

"What ya doin' here, boy? You been drinkin'?"

Shadow had a headache. He squinted his eyes as he looked for Zulmary's car. It was gone. So was Zulmary.

"No sir. I fell asleep."

"Strange place to fall asleep."

"I guess the lack of sleep caught up with me."

"Where's your partner?"

Shadow knew he meant Lamar. "I still haven't found him." Shadow did not want to talk to the lawman.

"That boy flew the chicken coop. He musta done somethin' real bad to leave you like this. Hell, you probably know where he is right now. You just actin' like you're on the hunt." Shadow did not respond. "I figured you'd be runnin', too."

"I have nothing to run from. If I did I still wouldn't run."

"Is that a fact?" Shadow did not respond. Mr. Butler looked down into the truck and smiled. "Damn boy, you had a hell of a daydream here, didn't ya? You need to zip them pants up before one of our big blue crabs bite that thing of yours off."

Shadow looked down at his limp exposure. He hated the white lawman seeing him like that. Mr. Butler had an interesting observation while Shadow fixed his pants.

"Damn, you smell good, boy."

Jason walked up the front steps of John King's front porch. He was going to get his son and take the child back to the boat so Tom Green could see him. He knew he would have to lie to his mother in order to take Billy out of the house.

Shadow Martin stood next to his truck while Mr. Butler patted him down. "You're clean, ain't ya boy?"

"I've already told you I don't want any trouble. I came here for a funeral and I haven't done anything wrong. I'm not sure why you want to do something to me. And yet, I probably do know why."

Mr. Butler's eyes widened. "And why is that?"

Shadow had to make his stand. "I'm real scared, mister. I think you can see that. I'm a black man in your town and you don't like me at all. You have a gun and a stick that says you can do what ever you want to me. You can tell any story you want and folks will believe you. All I can say to you is that I am one scared man. I have a bad feeling I won't leave this town. I hope I'm wrong."

Mr. Butler loved it when the young black man admitted his fear. He thrived on creating fear and discomfort in the black citizens of Mayport. Scaring the young black college man was a thrill for Mr. Butler. He was like a dog that sensed fear. Mr. Butler would not let up on his new victim. Shadow's eyes widened when he saw Mr. Butler unhook the leather cord that locked down the hammer on his pistol. His heart raced in his chest and the juices in his stomach went sour. Shadow thought he was going to have to defend himself or die at the hands of the awful lawman. He did not want to die at the little jetties outside the town of Mayport, Florida.

The noise of a car engine stopped Mr. Butler's deadly movement. Shadow and Mr. Butler turned to see a marked police car turning onto the white crushed shell road of the little jetties. Shadow was not sure if the arrival of the police car would change his drastic and life threatening situation. He did feel better when he saw Mr. Butler place the safety cord back onto his gun as Officers Boos and Short stepped out of the police car. Officer Boos' voice was music to Shadow's ears.

"Mr. Butler, everything okay, sir?"

Mr. Butler turned away from Shadow and faced Officer Boos. "Yes, I'm fine. Our boy here was takin' a nap. I stopped to check it out. I think he was playin' with himself and fell asleep." Only Mr. Butler and Shadow understood the statement. David Boos walked closer to Shadow's truck.

"Can we help you, sir?"

Mr. Butler looked at Shadow. "No. I'm makin' sure he leaves town. He was just tellin' me that he was leavin' and won't be back. With Lamar runnin' away like he did, I thought this boy would run, too. He was probably runnin' when he had to pull off the road and jerk off. He's one strange black bird."

Shadow could not believe David Boos' next question to Mr. Butler. "Would you like us to be sure he leaves, sir? We can escort him to the county line."

Mr. Butler looked into Shadow's eyes and whispered. "You need killin', boy. I think you'll be a thorn in the white man's side as long as you're alive. Don't cross my path again. Now get in that truck."

Shadow did not hesitate. He got into the truck and started the engine. Mr. Butler had instructions for the other officers. "Y'all don't have to follow him. This boy's scared enough to keep on ridin'."

Shadow hated the evil lawman. He drove his truck away from the little jetties and out onto Mayport Road. He was careful to drive slowly and not kick up dust or spin the tires. He did not want to give Mr. Butler any reason to pursue him.

Mary C. looked down from Mr. King's upstairs balcony as her son, Jason, stepped out of her brother Bobby's truck. Jason didn't look up. Mary C. knew he did not see her. He looked up when he heard his mother's cold-hearted voice. "Well, well, if it ain't my seasick boy. You get paid, yet?"

"No ma'am. I thought maybe Chichemo brought it to you."

Mary C. shook her head. "No. I ain't seen a dollar, yet. Al Leek didn't pay you?"

"No ma'am. I'm sure he paid Chichemo. I didn't go to the office."

Mary C. shook her head. "You gotta get more involved in the business, son. Chichemo works for us. We don't work for him."

Jason didn't know what to say. He had not heard his mother talk that way about Chichemo before. He put his head down as Mary C. continued. "Now ya know ol' Chichemo's been known to go on a booze binge every now and then. I hope he ain't fell off the wagon with all our money."

Jason kept his head down. "I don't know mama. I'm sure he'll be here soon to settle up."

"I hope so, son."

Shadow Martin took his foot off of the gas pedal of his Ford truck as he approached the end of Mayport Road. He turned the steering wheel to the right and drove into the gravel parking lot of Silver's bar and package store. Shadow stopped the truck and put his head down against the steering wheel. His heart raced in his chest. He hated the fact he was actually running away. He hated the fact the "White Cracker" lawman was running him out of town. He hated the fact he had admitted his fear to Mr. Butler. He hated the fact he knew in his heart something awful had happened to his friend, Lamar Harris. As his thoughts slammed against the inside of his head, a knock on the driver's side window of the truck startled him. He lifted his head off of the steering wheel quickly. Shadow turned to the intruder. It was Zulmary.

"Hey Shadow Martin. I knew you would stop here."

Jason stood next to his son's bassinet. Mary C. stood behind him. She was too smart for Jason. "What's on your mind, son? You scared Chichemo's runoff with all our money?" Her two questions surprised him. He had not thought of Chichemo at all.

"No ma'am. He'll come with the money. I was just thinking about spending some time with Billy, that's all."

Mary C.'s next comment caught Jason completely off guard.

"Why don't you take him for a ride. Go somewhere and be alone with him. You might even consider visiting your crazy circus friends. They seem to love you two like y'all was family. Let all this stuff blow over here. He'll be safe there."

Jason turned to his mother. "You don't even like those people, Mama. What's gonna happen here? It must be somethin' awful bad for you to want to send us away."

Mary C. smiled. "If I'm here alone nothin' can hurt me. Having you and Billy here makes me care too much. Y'all make me weak and I'll make mistakes. Please take him away and I'll send word when you can come back."

"This is crazy, Mama. I should be here if you need me. I can't just leave. The last time I left you needed me and I ain't forgave myself for not bein' here with you."

"When John let me come here, it gave me all I needed. You have to take Billy away. I'm not gonna talk about it no more. I'll get him ready and you go fill the truck up with gas. There's some money for y'all on the dresser.

Zulmary sat on the tailgate of Shadow Martin's truck. Shadow stood next to her.

"You seem vewy twoubled, Shadow Martin. I knew you would stop here."

Shadow looked into Zulmary's multi-colored eyes. "How did you know that?"

"I see it. You cannot pass by here and weave dis pwace. Even knowin' Laraw is gone, you can not weave."

Shadow pressed his lips together. "He is gone. Isn't he?"

Zulmary nodded. "He gone."

Shadow looked at Zulmary in a different way than he had before. She sensed the difference. "What is it, Shadow Martin?"

"What do you see, Zulmary? You came here to meet me for a reason. What do you see?"

Zulmary reached out her hand and touched Shadow's cheek. "I see a good and bwave man. It was you destiny to come. Lamaw was the instwament that bring you here. When the battle begin you future begin too."

Shadow shook his head. "I'm not very good at all this hocus-pocus stuff, you know? I have to admit, it all scares me."

"It good to be afwaid. It is the makin' of men."

Zulmary slid her body off the tailgate of the truck to stand with Shadow Martin. She reached down and placed the palm of her hand against his crotch. "Can I see "it" again?"

Jason couldn't believe his mother was standing on John King's front porch waving good-by to her son and grandson. Mary C. was smiling and waving. It didn't seem natural to Jason. It was her suggestion that they leave. It was as if she knew he wanted to take Billy away. Jason gave one last wave and the truck pulled away as Mary C. walked back in the haunted house. Jason drove the truck toward Mr. Leek's dock where Tom Green was waiting for him and the oak baby.

Mary C. walked directly to one of the upstairs bedrooms and closed the door. She undressed and lay naked across the big double bed. She reached up toward the magic music box carousel and turned it on. As the music started and the small lights began to flash, Mary C. closed her eyes and let the spinning carousel take her away.

Jason's stomach went sour when he drove the truck up to the steps of the fish house. A police car and Mr. Butler's unmarked car were parked next to the fish house. Jason's stomach burned even more when he saw two uniformed police officers and Mr. Butler walking out of the door of the fish house with Tom Green between them. Jason recognized officers Short and Boos.

Jason jumped from his truck and walked toward the foursome. Mr. Butler stepped to Jason. Jason looked into Tom Green's bloodshot eyes. Tom shook his head as a signal for Jason not to interfere. Mr. Butler spoke first.

"I'm sure you didn't know this fugitive was hiding on your boat. I would hate to think you were aiding and abetting a murderer."

Jason's heart was breaking. He had no words as the two officers put Tom Green into the back seat of the patrol car. Mr. Butler was not finished.

"It never fails. They always come back. It just took ol' Tom here a little longer than usual. I remember that night when Tom chopped sheriff Floyd up like he was butcherin' a hog. That was an awful night." Mr. Butler looked at Tom Green in the back seat of the car. "It didn't take your folks long to turn your black ass in, did it? I took the call, myself. And boy was I surprised to here a black woman's voice tellin' me your whereabouts. You got black and white enemies. You shoulda stayed gone, boy."

Tom Green knew his archenemy, Macadoo, had decided to punish him for not joining her evil quest of revenge. Mr. Butler opened the door of his car and looked back at Jason.

"I'll probably need to talk to you later, but for now we're gonna find a cell for ol' Tom to sleep in." Mr. Butler got into his car and led the patrol car away from the dock and onto the main street, leaving Jason in pain.

John King stopped in the upstairs hallway when he heard noises coming from behind one of the bedroom doors. There was a flickering light showing through the wide keyhole below the doorknob. He stepped closer to the door and he recognized the magical sounds from the carousel music box. His heart pounded in his chest as he realized Mary C. was in the bedroom with the carousel spinning. Mr. King knew she was trying to bring about a sexual encounter with the dead, but still very active, Lester "Hawk" Hawkins. The lights shinning through the keyhole beckoned Mr. King to take a peek. He could not help himself as he knelt down on one knee and placed one eye against the keyhole. He had no idea he was looking through the same keyhole used by Tom Thumb, when the circus midget watched Sandeep and Eve perform their tattoo swirling sex ritual. John King considered himself the ultimate Southern gentleman, but the temptation and the vision in his head of Mary C. using the carousel to bring her lover back from the dead to share her body and bed, was just too much for John King to take. His one eye widened to its fullest when he focused it on the movement in the room.

Mary C. lay naked face down in the middle of the bed. Her back and buttocks were visible. The lights from the spinning carousel bounced off the walls, the ceiling and Mary C.'s naked body. Mr. King watched in amazement as Mary C. pushed her pelvic area up and down against the mattress in a humping motion. His heart raced even more when she pushed up onto her knees elevating her butt cheeks higher than the rest of her body. Mary C. rocked back and forth on her knees and pushed back harder, as if there was resistance against her as she moved. She pushed herself up off the bed with her hands, arching her back and raising her head upward.

Mr. King had never actually seen Mary C. completely naked. He had seen her physical attributes throughout the years when she wore low-cut blouses, revealing her cleavage. He had seen her butt cheeks when she wore her white short-shorts. He knew when she was bra-less and her full round breasts pushed against a tight pullover shirt. But, he had never seen her completely naked. Mr. King and Mary C. were sharing a "first". Mary C. just didn't know it. He loved seeing her from behind, but his heart continued its abnormal beat in anticipation of a naked full frontal view.

Mary C. continued to thrust her hips up and down in a sexual pumping motion. Mr. King knew she was lost deep in the spell of the magic music box. Mary C.'s moans and groans of pleasure told of her satisfaction. If the ghost of Lester Hawkins was in that bed behind Mary C., John King could not see him, but he had no doubt Mary C. could feel the Hawk deep inside her. Mr. King also knew he was a witness to the ultimate dry-hump of the century. Mary C. grabbed the wooden headboard of the bed and began pushing her firm butt cheeks higher and harder into the air. Mr. King's manliness hardened as it filled with blood and pushed against the front of his pants. He wanted to stroke himself, but the lights of the carousel would not let him take his eyes away from the lust filled view of the keyhole. Mr. King's throat went dry when he heard Mary C. speak to her ghostly partner.

"Come on! That's it! Come on!"

The headboard began to slam against the wall as Mary C. held on tight with both hands. Something was sexually pounding her like a wild animal and Mary C. was giving no quarter. She was as much an animal as the apparition behind her. Mr. King knew the carousel had once again opened the door to the other side and let Hawk's wondering spirit return as Mary C. had predicted. He was shocked when Mary C. turned away from the headboard and sat up in the bed as if she had straddled her invisible visitor. She faced the door and the keyhole.

Mr. King's first frontal nude vision of Mary C. was before him. He was not disappointed. Even at her age, her breasts were full and firm. Her trademark stomach muscles rippled as she moved and her muscular legs added to the vision. Only her beautiful face rivaled her body. She was still perfect and John King considered it a privilege and honor to see her in that manner. His eye would not leave the keyhole until Hawk and Mary C. completed their ghostly ritual or the carousel stopped turning.

Jason held Billy in his arms as he knocked on Miss Margaret's front door. His aching heart jumped when his beautiful Sofia opened the front door. Her white porcelain flawless face lit up when she saw her visitor.

"Jason, what a pleasant surprise. And Billy, too. Oh my! This is truly wonderful."

Jason always loved the way Sofia talked. Her sky-blue eyes seemed to dance with excitement when he was with her.

"Come in, please. Let me hold Billy." Sofia took the child as they all moved into the living room of the house. "Everyone's gone, but me. I have to work later this evening. Mother will be back soon. I hope you'll stay so she can see Billy."

Tom Green's peril was on Jason's mind so he only gave her a half smile. "I was hoping Billy could stay here with you until I take care of some business."

Sofia's face lit up again. "Of course he can stay here. Mother will be thrilled, too." Sofia knew Jason's troubled look. "What is it, Jason? What's wrong?" She leaned forward and kissed Jason. "I can tell you need to go. What ever it is, please be careful. Billy and I need you to be safe."

Jason's heart raced with her caring words. He put his arm around her small waist and pulled her to him. Their kiss was filled with passion and was long and wet. Sofia held Billy and made sure not to squeeze the child between them. As the kiss lingered, Jason and Sofia both thought of their wild and recent sexual encounter at the store. They both had a tingling between their legs.

While Jason and Sofia were sharing tingles, Shadow Martin was also feeling a tingling sensation between his legs, as Zulmary's soft and hot lips encircled his manliness in the cab of his truck. She wanted to do more than just see "it".

The sweet aroma that had filled Shadow's nostrils before, once again filled the cab of the truck. Every breath he took, during Zulmary's oral demonstration, filled his lungs with the intoxicating aroma. His vision was blurred, but he could see the back of

Zulmary's head between his legs.

Sofia stepped away from Jason and lay Billy on the couch, placing a large cushion next to him so he would not fall. She turned back to Jason, reached for him and pulled him down with her to the floor. The sound of the engine of the family station wagon ended their passionate moment. Miss Margaret was home.

Shadow Martin tightened his stomach muscles to prolong the heat and sensation he was feeling from Zulmary's strategically placed lips. He did not want it to end. Shadow's noises of pleasure told them both he could not hold the explosion much longer. Zulmary surprised Shadow when she pulled her head and mouth away, exposing him to the sweet smelling air. Like before, she lifted her long dress and straddled him. He instantly penetrated deep inside her. The moisture and heat inside Zulmary was too much for him as he exploded again and filled her with his body fluids. Shadow opened his eyes and found himself once again eye-to-eye with the one black eye and one blue eye of Mayport's apprentice witchdoctor, Zulmary.

Miss Margaret stood in her living room holding the oak baby. "Of course he can stay here, Jason. Take your time and we'll see you when you get here."

Jason nodded. "Thank you. I'll try to be back before dark."

"Well, just take your time and just know he's here with us. Would you like to come back for supper? Sofia's making the banana pudding." Sofia's eyes lit up at her mother's invitation.

Jason nodded. "I'd like that."

Jason moved toward the front door, Miss Margaret sat down with Billy in her rocking chair, and Sofia followed Jason out onto the front porch.

"I'm worried about you, Jason. Something is dreadfully wrong. I can see it in your eyes."

Jason stepped off the porch and looked up at Sofia. "I'll tell you about it at supper time." He turned toward the truck. Sofia's next words caused chills to run through his body. "Please hurry back to us. I want to be with you again."

Shadow Martin opened his eyes and realized his face was pressed against the plastic seat covers. He sat up and tried to focus his blurry eyes. Shadow's head pounded from the remaining sweet aroma. When his vision cleared he realized Zulmary was gone again. Shadow looked out of the front windshield and saw two men coming toward the truck from Silver's bar and package store. The men passed the front of the truck and stepped to the passenger side window. One of the men looked into the cab of the truck.

"Damn, boy! Where'd the little lady go? Y'all was really puttin' on a show out here. I went and got Harvey, here. I didn't want him to miss out on you two wild rabbits. Right out here in the open. You people don't care where y'all do it, do ya?"

Shadow Martin started the truck engine and left Harvey and his red neck friend standing in the parking lot at Silver's bar and package store.

Mr. Butler's unmarked police car was leading the way past the little jetties with officer David Boos following behind in the patrol car. His partner, Paul Short sat in the passenger's seat. Tom Green was in the back seat with his hands in handcuffs behind him. Mr. Butler stuck his arm out of the window of the car and motioned for Officer Boos to follow him off the road next to the little jetties.

The two cars stopped on the shell road next to the small rocks. Mr. Butler stepped out of his car and walked to the patrol car. Officer Boos stepped out of his car to greet Mr. Butler.

"Something wrong, sir?"

Mr. Butler shook his head. "No, not at all. No sense in all of us taking him back to the station. Put him in my car and you two can stay here and make your rounds. Mayport's like a pot of boiling crabs right now. I don't want the lid to blow off. Somebody turned Tom in, that one boy's missin', that other boy's leavin' town, and Mary C.'s preparing for war. It's a powder keg I tell ya, a damn powder keg."

Officer Short stepped out of the car. He didn't like the strange and untimely change in procedure. "We can deliver him, sir and be back out here in half an hour."

Mr. Butler did not hesitate with his reply. "I'll take him in and you two stay in the area. Make yourself seen around here."

Mr. Butler opened the back door of the patrol car and pulled Tom Green out by his arm. The two officers did not assist him as Mr. Butler put his prisoner into the back seat of his car. Mr. Butler looked back at the two officers. "Keep me posted on your whereabouts and anything unusual."

Officer David Boos spoke under his breath in a low voice. "How about you taking our prisoner away, is that unusual enough for you?" Mr. Butler drove his car away from the little jetties with Tom Green handcuffed in the back seat.

Shadow Martin wasn't thinking very clearly as he drove his truck onto Mayport Road in the wrong direction. He was headed back to Mayport. He passed by Tony's Seafood Shack and then the Shady Oak gas station. When he realized he was headed back to Mayport he drove his truck off the main road and onto an open area. There were two narrow dirt roads in front of him. The roads were only wide enough for one vehicle. Thick underbrush and palmetto fans bordered both paths. Shadow drove his truck onto the road to his right. The plant growth concealed the truck from the main road. Shadow stopped the truck and turned off the engine. He wanted to stop moving and try and get his bearings before he continued. The sweet smell of Zulmary's potion was still in the cab of the truck, but it was not as heavy as before. He rolled both windows down, hoping to release the last of the lingering sweet odor. Shadow knew he could not continue until his head was clear and he would be able to make rational decisions again. His hiding place was perfect.

Mary C. lay naked in the bed. The music box was no longer spinning. Whatever ghostly spirit had ravished her was gone. She had no doubt it was Hawk. John King's eye was still filling the keyhole. He also knew the ravishing was over, but he still wanted to watch Mary C. It was a once in a lifetime experience and he was going to carry it to the hilt. Mr. King's keyhole eye widened when Mary C. reached for the carousel and flipped the "on" switch again. The carousel began to turn, the music began to play and the lights began bouncing off the walls. Mary C. was opening the door to the other side so Hawk could come back for more.

Jason went back to the boat and got the .45 caliber pistol Chichemo kept in a drawer near the bunk. He loaded the six empty chambers of the gun with bullets. Jason was not thinking clearly either as he left the boat and got into his truck. His thoughts were of saving his friend, Tom Green.

Shadow Martin reached for the key in the ignition of his truck. When he touched the key he heard the engine of another vehicle.

He took his hand away from the ignition and looked out the driver's side window. Shadow could see that a car had driven off the main road and was moving on the other narrow road that was parallel to the road he had taken. The car rolled past him and went deeper into the wooded area. Shadow knew the driver of the other car was unable to see his truck in the thick bushes. He saw red tail lights flash and go out as the car stopped about fifty yards down the narrow road. Shadow listened out of his opened window. The voice he heard was low, but the stillness around them carried the words to Shadow's ears.

"Get your black ass out of my car."

Shadow's heart raced in his chest. He knew something bad was going to happen. He did not want to leave the truck, but for some reason he opened the door and stepped out onto the ground.

The voice carried again. "I can't believe you're here. You got to be the dumbest black son-of-a-bitch on the face of the earth."

Shadow was trembling as he felt his feet moving toward the voice. The voice cut through the air again. "Get on your knees, boy, and tell me you're sorry you killed my friend." Shadow heard no other voice. "I said get on your knees!" Shadow looked through a group of palmetto fans to see Mr. Butler hit Tom Green in the face with his fist and knock Tom to the ground. Shadow was instantly sick to his stomach. Mr. Butler's voice made him even sicker. "Come on now, boy. Up on your knees and say you're sorry." Tom Green was still in handcuffs. He rolled to his side and stood up to face the evil lawman. "That a boy. Now on your knees." Tom did not move. He continued to stand and face his attacker. Mr. Butler realized his newest victim was standing in defiance before him. Mr. Butler pulled his revolver out of the holster at his side and pointed it at Tom Green's head, touching Tom's forehead with the end of the thin barrel.

"If you don't get down on your knees I will splatter what little brains you got all over these woods."

Shadow was surprised when he heard Tom Green's voice. "You gonna kill me anyway, boss. It don't matter if I'm on my knees or not. I'd much rather be lookin' you in the eyes when you pull that trigger."

Shadow Martin realized at that moment his destiny was to keep that brave black man alive. He was next to Mr. Butler in a split second. Shadow slammed his forearm and fist down on the gun in Mr. Butler's hand, knocking the pistol to the ground. The shocked lawman turned to face Shadow. Before he made the full turn, Shadow threw a clenched fist that landed on the bridge of Mr. Butler's nose. The tough lawman did not go down, but the young and strong, Shadow Martin, continued to throw heavy punches to his face and head. Mr. Butler was so dazed by the first punches that he never recovered and was unable to defend himself. Shadow kept swinging until Mr. Butler went down. Once Mr. Butler was on the ground, Shadow began kicking him in the chest and head. He kicked until there was no movement from the evil one. Tom Green stood back and watched the young black man's rage as Shadow picked up the gun and began pulling the trigger, emptying the six bullets from the six chambers into Mr. Butler's head and body. When all the bullets had left the gun Shadow continued to pull the trigger six more times. After hearing the six clicks of the hammer, Shadow threw the hot and empty gun at Mr. Butler just to be sure he was dead. Tom Green's voice brought Shadow Martin back from his temporary insanity.

"I think he's dead, son. Can ya get the key and get these things off me?" Shadow looked up at Tom Green. "I think he's got a key in his top shirt pocket." Shadow nodded and looked at the face down Mr. Butler. He took his foot and lifted Mr. Butler, rolling him over onto his back. Shadow bent down and reached into Mr. Butler's shirt pocket. He turned with the key to face Tom Green.

"I thought I was gonna die in these woods a few minutes ago. Thank ya, son. It wasn't my time to go. I don't think we need to stay here too long. When he don't show up at the police station, they'll be huntin' for him and me. I don't know what made you come out here and we ain't got time to ponder on it. You need to get as far away from here as you can as fast as you can. I won't ever forget this, Shadow Martin. I'm getting' pretty old now so "ever" ain't that long for me now. As long as I'm breathin' you will be in my beating heart. Now, unlock these things and get out of here."

Tom Green turned his back to Shadow so he could unlock the handcuffs. After two clicks Tom was free. He turned to face his deliverer. Shadow's head was clearing.

"What about you? You can't stay here. We can be in Daytona by night fall."

Tom shook his head. "They won't be looking for you. You've done enough. They might not look for him for a while. If and when they do find him they'll think I'm on the run. I've got enough time to take care of some unfinished business. I'd never forgive myself if I left without saying good-by to an old friend. Now, you go on."

John King alternated knees as he continued to watch Mary C.'s sexual ritual through the keyhole of the bedroom door. It was obvious to him that the magic music box had, once again, opened the door to the other side. Mary C. was moving, groaning, moaning, humping and having another bizarre encounter with someone or something. Mr. King was not sure if it was real or not, but he did know Mary C. thought it was really happening. She thrashed her body from one side of the big double bed to the other side.

John King thought the second encounter he was watching was much more intense than the first, if that was possible. It was as if there was more than one spirit enjoying the curves of Mary C.'s body. Mr. King thought perhaps Hawk had brought some new friends along to handle the wild animal, Mary C. Or perhaps, the others were not invited at all and were ghostly party crashers. Or better still, Hawk was not there at all and had never been there. Whatever was happening in that bed John King was not leaving the keyhole. He shifted knees again and continued his lustful observation.

Shadow Martin drove his truck out of the thick woods onto Mayport Road. He reluctantly left Tom Green behind standing at the edge of the woods. The small black man stepped toward the road and watched Shadow's truck move away until it disappeared at the curve before Tony's Seafood Shack.

Tom Green turned quickly and moved back into the wooded area when he heard the engine of an approaching vehicle. A truck went roaring by and rolled up next to the gas pumps at the Shady Oak gas station about a hundred yards from where Tom was standing. He shook his head as his fate and destiny continued to unfold. Jason stepped out of the truck and began pumping gas into an empty tank. Mr. Norberg stepped out of the station building and stood on the front steps. He was a short man, but had a thick and powerfully built body. He was in his mid-fifties. Mr. Norberg liked it when his customers pumped their own gas.

"You need help, boy?"

Jason shook his head and held the flowing nozzle. He stopped the flow of gas when the meter read three dollars. He replaced the hose and walked to Mr. Norberg. Jason handed him a five-dollar bill.

"I got three dollars worth, Mr. Norberg."

Mr. Norberg took the five. "Come on in, boy. I'll get your change." Jason followed Mr. Norberg into the small building. "How's that pretty mama of yours?" It never failed. Folks always asked Jason the same question, especially the men.

"She's fine, sir."

"I heard y'all had some bad times over there lately. I hope that's all over now."

"Me too, sir."

As Mr. Norberg was handing Jason the two dollars change, Tom Green was climbing into the back bed of Jason's truck. He picked up a dirty green army blanket and covered himself as he lay down in the back floor bed. Jason had used the blanket to cover boxes of fish and shrimp to keep the wind from melting the ice during the ride. The blanket smelled awful, but Tom Green did not care. It was the smell of freedom. His heart raced in his chest when he heard Jason open the door to the truck and he felt it when Jason climbed into the driver's seat. In a matter of seconds the truck was rolling away from the Shady Oak gas station.

Mary C. could not contain her audible outbursts of pleasure. Mr. King wanted to scream along with her. One time he almost opened the door so he could stop the carousel from spinning and release Mary C. from the hold of the sexual dream. But, that was just a fleeting thought. Real or not, it was the most exciting thing Mr. King had ever witnessed. He felt as if he was a participant even though he was on the other side of the door.

Jason reached down and touched the loaded pistol on the seat next to him. He was not sure what he would or could do when he got to the police station. His thoughts were still not very clear and he was acting on pure emotion. A noise startled him as Tom Green knocked on the back window of the truck cab.

Jason turned the steering wheel and the truck rolled to the shoulder of the road. When the truck stopped, Tom Green jumped from the back flat bed and opened the passenger side door. Jason's heart raced as his old friend climbed into the front seat. Jason was speechless, but not Tom Green.

"It's better if you don't know. Just take me back to Mayport."

Shadow Martin was about thirty miles away from Mayport. The events of the last few days were raging in his head. He was scared, sad and proud, if that was possible. He had lost his best friend, attended Miss Hattie's funeral, and put a beautiful stallion out of its misery. He met and bedded Chiquita Naomi. He had stood in the bedroom of Aunt Matilda, the Mayport witchdoctor. On two separate occasions he was seduced by Zulmary, the black and blue eyed, potion mistress, and heir apparent to the witchdoctor. Shadow Martin had no idea what would come from his actions and decisions. He was sure of one thing, his life had been changed forever.

Jason stopped his truck in front of Miss Margaret's house. Tom Green picked up the pistol and moved behind the steering wheel as Jason opened the driver's side door and stepped to the ground.

"You get Billy and I'll pick y'all up at the dock in half hour." Jason nodded to his friend. When Tom drove the truck away, Jason looked up to see the beautiful Sofia standing on the front porch.

Macadoo sat on her back porch with her huge fat feet wedged down into a bucket of warm water and Epson's salt. She was eating boiled peanuts. Two empty paper bags lay on the floor next to her and she held a full bag in her hand. There were so many empty shells on the floor it looked as if Miss Chick, the resident elephant at the Jacksonville Zoo, had just eaten lunch on Macadoo's porch.

Macadoo looked up from her third bag of boiled peanuts as Tom Green walked up the steps to her porch. Perhaps she changed her expression, but Tom did not see any movement in her fat and swollen face. He stepped to her and crushed a pile of the soft water soaked peanut shells under his feet. Macadoo saw the gun Tom Green held in his hand.

"Well, well. Tom Green. Did you come back to join me?"

Tom Green did not change his facial expression either. "No. I came back to kill you and end a lot a future misery for a lot a folks."

Macadoo lifted her huge right foot out of the bucket of water. "I got corns on my toes big as china berries." She lowered her swollen and cracked skin foot back down into the water. "Now Tom, you and me both know my destiny ain't to die on this back porch with a belly full of boiled peanuts and my corns soakin'. Sit with me and let's decide together how we'll rid this place we love of the evil white devil."

Tom Green raised the pistol and pointed at Macadoo's huge head. "I don't know about your destiny. I'm just here to fulfill mine."

Jason stood on Miss Margaret's front porch holding his son, Billy, in his arms. Sofia stood with him. "Why do you have to go away again? I don't think you'll come back this time." She touched Billy's little head. Jason saw Sofia's beautiful sky blue eyes fill with tears. At that moment Jason's words surprised them both.

"Why don't you come with us?"

The flow of blood in Sofia's perfect veins changed directions when she realized what Jason had said. He had more. "Please go with us. It's the only way for us to be together. Let's shock 'em all."

The only person in more shock than Sofia at that moment was Macadoo as three bullets from Chichemo's gun penetrated her huge forehead.

When the carousel stopped spinning for the second time, Mary C. and John King were both completely exhausted. Mr. King moved away from the door and sat with his back against the hallway wall. His one keyhole eye could take no more. Mary C. lay face down on the bed with one of her arms hanging off the edge of the bed dangling toward the wooden floor. She had no idea that in the course of a week the voluptuous and beautiful, Ruby, had poisoned and killed Mary C.'s vigilante, Lamar Harris. She had no idea Shadow Martin had filled Mr. Butler's body with bullets. She had no idea Tom Green had put three bullets into Macadoo's hundred pound head. She had no idea all her present enemies had been eliminated and she did not have to lift one of her evil fingers.

John King pushed himself up off the hallway floor. His back was sore and his knees throbbed. He did not want Mary C. to discover his presence outside the bedroom. He moved quickly and quietly down the hall and out onto the upstairs balcony of his haunted house. Mr. King took a deep breath of the fresh Mayport air as he looked out over the St. Johns River. His nose told him it was low tide. There was movement below and Mr. King looked down to see the monster devil dog, Abaddon, walking up to the steps of his front porch. The mutant canine sat down on the top step. The dog was one of many protectors for Mary C.

The remains of Lamar Harris would never be found. The Mayport buzzards would pick Mr. Butler's bones clean of all organs and flesh before his bones were discovered by one of the Steen boys while he was cutting palmetto buds for the Palm Sunday celebration at the St. John's Catholic Church. Macadoo would be found in two days when a group of ladies from the New Zion Church on Girvin Road came to visit and pray together. When they got her feet out of the bucket of water they looked like two twenty pound purple prunes. Jason, Tom Green, Billy and Sofia were all sitting in the cab of Uncle Bobby's truck. They were passing the curve at the little jetties. The Mayport foursome was headed to the Giant's Motel in Gibsonton, Florida U.S.A.